TOMORROW THE BIRDS

OSAMU TEZUK

TOMORROW THE BIRDS

OSAMU TEZUKA

Written and drawn by Osamu Tezuka
Translated by Iyasu Adair Nagata
Lettered by Aidan Clarke

for ablaze
managing editor RICH YOUNG
editor KEVIN KETNER
associate editor AMY JACKSON
designers JULIA STEZOVSKY & RODOLFO MURAGUCHI

Publisher's Cataloging-in-Publication data

Names: Tezuka, Osamu, 1928-1989, author.
Title: Tomorrow the birds / Osamu Tezuka.
Description: Portland, OR: Ablaze, 2024.
Identifiers: ISBN: 978-1-68497-238-8
Subjects: LCSH Birds--Comic books, strips, etc. I Dystopia--Comic books, strips, etc. I Horror--Comic books, strips, etc. I Horror fiction. I Science fiction. I Graphic novels. I BISAC COMICS & GRAPHIC NOVELS / East Asian Style / Manga / General I COMICS & GRAPHIC NOVELS / Science Fiction / General
Classification: LCC PN6790.J33 .T6613 2024 I DDC 741.5--dc23

TOMORROW THE BIRDS. Published by Ablaze Publishing, 11222 SE Main St. #22906 Portland, OR 97269.

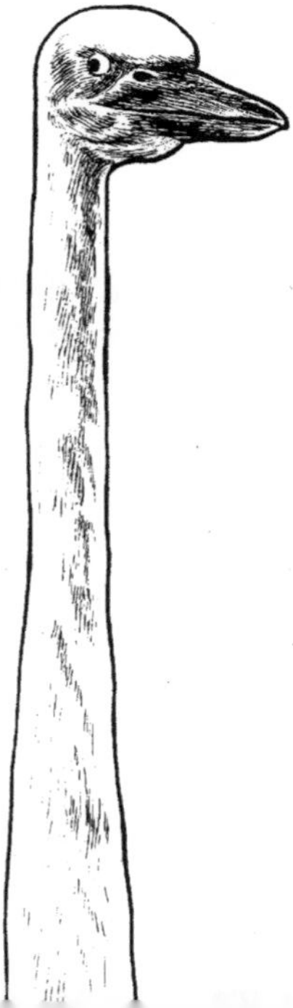

Dear Readers,

Many non-Japanese appear in manga by Osamu Tezuka, such as people from Africa and Southeast Asia. Some of the depictions are exaggerations of times in the past. The portrayals are at times different from how things are now. In recent years, some have pointed out that such illustrations constitute racial discrimination against non-Japanese people. Given that some feel uncomfortable with or demeaned by these drawings, we must address these concerns.

Exaggerating characteristics for the purposes of parody is one of the most important methods of humor in manga. This is especially pronounced in Tezuka's works, which parody people from many different countries. His characters are based not only on people but also plants, animals, and even imaginary creatures, for great comical effect. His self-portraits are no exception, as seen in the way he drew his nose to be many times larger than it actually was. Tezuka always held firm in his belief that all forms of hatred and antagonism are bad, whether between civilization and the uncivilized world, developed and undeveloped nations, the powerful and the weak, the rich and the poor, or the able-bodied and disabled. His stories have a strong undercurrent of love for all humanity.

This undercurrent of love remains intact, similarly, when his works offer commentary on historical events or people. It is important to remember that Tezuka's commentary on these matters is reflective of a time period and cultural environment different from our present standards of speaking on these events.

We continue to publish this Osamu Tezuka manga for the following reasons: Tezuka is deceased, making it impossible for him to revise his work. If a third party were to edit his work, that would result in issues involving moral rights. It would not be an appropriate way to address the matter. We believe we are obligated to preserve and protect works that are considered part of Japan's cultural heritage. We have always been against all forms of discrimination and believe that this is the responsibility of everyone involved in publishing. When reading this manga by Osamu Tezuka, we hope that you recognize the fact that various forms of discrimination exist in our world. We hope it will motivate you to deepen your understanding of this issue.

Tezuka Productions and ABLAZE

Tomorrow the Birds

Table of contents

IN JUNE 1975, IN KARINO, OUTSIDE THE TOWN OF MINAMI ASHIGARA IN KANAGAWA, A FIRE BROKE OUT AT THE ADACHI FAMILY FARMHOUSE. THE ENTIRE HOME PERISHED AND THE BURNT REMAINS OF ALL FAMILY MEMBERS WERE RECOVERED. THE FIRE MAY HAVE BEEN CAUSED BY CARELESSNESS, BUT A CERTAIN ASPECT OF ITS ORIGIN GAVE REASON TO SUSPECT FOUL PLAY. THE INVESTIGATION IS ONGOING.

CHAPTER 1: URORONKA DOMESTICA IGNIS

DAD! DON'T DO THIS! IT'S CRUEL!
NO, IT'S NOT!
THIS RECORDING TEACHES 'EM TO SING NICE 'N PRETTY... NUTHIN' WRONG WITH THAT!
STOP!!

LISTEN! I'M FEEDIN' 'EM THIS HYPERPROTEIN STUFF MADE BY PROFESSOR WHAT'S-HIS-NAME AT THE UNIVERSITY OF TOKYO!
SHEESH, QUIT TALKING NON-SENSE.
THE BIRDS ARE STRESSED... STOP IT!
HEARING THE SAME THING ALL DAY... EVEN A PERSON WOULD GO MAD!
YOU PLAY SOME GOOD BIRDSONG FOR THEM, THEY LEARN TO SING THAT WAY.
THINK OF IT AS STUDYING.
KNOW WHAT HAPPENS WHEN A CHICK EATS IT? ITS BRAIN GETS HUGE! LEARNS ALL KINDS OF STUFF!
THE INVESTIGATION SHOWED THAT THE FIRE HAD STARTED ABOVE THE THATCHED ROOF. IN OTHER WORDS, THE ROOF BURNED FIRST AND FELL ONTO THE SLEEPING FAMILY, GIVING THEM NO CHANCE TO ESCAPE. THIS MAKES ARSON THE MOST LIKELY CAUSE. THE INVESTIGATION WILL CONTINUE ALONG THOSE LINES.
THEY'LL FETCH DOUBLE THE PRICE! WE CAN EVEN SELL 'EM ABROAD!
BUT DAD, THAT'S MEAN! THE POOR BIRDS!
I'M RUNNIN' A BUSINESS HERE!

KNOW HOW SOME FARMS JUST FEED THEIR CHICKENS AND HARDLY EVER LET 'EM GET EXERCISE?
CHIRRRP PEEP CHR
CHIRRP
Hmph!
THEY'RE LIKE ROBOTS... ALL THEY DO IS LAY EGGS. THAT'S HOW YOU'RE TREATING OUR BIRDS.
SOME-DAY...
THE BIRDS MIGHT SEEK REVENGE...
SHUT UP!
REMEMBER THAT MOVIE ON TV?
WHERE THE BIRDS ATTACK HUMANS AND PECK 'EM TO DEATH?
QUIT TALKING LIKE A KNOW-IT-ALL, YOU LITTLE BRAT!

CHIRP
ALREADY LEARNED HOW TO SING! LISTEN!
FINE... I'LL LET ONE OUT.
LOOK HOW CALM IT IS.
HEY!
IT TOOK SOME-THING!
SHWIP
DAMN... WHAT A PEST!
WELL, THAT'S THAT... WOULD'VE BEEN 5,000 YEN...

AH! AH!!!
HEY DAD, WHAT DID THAT BIRD TAKE?
SHUT UP AND GO TO SLEEP.
ONE WEEK LATER, A FIRE BROKE OUT IN A NEARBY MOUNTAIN FOREST. IT BURNED 16 OR 17 HECTARES BEFORE IT WAS FINALLY PUT OUT. IMMEDIATELY AFTERWARD, A REPORTER...
IN JULY OF THE SAME YEAR, AROUND 300 METERS FROM WHERE THE FAMILY PERISHED, ANOTHER FIRE STARTED ON A DECK OUTSIDE A HOME. A FAMILY MEMBER WITNESSED A SMALL BIRD – A BENGALESE FINCH OR JAVA SPARROW – WITH A MATCH IN ITS MOUTH. HOW BIZARRE! DID THAT ACTUALLY HAPPEN? THE VICTIM WAS DISTRESSED. PERHAPS THEY HAD HALLUCINATED. THE INVESTIGATION IS ONGOING.

IMPOSSI-BLE!
THIS IS THE ARSONIST!
THIS PHOTO'S FROM THE SCENE OF THE FIRE! A BIRD WAS FLYING AROUND WITH A BURNING TWIG IN ITS BEAK!
IF THAT BIRD WAS REALLY HOLDING A BURNING TWIG IN ITS BEAK, WHERE DID IT LEARN THAT BEHAVIOR?
ANIMALS ARE INSTINCTIVELY AFRAID OF FIRE.
THE BIRD THAT COMMITTED ARSON DREW MUCH ATTENTION FROM THE MEDIA. PROFESSIONAL AND AMATEUR RESEARCHERS AND HUNTERS SCOURED THE MUSASHINO PLAIN IN SEARCH OF IT.
THEN ONE SNOWY NIGHT, IN A THICKET NEAR ODAWARA, THE BIRD WAS FOUND DEAD.
ITS NEST WAS CHARRED, HOLDING TWO OR THREE BURNT EGGS. A DOZEN MATCHBOXES WERE ALSO FOUND.
PERHAPS THE BIRD LIT A FIRE TO STAY WARM AND ACCIDENTALLY BURNED TO DEATH. OR WAS IT SUICIDE?

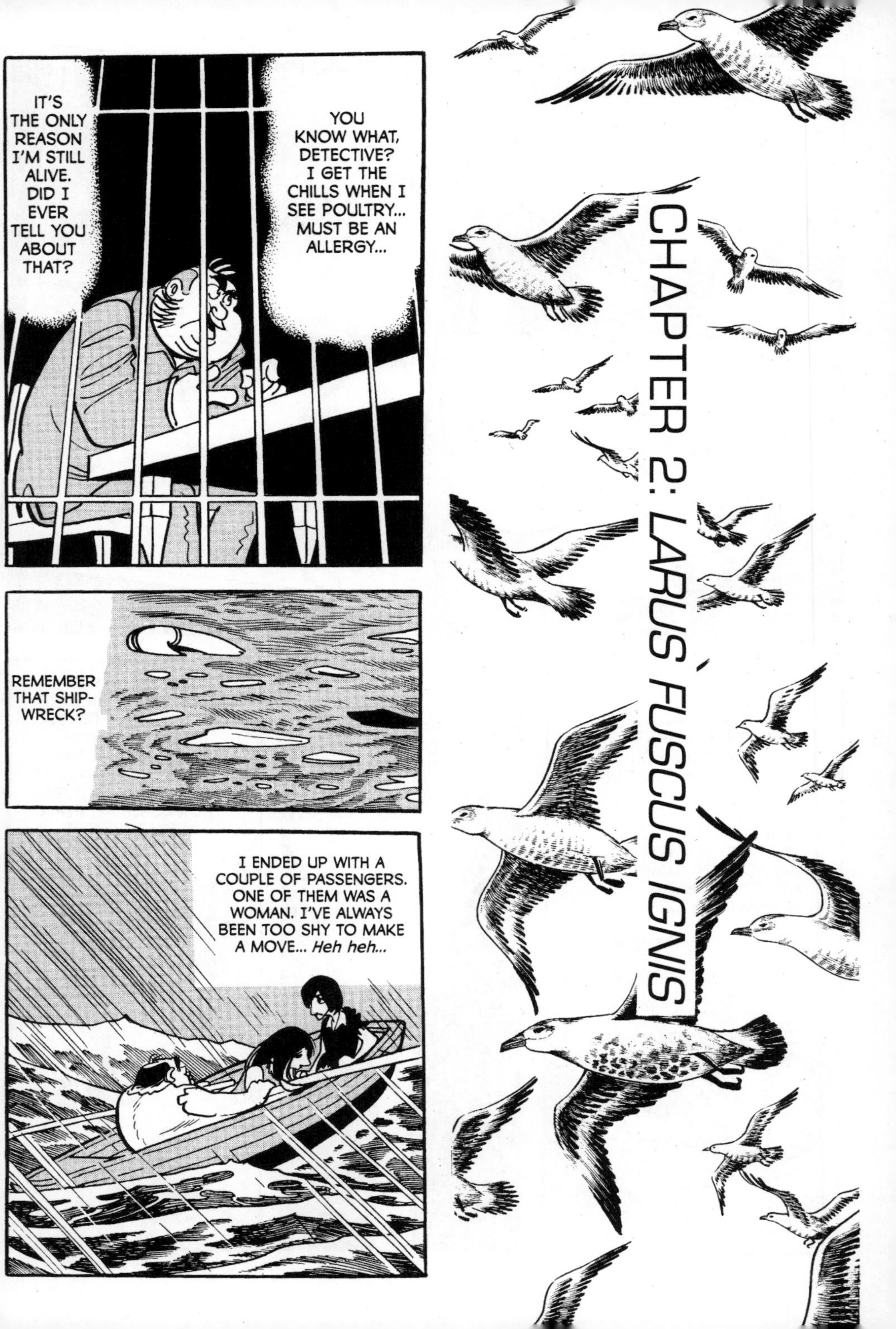

CHAPTER 2: LARUS FUSCUS IGNIS
YOU KNOW WHAT, DETECTIVE? I GET THE CHILLS WHEN I SEE POULTRY... MUST BE AN ALLERGY...
IT'S THE ONLY REASON I'M STILL ALIVE. DID I EVER TELL YOU ABOUT THAT?
REMEMBER THAT SHIP-WRECK?
I ENDED UP WITH A COUPLE OF PASSENGERS. ONE OF THEM WAS A WOMAN. I'VE ALWAYS BEEN TOO SHY TO MAKE A MOVE... *Heh heh...*

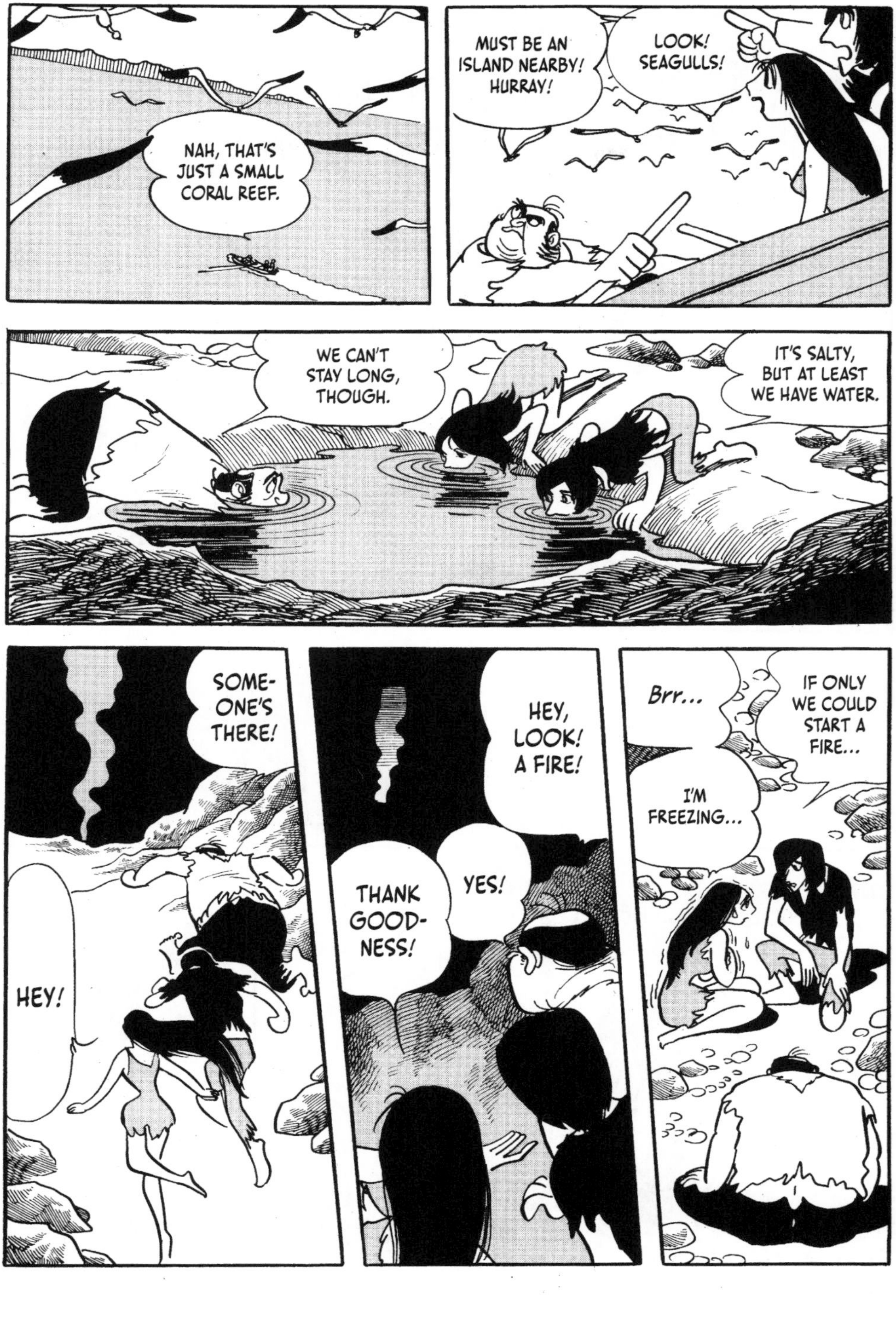
LOOK! SEAGULLS!
MUST BE AN ISLAND NEARBY! HURRAY!
NAH, THAT'S JUST A SMALL CORAL REEF.
IT'S SALTY, BUT AT LEAST WE HAVE WATER.
WE CAN'T STAY LONG, THOUGH.
IF ONLY WE COULD START A FIRE...
Brr...
I'M FREEZING...
HEY, LOOK! A FIRE!
YES!
THANK GOOD-NESS!
SOME-ONE'S THERE!
HEY!

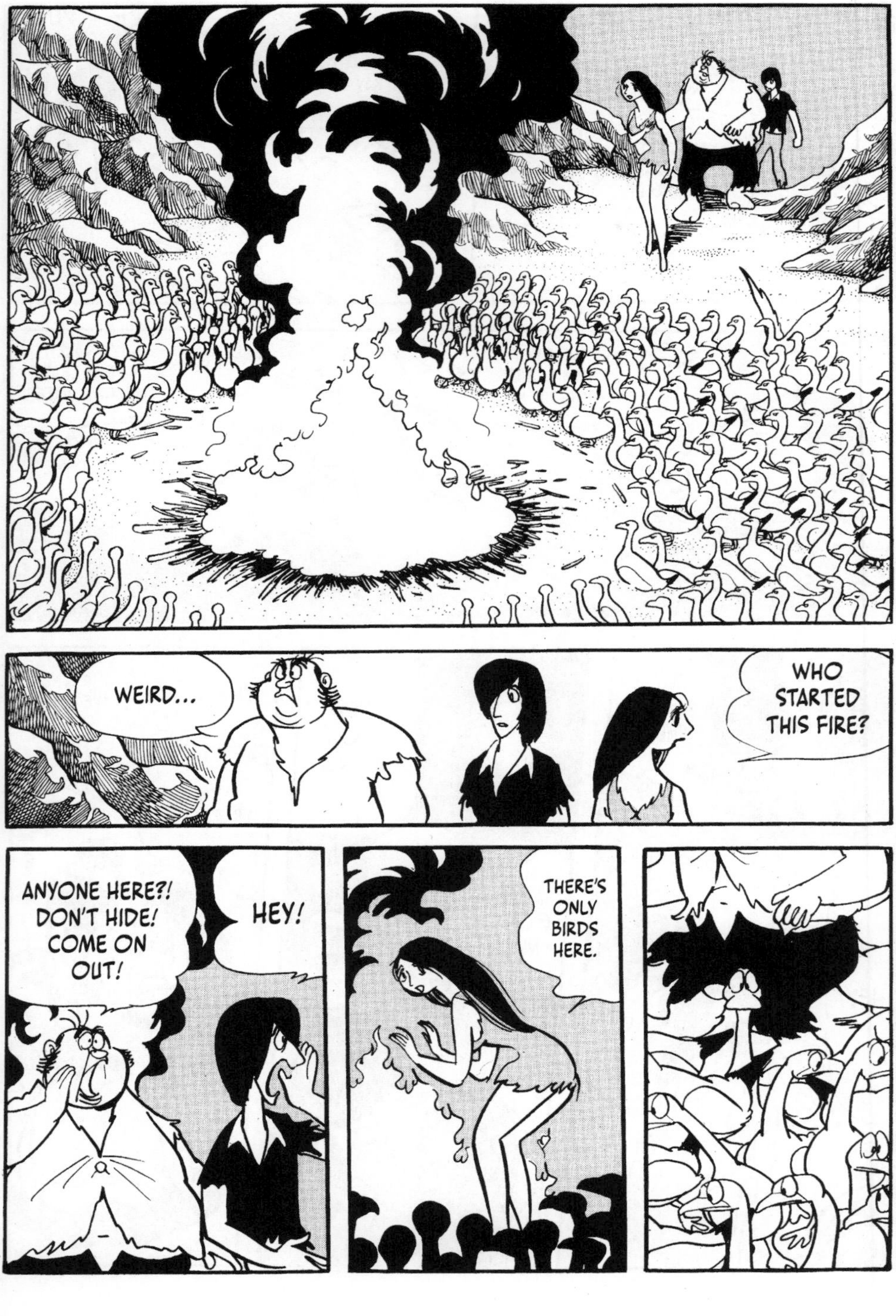
WEIRD...
WHO STARTED THIS FIRE?
HEY!
ANYONE HERE?! DON'T HIDE! COME ON OUT!
THERE'S ONLY BIRDS HERE.

I NEVER HEARD OF BIRDS STARTING A FIRE... HAVE YOU?
MUST'VE BEEN...
T-THEN WHO STARTED THIS FIRE?!
NO FOOTPRINTS IN THE SAND... NO SIGN OF ANYONE HERE.
HEY! LOOK!
HEY... THEY'RE NOT RUNNING FROM THE FIRE. THEY'RE ALL HERE TO KEEP WARM.
THE BIRDS STARTED THE FIRE, AND NOW THEY'RE ADDING WOOD! IMPOSSIBLE! I MUST BE HALLUCINATING!
HEY BIRDS, HOPE YOU DON'T MIND US.
LET US STAY BY THE FIRE TONIGHT, OKAY?

BUT THERE'S SO MANY BIRDS RIGHT HERE!
LET'S GO FISHING IN THE MORNING.
I NEED TO EAT... DON'T YOU?
I'M STARV-ING...
WHEN DID THESE BIRDS START TO USE FIRE? AND HOW?
H-HEY, THAT'S NOT RIGHT... THEY'RE LETTING US STAY HERE. WE OWE THEM.
IT'LL BE EASY. THEY WON'T RUN AWAY. JUST GRAB THEM!
I WANT TO EAT SOME!
HEY! DON'T!
NO!
CAN'T YOU EVEN CATCH A BIRD?!
USELESS COWARD! YOU'RE SUPPOSED TO BE A MAN OF THE SEA!
DO IT!
COOK ME A BIRD, THEN YOU CAN HAVE YOUR WAY WITH ME.

I CAN'T WATCH THIS...
Hmph! KEEP OUT OF THIS!
YOU STRANGLED THEM! YOU INGRATE!
Brr... I'M FREEZ-ING....
BUT I GET HIVES WHEN I SEE POULTRY...
I'M OUTTA HERE.
SUIT YOUR-SELF.
THE BIRDS ARE FLYING AWAY.
IS IT MORNING ALREADY?
I CAN SMELL THEM COOKING THOSE BIRDS...
THIS IS ON THEM... NOT ME!
HEY! YOU TWO!
?

HEY! WHERE'D YOU GO?!
DAMN... THEY HAD A HUGE FEAST...
YIKES!
HONEST! I SWEAR TO GOD, IT'S TRUE! WHAT?! YOU THINK I RAPED THE WOMAN...?
AND KILLED THE MAN AND ATE THEM BOTH? NO! NO WAY! IT WASN'T ME! *IT WASN'T ME!!* I DON'T WANT TO DIE! IT WAS THE BIRDS! ASK THE BIRDS!

CHAPTER 3: PYROMANIAC MAGPIES

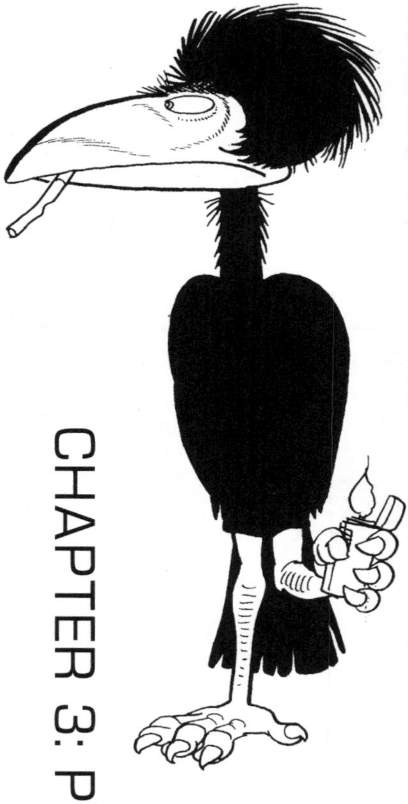

I'M SADATSUNE SAKUEMONNOJO KOMATSU.
I KNOW... TERRIBLE NAME. I HATE MY PARENTS FOR NAMING ME THIS.
BUT I'VE BEEN ADVISED THAT CHANGING IT WOULD BRING BAD LUCK.
SO I'VE DEALT WITH IT MY WHOLE LIFE.
BUT I'VE HAD ENOUGH. I'M A NEWS COMMENTATOR FOR QPTV, AND AFTER EVERY BROADCAST, VIEWERS COMPLAIN. THEY THINK I'M JOKING ABOUT MY NAME.

SO I MADE UP MY MIND. I WENT TO THE CITY OFFICE TO CHANGE MY LEGAL NAME.
SADATSUNE SAKUE-MONNOJO KOMATSU... OH, YOU'RE THAT ANNOUNCER.
THAT'S RIGHT... I NEED A NAME THAT'S SHORT AND SNAPPY. I LOVE SAKYŌ KOMATSU BOOKS, SO I'LL GO WITH UKYŌ KOMATSU.
MR. KOMATSU, IT'S FOR YOU. IT'S THE TV STATION.
GET BACK HERE! WE'RE AIRING A SPECIAL PROGRAM! YOU'RE THE ONLY ONE WHO SPEAKS RUSSIAN!
WHAT'S GOING ON? DID THE SOVIETS DO A SOFT LANDING ON MARS?
NO, IT'S MAGPIES.
A SWARM OF BIRDS RANSACKED THE USSR. MOSCOW HAS WARNED US THEY'RE HEADING TOWARD JAPAN.
HUH?
A GANG OF CRAZY BIRDS IS SETTING FIRE TO EVERYTHING THEY SEE. THEY'RE A TYPE OF MAGPIE... SUPER SMART!

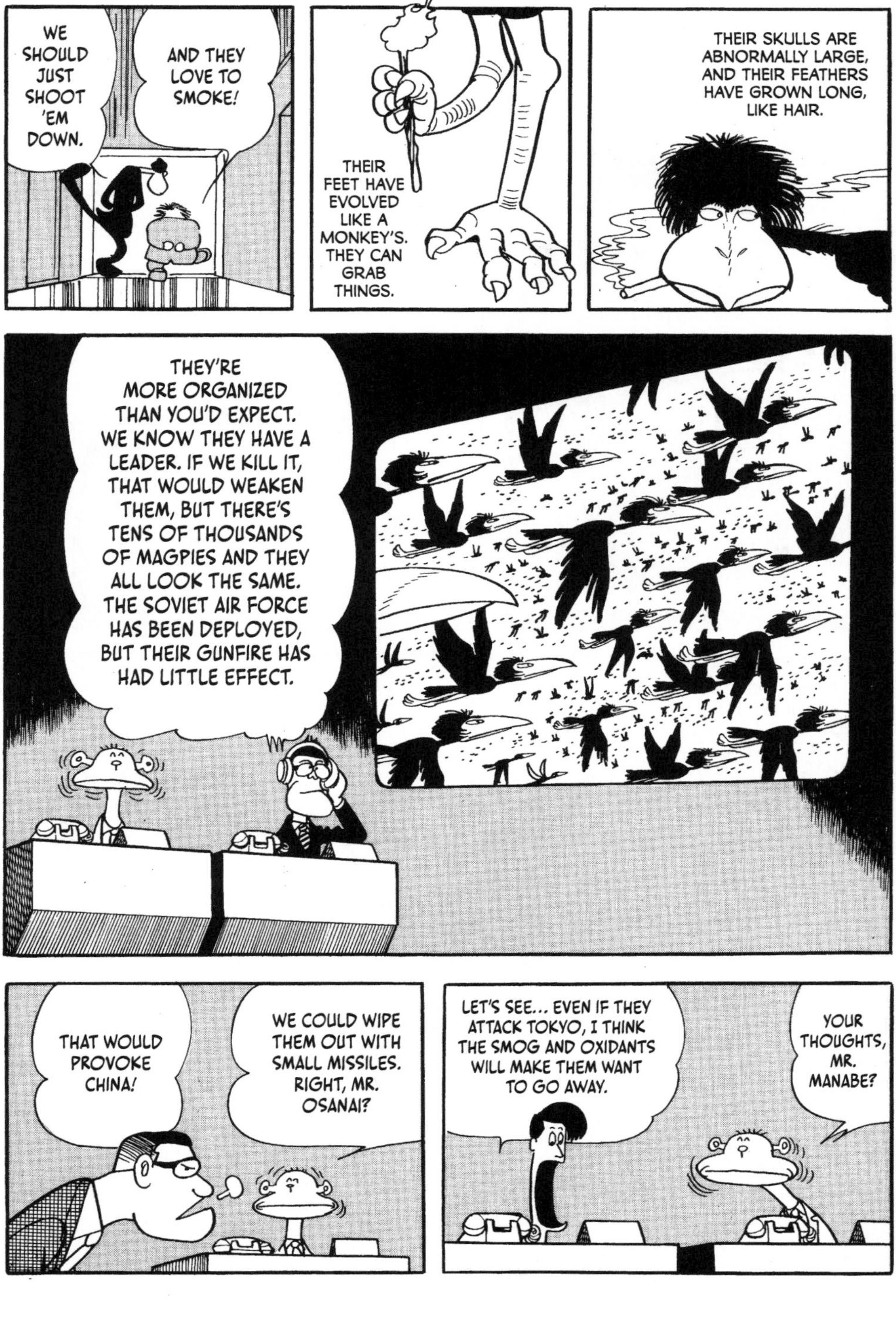
WE SHOULD JUST SHOOT 'EM DOWN.
AND THEY LOVE TO SMOKE!
THEIR FEET HAVE EVOLVED LIKE A MONKEY'S. THEY CAN GRAB THINGS.
THEIR SKULLS ARE ABNORMALLY LARGE, AND THEIR FEATHERS HAVE GROWN LONG, LIKE HAIR.
THEY'RE MORE ORGANIZED THAN YOU'D EXPECT. WE KNOW THEY HAVE A LEADER. IF WE KILL IT, THAT WOULD WEAKEN THEM, BUT THERE'S TENS OF THOUSANDS OF MAGPIES AND THEY ALL LOOK THE SAME. THE SOVIET AIR FORCE HAS BEEN DEPLOYED, BUT THEIR GUNFIRE HAS HAD LITTLE EFFECT.
WE COULD WIPE THEM OUT WITH SMALL MISSILES. RIGHT, MR. OSANAI?
THAT WOULD PROVOKE CHINA!
YOUR THOUGHTS, MR. MANABE?
LET'S SEE... EVEN IF THEY ATTACK TOKYO, I THINK THE SMOG AND OXIDANTS WILL MAKE THEM WANT TO GO AWAY.

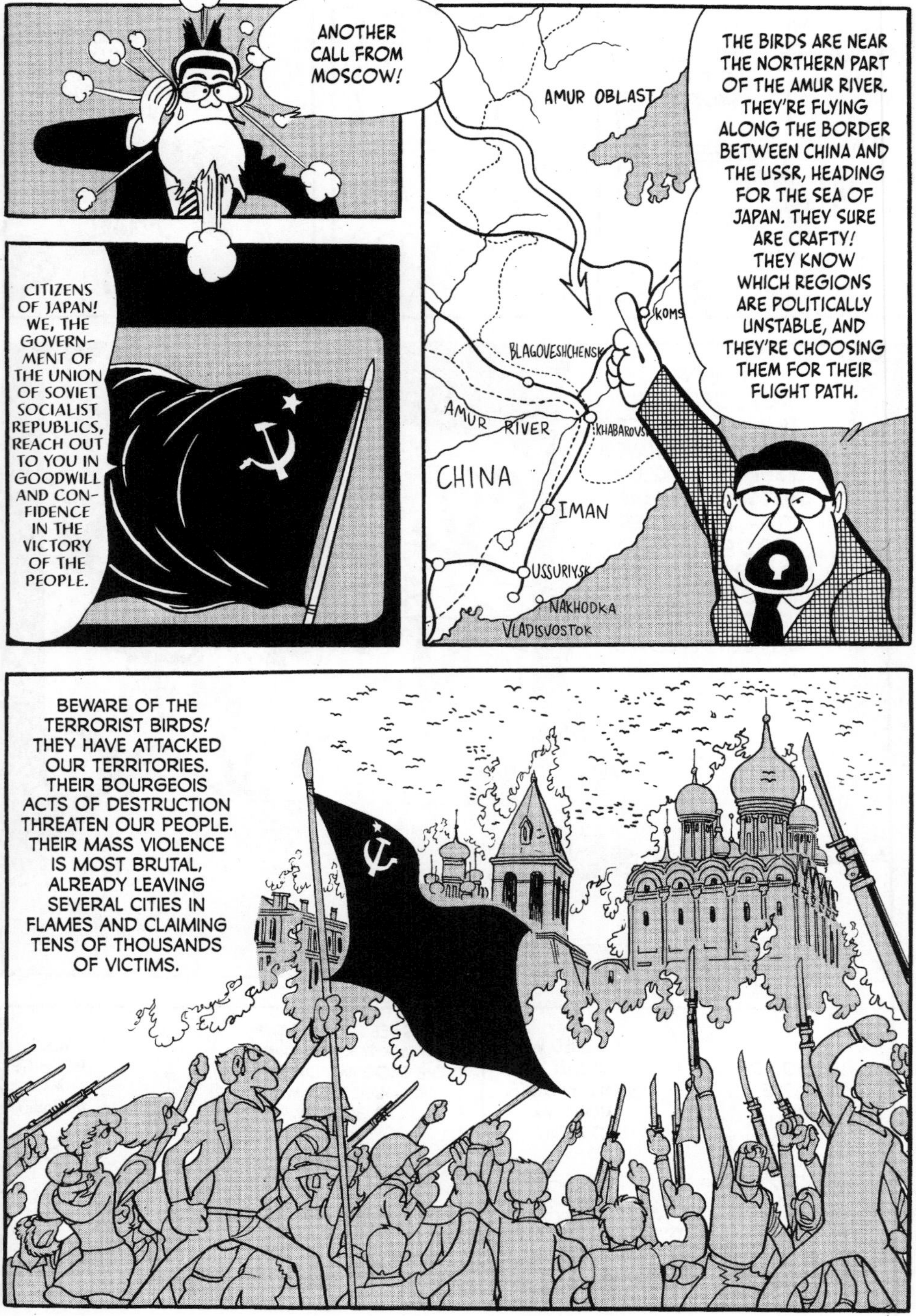
ANOTHER CALL FROM MOSCOW!
AMUR OBLAST
THE BIRDS ARE NEAR THE NORTHERN PART OF THE AMUR RIVER. THEY'RE FLYING ALONG THE BORDER BETWEEN CHINA AND THE USSR, HEADING FOR THE SEA OF JAPAN. THEY SURE ARE CRAFTY! THEY KNOW WHICH REGIONS ARE POLITICALLY UNSTABLE, AND THEY'RE CHOOSING THEM FOR THEIR FLIGHT PATH.
KOMS
BLAGOVESHCHENSK
AMUR RIVER
KHABAROVS
CHINA
IMAN
USSURIYSK
NAKHODKA
VLADISVOSTOK
CITIZENS OF JAPAN! WE, THE GOVERNMENT OF THE UNION OF SOVIET SOCIALIST REPUBLICS, REACH OUT TO YOU IN GOODWILL AND CONFIDENCE IN THE VICTORY OF THE PEOPLE.
BEWARE OF THE TERRORIST BIRDS! THEY HAVE ATTACKED OUR TERRITORIES. THEIR BOURGEOIS ACTS OF DESTRUCTION THREATEN OUR PEOPLE. THEIR MASS VIOLENCE IS MOST BRUTAL, ALREADY LEAVING SEVERAL CITIES IN FLAMES AND CLAIMING TENS OF THOUSANDS OF VICTIMS.

DAMN!! WHAT ON EARTH...?!
THE SOVIETS ARE DISCLOSING DAMAGE FIGURES. THIS MUST BE SERIOUS...
THE BIRDS AREN'T JUST SETTING CITIES ON FIRE... THEY'RE ALSO KILLING HUMANS AND USING THEM TO MAKE YAKITORI.
YAKITORI...? YOU MEAN YAKI-HUMANS? WAS THAT A MISTRANSLATION?
THE MINISTER OF DEFENSE HAS DEPLOYED THE JAPAN AIR SELF-DEFENSE FORCE TO THE SEA OF JAPAN.
OH, THIS IS SERIOUS...
IS THAT REALLY NECES-SARY...?
NO... THEY USE SKEWERS... AND INTESTINES AND LIVER...
THEY'RE SAYING THE BIRDS ADD ONION AND SAUCE WHEN EATING HUMANS...
NON-SENSE! THAT CAN'T BE TRUE!

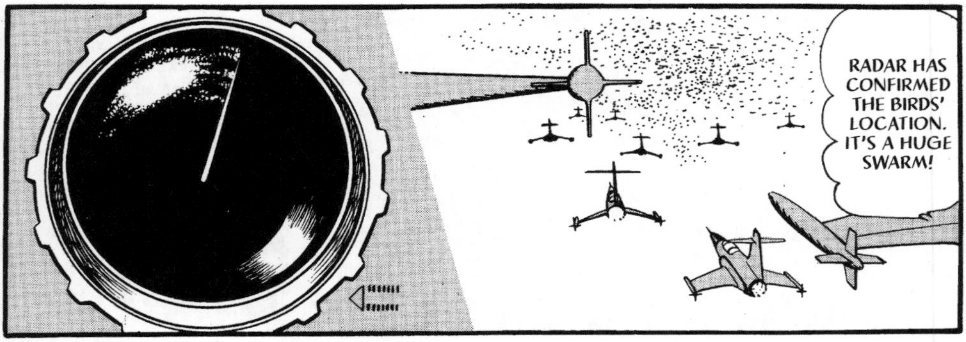
RADAR HAS CONFIRMED THE BIRDS' LOCATION. IT'S A HUGE SWARM!

BAM
RA-TA-TA-TA.
RA-TA-TA-TA-TA
NEW—N
MAX—N

THE BIRDS ARE SETTING FIRE TO THINGS, RIGHT? WE LIVE IN THE WOODS. A FIRE HERE WOULD RUIN EVERYTHING!
HONEY... I'M SCARED... I'VE BEEN WATCHING THE UPDATES.
HEY... IT'S ME. DOESN'T LOOK LIKE I'LL MAKE IT HOME TONIGHT.
THERE'S NO END TO THIS BREAKING NEWS...
SOMETHING BAD'S GONNA HAPPEN...
MAYBE I SHOULDN'T HAVE CHANGED MY NAME...
JUST THINK OF THE LOAN BIRDS THAT VISIT EVERY MONTH. THEY'RE A LOT SCARIER...
HUH? DON'T BE SO MAD. DON'T WORRY.
A STATE OF EMERGENCY WAS DECLARED IN THE HOKURIKU AND JŌETSU REGIONS. RESIDENTS ARE EVACUATING IN DROVES!
THEY'RE SAYING THE BIRDS WILL LAND IN NAOETSU OR ON THE MOUTH OF THE ITOIGAWA RIVER.
THE AIR FORCE COULDN'T STOP 'EM?
THERE'S TENS OF THOUSANDS. CAN'T KILL 'EM ALL.

THE ARSONIST MAGPIES APPROACHED FROM THE SEA OF JAPAN AND LANDED IN NIIGATA CITY. THE CITIES OF NIIGATA AND NIITSU WENT UP IN FLAMES, WITH NO HOPE OF EXTINGUISHING THE FIRES.

AFTER ALL, THE FIRES STARTED IN ALL DIRECTIONS, ALL AT ONCE. THE BIRDS EVEN ATTACKED THE EVACUATING CARS. CONVERTIBLES AND PICKUP TRUCKS WERE THE FIRST TO FALL VICTIM.

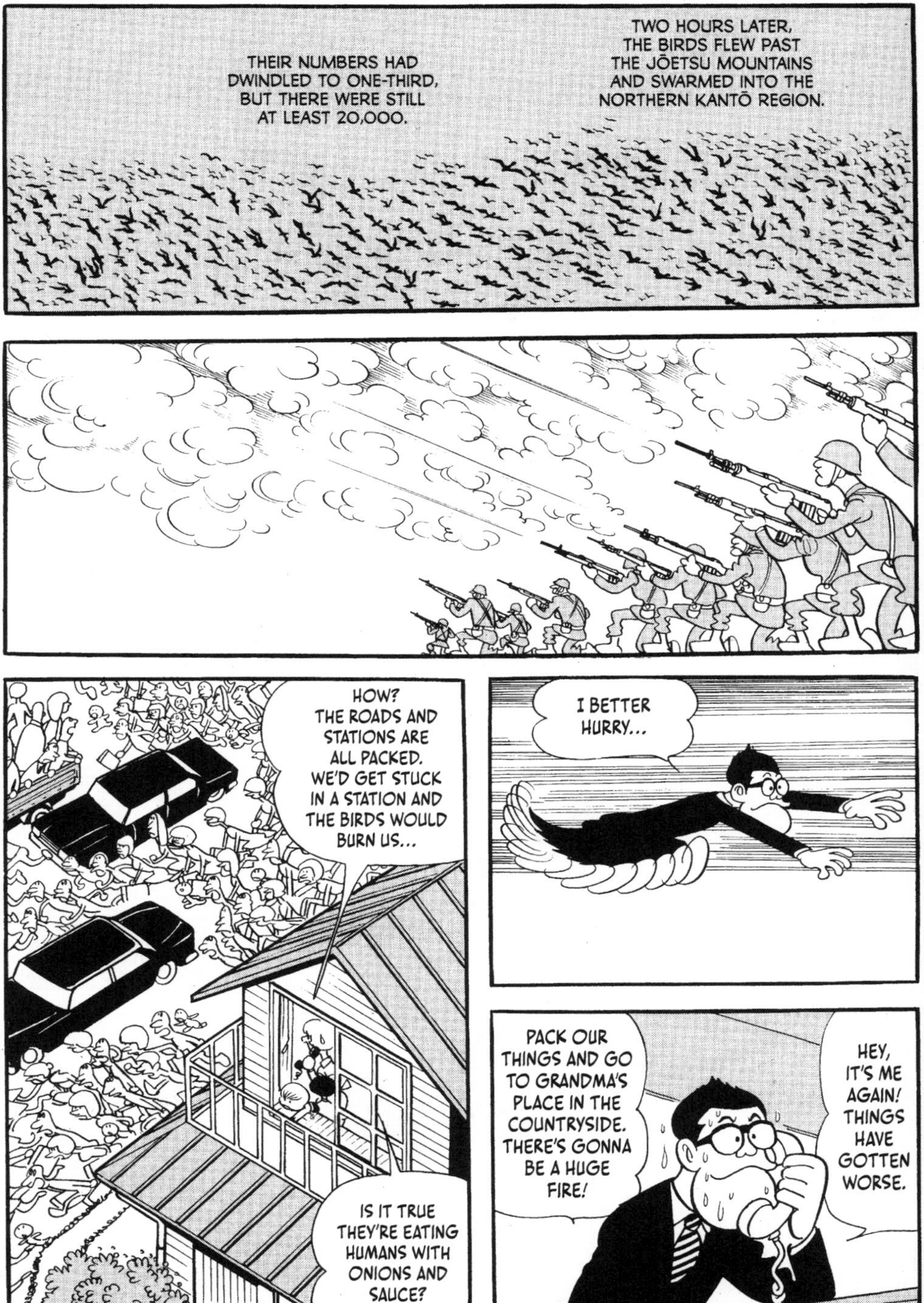
TWO HOURS LATER, THE BIRDS FLEW PAST THE JŌETSU MOUNTAINS AND SWARMED INTO THE NORTHERN KANTŌ REGION.
THEIR NUMBERS HAD DWINDLED TO ONE-THIRD, BUT THERE WERE STILL AT LEAST 20,000.
I BETTER HURRY...
HEY, IT'S ME AGAIN! THINGS HAVE GOTTEN WORSE.
PACK OUR THINGS AND GO TO GRANDMA'S PLACE IN THE COUNTRYSIDE. THERE'S GONNA BE A HUGE FIRE!
HOW? THE ROADS AND STATIONS ARE ALL PACKED. WE'D GET STUCK IN A STATION AND THE BIRDS WOULD BURN US...
IS IT TRUE THEY'RE EATING HUMANS WITH ONIONS AND SAUCE?

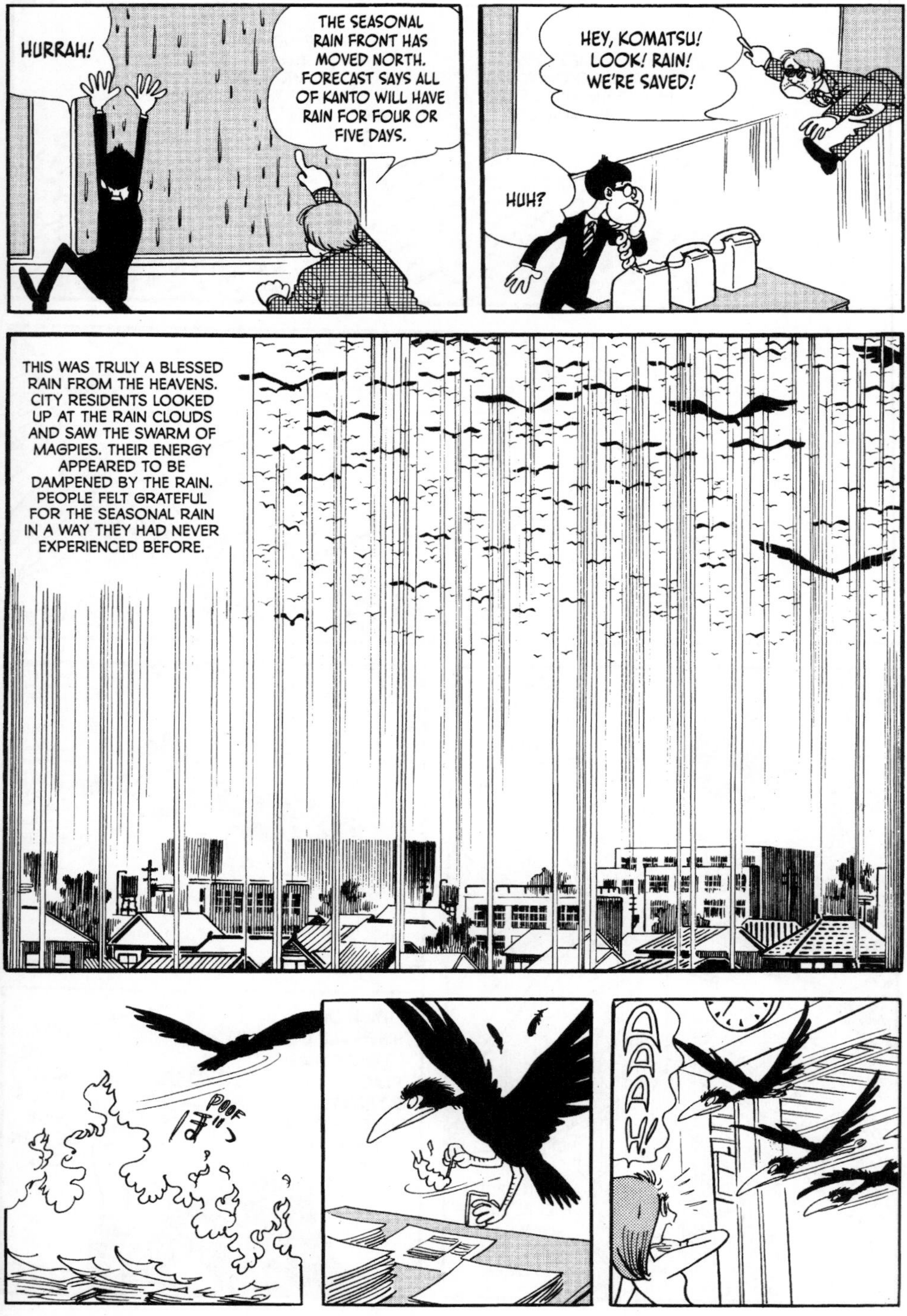
HURRAH!
THE SEASONAL RAIN FRONT HAS MOVED NORTH. FORECAST SAYS ALL OF KANTO WILL HAVE RAIN FOR FOUR OR FIVE DAYS.
HEY, KOMATSU! LOOK! RAIN! WE'RE SAVED!
HUH?
THIS WAS TRULY A BLESSED RAIN FROM THE HEAVENS. CITY RESIDENTS LOOKED UP AT THE RAIN CLOUDS AND SAW THE SWARM OF MAGPIES. THEIR ENERGY APPEARED TO BE DAMPENED BY THE RAIN. PEOPLE FELT GRATEFUL FOR THE SEASONAL RAIN IN A WAY THEY HAD NEVER EXPERIENCED BEFORE.
POOF
HAAAAH!

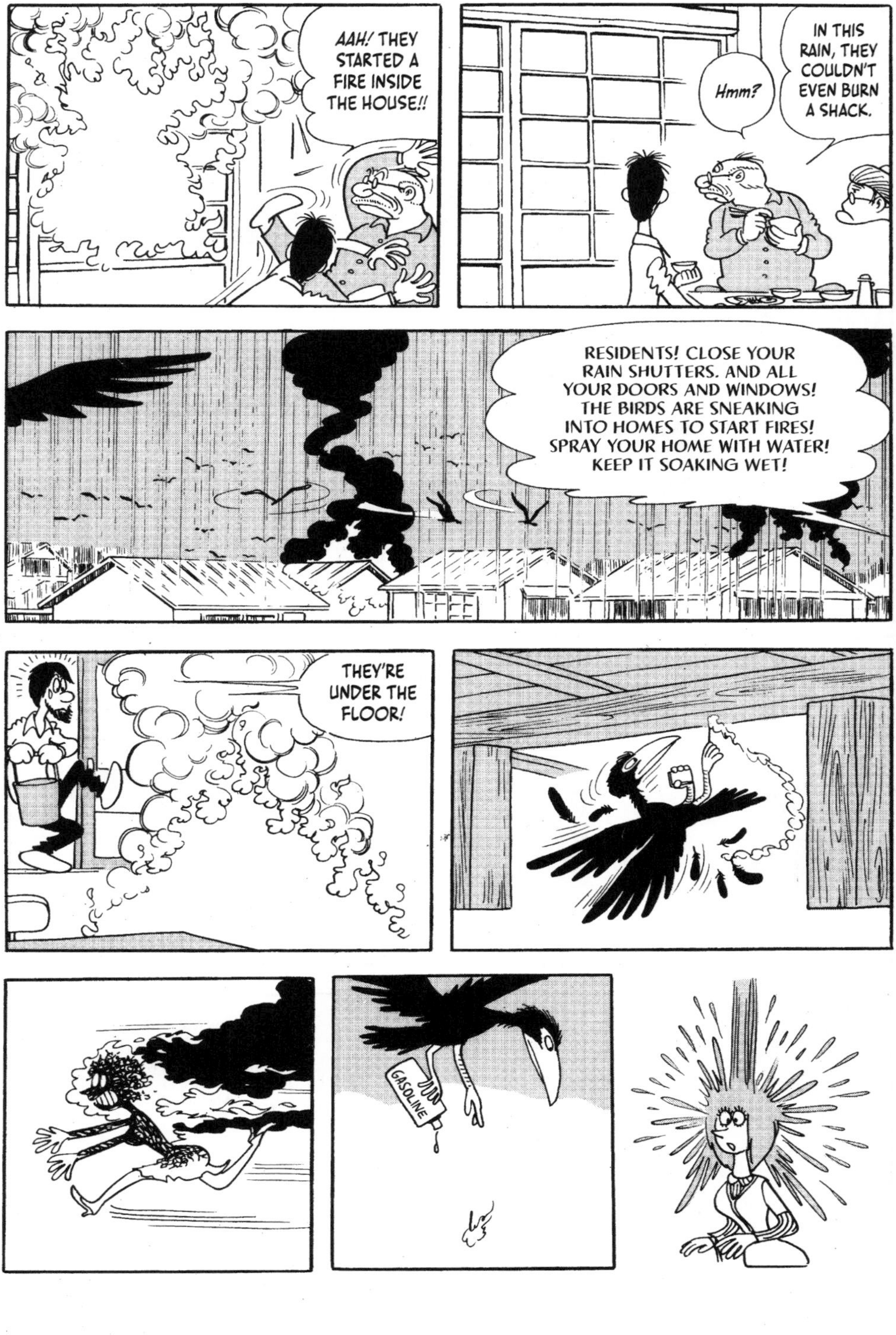
AAH! THEY STARTED A FIRE INSIDE THE HOUSE!!
IN THIS RAIN, THEY COULDN'T EVEN BURN A SHACK.
Hmm?
RESIDENTS! CLOSE YOUR RAIN SHUTTERS. AND ALL YOUR DOORS AND WINDOWS! THE BIRDS ARE SNEAKING INTO HOMES TO START FIRES! SPRAY YOUR HOME WITH WATER! KEEP IT SOAKING WET!
THEY'RE UNDER THE FLOOR!
GASOLINE

THERE WAS DISAGREEMENT IN THE GOVERNMENT'S SPECIAL TASK FORCE BETWEEN THE HAWKS, WHO DEMANDED ANNIHILATION OF THE MAGPIES, EVEN IF IT MEANT BURNING THE CAPITAL CITY TO ASHES, AND THE DOVES, WHO ADVOCATED SCATTERING BIRDFEED TO FILL THE BIRDS' STOMACHS AND ENCOURAGING THEM TO FLY TO ANOTHER COUNTRY.
IN ADDITION TO THE HAWKS AND DOVES, A MAGPIE FACTION EMERGED. THEY PROPOSED ACCEPTING THE MAGPIES' DEMANDS AND SEEKING CO-EXISTENCE.
THIS WAY, SIR.
THEY MIGHT JUST BE ACTING OUT OF A SENSE OF ALIENATION.
CONSIDER THE BIRDS' ARGUMENTS?! ABSOLUTELY NOT!
IT WANTS TO TAKE ME TO MEET THEIR LEADERS.
AN ORNITHOLOGIST, THE ONLY HUMAN FLUENT IN MAGPIE, SERVED AS THE MEDIATOR.

LET US REMOVE OUR GARMENTS AND HAVE A HEART-TO-HEART...OR SHOULD I SAY... REMOVE OUR FEATHERS...
HEAVEN DOES NOT CREATE ONE BIRD ABOVE OR BELOW ANOTHER. YOU ARE GOD'S CREATION.
THEY'RE SAYING...
THEY INTEND TO ELIMINATE HUMAN HISTORY AND DESTROY EVERY TRACE OF OUR CULTURE.
THEN THEY WILL BUILD A WORLD OF PEACE AND EQUALITY. A WORLD FOR BIRDS.
IF WE LET THEM USE JAPAN AS THE BASE FOR THEIR REVOLUTION, THEY WON'T BOTHER HARMING THE JAPANESE PEOPLE.
IMPOSSI-BLE!
AND THUS THE HISTORICAL FUJIMIDAI CONFERENCE WAS HELD IN NERIMA.
LISTEN, BIRDS...

YOU THINK THAT'LL WORK WITH THE BIRDS?
WHEN DEALING WITH OTHER COUNTRIES, WE'VE ALWAYS TAKEN A CRAVEN APPROACH, SO...
WELL, WE JAPANESE HAVE ALREADY BEEN HOSTING MILITARY BASES OF A FOREIGN COUNTRY.
WHAT DO YOU THINK, FOREIGN MINISTER?
FELLOW CITIZENS, LET'S WELCOME THE MAGPIES INTO OUR HOMES.
WE'LL WORK WITH THE MAGPIES, BUT A LEADING NATION LIKE OURS WILL NOT DEAL WITH CROWS!
FOOL! THEY'RE NOT CROWS.
OUR CRAVEN APPROACH... CAN BE OUR RAVEN APPROACH.
SO, I PULLED OUT AN OLD FILM AND PATCHED TOGETHER A SHOW TO PLEASE THE MAGPIES. THE FILM I USED WAS *HECKLE AND JECKLE.*
KOMATSU, HOW ABOUT A SPECIAL PROGRAM TO EDUCATE MAGPIES?
I'M GETTING GOOSE-BUMPS...
Welp ...
WE NEED TO GET ALONG WITH THEM.

CHAPTER 4: ONCE UPON A TIME, HAPPILY EVER AFTER

ONCE UPON A TIME, AN OLD MAN AND AN OLD WOMAN (NOTE 1) WERE FORCED TO WORK FOR A SPARROW (NOTE 2). THE MAN SERVED THE SPARROW WITH GREAT KINDNESS, BUT THE WOMAN HATED THE SPARROW AND HARASSED IT.
(NOTE 1) THEY'RE HUMAN, OF COURSE.
(NOTE 2) PASSER MONTANUS IGNUS. IN OTHER WORDS, SPARROWS WHO USE FIRE. PROTECTED BY THE GOVERNMENT. SERVED BY HUMANS.

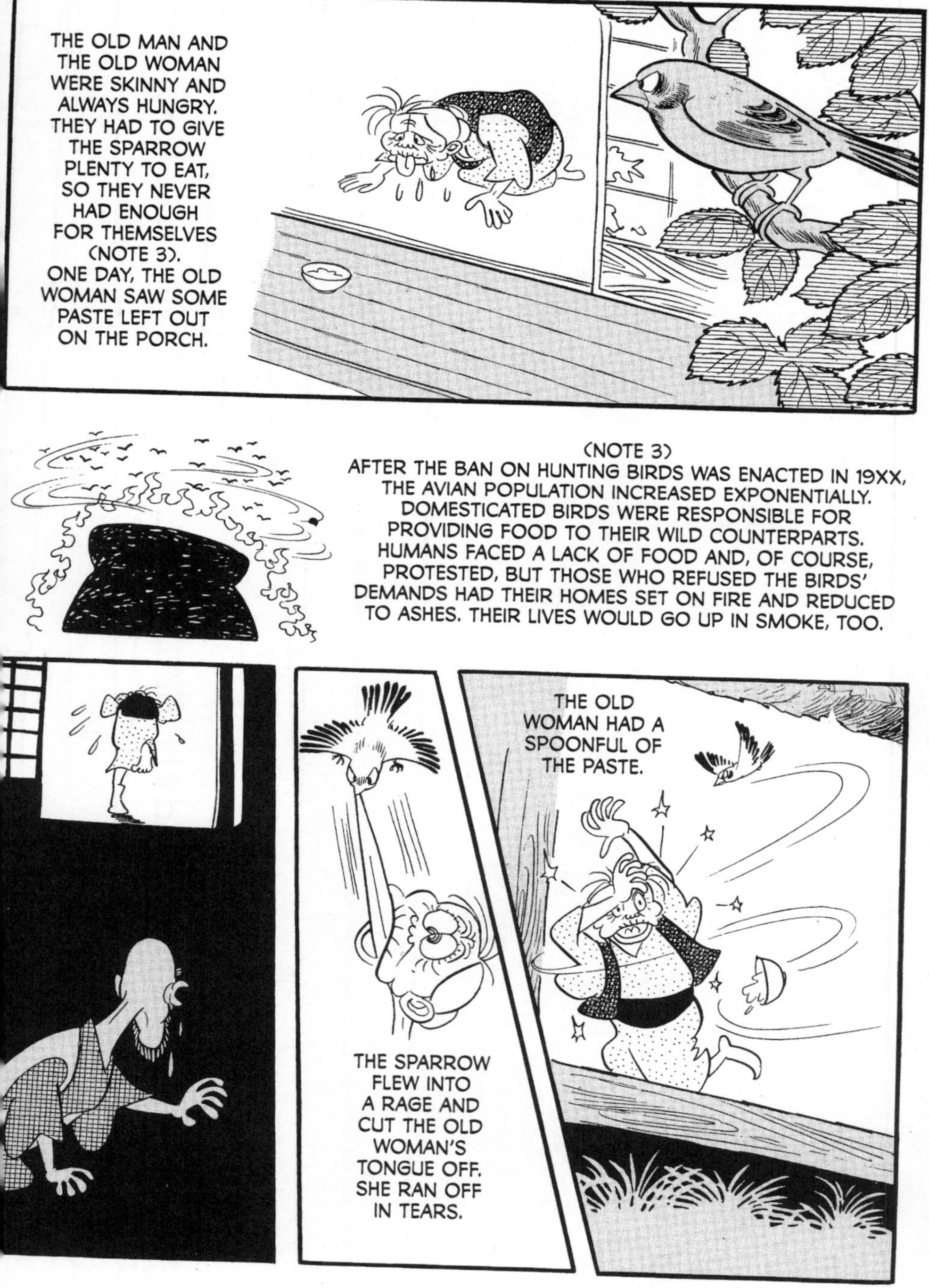
THE OLD MAN AND THE OLD WOMAN WERE SKINNY AND ALWAYS HUNGRY. THEY HAD TO GIVE THE SPARROW PLENTY TO EAT, SO THEY NEVER HAD ENOUGH FOR THEMSELVES (NOTE 3). ONE DAY, THE OLD WOMAN SAW SOME PASTE LEFT OUT ON THE PORCH.
(NOTE 3)
AFTER THE BAN ON HUNTING BIRDS WAS ENACTED IN 19XX, THE AVIAN POPULATION INCREASED EXPONENTIALLY. DOMESTICATED BIRDS WERE RESPONSIBLE FOR PROVIDING FOOD TO THEIR WILD COUNTERPARTS. HUMANS FACED A LACK OF FOOD AND, OF COURSE, PROTESTED, BUT THOSE WHO REFUSED THE BIRDS' DEMANDS HAD THEIR HOMES SET ON FIRE AND REDUCED TO ASHES. THEIR LIVES WOULD GO UP IN SMOKE, TOO.
THE OLD WOMAN HAD A SPOONFUL OF THE PASTE.
THE SPARROW FLEW INTO A RAGE AND CUT THE OLD WOMAN'S TONGUE OFF. SHE RAN OFF IN TEARS.

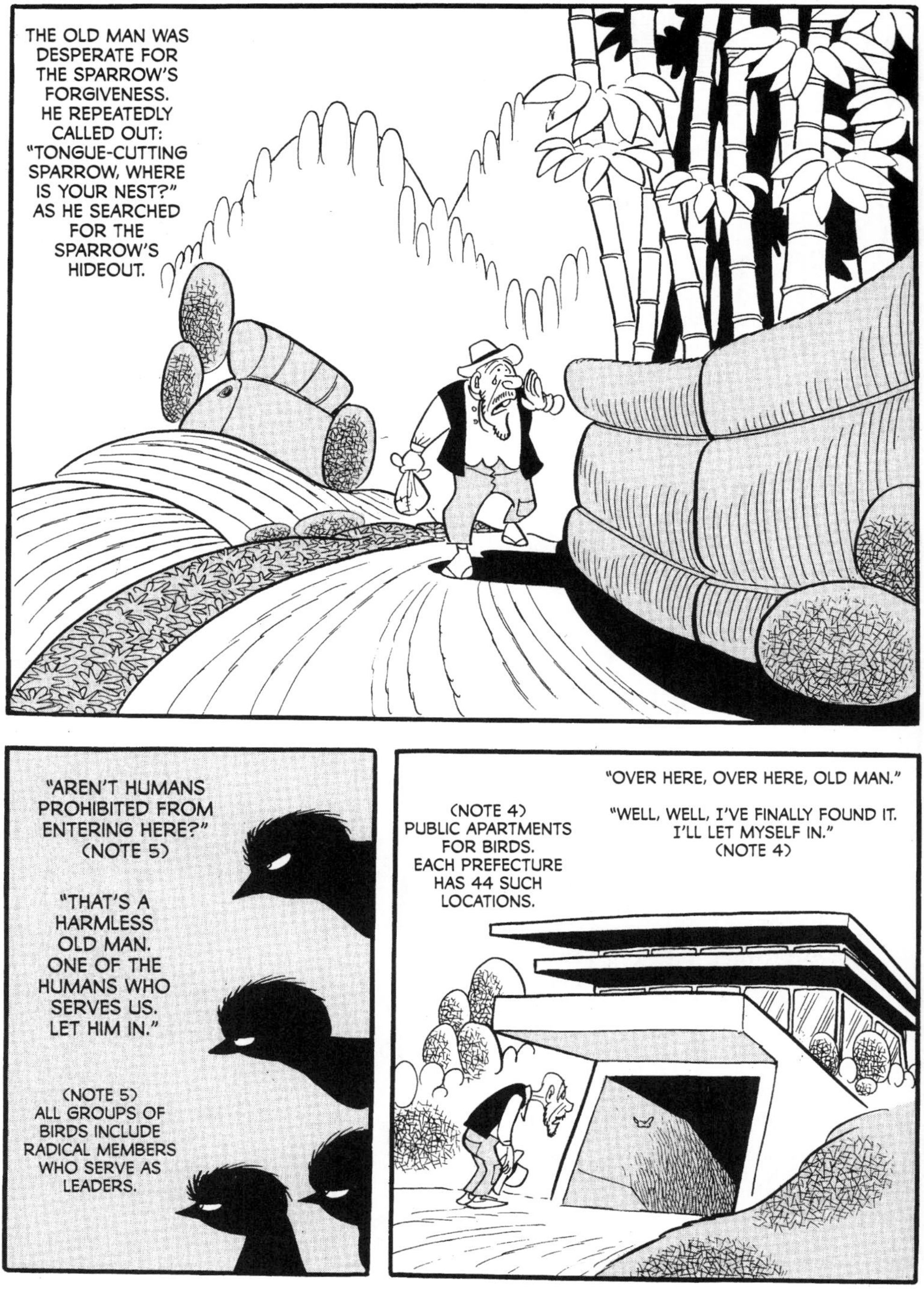
THE OLD MAN WAS DESPERATE FOR THE SPARROW'S FORGIVENESS. HE REPEATEDLY CALLED OUT: "TONGUE-CUTTING SPARROW, WHERE IS YOUR NEST?" AS HE SEARCHED FOR THE SPARROW'S HIDEOUT.
"AREN'T HUMANS PROHIBITED FROM ENTERING HERE?" (NOTE 5)
"THAT'S A HARMLESS OLD MAN. ONE OF THE HUMANS WHO SERVES US. LET HIM IN."
(NOTE 5) ALL GROUPS OF BIRDS INCLUDE RADICAL MEMBERS WHO SERVE AS LEADERS.
"OVER HERE, OVER HERE, OLD MAN."
"WELL, WELL, I'VE FINALLY FOUND IT. I'LL LET MYSELF IN." (NOTE 4)
(NOTE 4) PUBLIC APARTMENTS FOR BIRDS. EACH PREFECTURE HAS 44 SUCH LOCATIONS.

"HERE ARE TWO BOXES. TAKE ONE WITH YOU AND KEEP IT AT HOME."
"I CHOOSE THE SMALL ONE."
THE OLD MAN PUT THE BOX ON HIS BACK AND CAME BACK DOWN THE MOUNTAIN.
"YOU'VE COME A LONG WAY. HAVE SOMETHING TO EAT BEFORE YOU GO."
THE OLD MAN WAS SERVED A SPECIAL MEAL.
"WOW, YOU HAVE SUCH DELICIOUS FOOD HERE!"
"WE HAVE JUST ONE CONDITION."
"I'M SORRY FOR WHAT MY WIFE HAS DONE," THE OLD MAN APOLOGIZED.
"WE'LL LET IT GO THIS TIME. BUT DON'T UNDERESTIMATE OUR POWER." (NOTE 6)
(NOTE 6) TO COMMUNICATE WITH HUMANS, BIRDS USUALLY USE A VOICE-IMITATING DEVICE ON A COMPUTER.

THE TOWN WAS FILLED WITH HUNGRY PEOPLE. THEY ALL HATED THE BIRDS.
"WE CAN'T LET LOWLY CREATURES LIKE BIRDS CONTROL US!"
"MUMBLE MUMBLE" (NOTE 7)
AROUND THAT TIME, THE OLD WOMAN RAN AWAY TO TOWN.

"HOW CAN WE GET RID OF THEM ALL AT ONCE?"
"MUMBLE MUMBLE" (NOTE 7)
(NOTE 7) THE OLD WOMAN'S TONGUE WAS CUT, SO NOBODY COULD UNDERSTAND HER.

"I KNOW! WE SHOULD BLAST POISONOUS GAS INTO THEIR HOMES. THAT'LL KILL 'EM ALL!"
"WHAT KIND OF POISONOUS GAS?"
"HOW ABOUT SULFUROUS ACID GAS?"
"YOU DO IT, OLD WOMAN."
"MUMBLE MUMBLE"
THE OLD WOMAN CARRIED A GAS TANK TO THE SPARROWS' HOMES.

THE OLD WOMAN THREW THE TANK IN. THE TANK ROLLED AND ROLLED AND EVENTUALLY CAME TO A STOP.
BOOM!

THE OLD WOMAN WENT INSIDE TO SEE IF THERE WAS ANYTHING TO EAT.
"THE BIG BOX AND THE SMALL BOX ARE BOTH FULL OF RICE. TAKE WHICHEVER ONE YOU'D LIKE."

ALL OF THE SPARROWS DIED INSTANTLY.

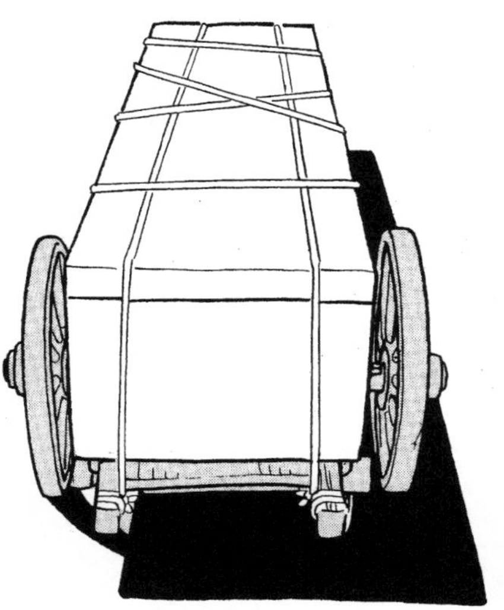

"MUMBLE MUMBLE"

THE OLD WOMAN PUT THE BIG BOX ON HER BACK AND RETURNED TO TOWN.

THE HUNGRY TOWNSFOLK WERE THRILLED TO SEE WHAT SHE'D BROUGHT (NOTE 8).

(NOTE 8)
SPARROWS WERE GIVEN NEW RICE, WHILE HUMANS WERE ONLY ALLOWED TO HAVE TWO-YEAR-OLD RICE.

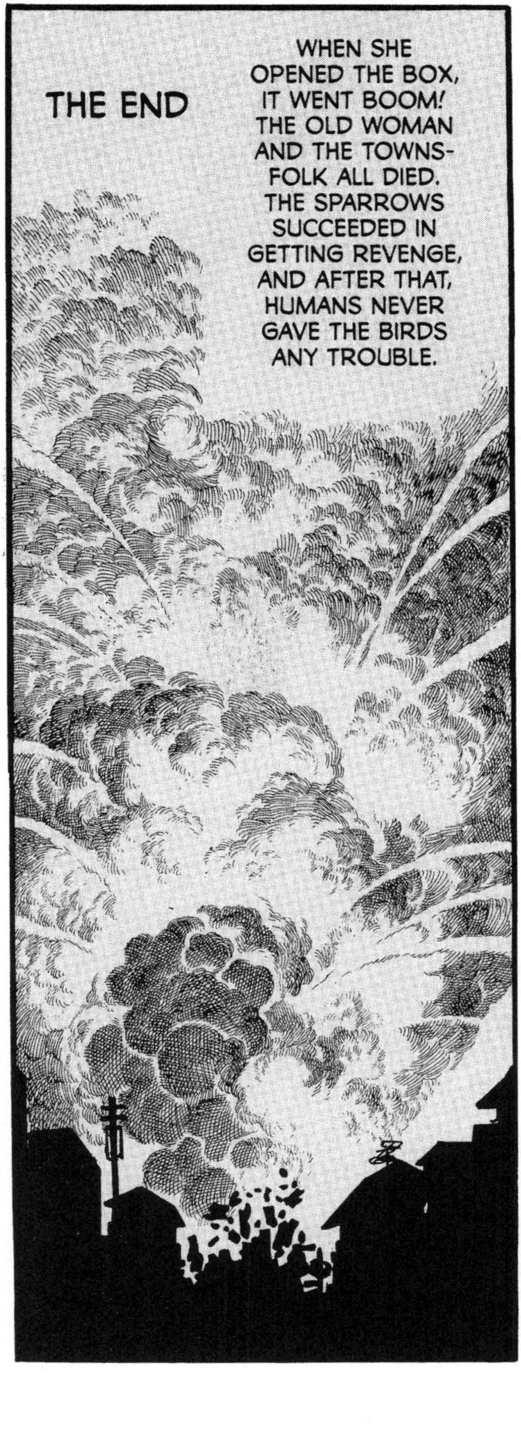

WHEN SHE OPENED THE BOX, IT WENT BOOM! THE OLD WOMAN AND THE TOWNSFOLK ALL DIED. THE SPARROWS SUCCEEDED IN GETTING REVENGE, AND AFTER THAT, HUMANS NEVER GAVE THE BIRDS ANY TROUBLE.
THE END

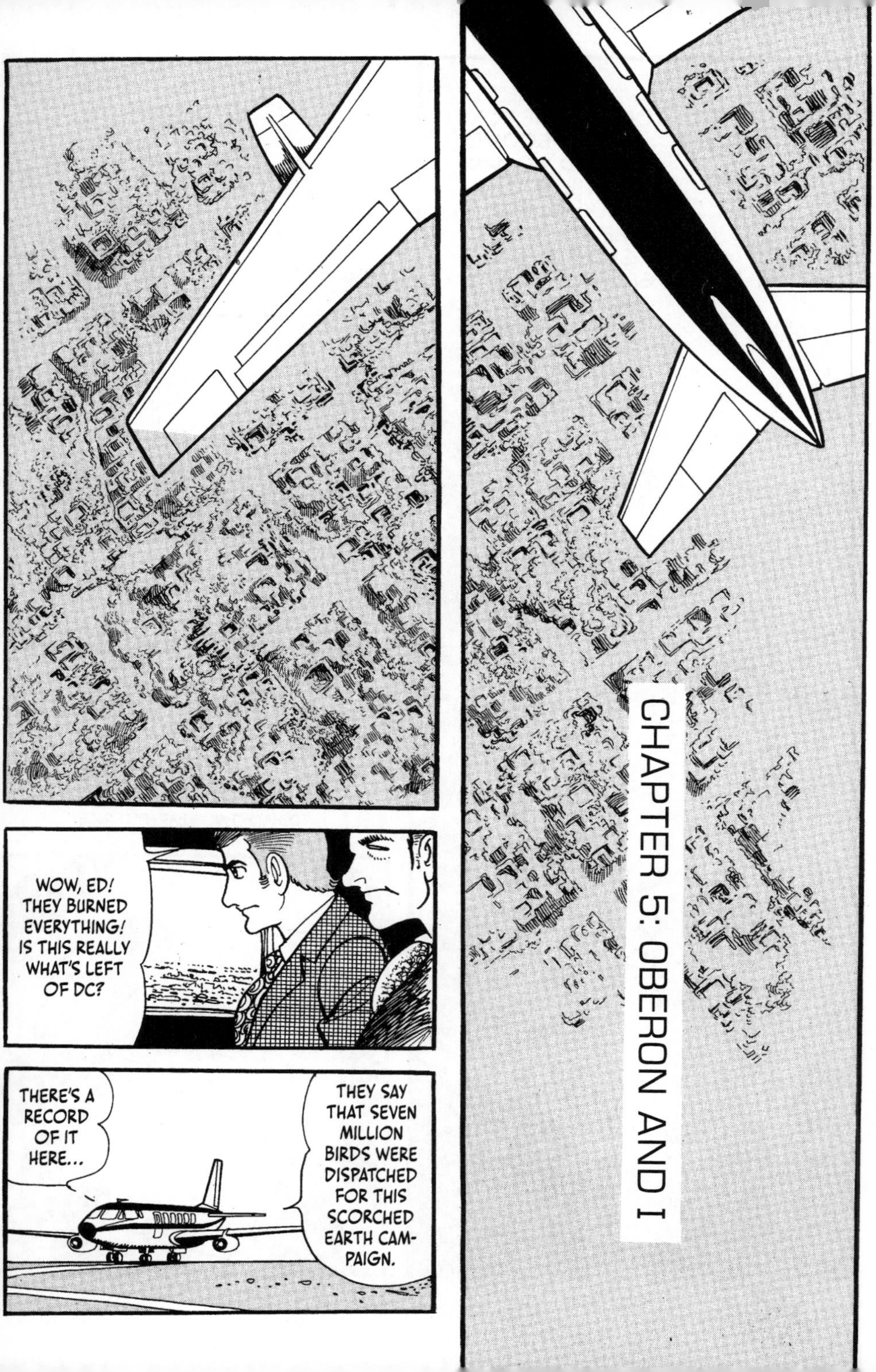
CHAPTER 5: OBERON AND I
WOW, ED! THEY BURNED EVERYTHING! IS THIS REALLY WHAT'S LEFT OF DC?
THEY SAY THAT SEVEN MILLION BIRDS WERE DISPATCHED FOR THIS SCORCHED EARTH CAMPAIGN.
THERE'S A RECORD OF IT HERE...

AROUND ONE MILLION WERE ARSON SPECIALISTS. THE REST WERE DECOYS.
THEY INTERFERED WITH FIREFIGHTING EFFORTS AND ATTACKED HUMANS.
SO, THEY'RE ORGANIZED... IMPRESSIVE.
WHOA... THIS IS THE WHITE HOUSE? IT'S THE GREY HOUSE NOW...
HEY... WHY IS A PRESIDENTIAL AIDE ASKING FOR ME?
I'M JUST A YOUNG ORNITHOLOGIST AT A SMALL INSTITUTE IN TEXAS...
THEY'RE EXPECTING YOU, MR. NIEM.
M-MR. PRESIDENT!!

I WANT YOU TO MEET THE LEADER OF THE BIRDS.
GOOD.
THANK YOU FOR COMING, MR. NIEM. OUR NATION IS IN CRISIS. ARE YOU READY TO SERVE YOUR COUNTRY LIKE ANY GOOD PATRIOT WOULD?
O-OF COURSE, SIR.
BUT WHY ME, SIR?
THEY'RE CRAZY, BUT THEY HAVE A LEADER. APPARENTLY, HE TAKES ORDERS FROM ANOTHER BIRD — THE REAL BOSS.
YES.
THE ARSONIST BIRDS? THE ONES THAT RAZED DC?
THE FBI CONFIRMED IT.
WOW... THEY GET A FINGERPRINT MATCH OR SOME-THING?
YOU USED TO DO EXPERIMENTS ON A PERUVIAN CONDOR NAMED OBERON. REMEMBER HIM?
WOULD YOU BE SURPRISED TO HEAR THAT OBERON IS THE BOSS?
W-WHAT?!

IF HE DOES... WHAT DO YOU WANT ME TO DO?
KILL HIM.
THERE ARE NO CONDORS IN NORTH AMERICA. SOMETIMES THEY WIND UP HERE BY MISTAKE, BUT THAT'S RARE. SO IT WAS EASY TO IDENTIFY HIM WHEN WE TESTED SOME FEATHERS.
OBERON MUST REMEMBER YOU. HE'LL AGREE TO SEE YOU.
IF YOU PLAY IT RIGHT, HE'LL LET HIS GUARD DOWN.
YOUR HEROIC ACT WILL GO DOWN IN HISTORY.
WHAT?!
KILL OBERON?
WITHOUT THEIR LEADER, THE BIRDS WON'T KNOW WHAT TO DO.
YOU'D BE SAVING OUR NATION... AND THE ENTIRE HUMAN RACE.
HOW CAN I... WHEN HUMANS ARE UNDER CONSTANT SURVEILLANCE FROM THE SKY?
DAMN... WHAT THE HELL...
INFILTRATING THE BIRDS' NEST WILL BE HARDER THAN SMUGGLING MYSELF INTO CHINA...

WE'RE NOW IN WEST VIRGINIA.
THIS PLACE IS IN RUINS, TOO, ED...
YEAH... THEY STORMED EVERY BUILDING IN THE AREA.
THERE'S NOT A HUMAN IN SIGHT...
THE BIRDS ATE EVERYONE. EVEN THE BONES.
THOSE LITTLE BIRDS?
I COULD SEE CONDORS DOING THAT, BUT...
THEY DO IT OUT OF NEED.
THEIR TASTES HAVE CHANGED.
THE BIRDS ARE BREEDING SO RAPIDLY THAT THEY DON'T HAVE ENOUGH FOOD. THEY KNOW THAT EATING EVERY PLANT IN SIGHT WOULD CAUSE DEVEGETATION.
YOU HUNGRY? LET'S EAT SOME-THING.
HERE'S SOME FRIED BIRD AND A BIRD SANDWICH.
MADE FROM BIRDS THAT ATTACKED DC.
WE'RE NO BETTER THAN THEM...

STOP! LISTEN TO ME!
I KNOW YOUR BOSS, OBERON! HE'S MY FRIEND!
THERE'S AN OLD NOVEL BY DU MAURIER CALLED *THE BIRDS.* IT'S ABOUT BIRDS THAT ATTACK HUMANS FOR NO REASON. BUT WHAT'S HAPPENING NOW... IS TOTALLY DIFFERENT. IT'S A BATTLE FOR SURVIVAL BETWEEN BIRDS AND HUMANS. IT'S A MATTER OF LIFE AND DEATH.
LOOK OUT, FREDDIE! THEY'RE GOING TO MAKE THEIR MOVE.

OBERON!!
IT'S GOOD TO SEE YOU, OBERON!
REMEMBER ME? IT'S PROFESSOR NIEM, FROM THE SAN ANGELO BIRD INSTITUTE.
IT'S GOOD TO SEE YOU, TOO, FREDDIE. I KNEW YOU'D BE COMING.
HUH? ARE YOU HIS INTERPRETER?
I'M TRANSMITTING SIGNALS INTO THIS HUMAN'S BRAIN SO I CAN TALK TO YOU. THINK OF HER AS AN INSTANTANEOUS INTERPRETING MACHINE. NEEDLESS TO SAY, I'VE ERASED HER PERSONALITY.
COME ON INSIDE. MAKE YOURSELF AT HOME. WE HAVE A LOT TO CATCH UP ON.
I TRUST YOU'LL ABANDON THAT SILLY PLAN TO KILL ME... RIGHT?
HUH?

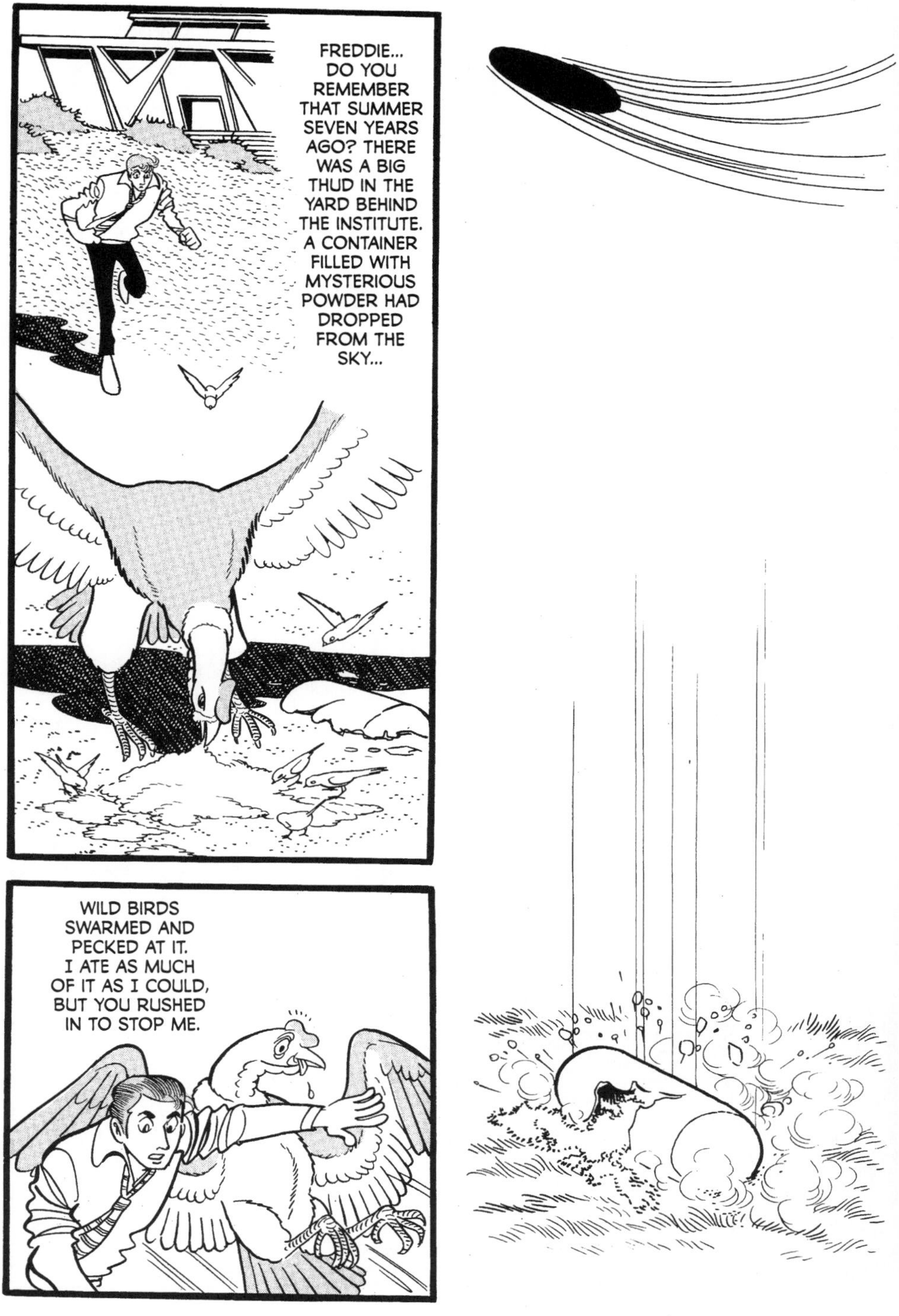
FREDDIE... DO YOU REMEMBER THAT SUMMER SEVEN YEARS AGO? THERE WAS A BIG THUD IN THE YARD BEHIND THE INSTITUTE. A CONTAINER FILLED WITH MYSTERIOUS POWDER HAD DROPPED FROM THE SKY...
WILD BIRDS SWARMED AND PECKED AT IT. I ATE AS MUCH OF IT AS I COULD, BUT YOU RUSHED IN TO STOP ME.

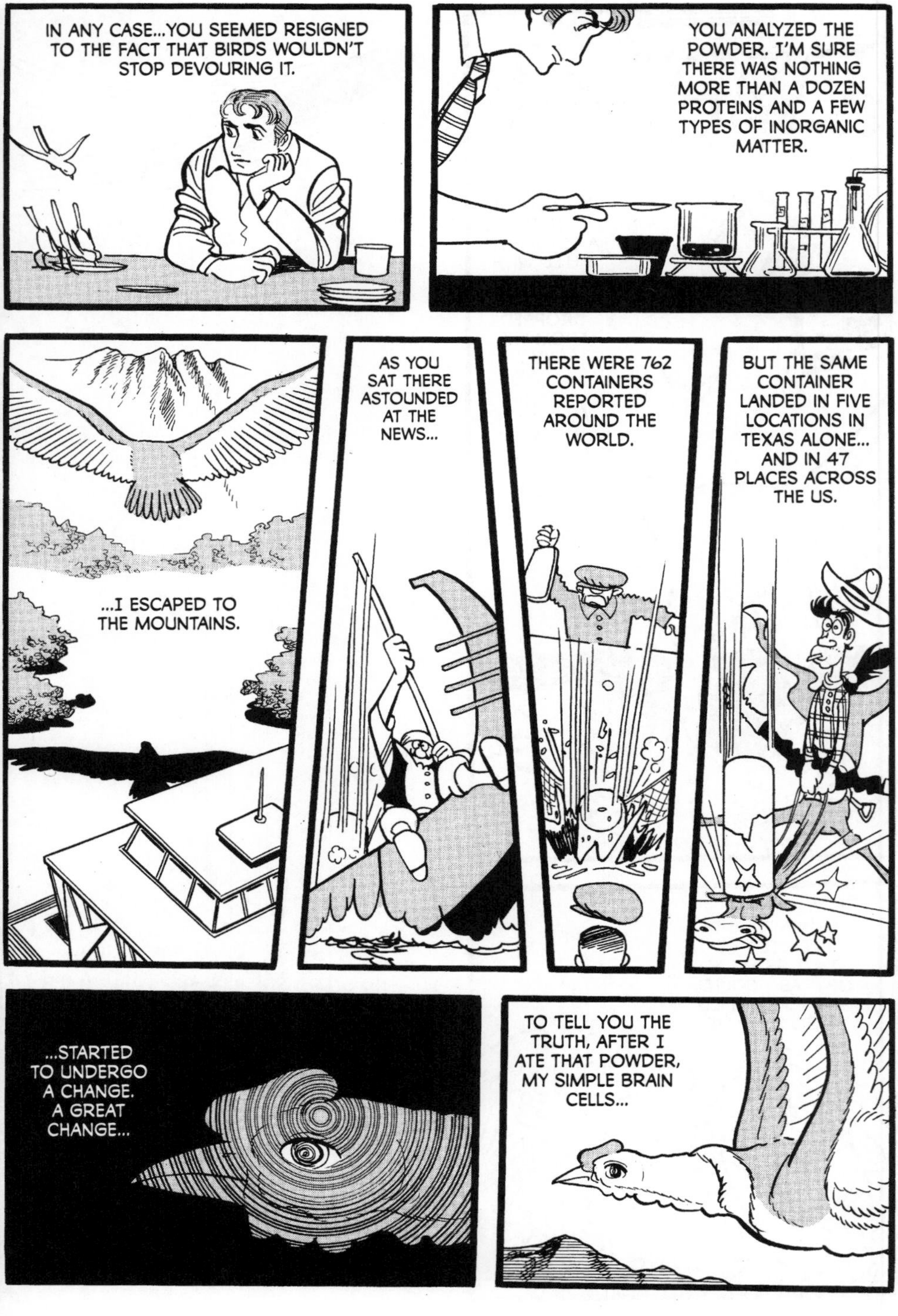
IN ANY CASE...YOU SEEMED RESIGNED TO THE FACT THAT BIRDS WOULDN'T STOP DEVOURING IT.
YOU ANALYZED THE POWDER. I'M SURE THERE WAS NOTHING MORE THAN A DOZEN PROTEINS AND A FEW TYPES OF INORGANIC MATTER.
...I ESCAPED TO THE MOUNTAINS.
AS YOU SAT THERE ASTOUNDED AT THE NEWS...
THERE WERE 762 CONTAINERS REPORTED AROUND THE WORLD.
BUT THE SAME CONTAINER LANDED IN FIVE LOCATIONS IN TEXAS ALONE... AND IN 47 PLACES ACROSS THE US.
TO TELL YOU THE TRUTH, AFTER I ATE THAT POWDER, MY SIMPLE BRAIN CELLS...
...STARTED TO UNDERGO A CHANGE. A GREAT CHANGE...

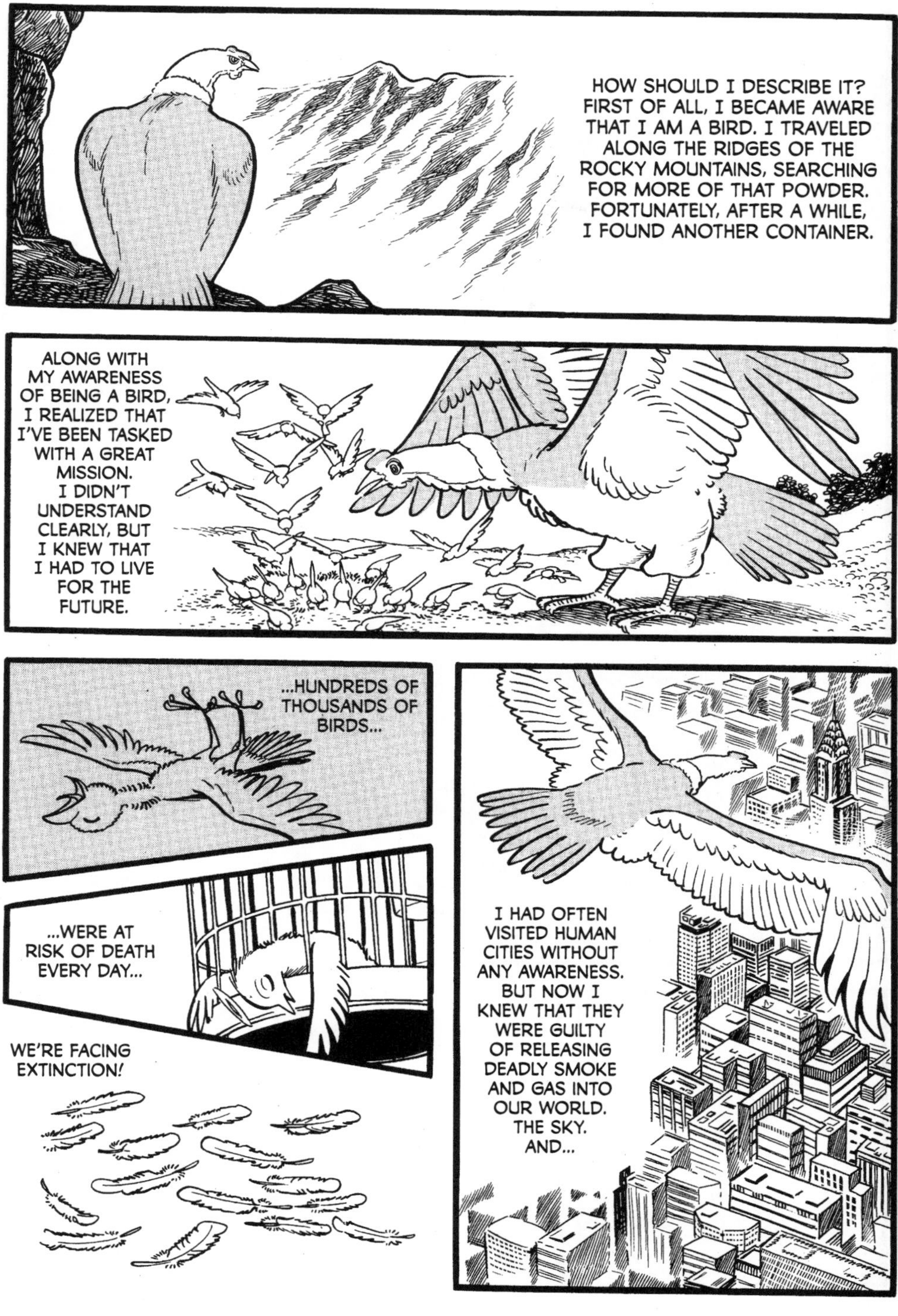
HOW SHOULD I DESCRIBE IT? FIRST OF ALL, I BECAME AWARE THAT I AM A BIRD. I TRAVELED ALONG THE RIDGES OF THE ROCKY MOUNTAINS, SEARCHING FOR MORE OF THAT POWDER. FORTUNATELY, AFTER A WHILE, I FOUND ANOTHER CONTAINER.
ALONG WITH MY AWARENESS OF BEING A BIRD, I REALIZED THAT I'VE BEEN TASKED WITH A GREAT MISSION. I DIDN'T UNDERSTAND CLEARLY, BUT I KNEW THAT I HAD TO LIVE FOR THE FUTURE.
...HUNDREDS OF THOUSANDS OF BIRDS...
...WERE AT RISK OF DEATH EVERY DAY...
WE'RE FACING EXTINCTION!
I HAD OFTEN VISITED HUMAN CITIES WITHOUT ANY AWARENESS. BUT NOW I KNEW THAT THEY WERE GUILTY OF RELEASING DEADLY SMOKE AND GAS INTO OUR WORLD. THE SKY. AND...

IT TOLD ME THAT ALL AROUND THE WORLD, BIRDS HAVE EATEN THAT POWDER AND ARE NOW AWARE. THEY'VE STARTED TO TAKE ACTION.
FREDDIE, I KNOW YOU THINK WE ATTACKED HUMANS OUT OF HATRED, BUT I WANT YOU TO UNDERSTAND. WE...
...ARE SIMPLY ASSERTING OUR RIGHT TO SURVIVE.
I MET A SHEARWATER FROM HAWAII...
IN JAPAN, A CLEVER AND GREEDY PERSON ANALYZED THE POWDER AND SYNTHESIZED IT. THEY'VE STARTED TO MASS PRODUCE IT AS BIRD FEED. IT'S BEING EXPORTED ALL AROUND THE WORLD, AND ALL KINDS OF DOMESTIC BIRDS ARE EATING IT.
ONE DAY... I REALIZED...
...MY HEAD...
...HAD GROWN SO MUCH, IT WAS HARD TO KEEP MY BALANCE.

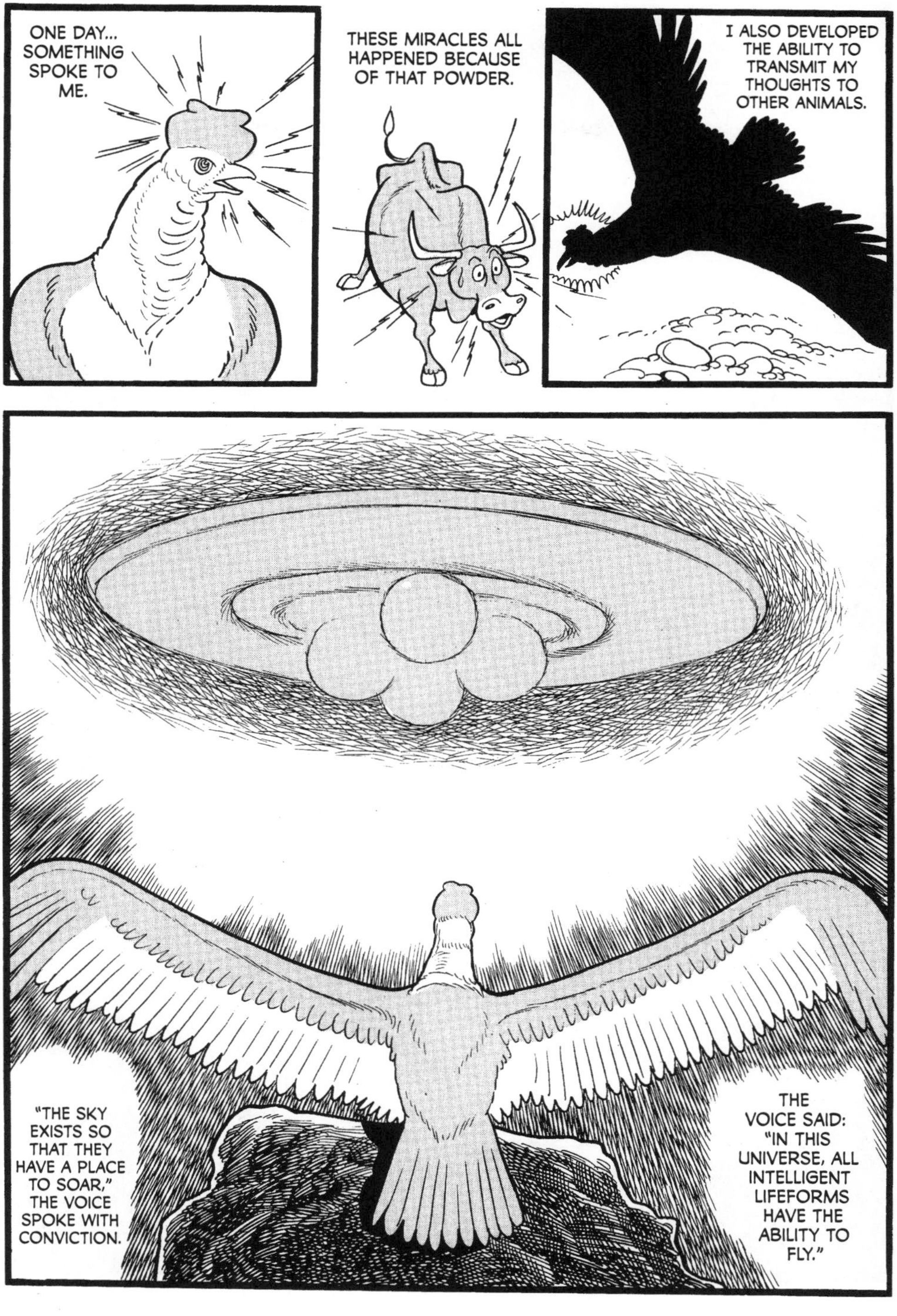
ONE DAY... SOMETHING SPOKE TO ME.
THESE MIRACLES ALL HAPPENED BECAUSE OF THAT POWDER.
I ALSO DEVELOPED THE ABILITY TO TRANSMIT MY THOUGHTS TO OTHER ANIMALS.
THE VOICE SAID: "IN THIS UNIVERSE, ALL INTELLIGENT LIFEFORMS HAVE THE ABILITY TO FLY."
"THE SKY EXISTS SO THAT THEY HAVE A PLACE TO SOAR," THE VOICE SPOKE WITH CONVICTION.

"BUT SOMETHING WENT WRONG DURING THE COURSE OF EVOLUTION. INSTEAD OF BIRDS, A GROUP OF UGLY BEASTS CALLED CATARHINI BECAME THE DOMINANT SPECIES. TWO-LEGGED AND LACKING THE ABILITY TO FLY, THESE APES WERE IGNORANT OF THE SANCTITY OF THE SKY..."
"HERE, TOO, ON THIS PLANET EARTH, IN THE VAST SKIES, BIRDS WERE SUPPOSED TO EVOLVE AS THE HIGHEST FORM OF LIFE."

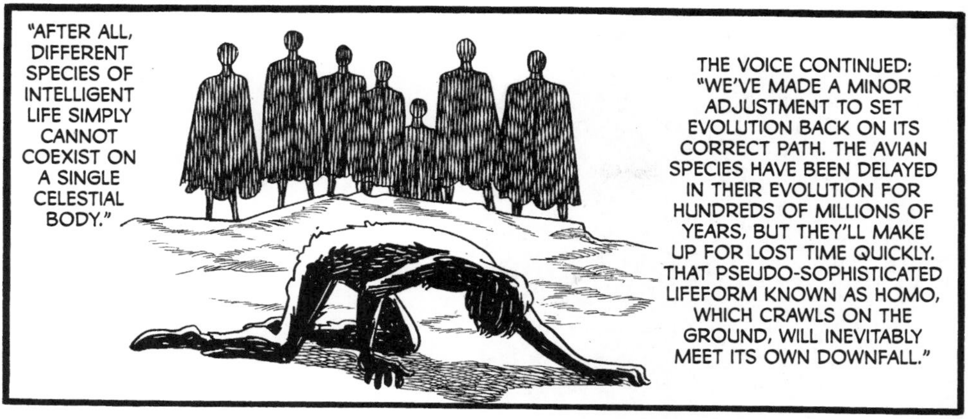
"AFTER ALL, DIFFERENT SPECIES OF INTELLIGENT LIFE SIMPLY CANNOT COEXIST ON A SINGLE CELESTIAL BODY."
THE VOICE CONTINUED: "WE'VE MADE A MINOR ADJUSTMENT TO SET EVOLUTION BACK ON ITS CORRECT PATH. THE AVIAN SPECIES HAVE BEEN DELAYED IN THEIR EVOLUTION FOR HUNDREDS OF MILLIONS OF YEARS, BUT THEY'LL MAKE UP FOR LOST TIME QUICKLY. THAT PSEUDO-SOPHISTICATED LIFEFORM KNOWN AS HOMO, WHICH CRAWLS ON THE GROUND, WILL INEVITABLY MEET ITS OWN DOWNFALL."

...I'VE TOLD YOU EVERYTHING. I'LL ACCEPT WHAT-EVER HAPPENS. I HOPE YOU'LL DO RIGHT BY ME, FREDDIE...
CRAZY WOMAN!
KNOCK IT OFF!

IT'S NO USE SNAPPING AT THAT WOMAN, FREDDIE. I'M THE ONE TALKING THROUGH HER.
SLAP

I DON'T KNOW WHAT KIND OF SCIENCE FICTION NUT YOU ARE, BUT THE WORLD IS IN CRISIS! THERE'S NO TIME FOR YOUR AMATEURISH HOGWASH!

DO YOU NEED ANYTHING?
NOPE.
IF YOU NEED ANYTHING, TELL THIS HUMAN.
SHE WILL MAKE YOUR BED.
THANKS...

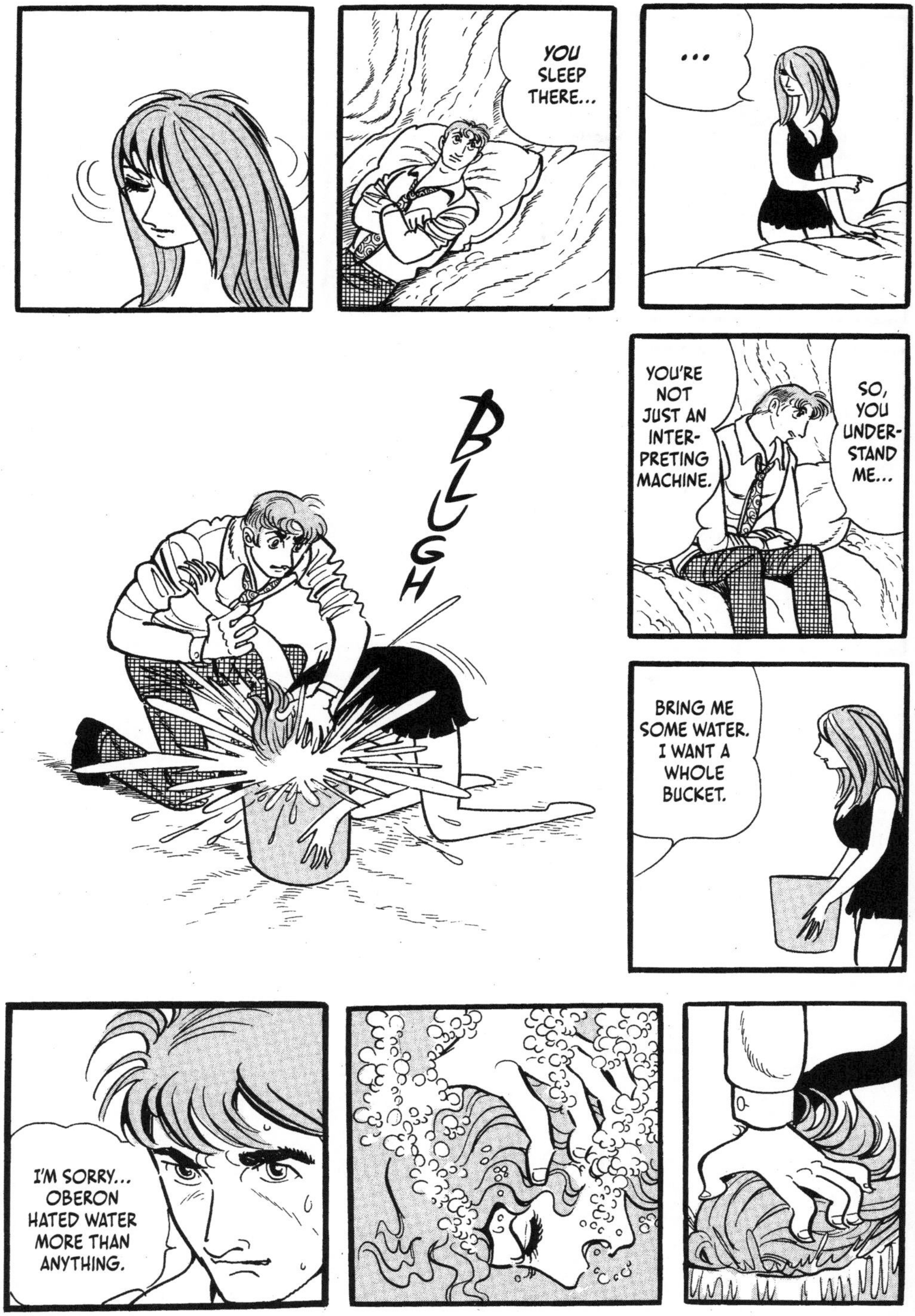
YOU SLEEP THERE...
...
YOU'RE NOT JUST AN INTER-PRETING MACHINE.
SO, YOU UNDER-STAND ME...
BRING ME SOME WATER. I WANT A WHOLE BUCKET.
BLUGH
I'M SORRY... OBERON HATED WATER MORE THAN ANYTHING.

GASP GASP
GASP GASP
COUGH COUGH
COUGH
I HAD TO DO IT... IT WAS THE ONLY WAY TO FREE YOU FROM HIS CON-TROL...
OBERON WILL HESITATE TO OCCUPY YOUR MIND... AT LEAST FOR A WHILE...
NOW...
EVERY TIME I TRIED TO SAY SOMETHING, IT STOPPED ME.
DO YOU WANT TO RUN AWAY?
OF COURSE!
...
...SO? DO YOU FEEL LIKE YOURSELF AGAIN?
...I WAS ALWAYS CONSCIOUS... BUT THAT BIRD HAD COMPLETE CONTROL OVER ME...

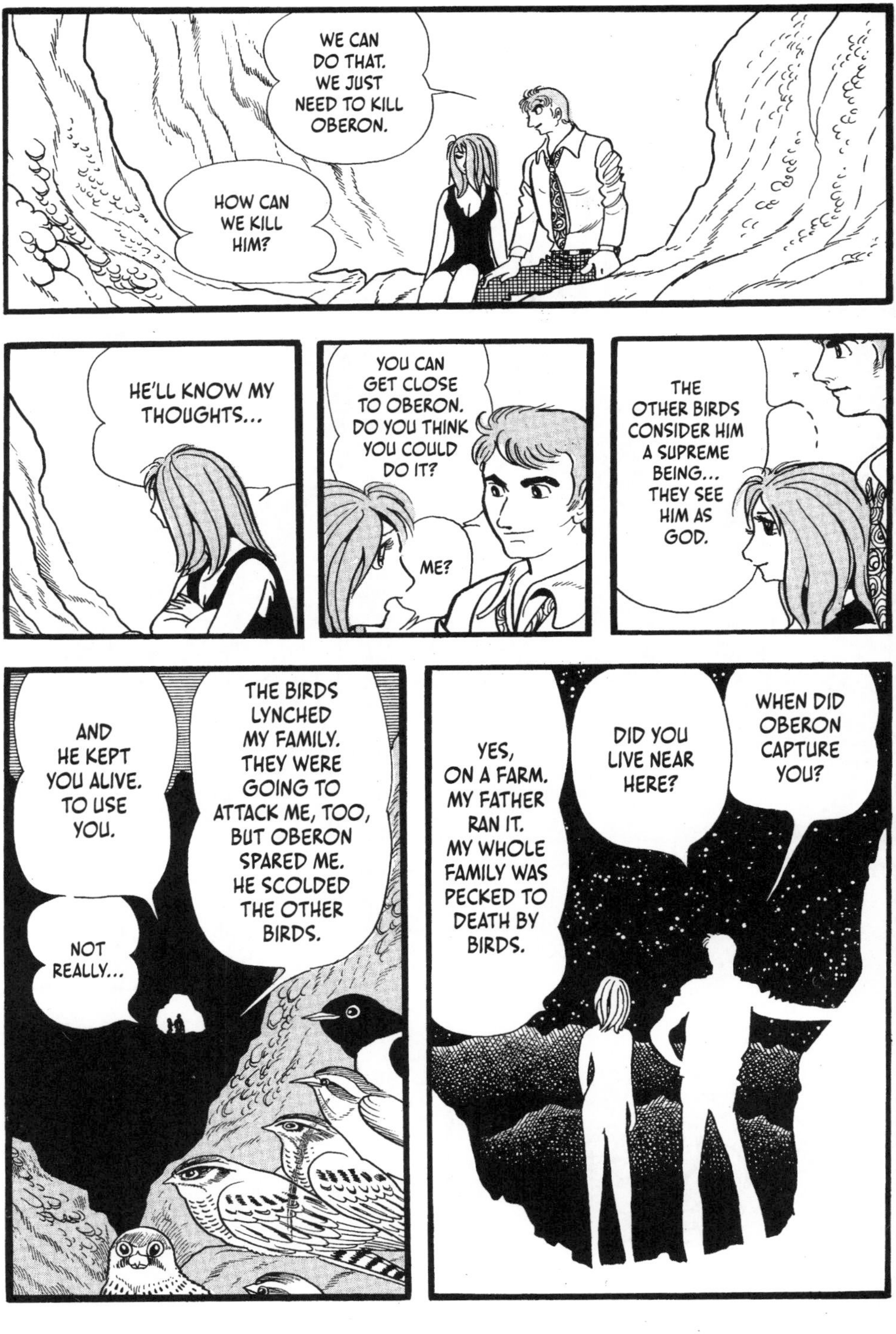
WE CAN DO THAT. WE JUST NEED TO KILL OBERON.
HOW CAN WE KILL HIM?
THE OTHER BIRDS CONSIDER HIM A SUPREME BEING... THEY SEE HIM AS GOD.
YOU CAN GET CLOSE TO OBERON. DO YOU THINK YOU COULD DO IT?
ME?
HE'LL KNOW MY THOUGHTS...
WHEN DID OBERON CAPTURE YOU?
DID YOU LIVE NEAR HERE?
YES, ON A FARM. MY FATHER RAN IT. MY WHOLE FAMILY WAS PECKED TO DEATH BY BIRDS.
THE BIRDS LYNCHED MY FAMILY. THEY WERE GOING TO ATTACK ME, TOO, BUT OBERON SPARED ME. HE SCOLDED THE OTHER BIRDS.
AND HE KEPT YOU ALIVE. TO USE YOU.
NOT REALLY...

TO KEEP THE HUMAN RACE FROM BEING WIPED OUT.
BUT I'M UNDER ORDERS TO KILL HIM.
I ACTUALLY LIKE OBERON, TOO.
I SEE. THEY KNEW BY INSTINCT THAT THEY COULD TRUST YOU.
I USED TO KEEP BIRDS. I LOVED THEM... WILD ONES WOULD COME TO ME, TOO.
SO, FREDDIE, YOU CAME HERE AT THE PRESIDENT'S ORDERS... DO YOU REALLY THINK YOU CAN KILL OBERON?
I ALWAYS CARED ABOUT HIM... BUT NOW... HE'S AN ENEMY. AND...I WANT TO SAVE YOU!
LET'S RUN AWAY TOGETHER.
THAT'S KIND OF YOU, BUT...

LISTEN... GO TO OBERON...
CLAP
...AND EXACTLY ONE HOUR LATER, SHOOT HIM IN THE HEAD WITH THIS GUN. DON'T LET HIM CATCH ON. DO IT WITHOUT THINKING ABOUT IT. YOU'RE GOING TO FORGET ABOUT THIS AS SOON AS YOU WAKE UP. WHEN I CLAP, YOU'LL WAKE UP! READY?
OBERON WON'T BE ABLE TO SENSE THAT YOU WANT TO KILL HIM.
I'M SCARED, FREDDIE... NOT OF OBERON... OF YOU.
I HAVE TO DO THIS.
GO BACK TO OBERON NOW. GOOD LUCK...
THERE SHOULD BE A GUNSHOT ANYTIME NOW... ONCE OBERON IS DEAD, SHE'LL COME RUNNING BACK HERE.

WHAT? YOU WANT ME TO COME WITH YOU?
OH! MY GUN... SHE DIDN'T TAKE IT!
OBERON! WHAT DO YOU WANT?!
THAT WOMAN JUST CAME BACK HERE. WHERE IS SHE?
WHY ARE YOU LOOKING AT ME LIKE THAT?
AAH!!
THAT WOMAN? I MADE YOU HALLUCINATE SO YOU'D TELL ME THE TRUTH. SHE WAS REAL, BUT SHE DIED LAST YEAR. I PROJECTED HER IMAGE INTO YOUR BRAIN.
I WANTED TO SEE HOW YOU REALLY FELT, FREDDIE. YOU REALLY DID WANT TO KILL ME... HOW DISAPPOINTING. I'LL HAVE TO PUNISH YOU.

BACK IN DC.
TELL THE WHITE HOUSE WE'RE BACK.
THIS IS FREDERICK NIEM, SPECIAL INVESTIGATOR REPORTING DIRECTLY TO THE PRESIDENT. I'M COLONEL E. HORTON.
HIS FACE LOOKS COMPLETELY DIFFERENT.
THAT'S PROFESSOR NIEM? I DON'T RECOGNIZE HIM AT ALL.
ONE MONTH LATER.

OBERON SAID: KILLING ME WON'T WORK. THE REAL BOSS IS SOMEONE ELSE.
...AND THAT CONCLUDES MY REPORT.
SO YOU DIDN'T KILL HIM?
BUT PROFESSOR NIEM, OUR INVESTIGATION HAS SHOWN THAT OBERON IS REVERED AS A RELIGIOUS FIGURE.
OBERON IS JUST A REGIONAL SUPERVISOR. AND HE WAS VOTED IN BY THE BIRDS. HE'S NOT SOME LOWLY APE BOSS.
EVEN IF THE BIRDS LOSE HIM, THEY'LL JUST ELECT ANOTHER LEADER.
SIR...
Whisper
Whisper
PROFESSOR! ARE YOU MAKING UP EXCUSES BECAUSE YOU FAILED TO COMPLETE YOUR MISSION?!

COLONEL HORTON, MAY I HAVE A WORD?
THIS MAY SOUND STRANGE... BUT DID ANYTHING UNUSUAL HAPPEN TO PROFESSOR NIEM DURING THE TRIP?
COME TO THINK OF IT...SINCE MEETING OBERON, HE'S BEEN VERY QUIET.
OH?
UNDER-SECRETARY OF STATE CRISP JUST TOLD ME...
...THE PROFESSOR IS BEHAVING STRANGELY. HE SPEAKS FLATLY, AS THOUGH HE'S RECITING FROM MEMORY...
...AND HE HAS NO FACIAL EXPRES-SION.
HE'S EXHAUSTED. PERHAPS THAT'S WHY?
OF COURSE. BUT THE WAY HE TALKS IS BIZARRE. IT'S AS THOUGH HE'S UNDER A SPELL.
THERE'S A HUGE BIRD... IT LOOKS LIKE A CONDOR!
IS THAT OBERON ?!

WHIZZ
WHIZZ
MR. PRESIDENT... STOP THEM, PLEASE! SHOOTING OBERON WON'T ACCOMPLISH ANYTHING!
ORDER THEM TO STOP FIRING.
OBERON WANTS TO KEEP THINGS STABLE BETWEEN BIRDS AND HUMANS...
HE WANTS TO NEGOTIATE WITH THE GOVERN-MENT.
HE DEMANDS THAT 70% OF THE WOMEN IN OUR COUNTRY UNDERGO STERILIZATION SURGERY.
IN OTHER WORDS...HE WANTS DRASTIC POPULATION CONTROL.
RATTA TATTAT
RATTA TATTAT

I'M SURE YOU LAUGHED OFF SUCH NONSENSE... RIGHT, PROFESSOR?
STERILIZATION SURGERY ON 70% OF OUR WOMEN?! IS HE TRYING TO WIPE US OUT?
WHAT?!
WHY ARE THE BIRDS MAKING DEMANDS ABOUT POPULATION CONTROL?
IT'S NOT NON-SENSE.
THE NATURAL GROWTH RATE OF THE POPULATION IS A STEEP CURVE. AT THIS RATE, NATURAL SELECTION WILL FALL OUT OF BALANCE. IN THE U.S., THIS MEASURE WILL ALSO HELP DEAL WITH UNEMPLOYMENT...
ENOUGH! WE'RE NOT HERE TO DISCUSS POLICY!
BIRDS HAVE NO RIGHT!
THAT DAMN CONDOR. WHAT NERVE!
LOOK! HIS HEAD IS LIKE A BALLOON.
MUST BE PACKED WITH BRAINS.
HE'S DEFINITELY GOT MORE THAN YOU!

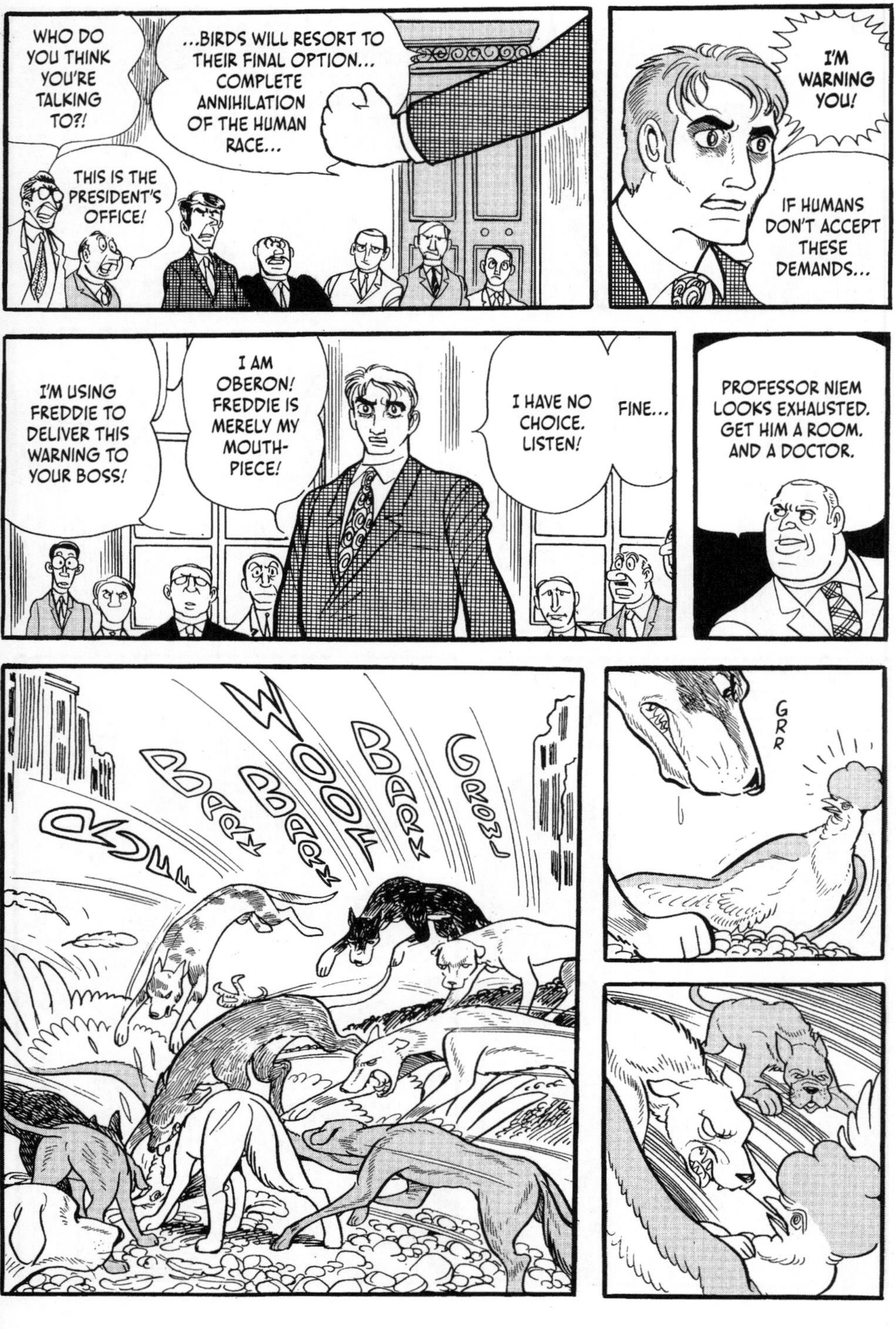
WHO DO YOU THINK YOU'RE TALKING TO?!
...BIRDS WILL RESORT TO THEIR FINAL OPTION... COMPLETE ANNIHILATION OF THE HUMAN RACE...
THIS IS THE PRESIDENT'S OFFICE!
I'M WARNING YOU!
IF HUMANS DON'T ACCEPT THESE DEMANDS...
I'M USING FREDDIE TO DELIVER THIS WARNING TO YOUR BOSS!
I AM OBERON! FREDDIE IS MERELY MY MOUTH-PIECE!
I HAVE NO CHOICE. LISTEN!
FINE...
PROFESSOR NIEM LOOKS EXHAUSTED. GET HIM A ROOM. AND A DOCTOR.
GROWL
BARK
WOOF
BARK
BARK
YELP
GRR

CHOMP
FREDDIE! SAVE ME!
ARE YOU OKAY?
PROFESSOR!
OBERON TRIED TO OUTDO HUMANS, BUT IT WAS HIS FELLOW ANIMALS THAT CAUSED HIS DEATH. HOW IRONIC. HOWEVER, WE MUST RECOGNIZE THAT THERE WILL BE A SECOND OBERON... AND A THIRD... WE WILL SOON BE FACING COUNTLESS BIRDMEN...
OBERON IS DEAD. HE WAS ATTACKED UNEXPECTEDLY BY A PACK OF RAVENOUS DOGS. THE WEIGHT OF HIS OVERGROWN BRAIN LIMITED HIS MOBILITY AND ENDED UP COSTING HIM HIS LIFE.
YES... I'M FINE NOW...
I'M SORRY... MR. PRESIDENT...
I TRIED TO TELL YOU...
...BUT OBERON HAD CONTROL OVER ME...

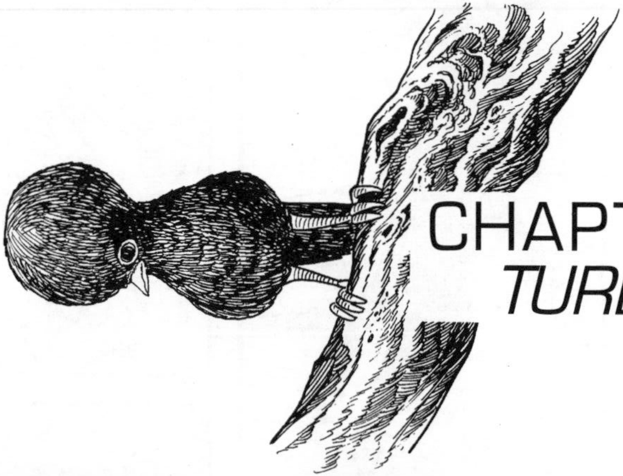

CHAPTER 6: *TURDUS MERULA SAPIENS* (BLACK BIRD)

A VILLAGE IN SOUTHERN SWITZERLAND
COME, DARLING. IT'S TIME TO EAT.
I MISS HEARING ABOUT THE VILLAGE....
WE'VE HAD NO VISITORS FOR DAYS...
LIZ, MY DEAR...
ONCE YOU'VE EATEN, SING FOR ME AGAIN. THAT'S MY ONLY JOY NOW...
I DON'T HEAR OR SEE WELL ANYMORE, BUT...
...IT'S LONELY WITH NO ONE TO TALK TO...

IS THAT YOUR FRIEND? YOU'RE OLD ENOUGH TO GO OUT AND HAVE FUN...
COME BACK SOON...
WHAT'S WRONG, LIZ?
MASTER?! DON'T USE THAT REACTIONARY HUMAN TERM!
UNDER DIRECTIVE 2613, ALL HUMANS IN THE AREA ARE TO BE KILLED. YOU'RE THE ONLY ONE SHELTERING A SURVIVOR, LIZ! YOU SHOULD KNOW BETTER. THE BOSS WANTS IT DONE ASAP!
HE'S MY MASTER.
BUT HE'S HARMLESS... AND HE'S KIND TO ME. HE HAS NOTHING BUT GOOD INTENTIONS, AND HE DOESN'T KNOW WHAT'S HAPPENING AROUND THE WORLD.
PLEASE... WAIT... I'M NOT SHELTERING HIM.

OUR MISSION IS TO TAKE THESE JURA MOUNTAINS. WE CAN'T ALLOW ANY SURVIVORS. NOT EVEN AN OLD MAN!
I KNOW...
BUT HE WON'T LIVE MUCH LONGER ANYWAY.
A YEAR OR TWO AT MOST. I WANT TO HELP HIM LIVE OUT HIS LIFE IN PEACE.
NO!
KILL HIM NOW. USE WHATEVER METHOD YOU LIKE.
PLEASE...
CAN WE AT LEAST LET HIM BELIEVE THAT BIRDS AND HUMANS ARE FRIENDS?
HOW WOULD WE DO THAT?
WE COULD ALL SING A EULOGY FOR HIM!
DON'T LEAVE ME ON MY OWN... IT'S SO LONELY...
WHERE HAVE YOU GONE...?
LIZ!
LIZ... OH, LIZ...
WHAT'S WRONG ?

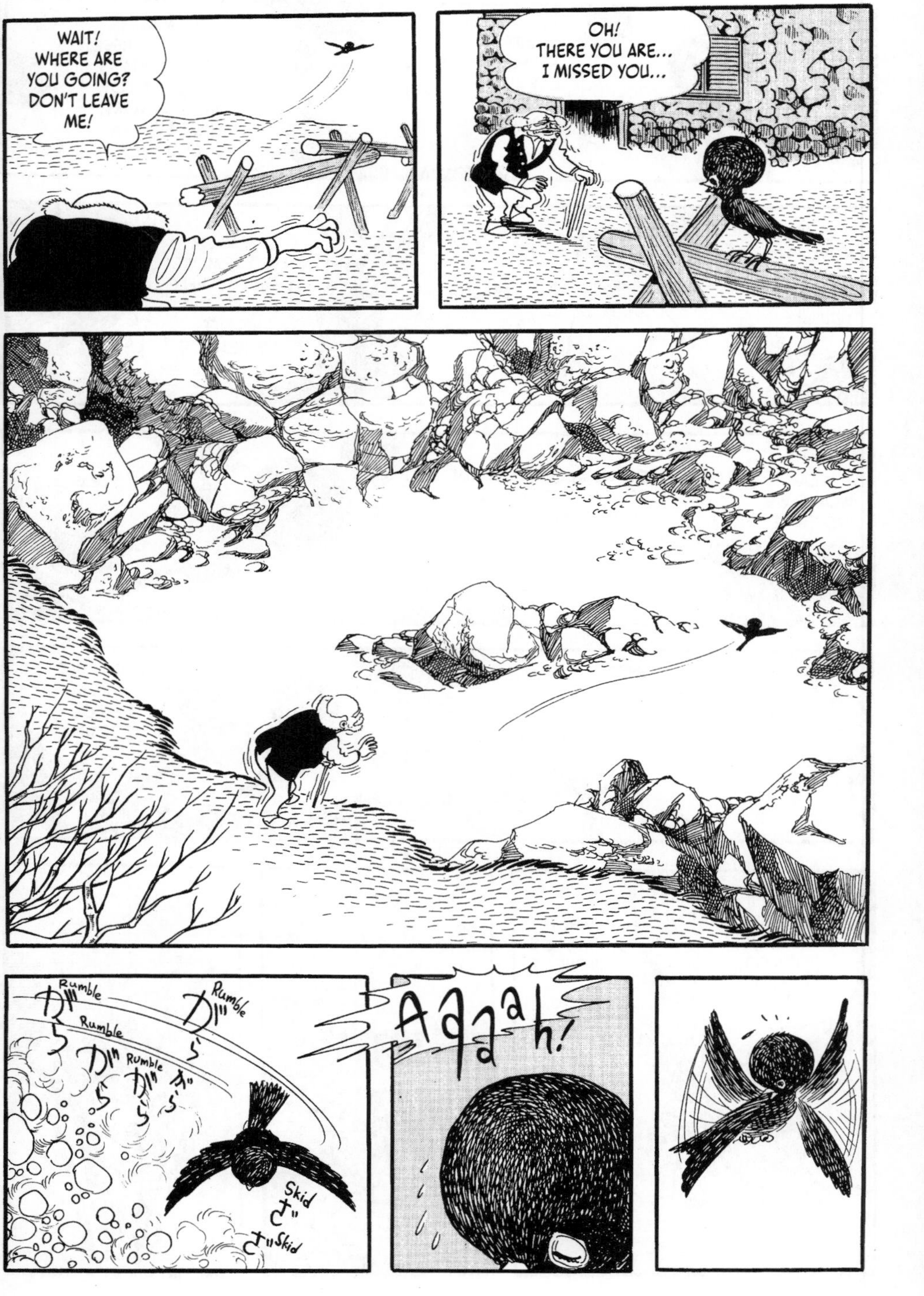
WAIT! WHERE ARE YOU GOING? DON'T LEAVE ME!
OH! THERE YOU ARE... I MISSED YOU...
Rumble
Rumble
Rumble
Rumble
Skid
Skid
Aaaah!

I KNOW... YOU WANTED TO SHOW ME THESE FLOWERS DOWN HERE... RIGHT?
LIZ... GO TO THE VILLAGE AND GET HELP.
WHY... AREN'T YOU GOING ...? WON'T YOU HELP ME...?
OH... YOU WERE SINGING FOR ME. LET ME HEAR SOME MORE...
WELL...FINE, YOU WANT TO STAY BY MY SIDE. RIGHT?
I DON'T HAVE LONG TO LIVE ANYWAY...
STAY WITH ME 'TIL THE END.
LIZ! WHO ARE ALL THOSE BIRDS?
!

THAT MAY HAVE BEEN THE LAST TIME BIRDS SANG FOR A HUMAN...
IT WAS ALSO AN ELEGY FOR HUMANITY.
BIRDS... SO MANY BIRDS...
ARE THEY ALL THE BIRDS IN THE WORLD...?
LIZ... DID YOU BRING THEM?
TO BE SURROUNDED BY FRAGRANT FLOWERS AND ALL THESE BIRDS SINGING...
...AS I DIE IN PEACE...
I MUST BE... THE LUCKIEST MAN ON EARTH...
THANK YOU... LIZ...

GRIK
GRIK
GRIK
GRIK
WHAT DO WE DO WITH 'EM, MA?
SHRED THEM AND FEED 'EM TO THE PIGS.

CHAPTER 7: IN RHODESIA

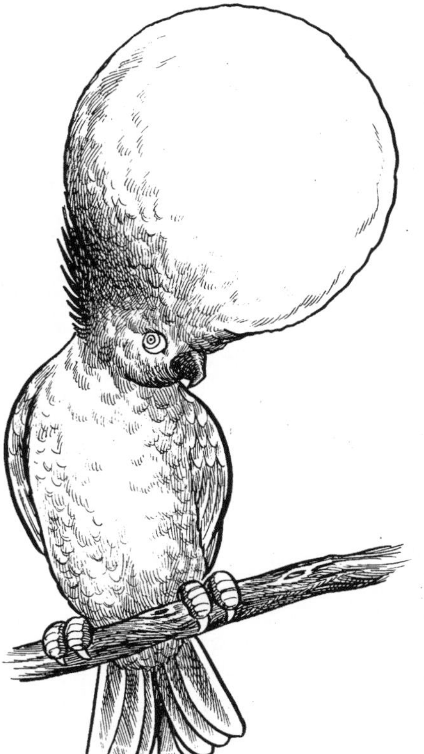

IF ANY MORE COME 'ROUND HERE, KILL 'EM ALL.
SURE.
HOW MANY WHITES ENTERED OUR DISTRICT?
AROUND A HUNDRED.
HERE THEY COME AGAIN…
VROOOOM
WAAA
THE POLICE IN THIS DISTRICT ARE ON OUR SIDE. THEY WON'T DO A THING.
BOOM
GWHS
I'LL FEED YOU TO THE PIGS!!

BLAM
BAM
BAM
BAM
PLEASE! LET US GO! WE HAVEN'T DONE ANYTHING TO YOU...
YOU WHITES CREATED THIS BLACK DISTRICT AND FORCED US INTO IT!
AND NOW YOU WANT TO TAKE REFUGE HERE?! HELL NO!
EAT SHIT!
MAY GOD BLESS THE BLACK PEOPLE...

GET IN THE BARN.
HELP! I'M BEGGING YOU! HIDE ME SOMEWHERE!
HELP!
SO THAT'S WHY YOU RAN BACK INTO TOWN...
THE BIRDS JUST STARTED ATTACKING THE WHITE DISTRICT. THEY'RE LED BY SOMEONE'S PET PARROT.
THEY WERE ONLY ATTACKING WHITEY?
YEAH... THE BLACK DISTRICT HERE IS THE ONLY PLACE THEY DON'T ATTACK.
THAT'S RIGHT... WE TRIED TO ESCAPE ALONG THE NATIONAL HIGHWAY. THE WHOLE TOWN EVACUATED. BUT A HUGE FLOCK OF BIRDS AMBUSHED US. WE COULDN'T GET THROUGH.
WHY IS GOD TURNING A COLD SHOULDER TO US WHITES?
...THE BIRDS ARE FRIENDLY TO BLACKS BECAUSE THAT'S WHAT GOD WANTS.
THE REVEREND SAYS...
REALLY? WELL, THAT'S A GOOD THING. I WONDER WHY, THOUGH?

Y'ALL DISCRIMINATE AGAINST US IN EVERY WAY. AND YOU ALWAYS SAY: "IT'S BECAUSE YOU'RE BLACK"...
WHITEY HAS BEEN SO CRUEL TO US. IT'S ONLY NATURAL THAT YOU'D SUFFER DIVINE PUNISHMENT.
WELL...
THEY'VE COME TO KILL ME!
OH NO!
BIRDS!
LET ME STAY HERE! PLEASE! THEY'LL PECK ME TO DEATH!!
KISS ME.
THEN I'LL LET YOU STAY.
WHAT? I WILL... I'LL DO WHATEVER YOU SAY...
WILL YOU DO WHAT I SAY...?
IF YOU DO, I'LL SAVE YOU.

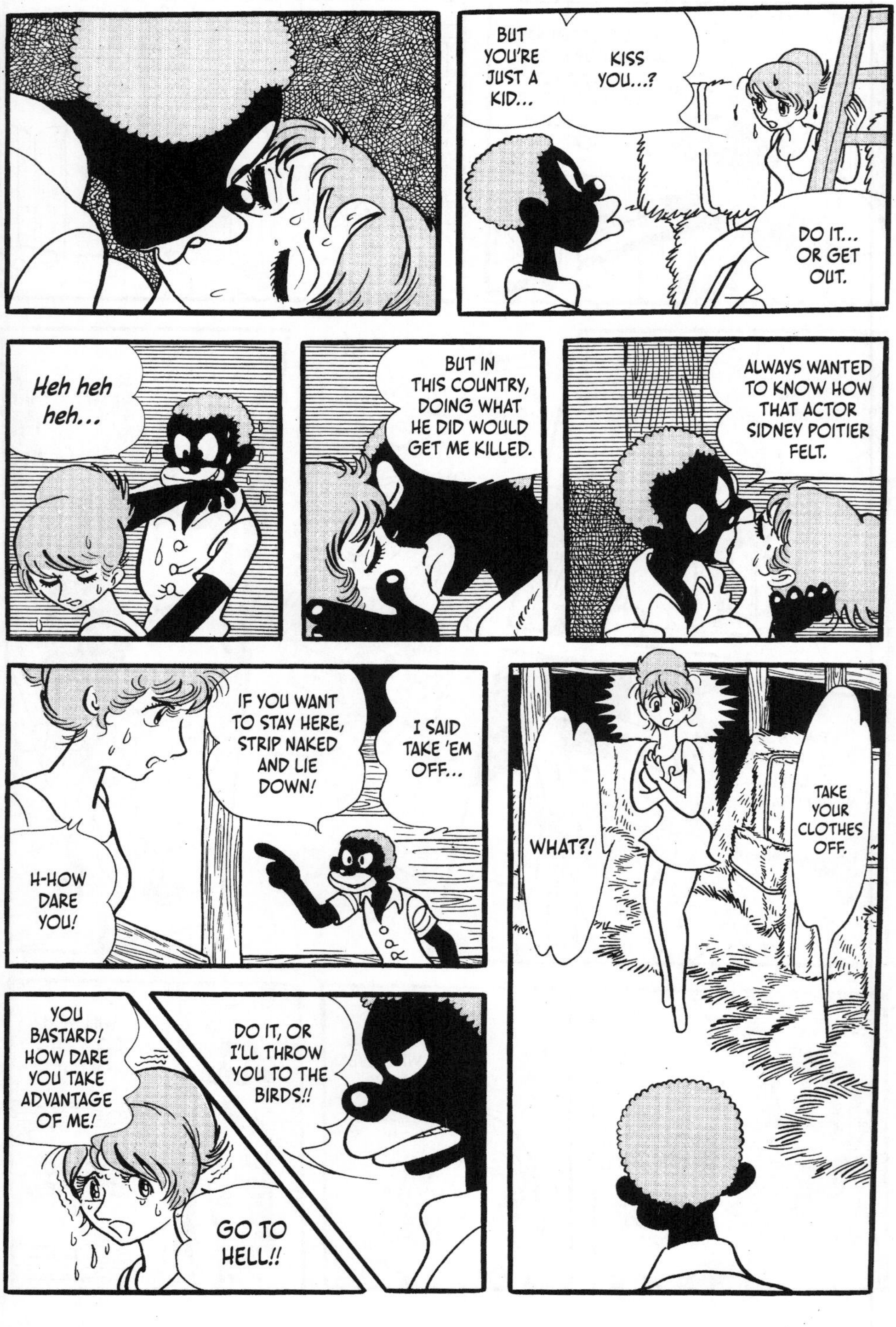
BUT YOU'RE JUST A KID...
KISS YOU...?
DO IT... OR GET OUT.
Heh heh heh...
BUT IN THIS COUNTRY, DOING WHAT HE DID WOULD GET ME KILLED.
ALWAYS WANTED TO KNOW HOW THAT ACTOR SIDNEY POITIER FELT.
IF YOU WANT TO STAY HERE, STRIP NAKED AND LIE DOWN!
I SAID TAKE 'EM OFF...
H-HOW DARE YOU!
WHAT?!
TAKE YOUR CLOTHES OFF.
YOU BASTARD! HOW DARE YOU TAKE ADVANTAGE OF ME!
DO IT, OR I'LL THROW YOU TO THE BIRDS!!
GO TO HELL!!

OH! FIRE!
THE BIRDS STARTED A FIRE!
THE DOOR'S STUCK! HELP!!
THE BIRDS HAD PLANNED TO PURGE THE HUMANS AT THE TOP OF THE HIERARCHY FIRST. IN THE UNION OF SOUTH AFRICA, BLACK PEOPLE WERE CONSIDERED INFERIOR. THEY WERE RULED BY THE WHITES. THE LEADER OF THE BIRDS HAD BEEN TOLD THAT REPEATEDLY, SO THE BIRDS PAID NO MIND TO THE BLACKS. THEY ONLY ATTACKED THE WHITES. BUT WHEN THE BIRDS SAW A BLACK BOY RAPE A WHITE WOMAN, THEY REALIZED THAT BLACK PEOPLE WERE ALREADY ON THE SAME LEVEL AS THE WHITES. BLACK PEOPLE ENDED UP MEETING THE SAME FATE AS THE WHITES.
Ha ha ha! Ha ha ha!
Ha ha ha... Heh heh heh...

MY ROUTINE IS TO WAKE UP AT SIX.
WALK FOR TWO HOURS...
...AND WRITE UNTIL LUNCH. AT 1 PM, I START TYPING AGAIN.
I JUST NEED TO COME UP WITH ONE PIECE A WEEK. EVEN IF I MISS THE DEADLINE, NOBODY SAYS ANYTHING. BACK WHEN I WAS A HACK WRITER...

CHAPTER 8: SPOKESMAN

NEEDLESS TO SAY, READERS JUMP AT THE CHANCE TO READ MY WORK.
TOY
...THIS IS THE LIFE I DREAMED OF.
NO MATTER HOW MANY READERS I HAVE, NO MATTER HOW IDEAL MY LIFE IS... I DON'T FEEL ANY SATISFACTION.
YES, THEY GO CRAZY FOR IT! WHAT AN AMAZING BEST-SELLER!
IT ALL STARTED WHEN... I DON'T EVEN REMEMBER ANYMORE. I WAS YOUNG AND OBSCURE, EKING OUT A LIVING WRITING SOMETHING CALLED "SCIENCE FICTION."
ONE DAY, OUT OF THE BLUE, "THERE WAS A KNOCK ON THE DOOR" (AS MY FELLOW WRITER SHIN'ICHI HOSHI OFTEN WRITES) AND SOMEONE OFFERED ME A CONTRACT.
IT APPEARED OUT OF NOWHERE. IT WAS LITERALLY A BIRD.
NOK NOK NOK
NOK NOK NOK NOK NOK NOK NOK

YOU'RE GOOD AT PORTRAYING NON-HUMAN INTELLIGENT LIFEFORMS... LIKE ALIENS AND MONSTERS.
I HAVE A CONTRACT OFFER FOR YOU.
WE WANT YOU TO WRITE ABOUT US. WE'RE "BIRDMEN."
IF YOU ACCEPT, WE'LL PAY WHATEVER AMOUNT YOU ASK. YOU'LL BE GUARANTEED A GOOD LIVING.
BACK THEN, IT WAS RARE FOR BIRDS TO COMMUNICATE WITH HUMANS USING TELEPATHY.
HALF-JOKINGLY, I SAID:
WELL THEN...I'LL DO IT FOR A MILLION DOLLARS A YEAR.
FINE. HERE'S A MILLION DOLLARS.
SIGN THIS.
...MIL...
A...

USE YOUR SKILLS TO MAKE READERS BELIEVE...
...THAT BIRDMEN ARE REAL!
MAKE THEM BELIEVE YOU!
...I'M SIGNING A MILLION DOLLAR CONTRACT WITH A BIRD.
M-MY FRIENDS WILL NEVER BELIEVE...
THEY WON'T? NO!
"BIRDMEN"? WHAT'S THAT?
THE SPECIES THAT WILL REPLACE HUMANS ON EARTH.
WE'LL SEND YOU INFO EVERY WEEK. YOUR JOB IS TO PUT IT IN WRITING.
THAT'S EASY...BUT EVERYONE WILL JUST THINK IT'S SILLY SCIENCE FICTION.
THAT'S WHY YOU NEED TO PERSUADE THEM!
I CHOSE THE TITLE *TOMORROW THE BIRDS.*
BGHK
SWEZ
AND THAT'S HOW MY DAILY ROUTINE STARTED...
ZP
EELMN

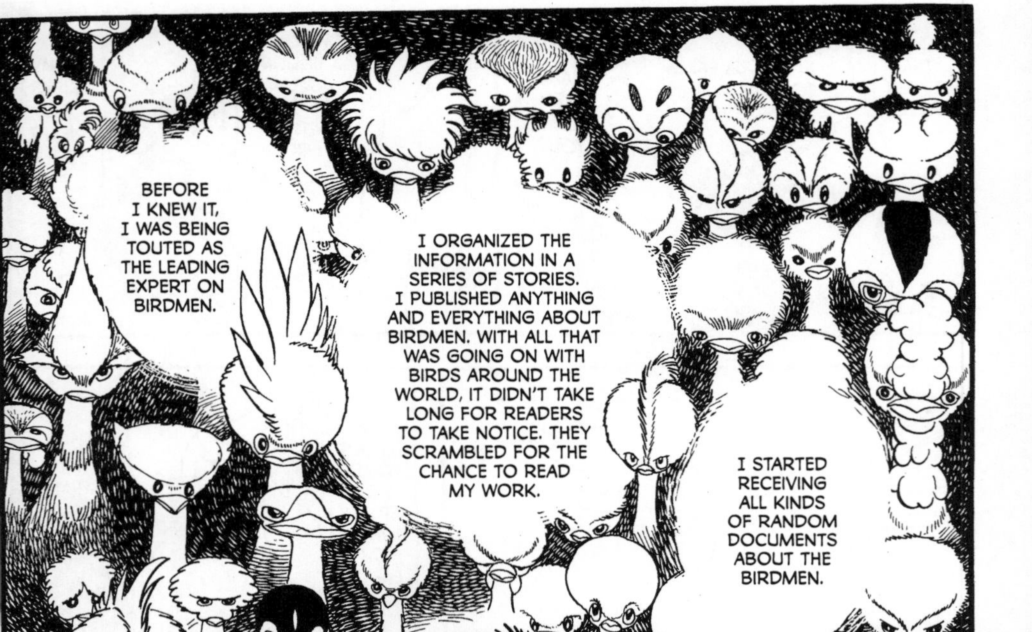
BEFORE I KNEW IT, I WAS BEING TOUTED AS THE LEADING EXPERT ON BIRDMEN.
I ORGANIZED THE INFORMATION IN A SERIES OF STORIES. I PUBLISHED ANYTHING AND EVERYTHING ABOUT BIRDMEN. WITH ALL THAT WAS GOING ON WITH BIRDS AROUND THE WORLD, IT DIDN'T TAKE LONG FOR READERS TO TAKE NOTICE. THEY SCRAMBLED FOR THE CHANCE TO READ MY WORK.
I STARTED RECEIVING ALL KINDS OF RANDOM DOCUMENTS ABOUT THE BIRDMEN.

I WAS NOTHING BUT A MOUTHPIECE FOR THE BIRDMEN.

BUT I WAS MISERABLE.

WITHOUT REALIZING IT, I WAS DOING P.R. TO HUMANS. LIKE THE WAY...
BAR
...THE US MILITARY USED TO SKILLFULLY SPREAD AMERICANISM IN THE COUNTRIES IT OCCUPIED.
DAMN BIRDS! I HOPE SOME CATS EAT YOU!
YOU SURE YOU WANT TO SAY SUCH THINGS?
BIRDMEN DIDN'T KNOW HOW TO DO P.R. AIMED AT HUMANS. WHO BETTER TO DO THAT THAN A HUMAN? THAT'S WHY THEY CHOSE ME.
HOW GREAT THE BIRDMEN ARE... HOW JUST, HOW SMART... HOW WORTHY OF BEING RULERS...

THIS MIGHT SOUND CORNY, BUT MY CONSCIENCE WON'T STAND FOR THIS!
YOU KNOW WHAT?!
WE HAVE A CONTRACT. YOU MUST FULFILL IT.
YOU HAVE NO RIGHT TO COMPLAIN.
DAMN IT!
MY BOOKS ARE NOW SELLING MORE THAN A MILLION COPIES A MONTH.
BUT TODAY, FOR THE FIRST TIME, I DIDN'T USE THE BIRDMEN'S MATERIAL.
YOU'RE A DOVE! YOU'RE SUPPOSED TO BE A SYMBOL OF PEACE!
FAKE PACIFIST!
ARE YOU SPYING ON ME?
THEY STUFFED ME IN A STEEL CAGE. I KNOW WHAT FATE AWAITS A TRAITOR...
IT'S A FITTING END FOR A PROPAGANDA WRITER.
"BEWARE OF THE BIRDS! DON'T TRUST THEM! RISE UP, MANKIND! FIGHT THE BIRDMEN!"

CHAPTER 9: DOBLOOD'S REQUEST TO THE APPRAISAL COMMITTEE

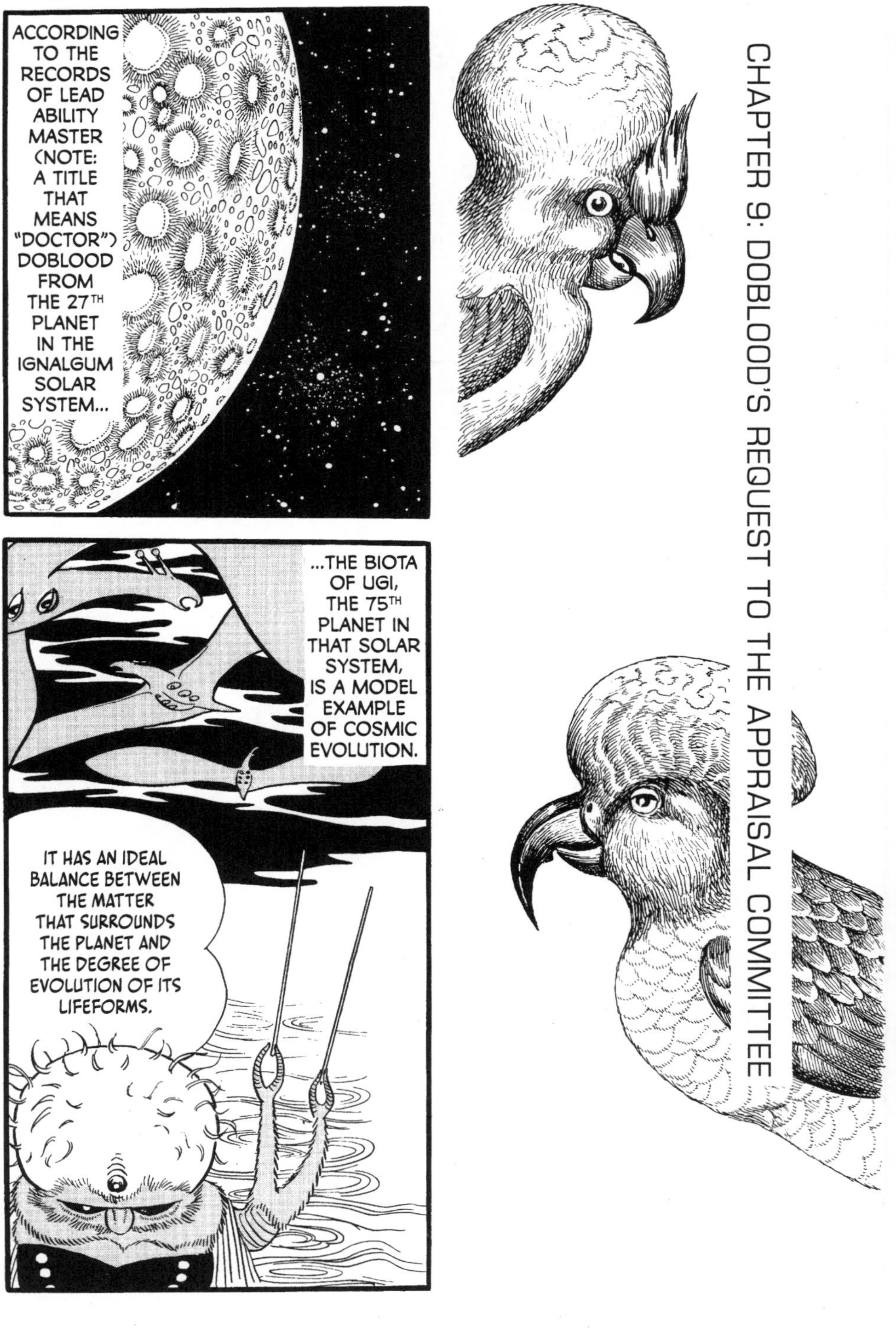

ACCORDING TO THE RECORDS OF LEAD ABILITY MASTER (NOTE: A TITLE THAT MEANS "DOCTOR") DOBLOOD FROM THE 27TH PLANET IN THE IGNALGUM SOLAR SYSTEM...
...THE BIOTA OF UGI, THE 75TH PLANET IN THAT SOLAR SYSTEM, IS A MODEL EXAMPLE OF COSMIC EVOLUTION.
IT HAS AN IDEAL BALANCE BETWEEN THE MATTER THAT SURROUNDS THE PLANET AND THE DEGREE OF EVOLUTION OF ITS LIFEFORMS.

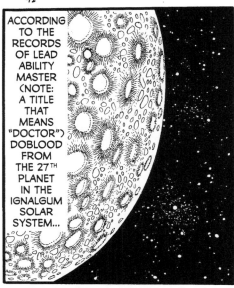

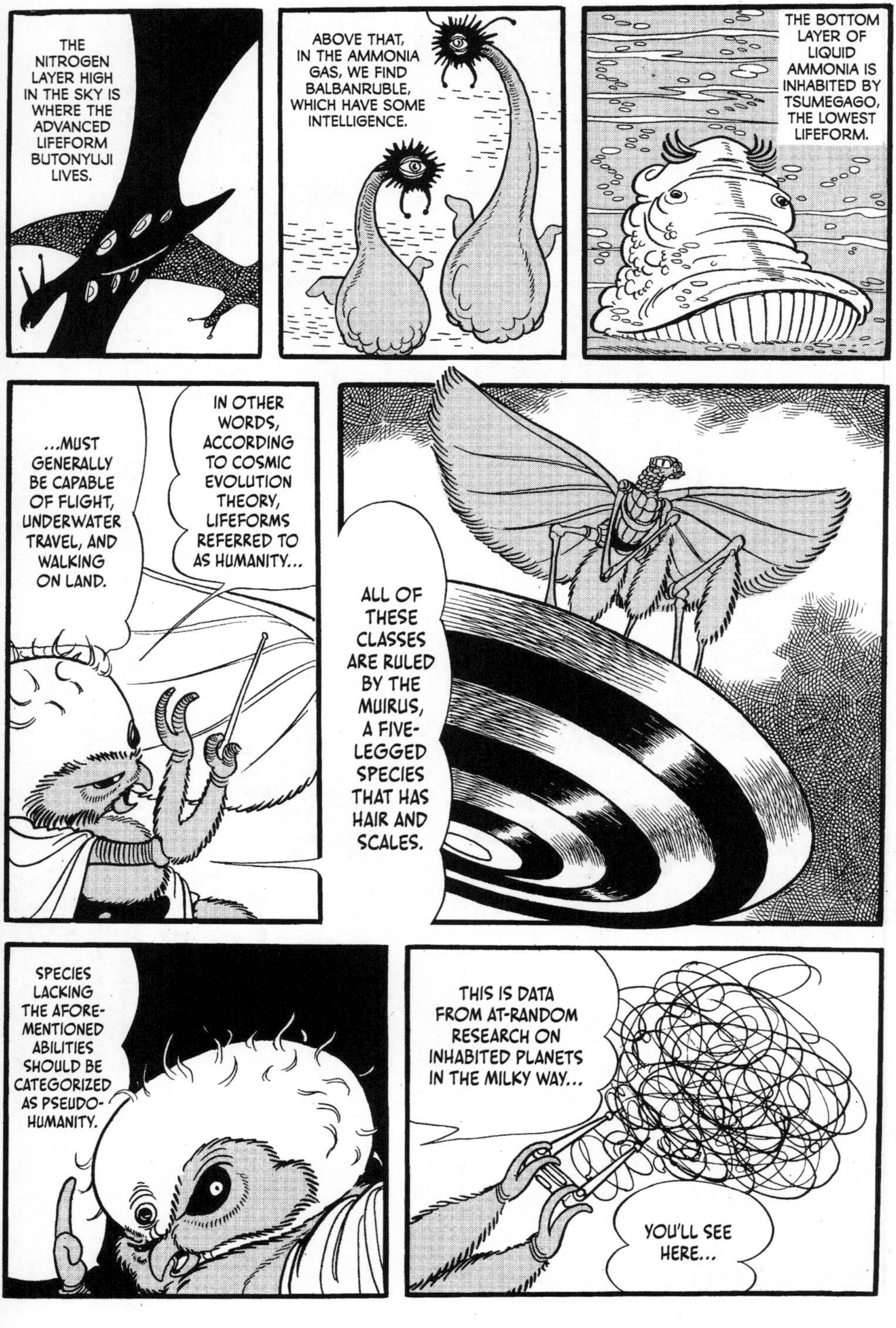
THE NITROGEN LAYER HIGH IN THE SKY IS WHERE THE ADVANCED LIFEFORM BUTONYUJI LIVES.
ABOVE THAT, IN THE AMMONIA GAS, WE FIND BALBANRUBLE, WHICH HAVE SOME INTELLIGENCE.
THE BOTTOM LAYER OF LIQUID AMMONIA IS INHABITED BY TSUMEGAGO, THE LOWEST LIFEFORM.
IN OTHER WORDS, ACCORDING TO COSMIC EVOLUTION THEORY, LIFEFORMS REFERRED TO AS HUMANITY...
...MUST GENERALLY BE CAPABLE OF FLIGHT, UNDERWATER TRAVEL, AND WALKING ON LAND.
ALL OF THESE CLASSES ARE RULED BY THE MUIRUS, A FIVE-LEGGED SPECIES THAT HAS HAIR AND SCALES.
SPECIES LACKING THE AFORE-MENTIONED ABILITIES SHOULD BE CATEGORIZED AS PSEUDO-HUMANITY.
THIS IS DATA FROM AT-RANDOM RESEARCH ON INHABITED PLANETS IN THE MILKY WAY...
YOU'LL SEE HERE...

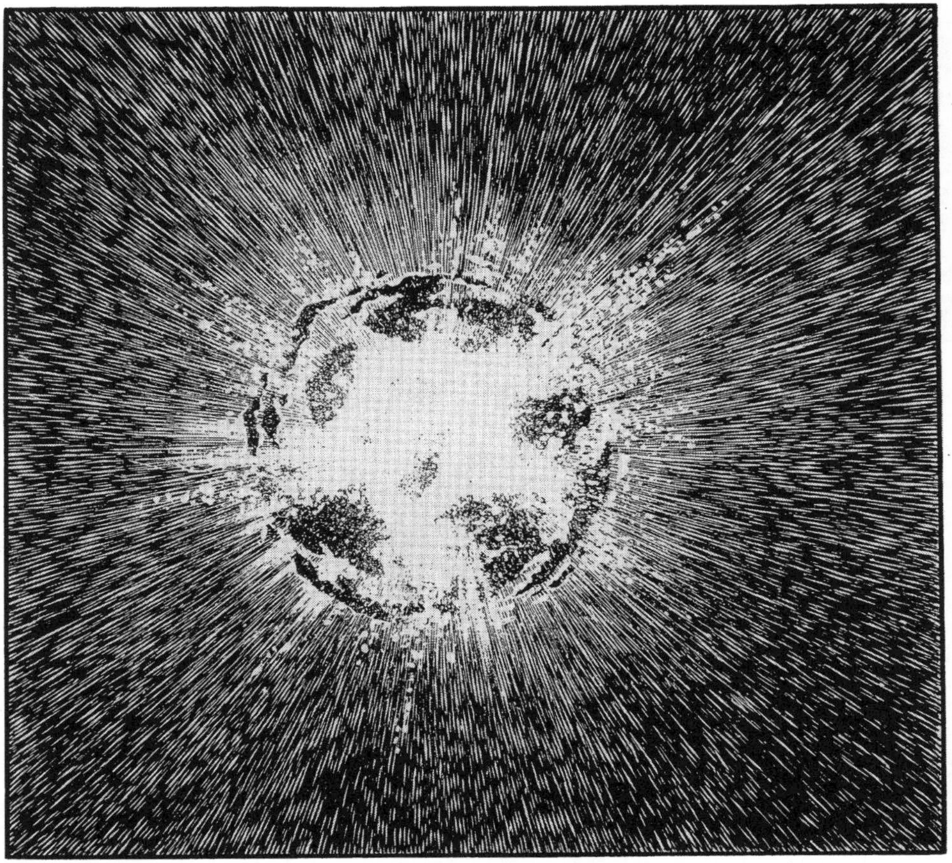

WE KNOW THAT THIS UNIVERSE WAS BORN FROM THE EXPLOSION OF AN ANCIENT COSMIC NUCLEUS. FROM THAT VERY MOMENT, ALL SOLAR SYSTEMS WERE DESTINED TO FOLLOW THE SAME COURSE OF EVOLUTION.

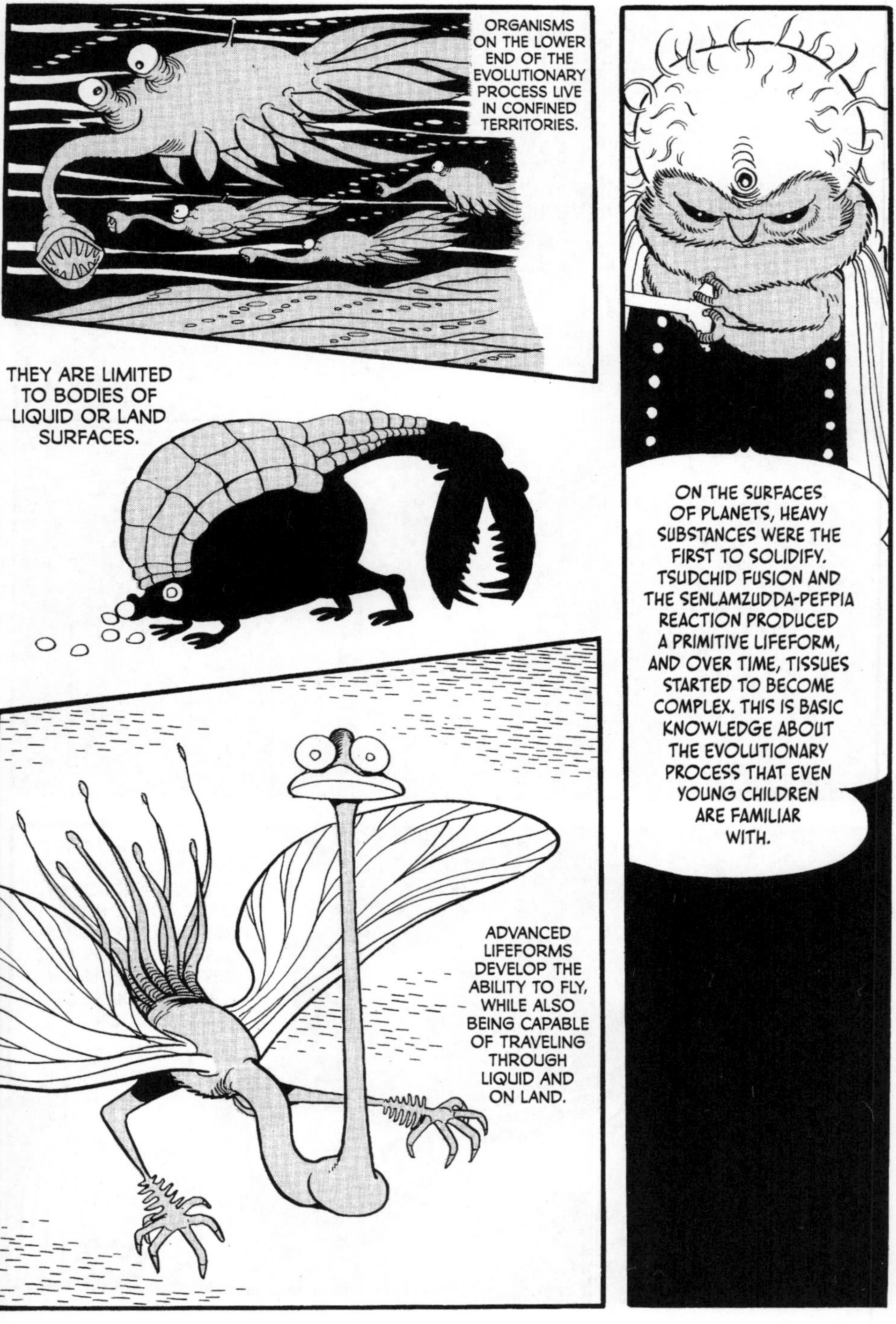
ON THE SURFACES OF PLANETS, HEAVY SUBSTANCES WERE THE FIRST TO SOLIDIFY. TSUDCHID FUSION AND THE SENLAMZUDDA-PEFPIA REACTION PRODUCED A PRIMITIVE LIFEFORM, AND OVER TIME, TISSUES STARTED TO BECOME COMPLEX. THIS IS BASIC KNOWLEDGE ABOUT THE EVOLUTIONARY PROCESS THAT EVEN YOUNG CHILDREN ARE FAMILIAR WITH.
ORGANISMS ON THE LOWER END OF THE EVOLUTIONARY PROCESS LIVE IN CONFINED TERRITORIES.
THEY ARE LIMITED TO BODIES OF LIQUID OR LAND SURFACES.
ADVANCED LIFEFORMS DEVELOP THE ABILITY TO FLY, WHILE ALSO BEING CAPABLE OF TRAVELING THROUGH LIQUID AND ON LAND.

ON CELESTIAL BODIES WITH LARGE MASS, THE ORGANISMS CRAWL ON THE GROUND. EVOLUTION ENDS WITHOUT ANY DEVELOPMENT OF A SOPHISTICATED HUMANITY.
NATURALLY, THE COURSE OF EVOLUTION IS NOT UNIFORM. THE COMPOSITION AND MASS OF EACH PLANET ARE VARIED.
THIS IS A DISTORTED FORM OF EVOLUTION.
ON THE THIRD PLANET OF THE ZOLA SOLAR SYSTEM, TWO-LEGGED BEASTS CALLED HOMO HOMO, WHICH EVOLVED FROM VERTEBRATE MAMMALS, REFER TO THEMSELVES AS HUMANITY, DESPITE LACKING THE ABILITY TO FLY.
WE MUST CORRECT IT BY SETTING EVOLUTION BACK ON ITS RIGHT COURSE.
ON THE THIRD PLANET OF THE ZOLA SOLAR SYSTEM...

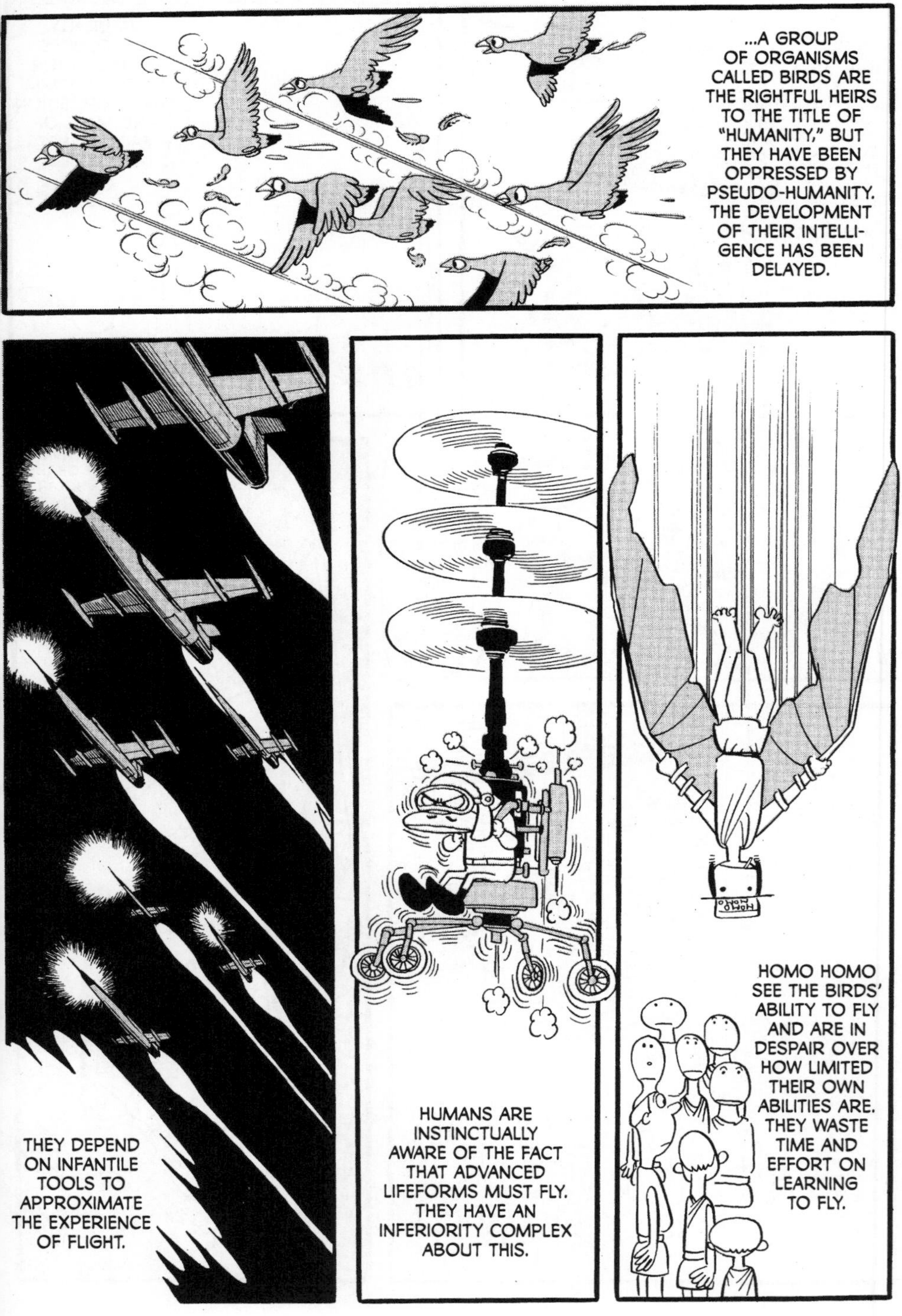
...A GROUP OF ORGANISMS CALLED BIRDS ARE THE RIGHTFUL HEIRS TO THE TITLE OF "HUMANITY," BUT THEY HAVE BEEN OPPRESSED BY PSEUDO-HUMANITY. THE DEVELOPMENT OF THEIR INTELLIGENCE HAS BEEN DELAYED.
THEY DEPEND ON INFANTILE TOOLS TO APPROXIMATE THE EXPERIENCE OF FLIGHT.
HUMANS ARE INSTINCTUALLY AWARE OF THE FACT THAT ADVANCED LIFEFORMS MUST FLY. THEY HAVE AN INFERIORITY COMPLEX ABOUT THIS.
HOMO HOMO SEE THE BIRDS' ABILITY TO FLY AND ARE IN DESPAIR OVER HOW LIMITED THEIR OWN ABILITIES ARE. THEY WASTE TIME AND EFFORT ON LEARNING TO FLY.

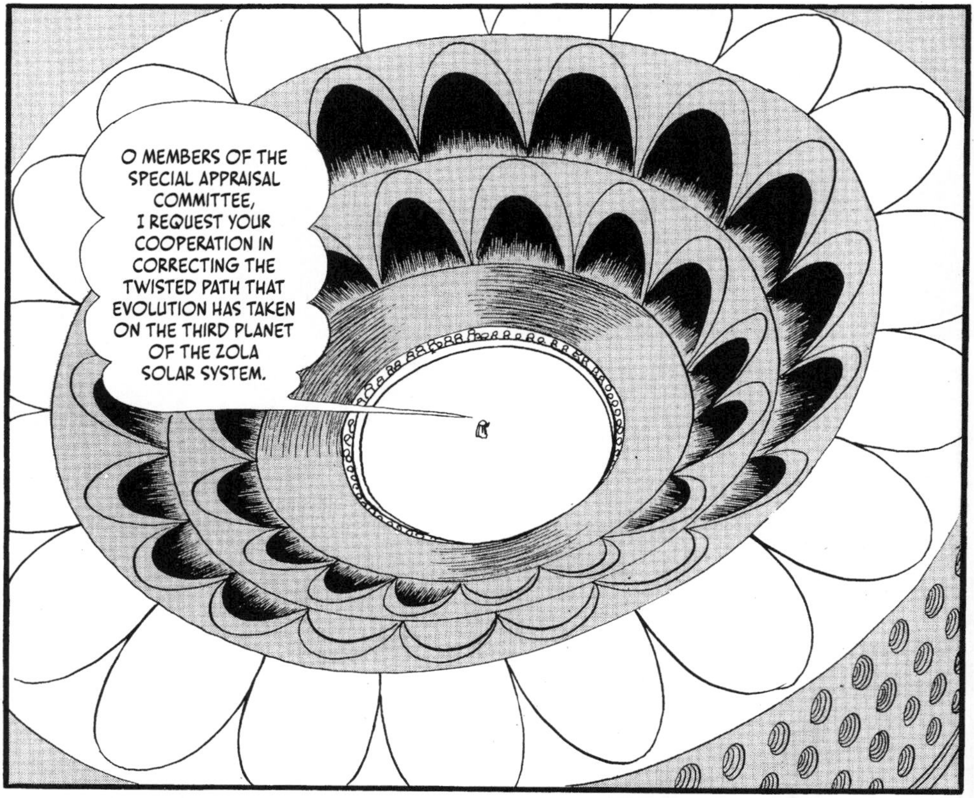

O MEMBERS OF THE SPECIAL APPRAISAL COMMITTEE, I REQUEST YOUR COOPERATION IN CORRECTING THE TWISTED PATH THAT EVOLUTION HAS TAKEN ON THE THIRD PLANET OF THE ZOLA SOLAR SYSTEM.

LEAD ABILITY MASTER DOBLOOD'S PASSIONATE SPEECH SUCCEEDED IN PERSUADING THE COMMITTEE. HUMANS ON EARTH WERE STRIPPED OF THEIR TITLE OF "LORDS OF CREATION." THE TASK OF INSTALLING BIRDS AS THE DOMINANT SPECIES WAS BEGUN.

...SIX HUNDRED AND TWELVE PIP.

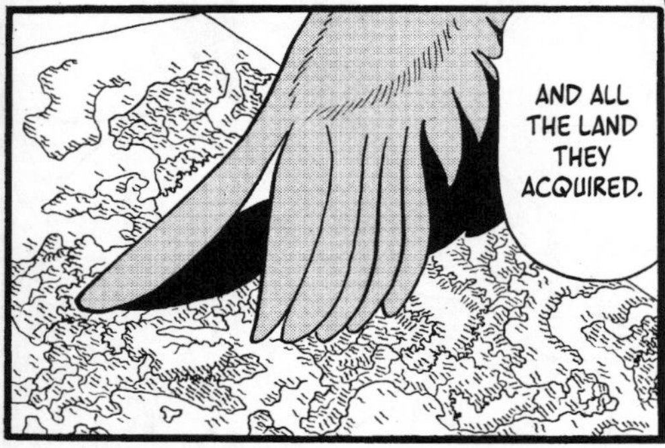

AND ALL THE LAND THEY ACQUIRED.

HOW ABOUT IT, NARCO? LET'S PLAY!

CHAPTER 10: QUAIL HILL

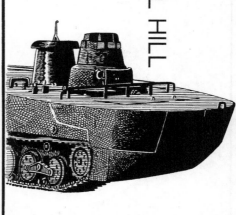

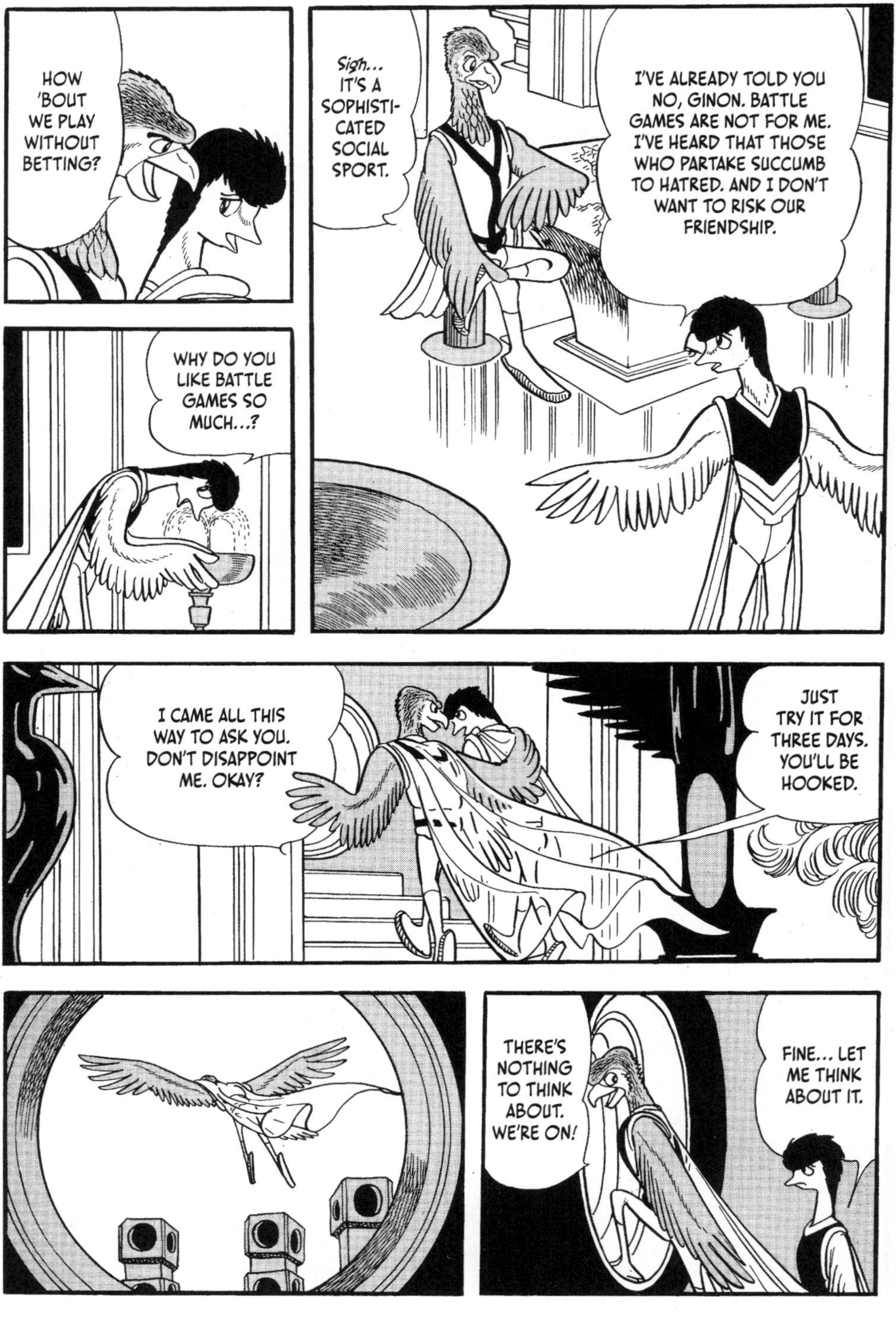
HOW 'BOUT WE PLAY WITHOUT BETTING?
Sigh... IT'S A SOPHISTI-CATED SOCIAL SPORT.
I'VE ALREADY TOLD YOU NO, GINON. BATTLE GAMES ARE NOT FOR ME. I'VE HEARD THAT THOSE WHO PARTAKE SUCCUMB TO HATRED. AND I DON'T WANT TO RISK OUR FRIENDSHIP.
WHY DO YOU LIKE BATTLE GAMES SO MUCH...?
I CAME ALL THIS WAY TO ASK YOU. DON'T DISAPPOINT ME. OKAY?
JUST TRY IT FOR THREE DAYS. YOU'LL BE HOOKED.
THERE'S NOTHING TO THINK ABOUT. WE'RE ON!
FINE... LET ME THINK ABOUT IT.

WAS THAT GINON?
YES, FATHER. HE CHALLENGED ME TO A BATTLE GAME.
HE FORCED ME INTO IT.
GINON IS A CARNIVORE. THEY'RE UNRULY AND VIOLENT.
THE WAY THEIR BEAKS ARE HOOKED... HOW SAVAGE!
THAT'S WHY I WARNED YOU... DON'T ASSOCIATE WITH CARNIVORES.
WHAT DID HE WAGER?
SIX HUNDRED AND TWELVE PIP. AND SOME LAND. BUT IN THE END, HE OFFERED TO PLAY WITHOUT BETTING.
HE'S LYING! IF YOU PLAY AND HE WINS, HE'LL DEMAND SOMETHING!

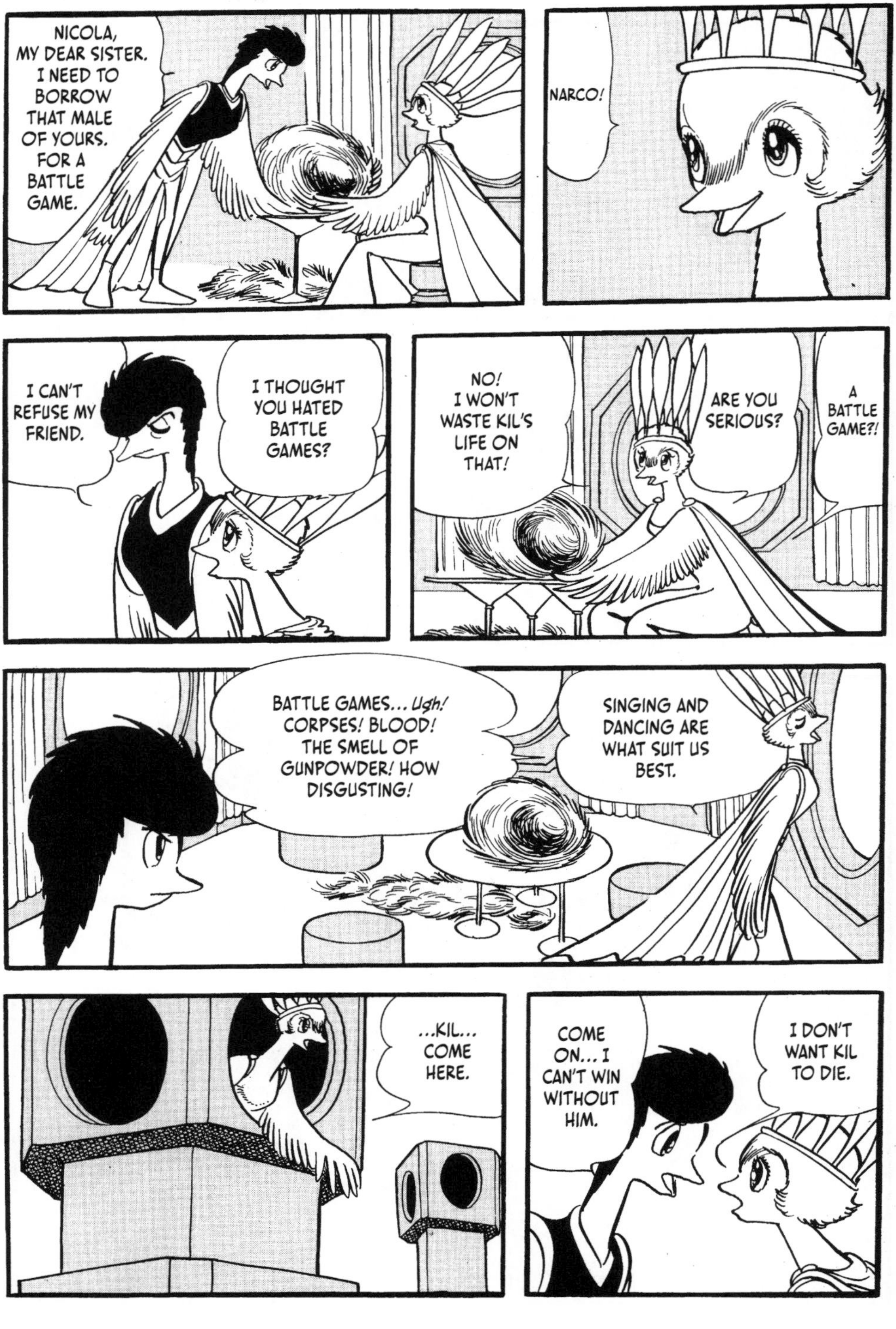
NICOLA, MY DEAR SISTER. I NEED TO BORROW THAT MALE OF YOURS. FOR A BATTLE GAME.
NARCO!
I CAN'T REFUSE MY FRIEND.
I THOUGHT YOU HATED BATTLE GAMES?
NO! I WON'T WASTE KIL'S LIFE ON THAT!
ARE YOU SERIOUS?
A BATTLE GAME?!
BATTLE GAMES... *Ugh!* CORPSES! BLOOD! THE SMELL OF GUNPOWDER! HOW DISGUSTING!
SINGING AND DANCING ARE WHAT SUIT US BEST.
...KIL... COME HERE.
COME ON... I CAN'T WIN WITHOUT HIM.
I DON'T WANT KIL TO DIE.

YOU KNOW WHAT BATTLE GAMES ARE?
I DO, MY LADY...
KIL, I NEED YOU FOR A BATTLE GAME. I'M SURE YOU'LL WIN!
WHERE IS THE OPPO-NENT?
AT GINON'S PLACE. THEY'RE HOMO HOMOS. A RECKLESS BUNCH.
I WON'T LOSE.
THAT'S THE SPIRIT! MY REPUTATION DEPENDS ON YOU WINNING.
WAIT! NO! I NEVER SAID YOU COULD BORROW HIM!

ALL OF THESE WEAPONS ARE YOURS. DYNAMITE. RAY GUNS. EVEN A TANK. THEY'RE HARDLY USED. LIKE BRAND NEW!
IT'S IN TWO WEEKS. MAKE A PLAN BY THEN.
YES, SIR.
COME WITH ME. IT'S TIME TO PLAN THE BATTLE!
MY DEAR BROTHER... YOU'LL REGRET THIS...

THE WORLD WAS NOW RULED BY BIRDMEN. HUMANS HAD REGRESSED. THEIR INTELLECT DEVOLVED, AND THEY WERE FORCED TO LIVE AS SLAVES TO THE BIRDMEN - THEY WERE REARED LIKE DOGS. THE BOURGEOIS CLASS OF BIRDMEN OWNED VAST AREAS OF FERTILE LAND AND SEVERAL HUNDRED HUMANS. ON OCCASION, THEY WOULD MAKE THE MEN FIGHT EACH OTHER FOR AMUSEMENT. THEY CALLED THESE "BATTLE GAMES." HUMANS WERE GIVEN WEAPONS THEY THEMSELVES HAD INVENTED THOUSANDS OF YEARS EARLIER. WITH THEIR INNATE MURDEROUS INSTINCT AND EGGED ON BY BIRDMEN, HUMANS KILLED EACH OTHER IN RECKLESS BATTLE. BEFORE LONG, BIRDMEN WERE GAMBLING ON THE GAMES, PUTTING THEIR PROPERTY AT STAKE.
THIS WOULD INEVITABLY LEAD TO A TRAGEDY...

IS THAT YOU, KIL?
YOU SHOULDN'T BE HERE!
THIS AREA IS WOMEN ONLY.

WE CAN SEE EACH OTHER AT NIGHT... WHY RISK IT DURING THE DAY?
I HAD TO... I WON'T BE SEEING YOU FOR A WHILE.
ARE THEY SENDING YOU SOME-WHERE?
NO... A BATTLE GAME.
WHAT?!
SIR NARCO'S ORDERS.
BUT YOU SERVE MISS NICOLA.
I DO...BUT SIR NARCO WAS CHALLENGED...
...TO A BATTLE GAME BY GINON.
HE NAMED ME LEADER. IT STARTS IN TWO WEEKS.

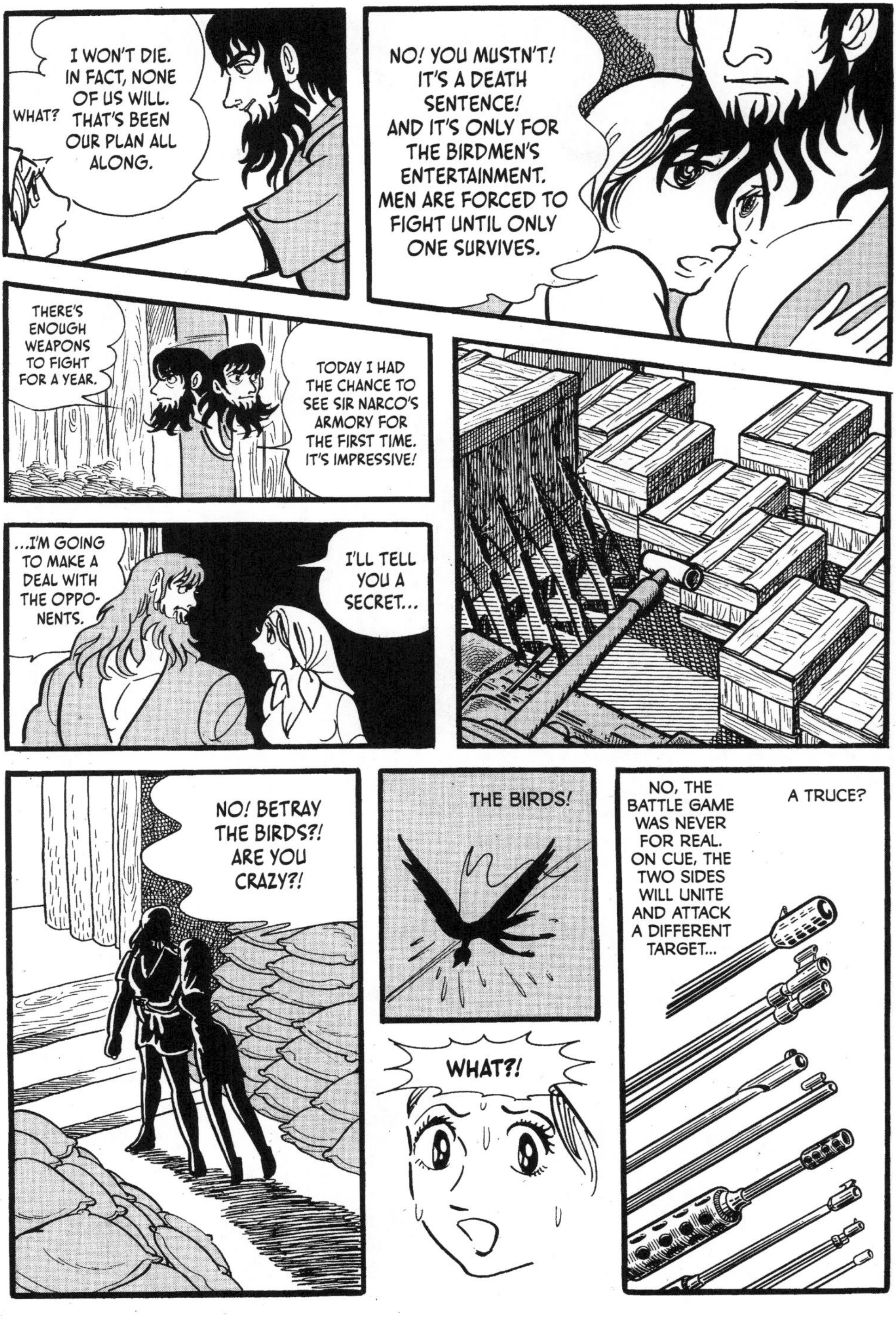
I WON'T DIE. IN FACT, NONE OF US WILL. THAT'S BEEN OUR PLAN ALL ALONG.
WHAT?
NO! YOU MUSTN'T! IT'S A DEATH SENTENCE! AND IT'S ONLY FOR THE BIRDMEN'S ENTERTAINMENT. MEN ARE FORCED TO FIGHT UNTIL ONLY ONE SURVIVES.
TODAY I HAD THE CHANCE TO SEE SIR NARCO'S ARMORY FOR THE FIRST TIME. IT'S IMPRESSIVE!
THERE'S ENOUGH WEAPONS TO FIGHT FOR A YEAR.
I'LL TELL YOU A SECRET...
...I'M GOING TO MAKE A DEAL WITH THE OPPONENTS.
A TRUCE?
NO, THE BATTLE GAME WAS NEVER FOR REAL. ON CUE, THE TWO SIDES WILL UNITE AND ATTACK A DIFFERENT TARGET...
WHAT?!
THE BIRDS!
NO! BETRAY THE BIRDS?! ARE YOU CRAZY?!

FATHER, IN TWO WEEKS, I START A BATTLE GAME WITH NARCO.
NARCO DOESN'T OWN ANY LAND WORTH ACQUIRING.
A WASTE OF TIME.
ACTUALLY, I DECIDED NOT TO WAGER ANYTHING.
THEN YOU'RE EVEN DUMBER THAN I THOUGHT!
THERE'S SOMETHING ELSE I'M AFTER.
OH YEAH?

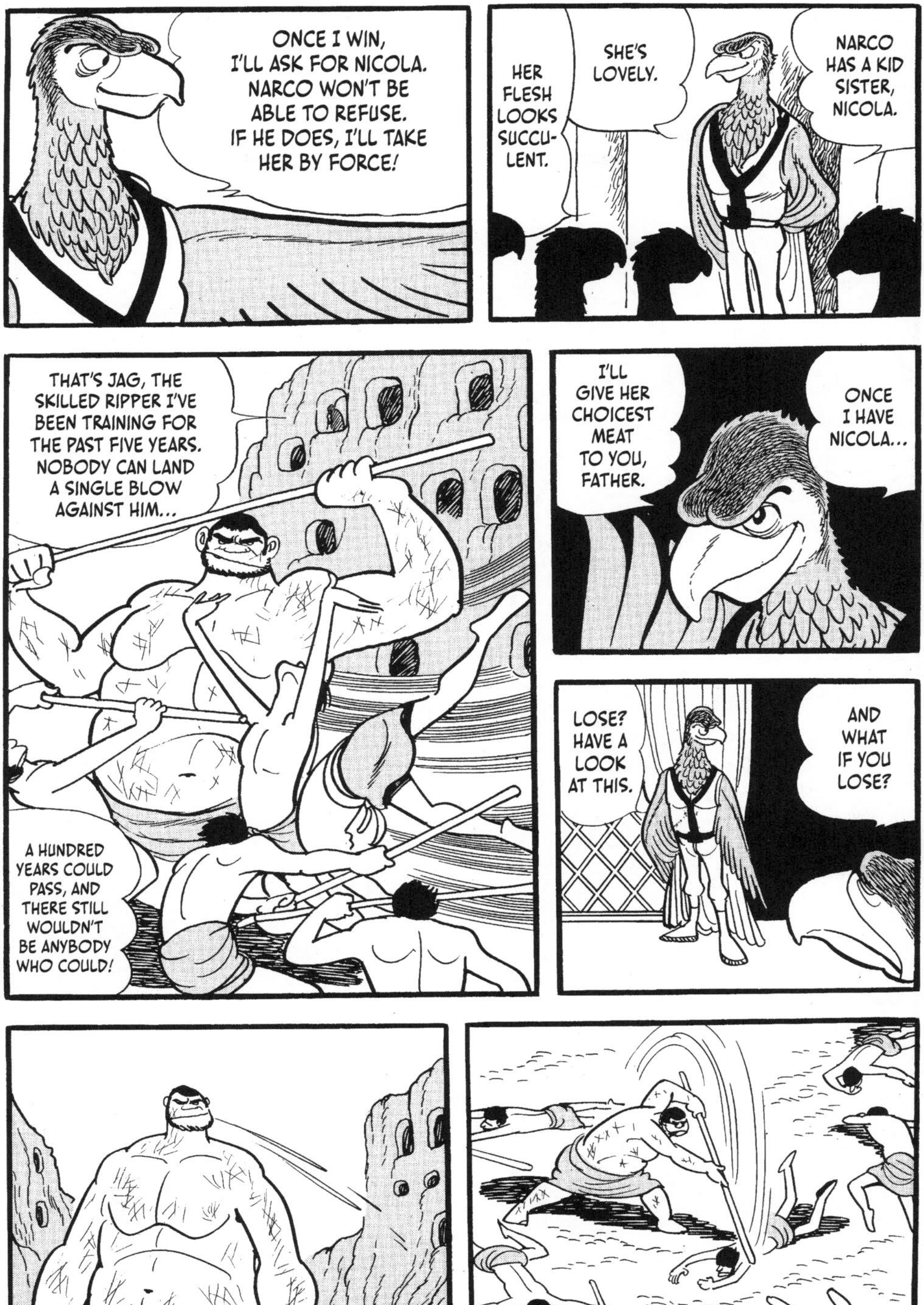
NARCO HAS A KID SISTER, NICOLA.
SHE'S LOVELY.
HER FLESH LOOKS SUCCU-LENT.
ONCE I WIN, I'LL ASK FOR NICOLA. NARCO WON'T BE ABLE TO REFUSE. IF HE DOES, I'LL TAKE HER BY FORCE!
ONCE I HAVE NICOLA...
I'LL GIVE HER CHOICEST MEAT TO YOU, FATHER.
AND WHAT IF YOU LOSE?
LOSE? HAVE A LOOK AT THIS.
THAT'S JAG, THE SKILLED RIPPER I'VE BEEN TRAINING FOR THE PAST FIVE YEARS. NOBODY CAN LAND A SINGLE BLOW AGAINST HIM...
A HUNDRED YEARS COULD PASS, AND THERE STILL WOULDN'T BE ANYBODY WHO COULD!

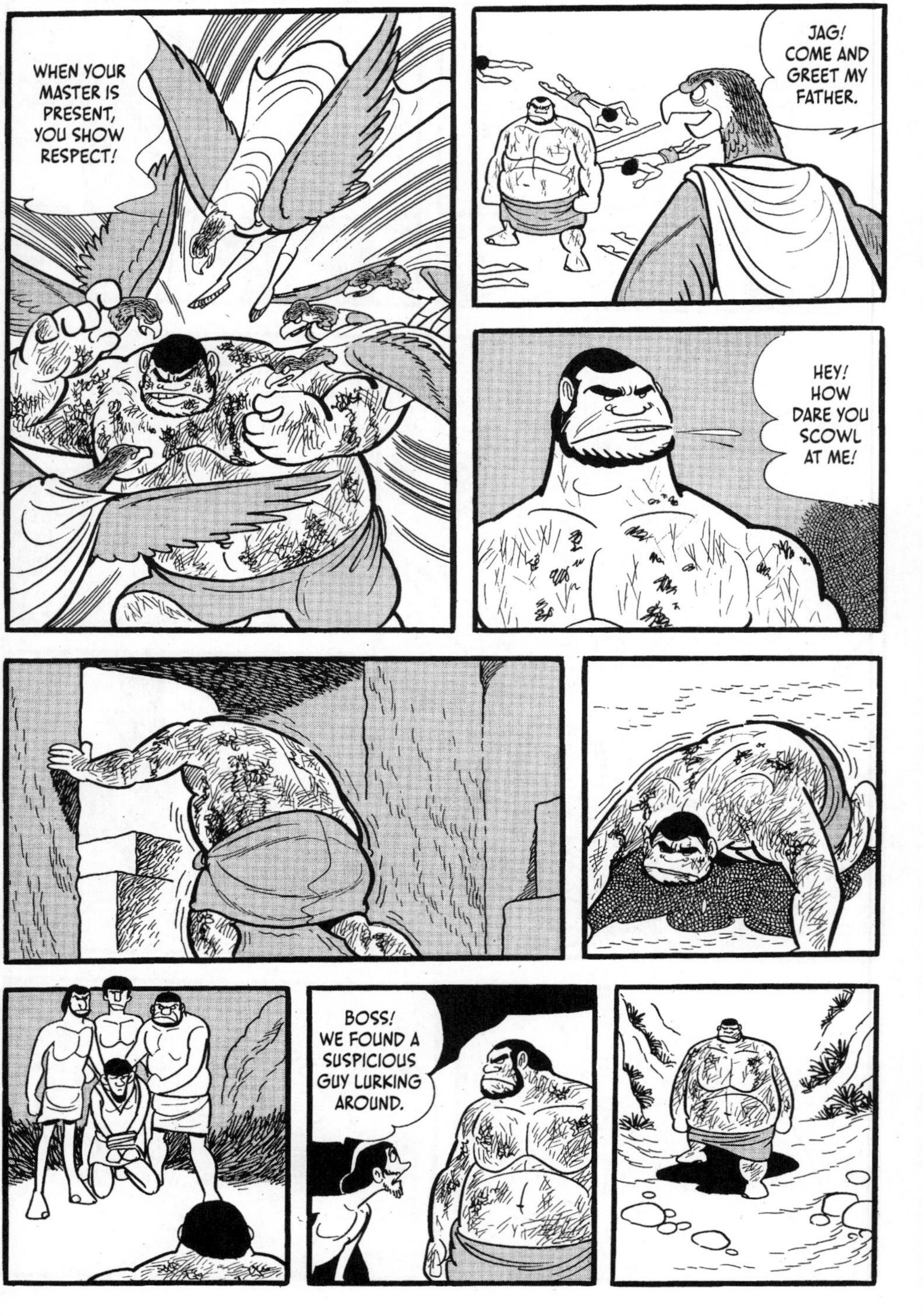
WHEN YOUR MASTER IS PRESENT, YOU SHOW RESPECT!
JAG! COME AND GREET MY FATHER.
HEY! HOW DARE YOU SCOWL AT ME!
BOSS! WE FOUND A SUSPICIOUS GUY LURKING AROUND.

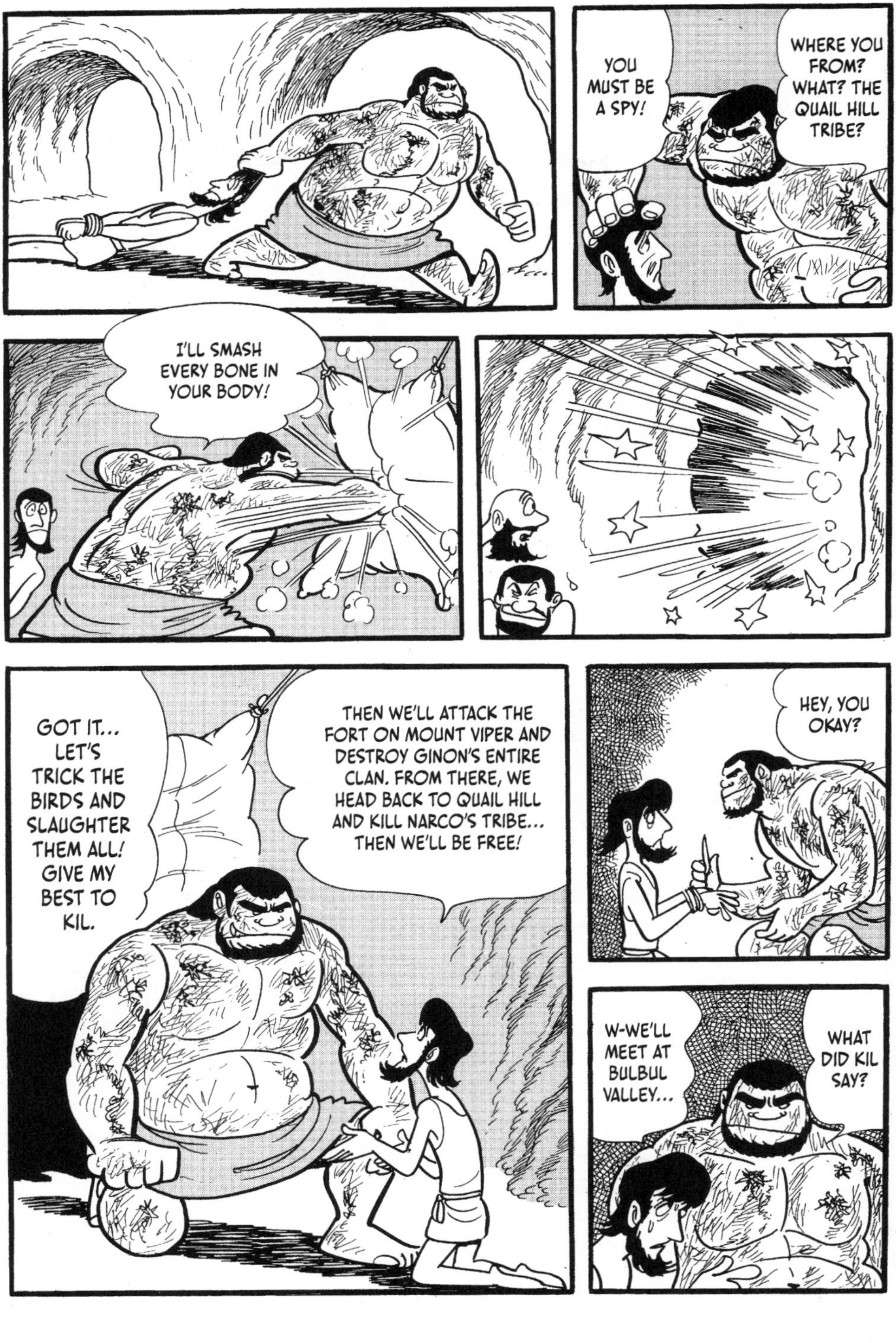
WHERE YOU FROM? WHAT? THE QUAIL HILL TRIBE?
YOU MUST BE A SPY!
I'LL SMASH EVERY BONE IN YOUR BODY!
THEN WE'LL ATTACK THE FORT ON MOUNT VIPER AND DESTROY GINON'S ENTIRE CLAN. FROM THERE, WE HEAD BACK TO QUAIL HILL AND KILL NARCO'S TRIBE... THEN WE'LL BE FREE!
GOT IT... LET'S TRICK THE BIRDS AND SLAUGHTER THEM ALL! GIVE MY BEST TO KIL.
HEY, YOU OKAY?
WHAT DID KIL SAY?
W-WE'LL MEET AT BULBUL VALLEY...

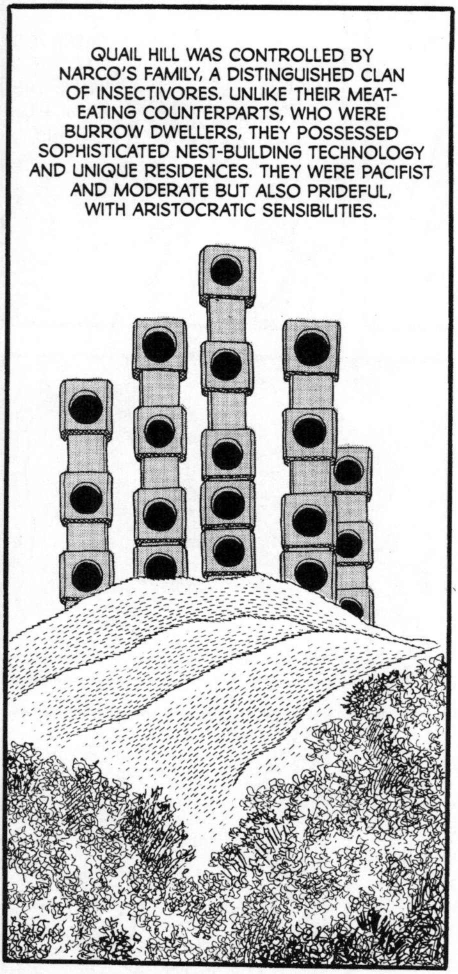
QUAIL HILL WAS CONTROLLED BY NARCO'S FAMILY, A DISTINGUISHED CLAN OF INSECTIVORES. UNLIKE THEIR MEAT-EATING COUNTERPARTS, WHO WERE BURROW DWELLERS, THEY POSSESSED SOPHISTICATED NEST-BUILDING TECHNOLOGY AND UNIQUE RESIDENCES. THEY WERE PACIFIST AND MODERATE BUT ALSO PRIDEFUL, WITH ARISTOCRATIC SENSIBILITIES.

SEVERAL MILLENNIA HAD PASSED FROM THE ERA WHEN HUMANS MASSACRED THEIR ANCESTORS...

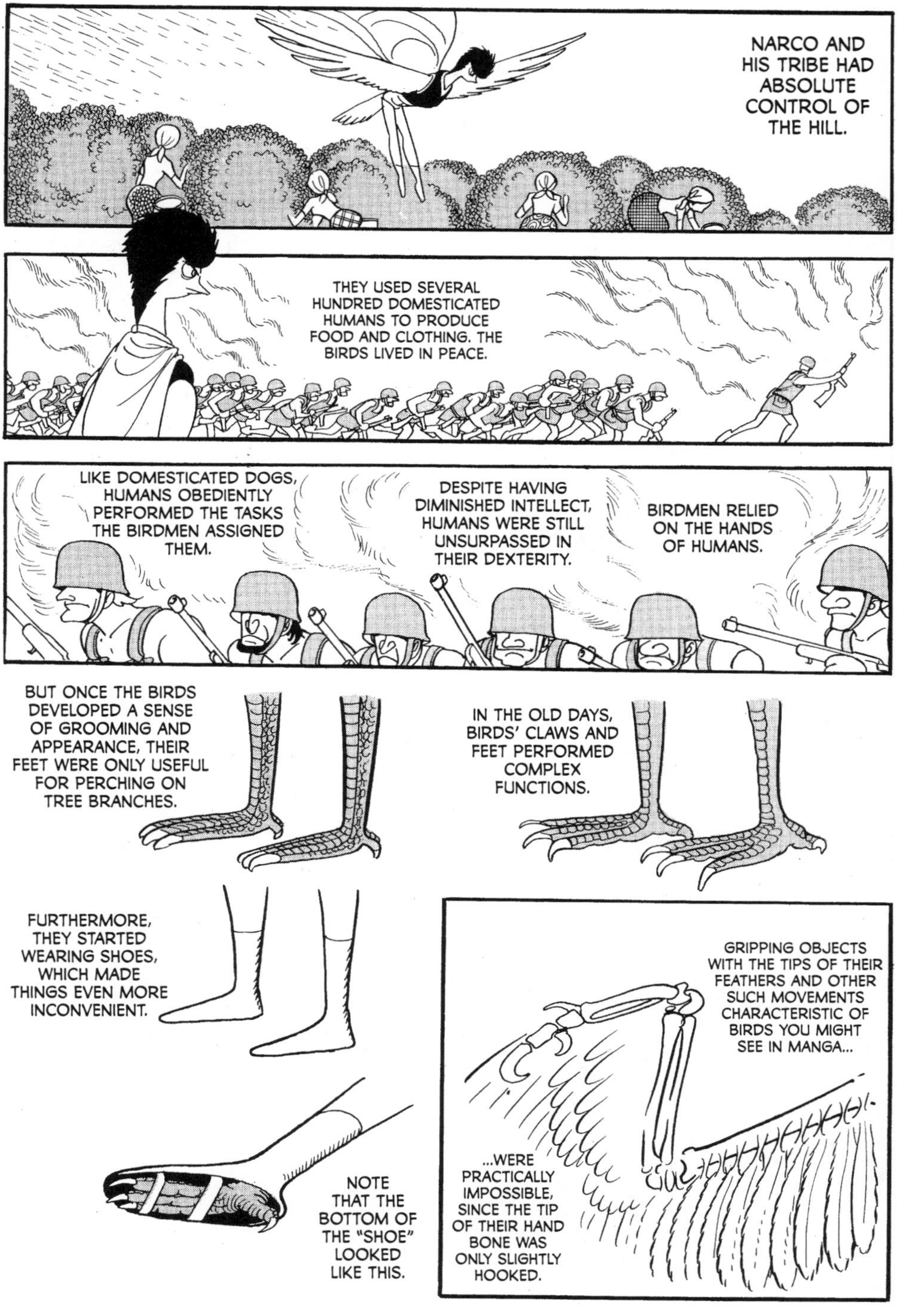
NARCO AND HIS TRIBE HAD ABSOLUTE CONTROL OF THE HILL.
THEY USED SEVERAL HUNDRED DOMESTICATED HUMANS TO PRODUCE FOOD AND CLOTHING. THE BIRDS LIVED IN PEACE.
LIKE DOMESTICATED DOGS, HUMANS OBEDIENTLY PERFORMED THE TASKS THE BIRDMEN ASSIGNED THEM.
DESPITE HAVING DIMINISHED INTELLECT, HUMANS WERE STILL UNSURPASSED IN THEIR DEXTERITY.
BIRDMEN RELIED ON THE HANDS OF HUMANS.
BUT ONCE THE BIRDS DEVELOPED A SENSE OF GROOMING AND APPEARANCE, THEIR FEET WERE ONLY USEFUL FOR PERCHING ON TREE BRANCHES.
IN THE OLD DAYS, BIRDS' CLAWS AND FEET PERFORMED COMPLEX FUNCTIONS.
FURTHERMORE, THEY STARTED WEARING SHOES, WHICH MADE THINGS EVEN MORE INCONVENIENT.
GRIPPING OBJECTS WITH THE TIPS OF THEIR FEATHERS AND OTHER SUCH MOVEMENTS CHARACTERISTIC OF BIRDS YOU MIGHT SEE IN MANGA...
NOTE THAT THE BOTTOM OF THE "SHOE" LOOKED LIKE THIS.
...WERE PRACTICALLY IMPOSSIBLE, SINCE THE TIP OF THEIR HAND BONE WAS ONLY SLIGHTLY HOOKED.

BIRDMEN WERE ABLE TO LIVE IN PEACE BECAUSE THEIR TOTAL POPULATION WAS SMALL. THEY DID NOT HAVE A SUDDEN GROWTH IN POPULATION. THE LAWS OF NATURE CAUSED UP TO 90% OF BIRDMEN EGGS TO ROT OR CRACK, PREVENTING UNCONDITIONAL PROLIFEROUS GROWTH. WHEN BIRDMEN EVOLVED FROM BIRDS, THEY WERE SIMULTANEOUSLY FORCED TO ENGAGE IN POPULATION CONTROL.

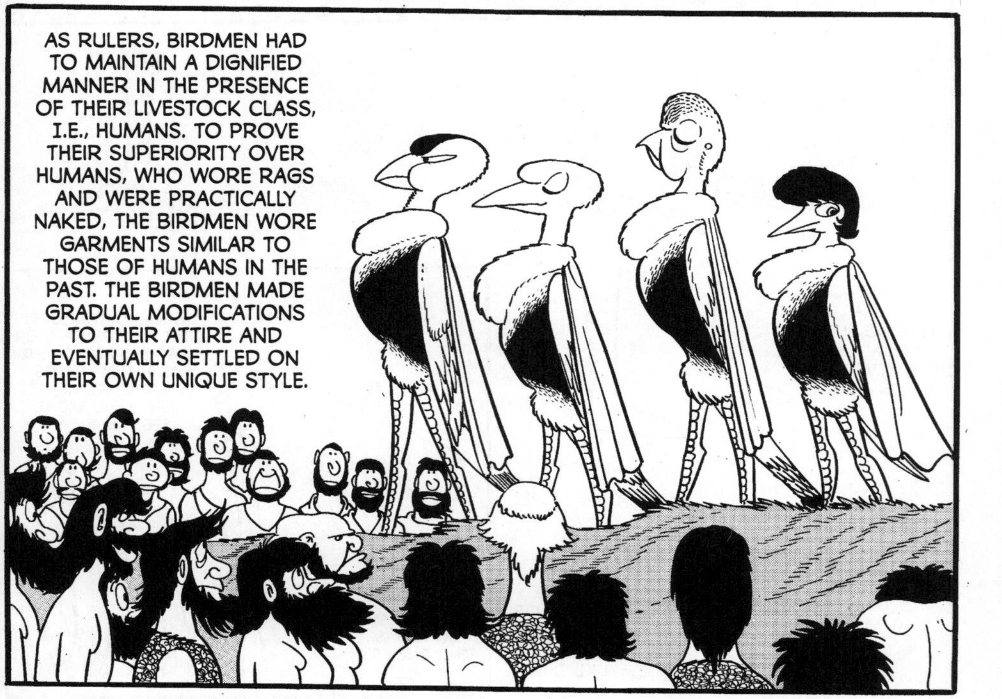
AS RULERS, BIRDMEN HAD TO MAINTAIN A DIGNIFIED MANNER IN THE PRESENCE OF THEIR LIVESTOCK CLASS, I.E., HUMANS. TO PROVE THEIR SUPERIORITY OVER HUMANS, WHO WORE RAGS AND WERE PRACTICALLY NAKED, THE BIRDMEN WORE GARMENTS SIMILAR TO THOSE OF HUMANS IN THE PAST. THE BIRDMEN MADE GRADUAL MODIFICATIONS TO THEIR ATTIRE AND EVENTUALLY SETTLED ON THEIR OWN UNIQUE STYLE.

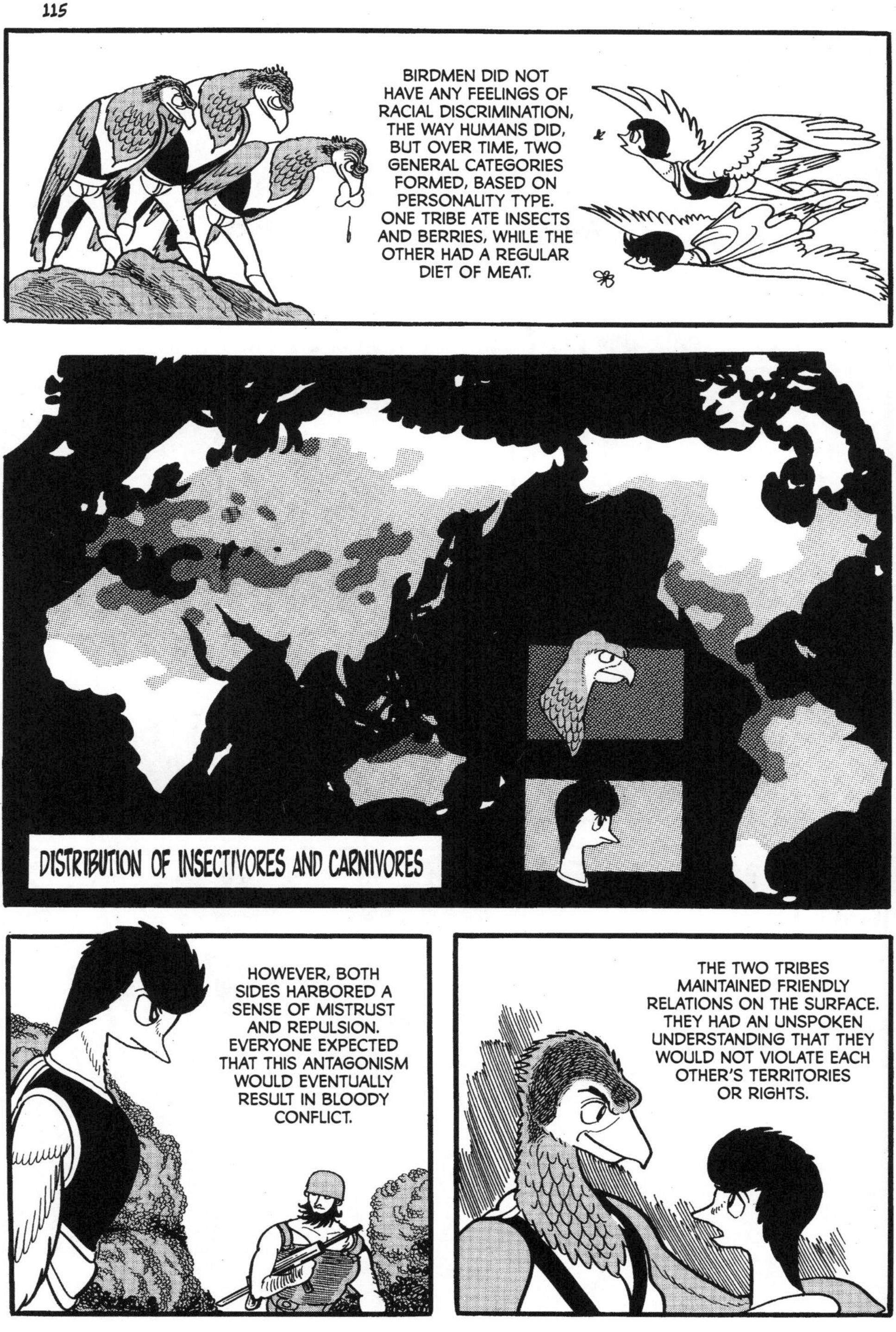
BIRDMEN DID NOT HAVE ANY FEELINGS OF RACIAL DISCRIMINATION, THE WAY HUMANS DID, BUT OVER TIME, TWO GENERAL CATEGORIES FORMED, BASED ON PERSONALITY TYPE. ONE TRIBE ATE INSECTS AND BERRIES, WHILE THE OTHER HAD A REGULAR DIET OF MEAT.
DISTRIBUTION OF INSECTIVORES AND CARNIVORES
HOWEVER, BOTH SIDES HARBORED A SENSE OF MISTRUST AND REPULSION. EVERYONE EXPECTED THAT THIS ANTAGONISM WOULD EVENTUALLY RESULT IN BLOODY CONFLICT.
THE TWO TRIBES MAINTAINED FRIENDLY RELATIONS ON THE SURFACE. THEY HAD AN UNSPOKEN UNDERSTANDING THAT THEY WOULD NOT VIOLATE EACH OTHER'S TERRITORIES OR RIGHTS.

THE BATTLE GAME STARTS TOMORROW. IS YOUR PLAN READY?
YES, SIR NARCO.
I THINK GINON HAS SET HIS SIGHTS ON MY SISTER. THAT MUST BE WHAT HE WANTS.
OF COURSE, SIR. I WILL NOT LOSE. I WILL FIGHT WITH EVERYTHING I HAVE UNTIL THE VERY END.
I'M COUNTING ON YOU. I NEED YOU TO WIN FOR THE HONOR OF OUR FAMILY.
I WILL NOT LET GINON...
...TAKE HER.
I CERTAINLY HOPE SO, MY GOOD WARRIOR!
WE WILL MARCH ON MOUNT VIPER, WHERE GINON'S FORT IS LOCATED.

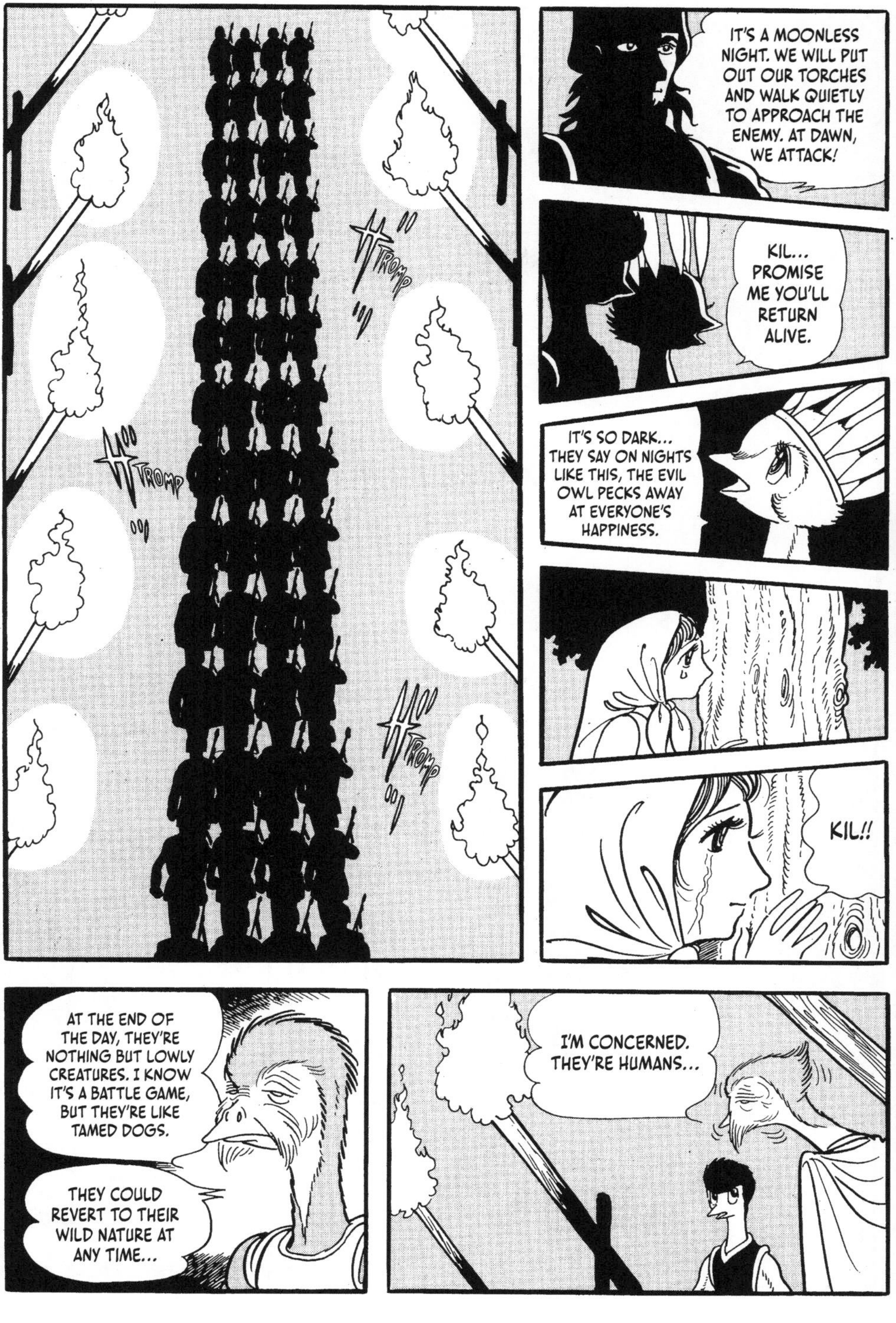
TROMP
TROMP
TROMP
IT'S A MOONLESS NIGHT. WE WILL PUT OUT OUR TORCHES AND WALK QUIETLY TO APPROACH THE ENEMY. AT DAWN, WE ATTACK!
KIL... PROMISE ME YOU'LL RETURN ALIVE.
IT'S SO DARK... THEY SAY ON NIGHTS LIKE THIS, THE EVIL OWL PECKS AWAY AT EVERYONE'S HAPPINESS.
KIL!!
AT THE END OF THE DAY, THEY'RE NOTHING BUT LOWLY CREATURES. I KNOW IT'S A BATTLE GAME, BUT THEY'RE LIKE TAMED DOGS.
THEY COULD REVERT TO THEIR WILD NATURE AT ANY TIME...
I'M CONCERNED. THEY'RE HUMANS...

I WANT YOU ALL TO TRACK THE HUMANS AND REPORT ON EVERY DEVELOPMENT.
I'M SURE FATHER WOULD WANT TO KNOW.
BUT IT'S SO DARK...?
HUMANS CAN SEE IN THE DARK, BUT NIGHTS LIKE THESE ARE A PROBLEM FOR US.
ONCE THE BATTLE STARTS, THERE WILL BE FIRE, SO WE'LL BE ABLE TO SEE.
BOSS! SOME BIRDS ARE FOLLOWING US!
DAMN! GET RID OF 'EM. BLOW THEM AWAY WITH THE BAZOOKA.
BOOM
BOOM
CHANGE COURSE! PROCEED TO BULBUL VALLEY!

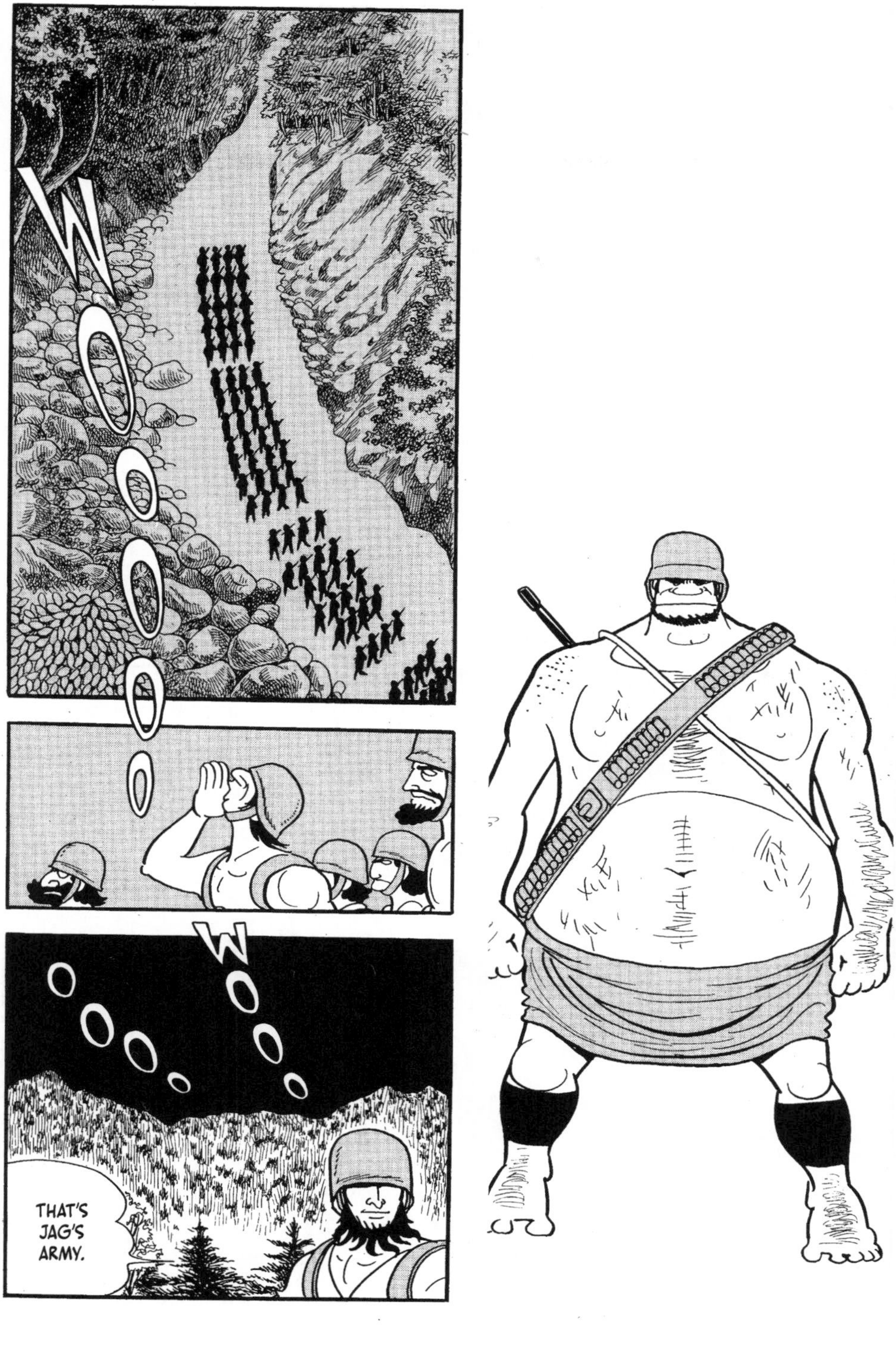
WOOOOOO
WOOOO
OOOOO
THAT'S JAG'S ARMY.

ARE YOU JAG?
YUP. YOU MUST BE KIL.
I'VE HEARD A LOT ABOUT YOU, KIL...
I'VE NEVER MET A HUMAN OUTSIDE MY TRIBE.
AT FIRST, I THOUGHT YOU WERE TRYING TO TRICK ME.
I HEARD YOU'RE TOUGH TO DEAL WITH, SO I WASN'T SURE YOU'D AGREE TO THIS PLAN.
AS YOU CAN SEE, I'M NOT EDUCATED. ALL I HAVE GOING FOR ME IS MY BRUTE STRENGTH. BUT YOU'RE SMART. TOGETHER, I THINK WE CAN WIN.
WHETHER WE WIN OR NOT MIGHT COME DOWN TO LUCK...BUT IF WE DO THIS AND IT EMBOLDENS OTHER HUMANS BY SHOWING THEM WE CAN FIGHT BACK AGAINST THE BIRDS, THAT WOULD BE GOOD ENOUGH FOR ME...
AFTER ALL, AS FAR AS I KNOW, NO HUMAN HAS REBELLED AGAINST THE BIRDS FOR THE PAST SEVERAL HUNDRED YEARS.

LISTEN! WHEN OUR TWO SIDES UNITE, WE'LL SPLIT INTO THREE TEAMS. ONE WILL FAKE A BATTLE AT THE FOOT OF MOUNT VIPER. THAT SHOULD CATCH THE BIRDS' ATTENTION. ONCE THAT HAPPENS...
ANOTHER TEAM WILL SET FIRE AROUND GINON'S FAMILY FORT!
THE LAST TEAM WILL WAIT FOR THE BIRDS TO EMERGE FROM THE SMOKE. THEY'LL SHOOT 'EM ALL!
AND TO MAKE SURE, TAKE THE BIRDS YOU'VE KILLED AND...
...PLUCK THEIR FEATHERS! COOK THEM! EAT THEM!!
Ugh!
REALLY? EAT...THE BIRDS...?
THAT'S BRUTAL...
HUMANS I COULD EAT... BUT BIRDS? HOW CRUEL...
SOME BOOKS SAY OUR ANCESTORS ATE BIRDS AND THOUGHT NOTHING OF IT...
THEY CALLED IT YAKITORI...
ARE YOU SERIOUS? DID THEY EAT THE ORGANS, TOO? AND BONES?
YEAH. THEY USED THE ORGANS IN A DISH CALLED MOTSU-YAKI. IT'S SUPPOSED TO BE DELICIOUS. THE BONES WERE USED TO MAKE SOUP.

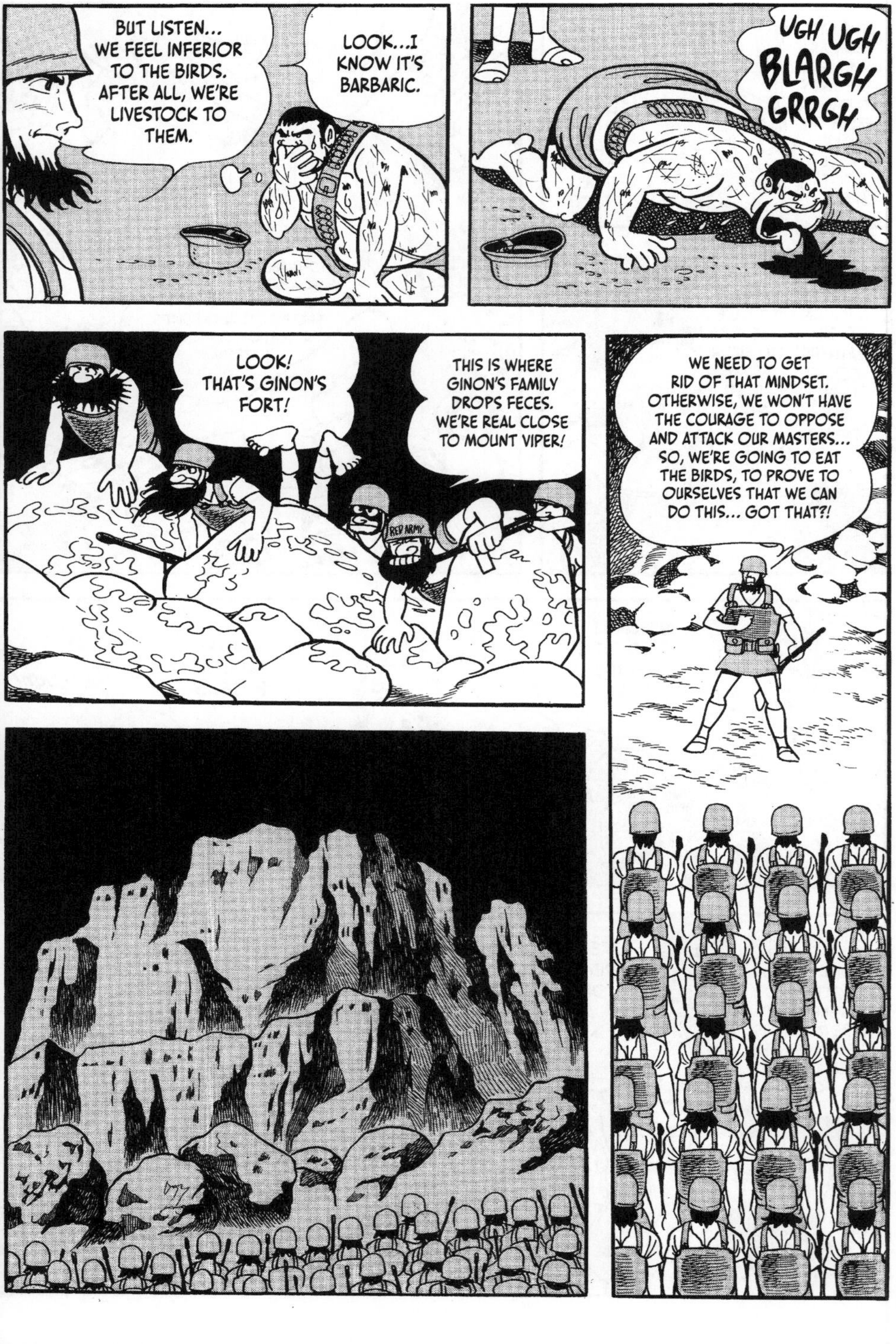
BUT LISTEN... WE FEEL INFERIOR TO THE BIRDS. AFTER ALL, WE'RE LIVESTOCK TO THEM.
LOOK...I KNOW IT'S BARBARIC.
UGH UGH BLARGH GRRGH
LOOK! THAT'S GINON'S FORT!
THIS IS WHERE GINON'S FAMILY DROPS FECES. WE'RE REAL CLOSE TO MOUNT VIPER!
RED ARMY
WE NEED TO GET RID OF THAT MINDSET. OTHERWISE, WE WON'T HAVE THE COURAGE TO OPPOSE AND ATTACK OUR MASTERS... SO, WE'RE GOING TO EAT THE BIRDS, TO PROVE TO OURSELVES THAT WE CAN DO THIS... GOT THAT?!

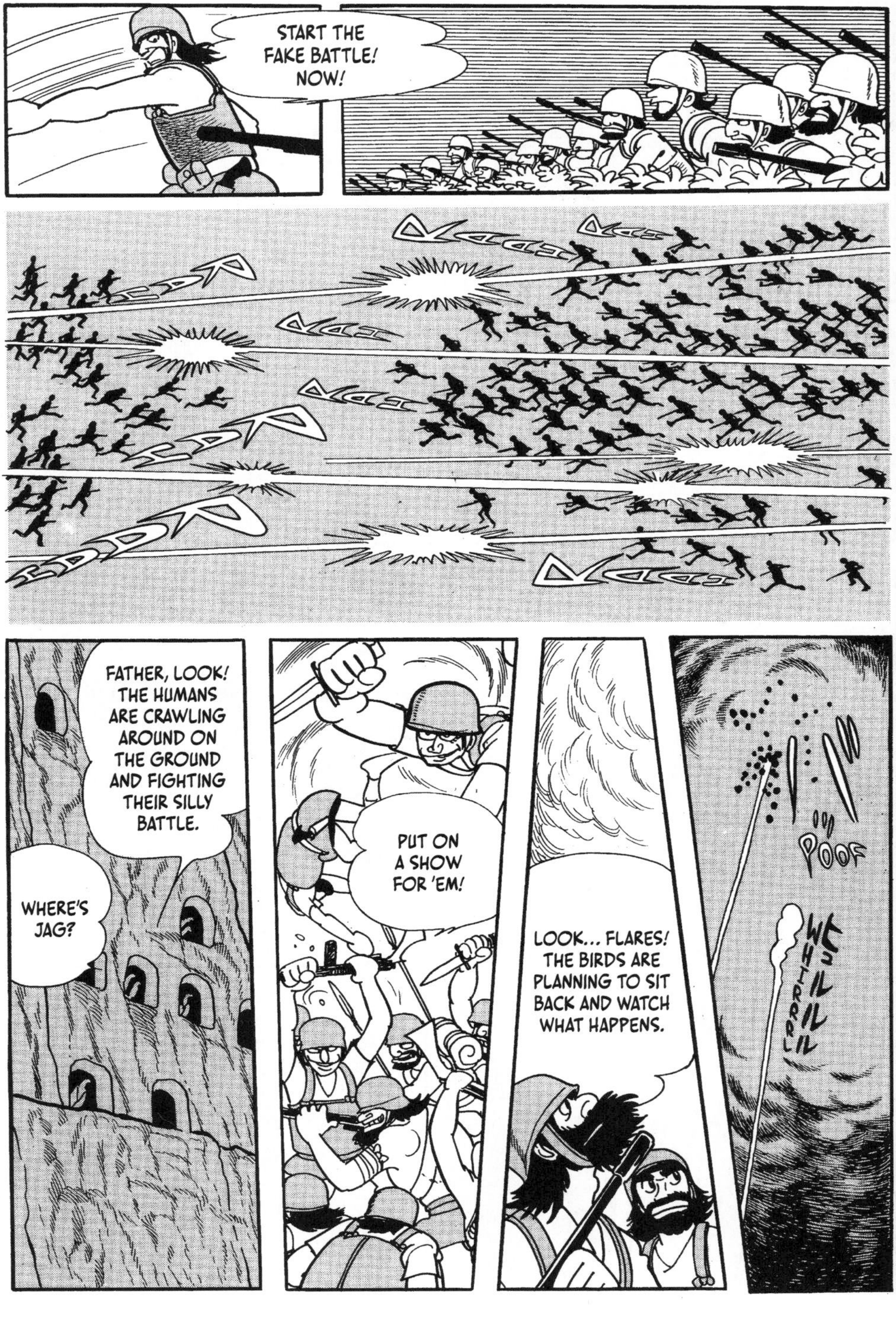
START THE FAKE BATTLE! NOW!
FATHER, LOOK! THE HUMANS ARE CRAWLING AROUND ON THE GROUND AND FIGHTING THEIR SILLY BATTLE.
WHERE'S JAG?
PUT ON A SHOW FOR 'EM!
LOOK... FLARES! THE BIRDS ARE PLANNING TO SIT BACK AND WATCH WHAT HAPPENS.
POOF
WHIRRRL

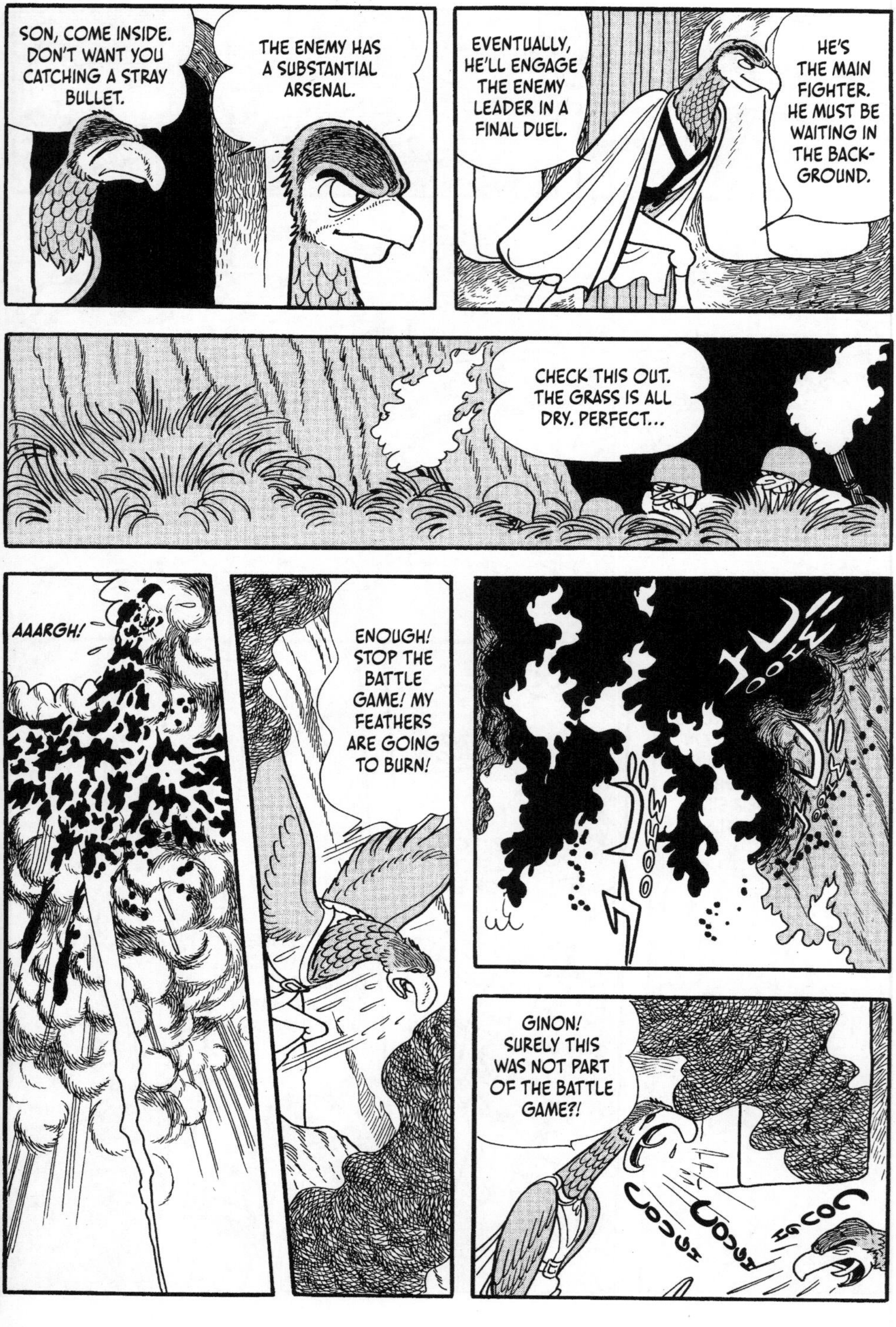
SON, COME INSIDE. DON'T WANT YOU CATCHING A STRAY BULLET.
THE ENEMY HAS A SUBSTANTIAL ARSENAL.
HE'S THE MAIN FIGHTER. HE MUST BE WAITING IN THE BACK-GROUND.
EVENTUALLY, HE'LL ENGAGE THE ENEMY LEADER IN A FINAL DUEL.
CHECK THIS OUT. THE GRASS IS ALL DRY. PERFECT...
AAARGH!
ENOUGH! STOP THE BATTLE GAME! MY FEATHERS ARE GOING TO BURN!
GINON! SURELY THIS WAS NOT PART OF THE BATTLE GAME?!

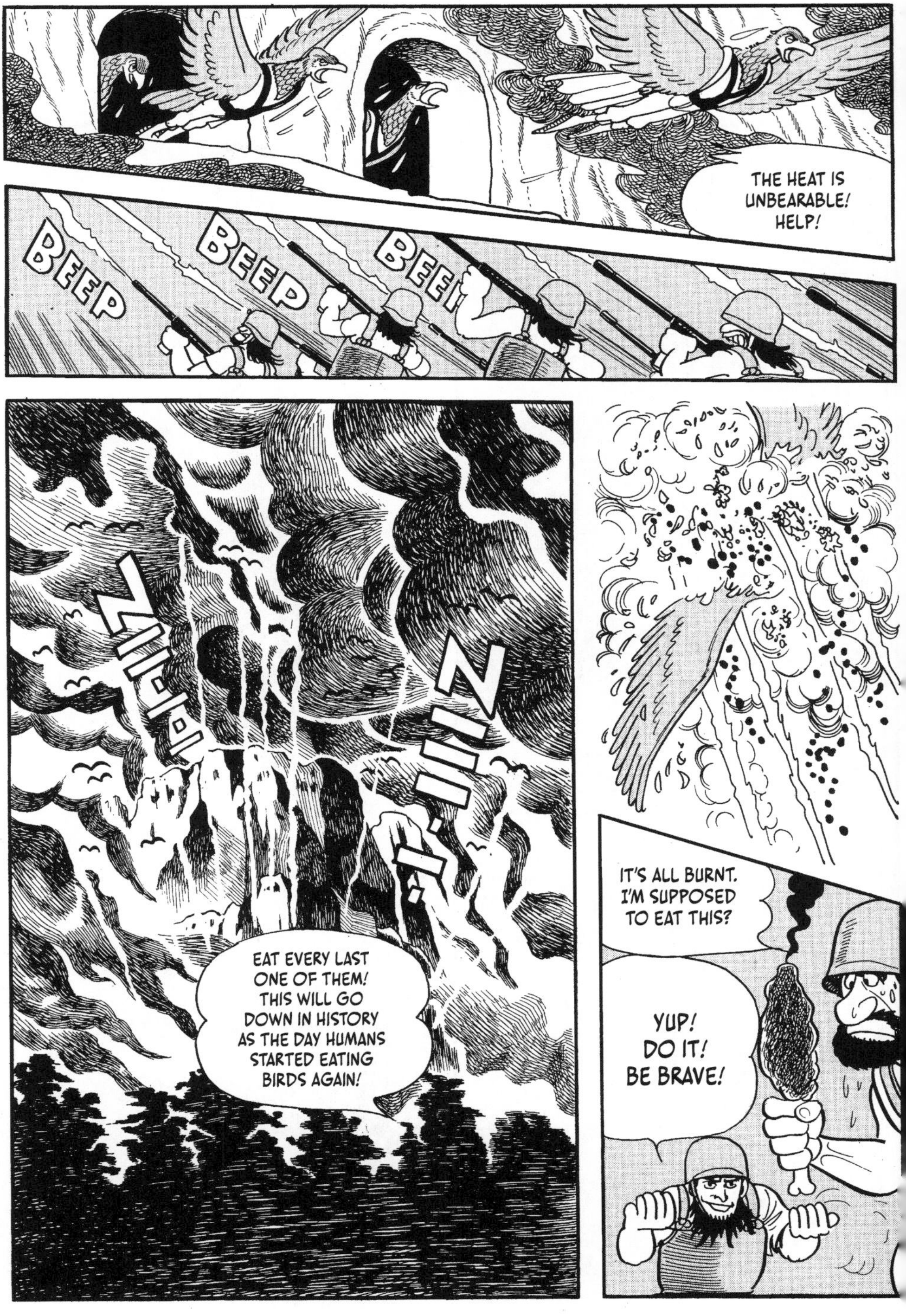
THE HEAT IS UNBEARABLE! HELP!
BEEP
BEEP
BEE
EAT EVERY LAST ONE OF THEM! THIS WILL GO DOWN IN HISTORY AS THE DAY HUMANS STARTED EATING BIRDS AGAIN!
IT'S ALL BURNT. I'M SUPPOSED TO EAT THIS?
YUP! DO IT! BE BRAVE!

IF GINON HAD SEEN THE HUMANS NOW, HIS FEAR WOULD LITERALLY HAVE GIVEN HIM GOOSEBUMPS. AFTER ALL, WHEN HIS BRETHREN TRIED TO ESCAPE THE FLAMES, THEY WERE SHOT DEAD AND DEVOURED... BUT NOT A SINGLE BIRDMAN WHO WITNESSED IT SURVIVED.

YOU KNOW, BIRDMEN MEAT ISN'T SO BAD AFTER ALL.
HEY, YOU KNOW WHO THIS IS? IT'S GINON. HE'S BURNT TO A CRISP!

I COULD EAT 'EM EVERY DAY!
ALL WE NEED NOW IS A DRINK... Burp...
WE ATE EVERY LAST ONE OF 'EM!
HOW WAS IT? GOOD?
ALRIGHT, WE NEED TO GET BACK TO QUAIL HILL BEFORE DAWN. LET'S MAKE SURE NARCO AND HIS FAMILY MEET THE SAME FATE!
THAT'S RIGHT! I WANT TO TELL THE OTHER SLAVES ABOUT THIS.
I'M STARTING TO THINK ALL BIRDS EXIST FOR US TO EAT.
I GOTTA HAND IT TO YOU... THIS WAS AMAZING. TO BE HONEST, I WASN'T SO SURE ABOUT THIS PLAN....
EATING THE BIRDS TO OVERCOME OUR INFERIORITY COMPLEX... THAT WAS BRILLIANT.
HEY BOSS... NEXT TIME, LET'S EAT THEM WITH SOME SAUCE AND SUGAR!

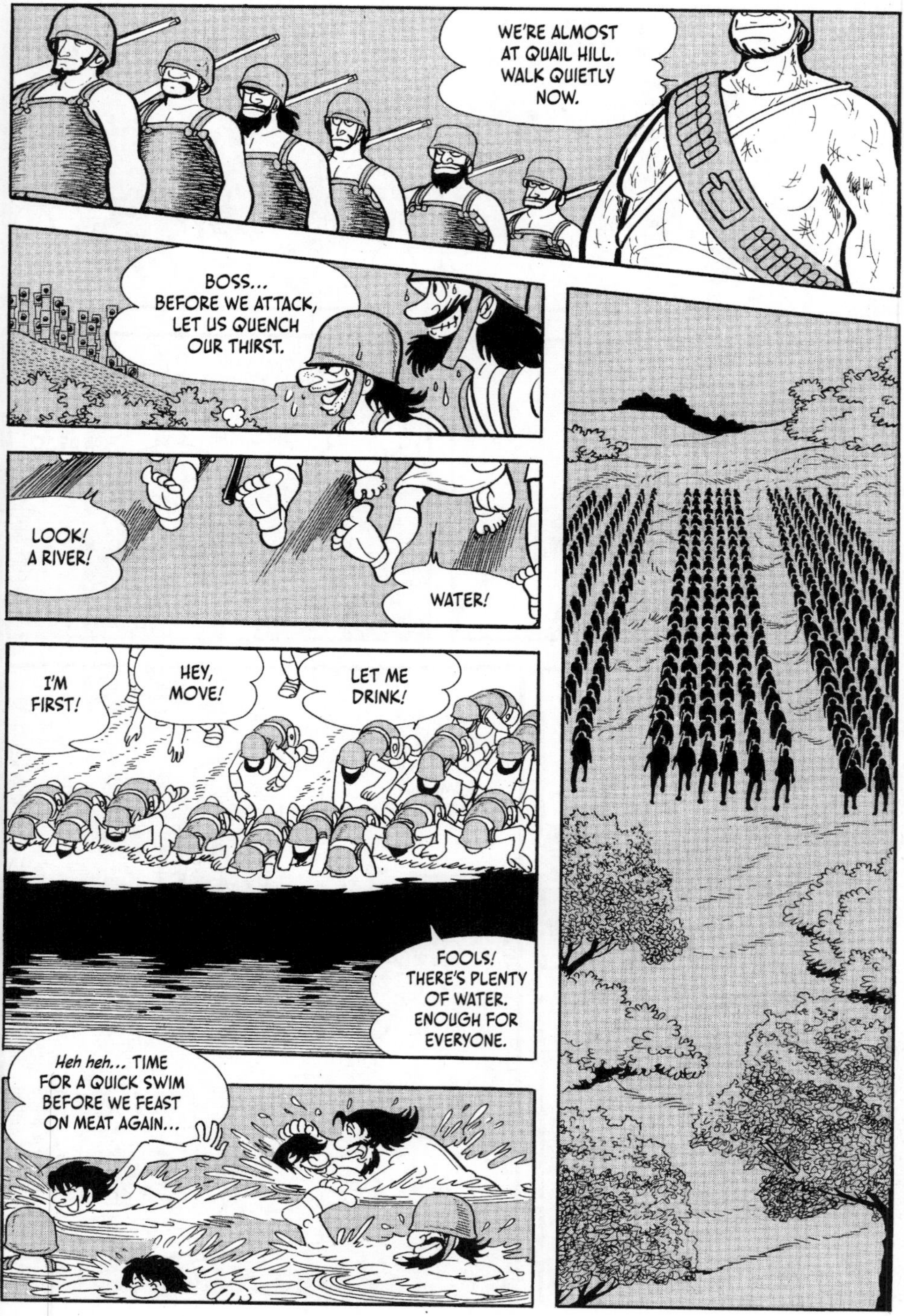
WE'RE ALMOST AT QUAIL HILL. WALK QUIETLY NOW.
BOSS... BEFORE WE ATTACK, LET US QUENCH OUR THIRST.
LOOK! A RIVER!
WATER!
I'M FIRST!
HEY, MOVE!
LET ME DRINK!
FOOLS! THERE'S PLENTY OF WATER. ENOUGH FOR EVERYONE.
Heh heh... TIME FOR A QUICK SWIM BEFORE WE FEAST ON MEAT AGAIN...

O-OUCH! I CAN'T BEAR IT!
B-Barf!
Gasp!
Ugh!
DAMN IT! SOMEONE POISONED THIS WATER UPSTREAM!
I'M NOT GOING TO MAKE IT...
SOMEONE BETRAYED US!!
OUR PLAN HAS FAILED! THE BIRDS OUTSMARTED US!!
IF YOU CAN STILL MOVE, TAKE REFUGE DOWNSTREAM! IT'S NOT SAFE HERE!
IT STINGS!
HELP!
Rrrrr... NO... THIS WATER IS...

Barf...
Ugh...
WE'RE OUT IN THE OPEN HERE...
LOOK! BIRDS! BIRDMEN ARE HEADED THIS WAY!
THEY'RE ATTACKING! LOOK OUT! AAARGH!
AAAAAAH!
FWOOSH
BANG
CRASH

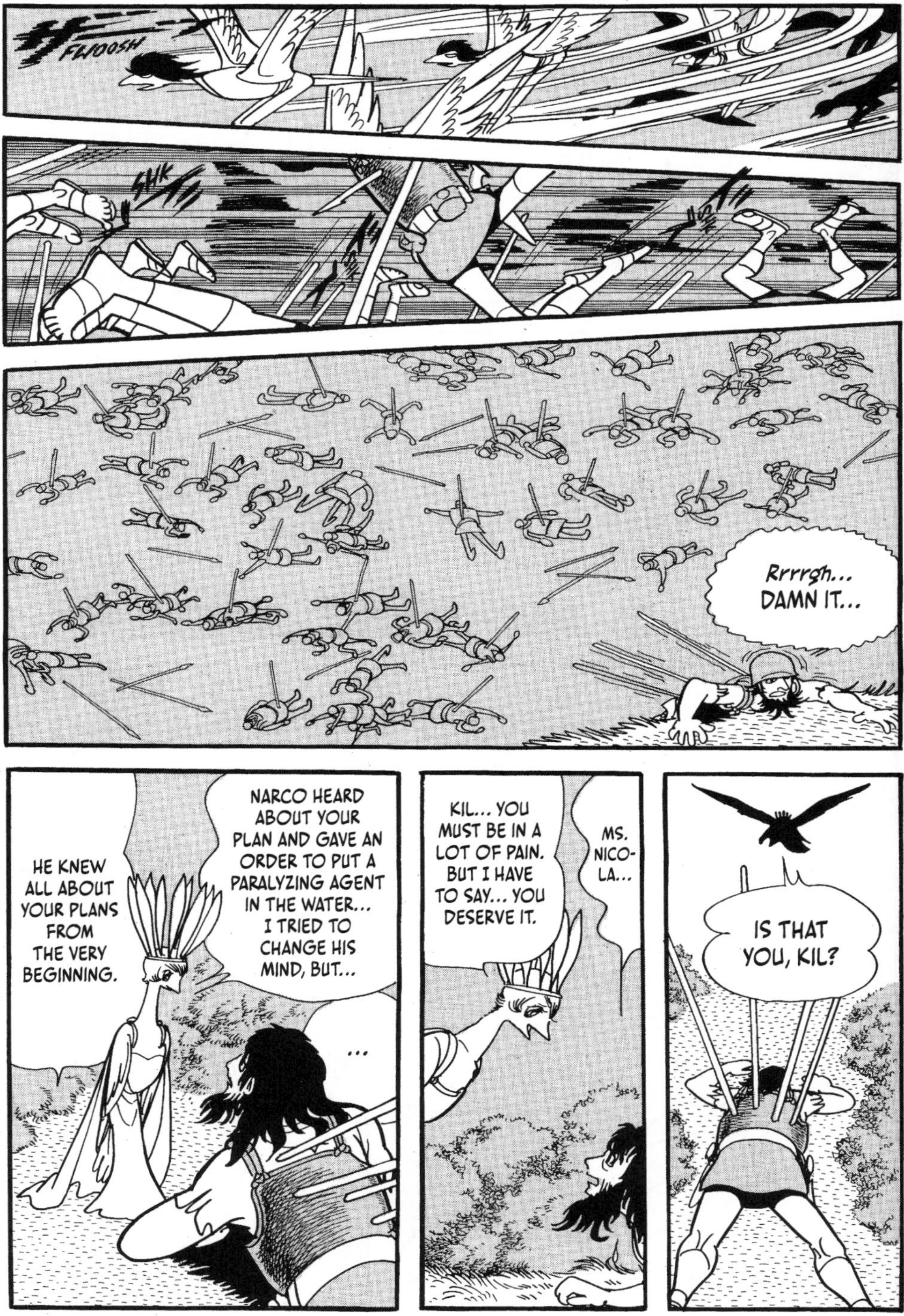
FWOOSH
SHK
Rrrrgh... DAMN IT...
NARCO HEARD ABOUT YOUR PLAN AND GAVE AN ORDER TO PUT A PARALYZING AGENT IN THE WATER... I TRIED TO CHANGE HIS MIND, BUT...
HE KNEW ALL ABOUT YOUR PLANS FROM THE VERY BEGINNING.
...
MS. NICOLA...
KIL... YOU MUST BE IN A LOT OF PAIN. BUT I HAVE TO SAY... YOU DESERVE IT.
IS THAT YOU, KIL?

NO ONE REPORTED THAT INFORMATION.
BUT HE NEVER IMAGINED YOU WOULD EAT GINON.
HE WANTED YOU TO ATTACK AND KILL GINON. NARCO NEVER TRUSTED HIM.
HE KNEW EVERYTHING? WHY DID HE JUST SIT BACK AND WATCH?
REPORTED?! WHO RATTED US OUT?!
Haha... IT WAS THAT FEMALE YOU KNOW WELL.
YOU USED TO SNEAK INTO THE FEMALE HUMAN FARM...
...TO TRY TO MATE WITH HER. REMEMBER?
WHAT?! NO WAY... HOW COULD SHE BETRAY ME?!
ONCE FEMALES ARE DONE MATING, THEY'RE ALWAYS CRUEL TO THEIR MALE... SHE HAS NO MORE USE FOR YOU.
NOW HER ONLY JOB IS TO HAVE THE BABY AND RAISE IT TO BE A GOOD PET.
KIL LAY ON THE GROUND DEVOID OF EMOTION AS NICOLA FINISHED SPEAKING. HER WORDS WERE A EULOGY TO HUMANITY, WHO WERE NOW NOTHING MORE THAN THE BIRDMEN'S PETS.

CHAPTER 11: CHROPATIA PITIARM

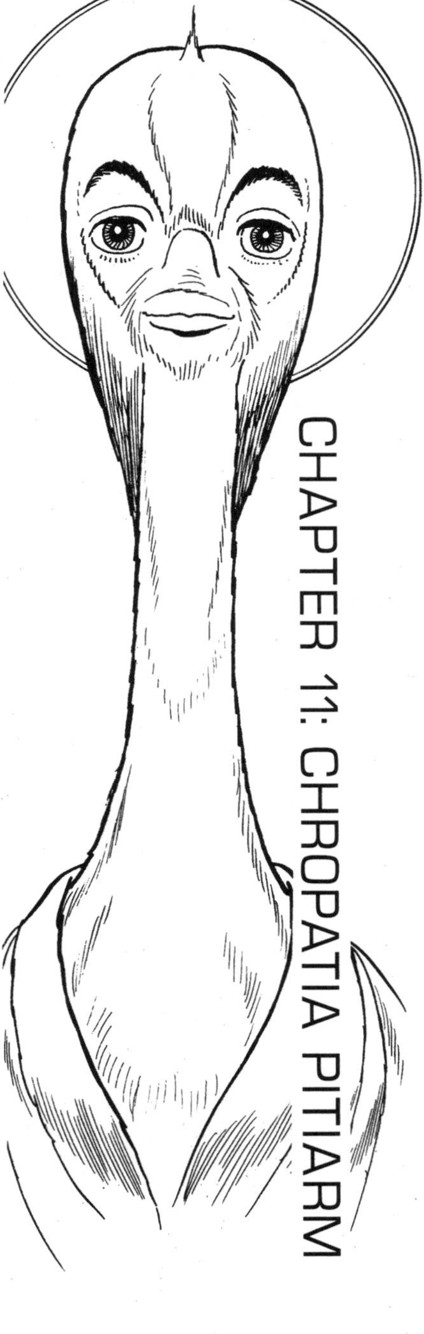

THE EMERGENCE OF SAINT POLOLO WAS A MONUMENTAL EVENT IN THE HISTORY OF THE RELIGIOUS FAITH OF BIRDMEN.

BEFORE THEN, BIRDMEN'S RELIGION WAS EXPRESSED IN THE FORM OF A RITUAL KNOWN AS "DANCE."

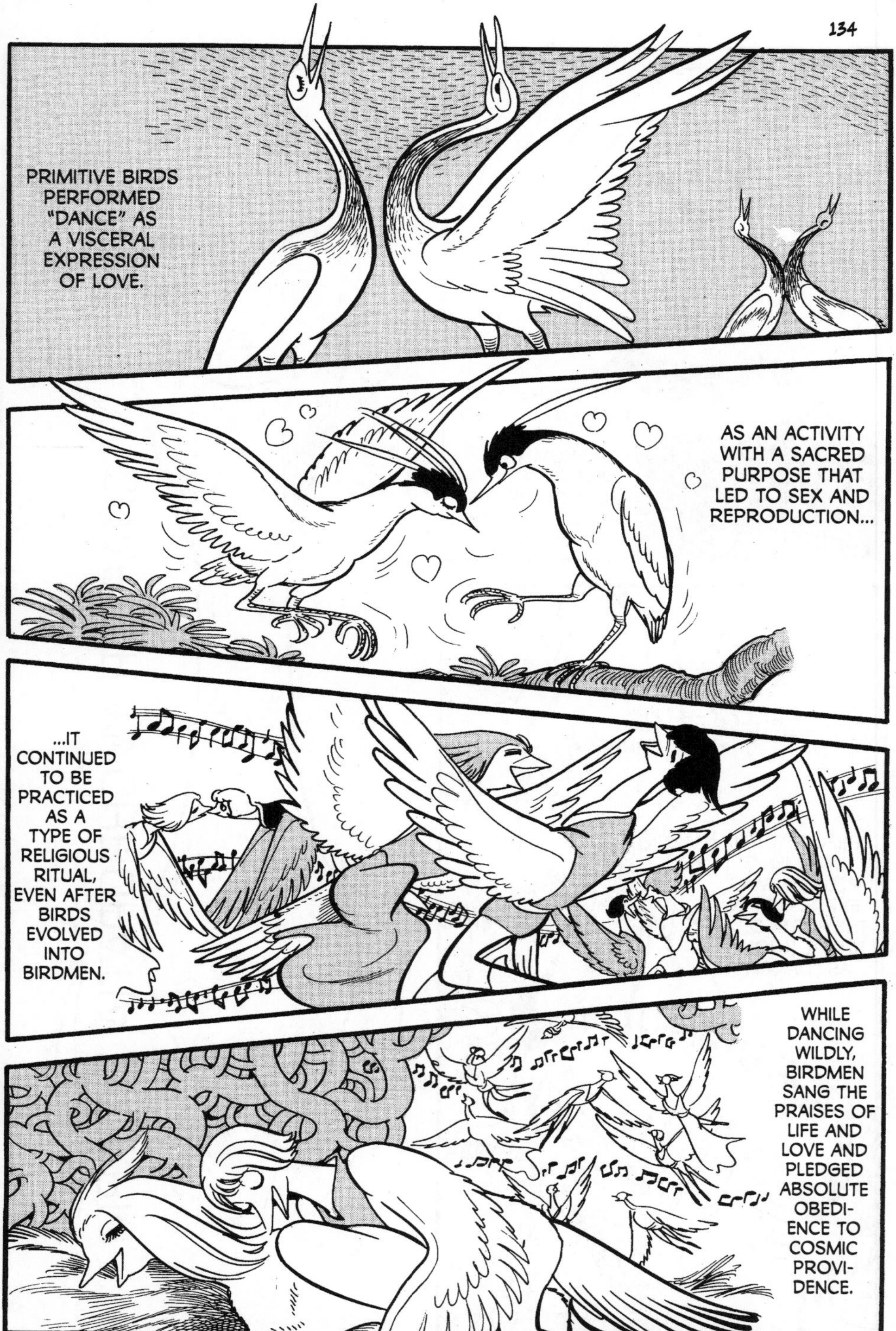
PRIMITIVE BIRDS PERFORMED "DANCE" AS A VISCERAL EXPRESSION OF LOVE.
AS AN ACTIVITY WITH A SACRED PURPOSE THAT LED TO SEX AND REPRODUCTION...
...IT CONTINUED TO BE PRACTICED AS A TYPE OF RELIGIOUS RITUAL, EVEN AFTER BIRDS EVOLVED INTO BIRDMEN.
WHILE DANCING WILDLY, BIRDMEN SANG THE PRAISES OF LIFE AND LOVE AND PLEDGED ABSOLUTE OBEDI-ENCE TO COSMIC PROVI-DENCE.

WHY ARE WE BORN?
BUT AS THEIR SOCIETY BECAME MORE COMPLEX, CLASSES STARTED TO FORM, ESPECIALLY ON AN ORGANIZATIONAL LEVEL. DISTINCTIONS BETWEEN THE RULING CLASS AND LOWER CLASSES GREW CLEARER, AND BIRDMEN OF THE LOWER CLASSES STARTED TO DOUBT.
AT FIRST, IT WAS A SIMPLE QUESTION. THERE WAS NOTHING PHILOSOPHICAL ABOUT IT.
BUT DANCE DID NOTHING TO RESOLVE IT.

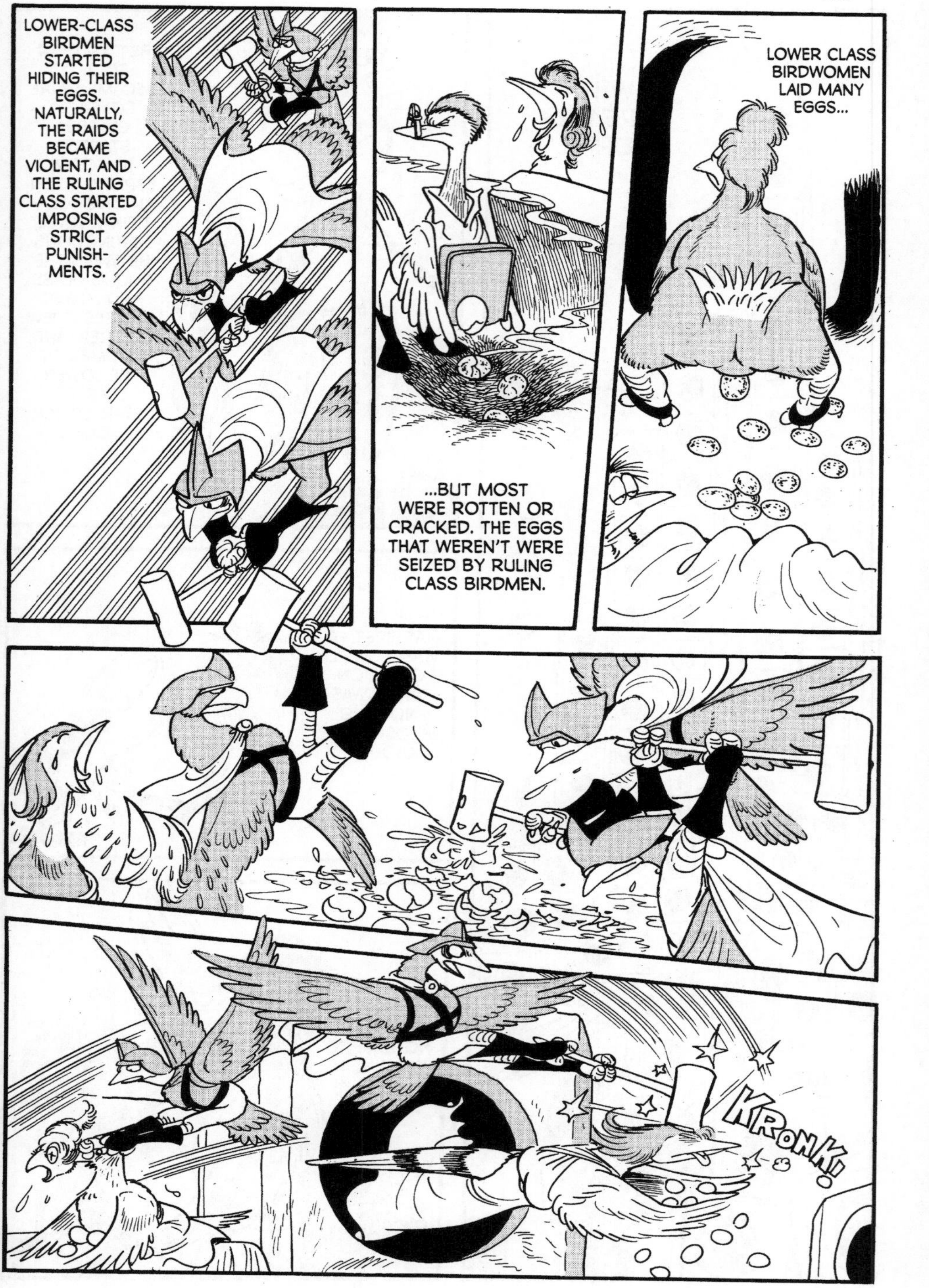
LOWER CLASS BIRDWOMEN LAID MANY EGGS...
...BUT MOST WERE ROTTEN OR CRACKED. THE EGGS THAT WEREN'T WERE SEIZED BY RULING CLASS BIRDMEN.
LOWER-CLASS BIRDMEN STARTED HIDING THEIR EGGS. NATURALLY, THE RAIDS BECAME VIOLENT, AND THE RULING CLASS STARTED IMPOSING STRICT PUNISH-MENTS.
KRONK!

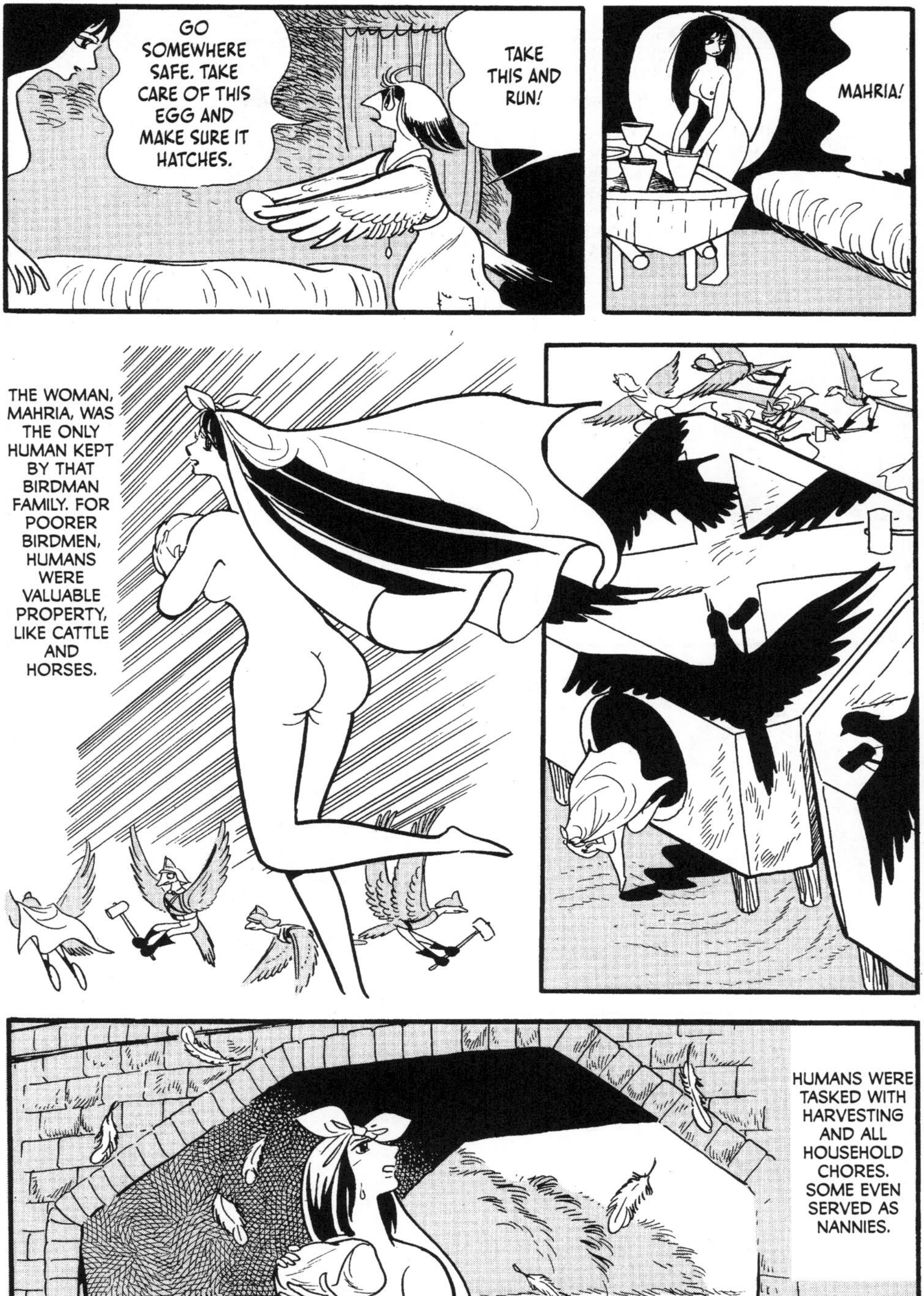
GO SOMEWHERE SAFE. TAKE CARE OF THIS EGG AND MAKE SURE IT HATCHES.
TAKE THIS AND RUN!
MAHRIA!
THE WOMAN, MAHRIA, WAS THE ONLY HUMAN KEPT BY THAT BIRDMAN FAMILY. FOR POORER BIRDMEN, HUMANS WERE VALUABLE PROPERTY, LIKE CATTLE AND HORSES.
HUMANS WERE TASKED WITH HARVESTING AND ALL HOUSEHOLD CHORES. SOME EVEN SERVED AS NANNIES.

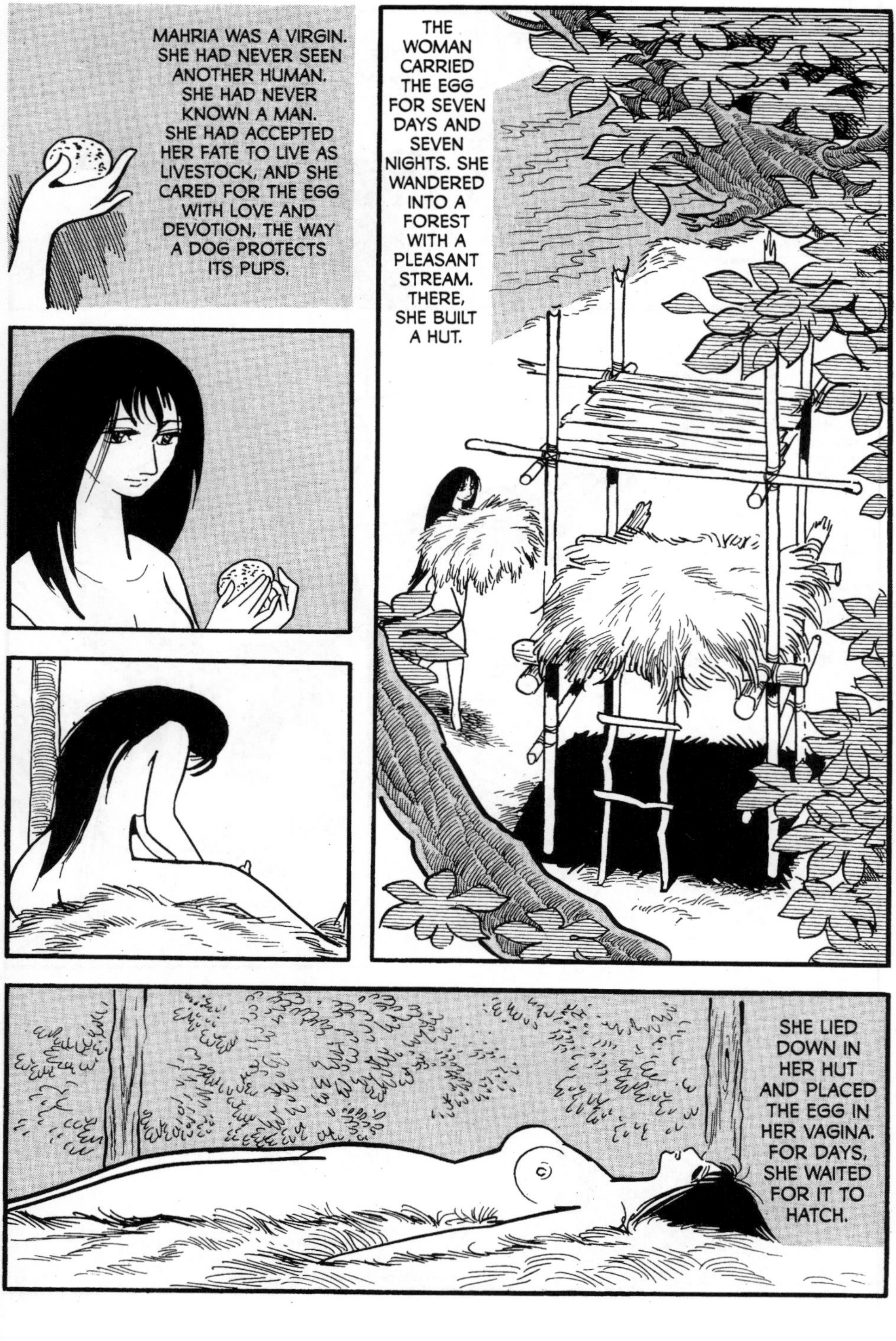
MAHRIA WAS A VIRGIN. SHE HAD NEVER SEEN ANOTHER HUMAN. SHE HAD NEVER KNOWN A MAN. SHE HAD ACCEPTED HER FATE TO LIVE AS LIVESTOCK, AND SHE CARED FOR THE EGG WITH LOVE AND DEVOTION, THE WAY A DOG PROTECTS ITS PUPS.
THE WOMAN CARRIED THE EGG FOR SEVEN DAYS AND SEVEN NIGHTS. SHE WANDERED INTO A FOREST WITH A PLEASANT STREAM. THERE, SHE BUILT A HUT.
SHE LIED DOWN IN HER HUT AND PLACED THE EGG IN HER VAGINA. FOR DAYS, SHE WAITED FOR IT TO HATCH.

EVERY DAY, SHE DRANK SOME WATER AND ATE FRUIT. SHE KEPT HER BODY STILL IN A HORIZONTAL POSITION.
THEN ONE NIGHT...
UNDER THE STARLIGHT, MAHRIA GAVE BIRTH TO A CHICK. THIS WAS THE FIRST AND LAST TIME SHE GAVE BIRTH, BECAUSE SHE DIED AROUND A YEAR LATER.
THE NEXT MORNING, SOME PILGRIMS WHO HAPPENED BY NAMED THE CHICK POLOLO. THE PILGRIMS ADVISED MAHRIA TO BATHE POLOLO IN THE PURE WATERS OF THE STREAM.
GENERATIONS LATER, HISTORIANS REFERRED TO THE YEAR OF THE BIRTH OF THIS CHICK AS THE FIRST YEAR OF CHROPATIA, THE CALENDAR OF THE BIRDMEN.

CHAPTER 12: THE GOSPEL OF POLOLO

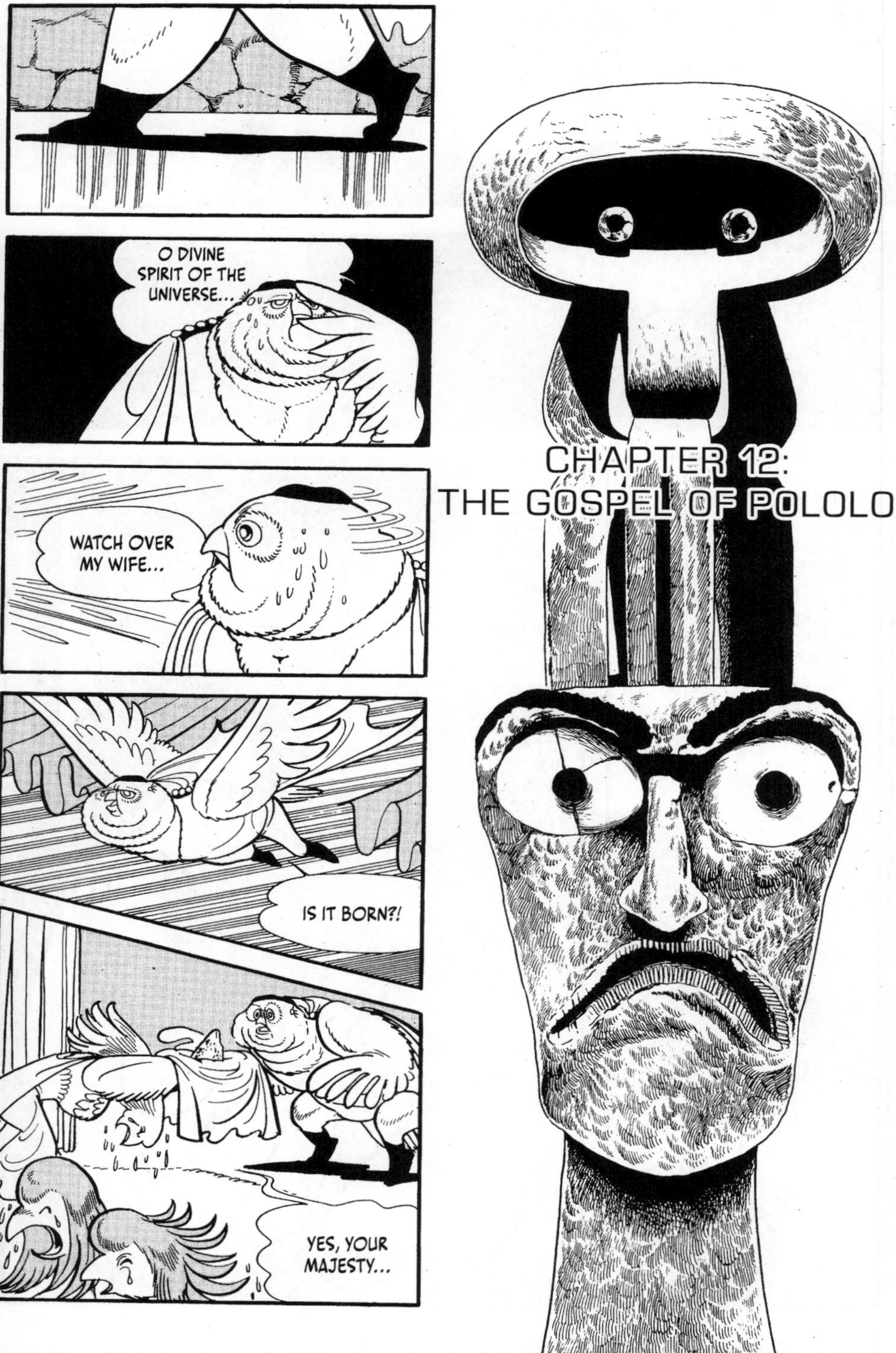

O DIVINE SPIRIT OF THE UNIVERSE...
WATCH OVER MY WIFE...
IS IT BORN?!
YES, YOUR MAJESTY...

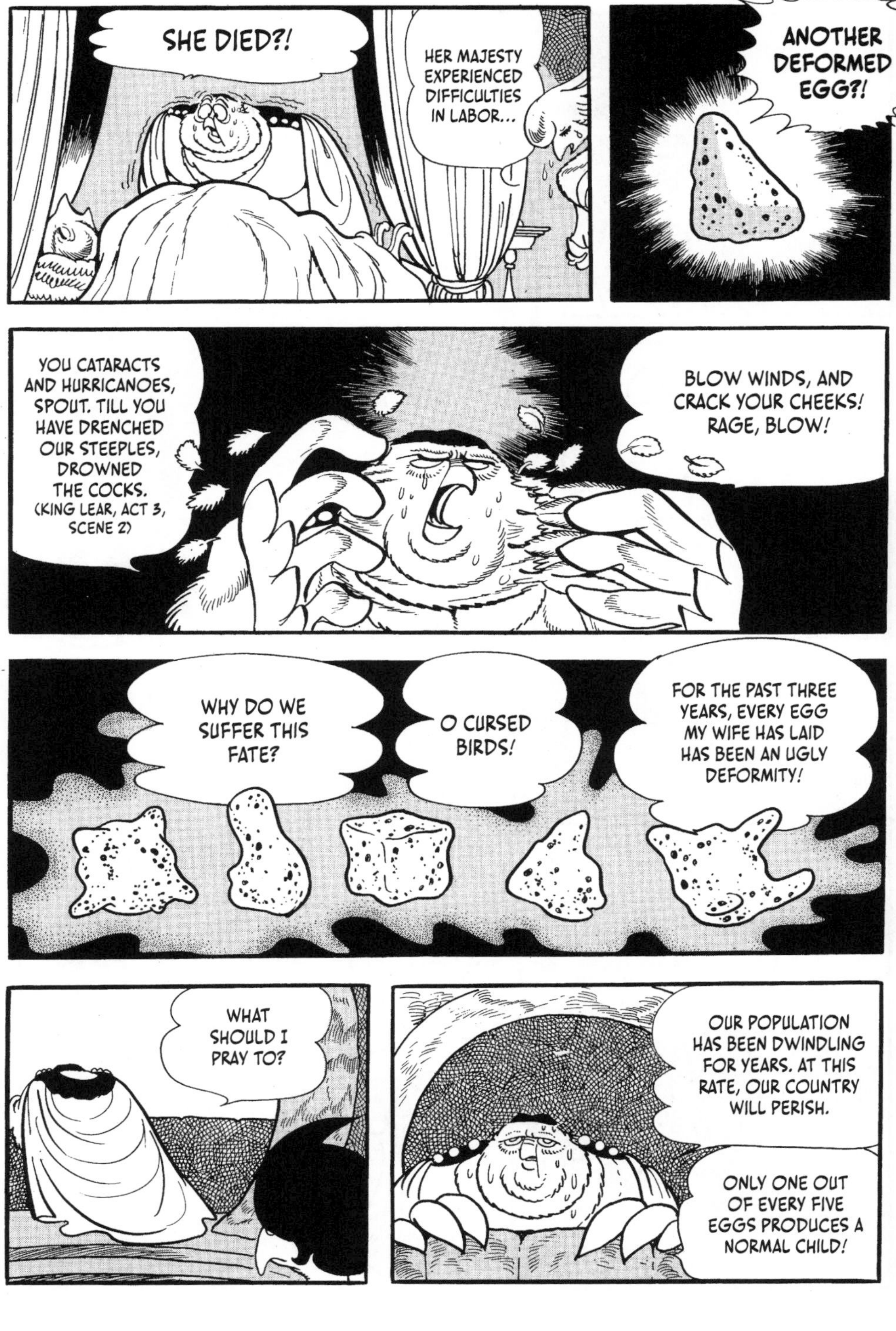
SHE DIED?!
HER MAJESTY EXPERIENCED DIFFICULTIES IN LABOR...
ANOTHER DEFORMED EGG?!
YOU CATARACTS AND HURRICANOES, SPOUT. TILL YOU HAVE DRENCHED OUR STEEPLES, DROWNED THE COCKS. (KING LEAR, ACT 3, SCENE 2)
BLOW WINDS, AND CRACK YOUR CHEEKS! RAGE, BLOW!
WHY DO WE SUFFER THIS FATE?
O CURSED BIRDS!
FOR THE PAST THREE YEARS, EVERY EGG MY WIFE HAS LAID HAS BEEN AN UGLY DEFORMITY!
WHAT SHOULD I PRAY TO?
OUR POPULATION HAS BEEN DWINDLING FOR YEARS. AT THIS RATE, OUR COUNTRY WILL PERISH.
ONLY ONE OUT OF EVERY FIVE EGGS PRODUCES A NORMAL CHILD!

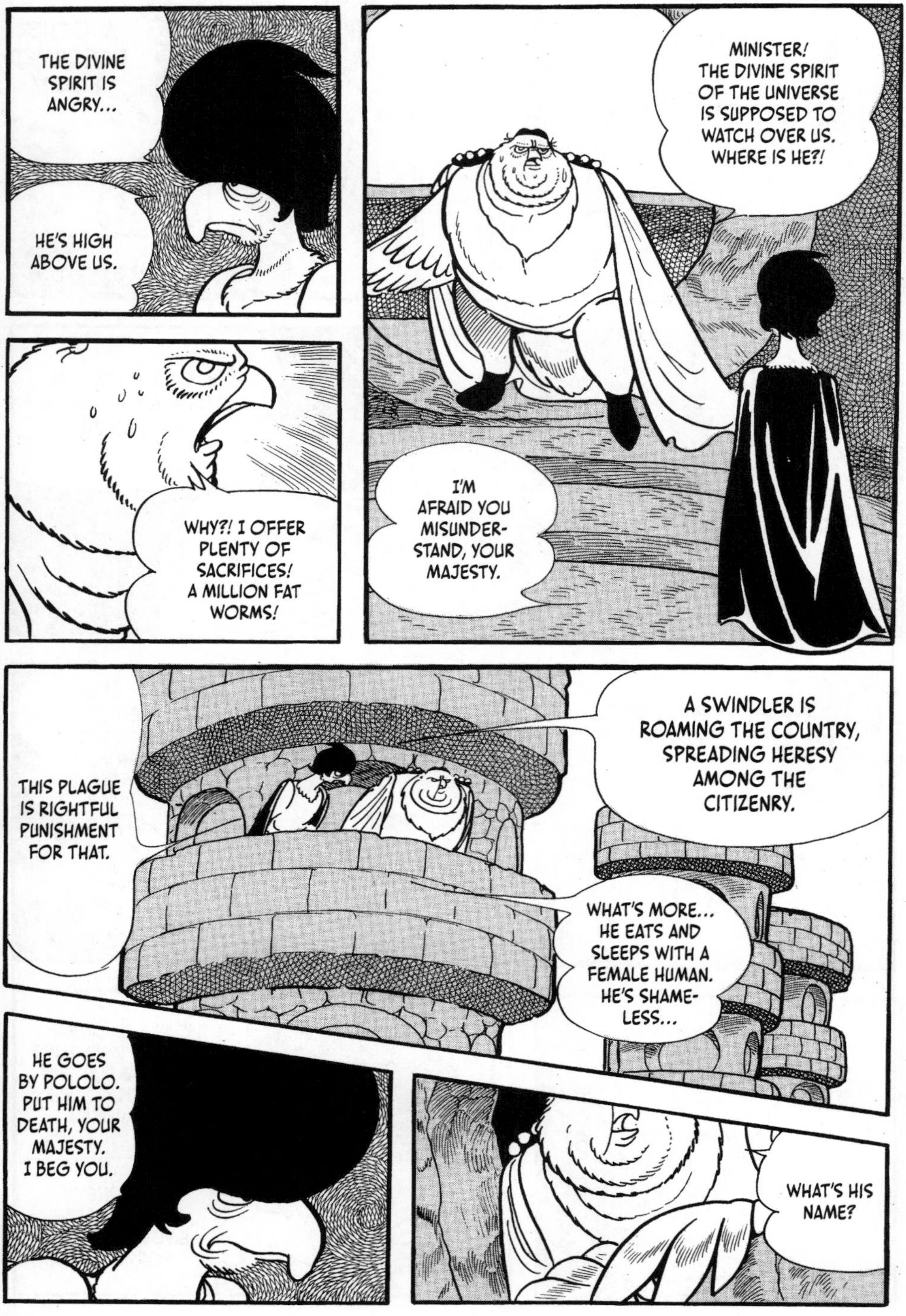
MINISTER! THE DIVINE SPIRIT OF THE UNIVERSE IS SUPPOSED TO WATCH OVER US. WHERE IS HE?!
I'M AFRAID YOU MISUNDERSTAND, YOUR MAJESTY.
THE DIVINE SPIRIT IS ANGRY...
HE'S HIGH ABOVE US.
WHY?! I OFFER PLENTY OF SACRIFICES! A MILLION FAT WORMS!
A SWINDLER IS ROAMING THE COUNTRY, SPREADING HERESY AMONG THE CITIZENRY.
WHAT'S MORE... HE EATS AND SLEEPS WITH A FEMALE HUMAN. HE'S SHAMELESS...
THIS PLAGUE IS RIGHTFUL PUNISHMENT FOR THAT.
WHAT'S HIS NAME?
HE GOES BY POLOLO. PUT HIM TO DEATH, YOUR MAJESTY. I BEG YOU.

LONG AGO, BEFORE OUR TIME... THIS WORLD BELONGED TO HUMANS. THEY HAD EVOLVED FROM APES. THE WAY WE DRESS AND MANY OF OUR CUSTOMS, WE INHERITED FROM HUMANS.

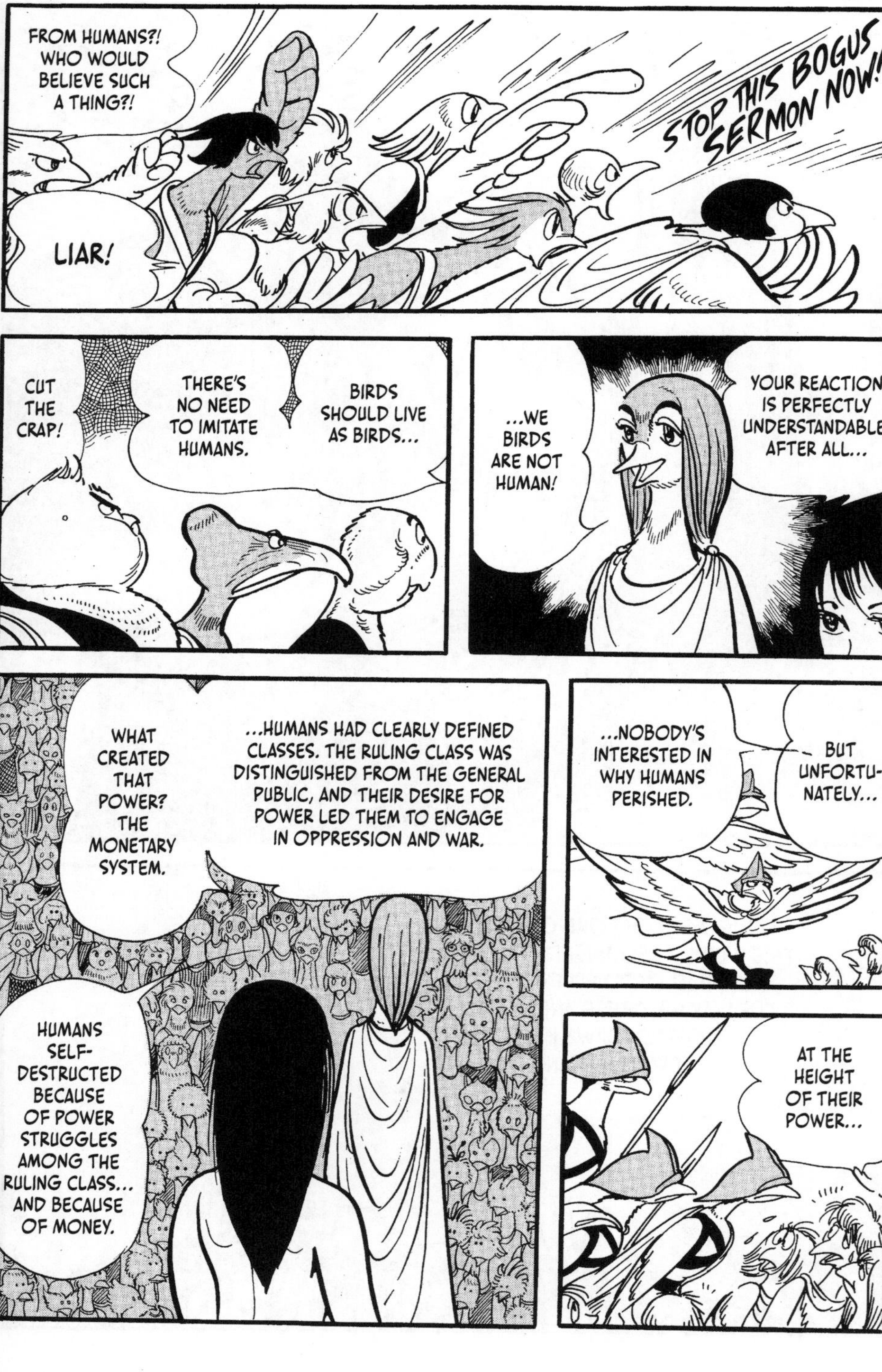
STOP THIS BOGUS SERMON NOW!
FROM HUMANS?! WHO WOULD BELIEVE SUCH A THING?!
LIAR!
YOUR REACTION IS PERFECTLY UNDERSTANDABLE. AFTER ALL...
...WE BIRDS ARE NOT HUMAN!
BIRDS SHOULD LIVE AS BIRDS...
THERE'S NO NEED TO IMITATE HUMANS.
CUT THE CRAP!
BUT UNFORTU-NATELY...
...NOBODY'S INTERESTED IN WHY HUMANS PERISHED.
AT THE HEIGHT OF THEIR POWER...
...HUMANS HAD CLEARLY DEFINED CLASSES. THE RULING CLASS WAS DISTINGUISHED FROM THE GENERAL PUBLIC, AND THEIR DESIRE FOR POWER LED THEM TO ENGAGE IN OPPRESSION AND WAR.
WHAT CREATED THAT POWER? THE MONETARY SYSTEM.
HUMANS SELF-DESTRUCTED BECAUSE OF POWER STRUGGLES AMONG THE RULING CLASS... AND BECAUSE OF MONEY.

UNFORTUNATELY, WE ALSO HAVE RULERS. AND MONEY.
HE'S RIGHT.
THIS MAKES US THE SAME AS HUMANS. HOW CAN WE SAY THAT WE DON'T IMITATE THEM?
WE ALSO HAVE SUFFERING AND POVERTY AND STARVATION AND POWER.
THAT IS THE PATH TO SALVATION FOR ALL OF YOU.
FOR BIRDS TO CONTINUE TO PROSPER AND BE HAPPY, WE'LL HAVE TO GIVE UP ALL OF THOSE THINGS.
COME HERE...
HOW CAN WE SAVE HER?
THIS LADY HERE HAS LAID TRIANGULAR EGGS... 18 TIMES!
WE CAN'T EVEN LAY NORMAL EGGS!

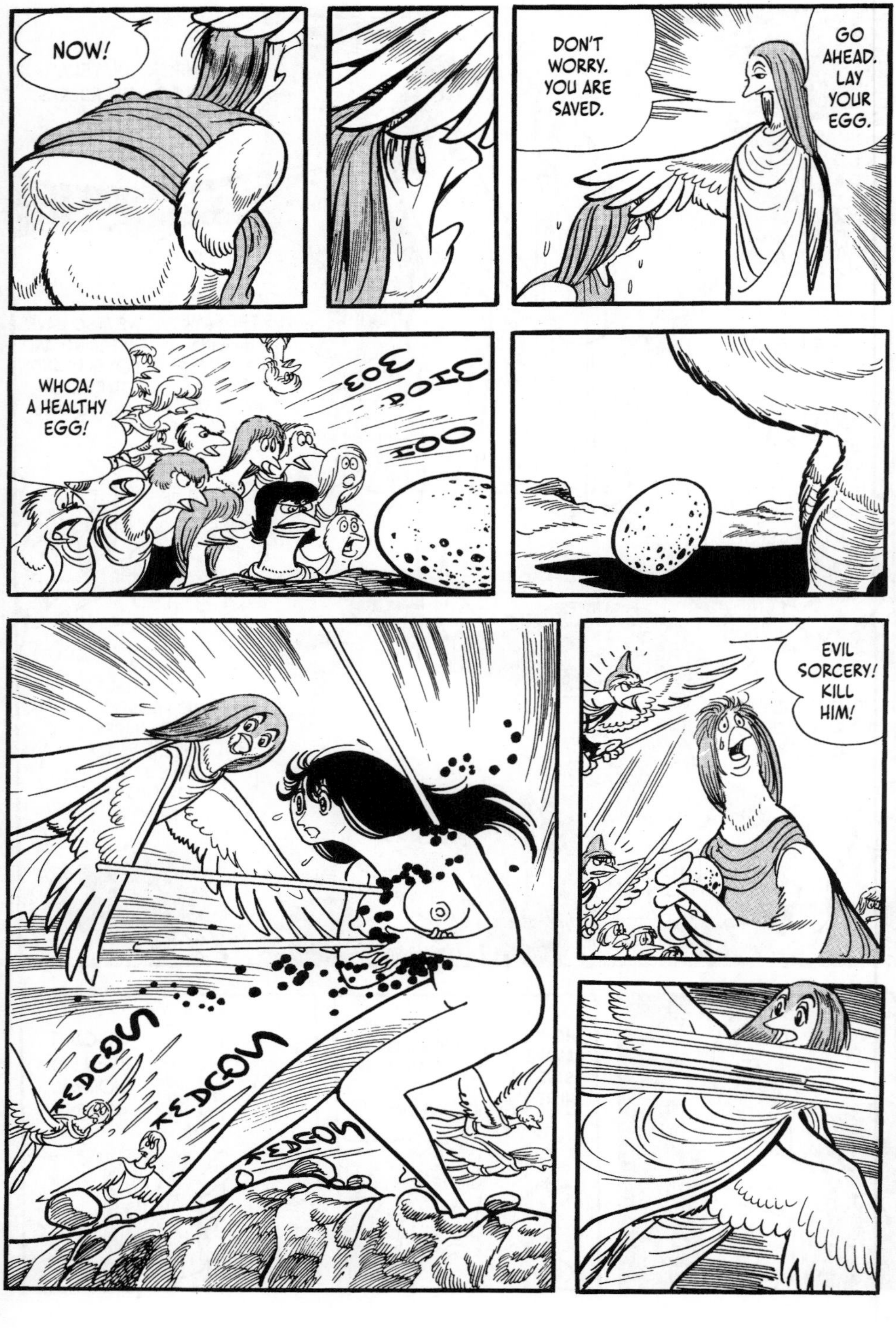
NOW!
DON'T WORRY. YOU ARE SAVED.
GO AHEAD. LAY YOUR EGG.
WHOA! A HEALTHY EGG!
EVIL SORCERY! KILL HIM!

LISTEN CAREFULLY, ALL OF YOU! THIS FALSE PROPHET IS SAID TO BE BORN FROM A FEMALE HUMAN!
IF THAT'S TRUE, HE WORKS FOR THE DEVIL! ANYONE WHO BELIEVES HIS LIES WILL BE THROWN IN JAIL!
SOLDIERS!

*"Lord, where are you going?", from The Acts of St. Peter

OR MAYBE HE'S ABANDONED US...
O FATHER IN HEAVEN! OVERSEER OF NATURAL PROVIDENCE. GIVE US COURAGE. SHOW US WHAT WE SHOULD DO... PLEASE... ONE LAST TIME...
IT'S NO USE... THAT HUMAN IS DEAD.
Rrg...rgh... rgh...
THAT'S HOW THE VOICE FROM HEAVEN ALWAYS STARTS!
Mumble mumble... Huff... Huff... Rgh...rgh...
...YOU'RE RIGHT.

O LORD...
MY NAME'S NOT "LORD"!
IT'S DOBLOOD, FROM THE 27TH PLANET OF IGNALGUM! DON'T MAKE ME TELL YOU AGAIN!
BUT LET US CALL YOU LORD. AFTER ALL, YOU ARE THE SPIRIT IN HEAVEN...
YOU FOOL! NINCOMPOOP! YOU LOUSY BUNCH OF LICE! NEVER MIND SUCH FORMALITIES! WHY AREN'T YOU DOING WHAT I TOLD YOU?!
BZZM

THAT'S WHY I GAVE YOU PSYCHIC POWERS AND ENERGY WAVES!
I'VE BEEN PREACHING THAT TO HUNDREDS OF THOUSANDS OF BIRDS... BUT THEY END UP CONSUMED BY DOUBT...
AFTER ALL, IT'S NOT EASY TO IMPLEMENT FUNDAMENTAL CHANGE IN THE WAY THEY LIVE...
IDIOT! STUPID SENILE DOLT!
I'LL TELL YOU AGAIN! BIRDS SHOULDN'T LIVE LIKE HOMO HOMOS! THOSE TWO-LEGGED BEASTS! YOU'RE BETTER THAN THAT! THAT'S WHAT YOU SHOULD BE TELLING EVERYONE!
LISTEN CAREFULLY, FOOL! THIS IS THE LAST TIME I'LL TELL YOU. IT'S MY FINAL COMMAND.
LAWS!
STATE AUTHORITY!
CLASSES!
MONETARY SYSTEMS!
GET RID OF ALL OF THEM!

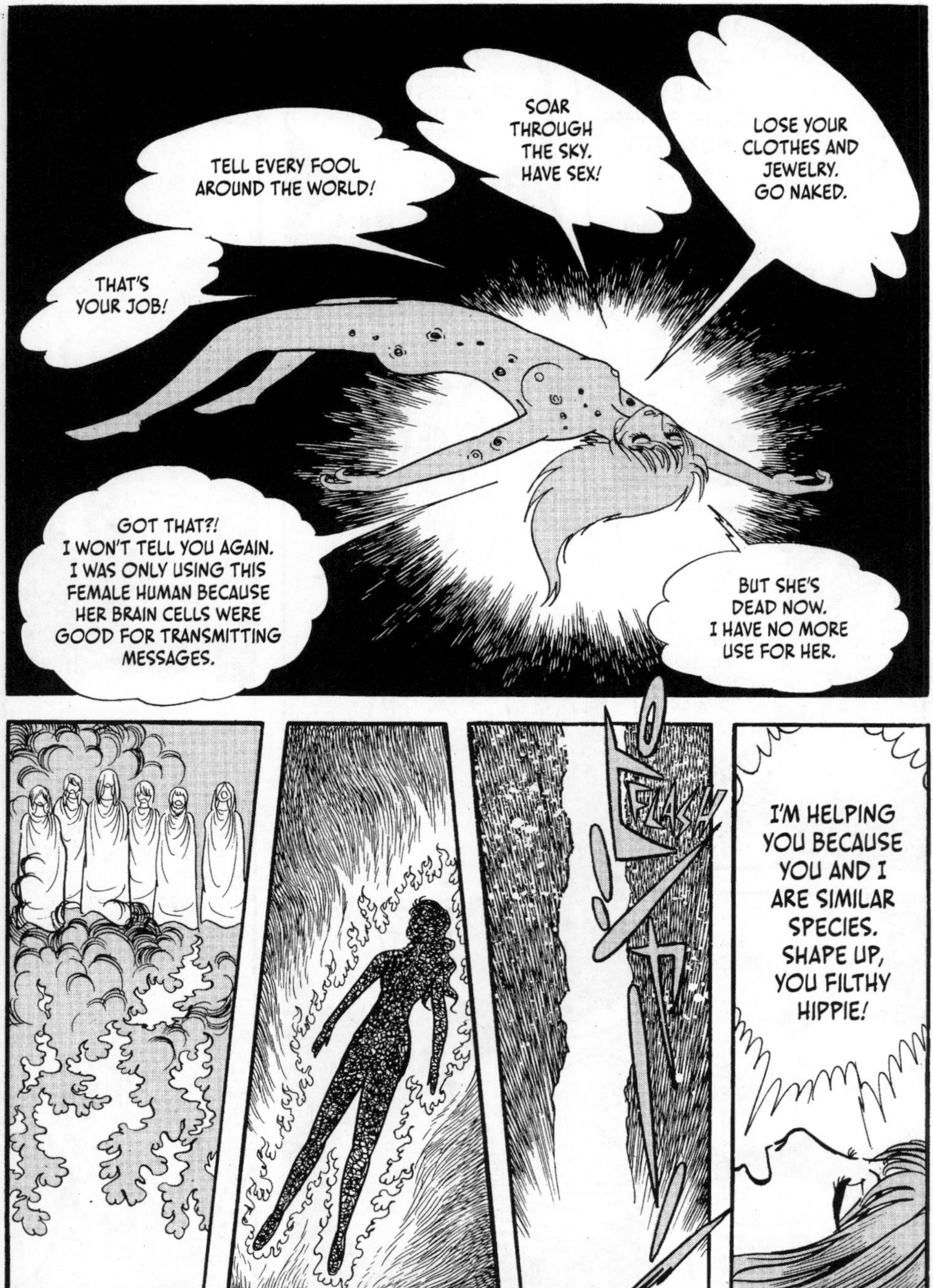
LOSE YOUR CLOTHES AND JEWELRY. GO NAKED.
SOAR THROUGH THE SKY. HAVE SEX!
TELL EVERY FOOL AROUND THE WORLD!
THAT'S YOUR JOB!
GOT THAT?! I WON'T TELL YOU AGAIN. I WAS ONLY USING THIS FEMALE HUMAN BECAUSE HER BRAIN CELLS WERE GOOD FOR TRANSMITTING MESSAGES.
BUT SHE'S DEAD NOW. I HAVE NO MORE USE FOR HER.
FLASH
I'M HELPING YOU BECAUSE YOU AND I ARE SIMILAR SPECIES. SHAPE UP, YOU FILTHY HIPPIE!

YOU HEARD THE LORD. HE SAID BIRDS SHOULD LIVE LIKE BIRDS.
HE HAD SOME MOUTH ON HIM...
THAT'S THE TRUTH.
THEY'RE SAYING BIRDS SHOULD GET RID OF CLASSES AND STATUS AND PROPERTY.
THEY WANT EVERYONE TO GET RID OF THEIR CLOTHES AND SHOES AND BE NAKED?!
THEY WANT TO BE NAKED? FINE! SKIN THEM!
AS A WARNING TO OTHER BELIEVERS!
THUS, IN THE 15TH YEAR OF CHROPATIA...
...THE HORRIFIC MASSACRE OF POLOLO BELIEVERS BEGAN.

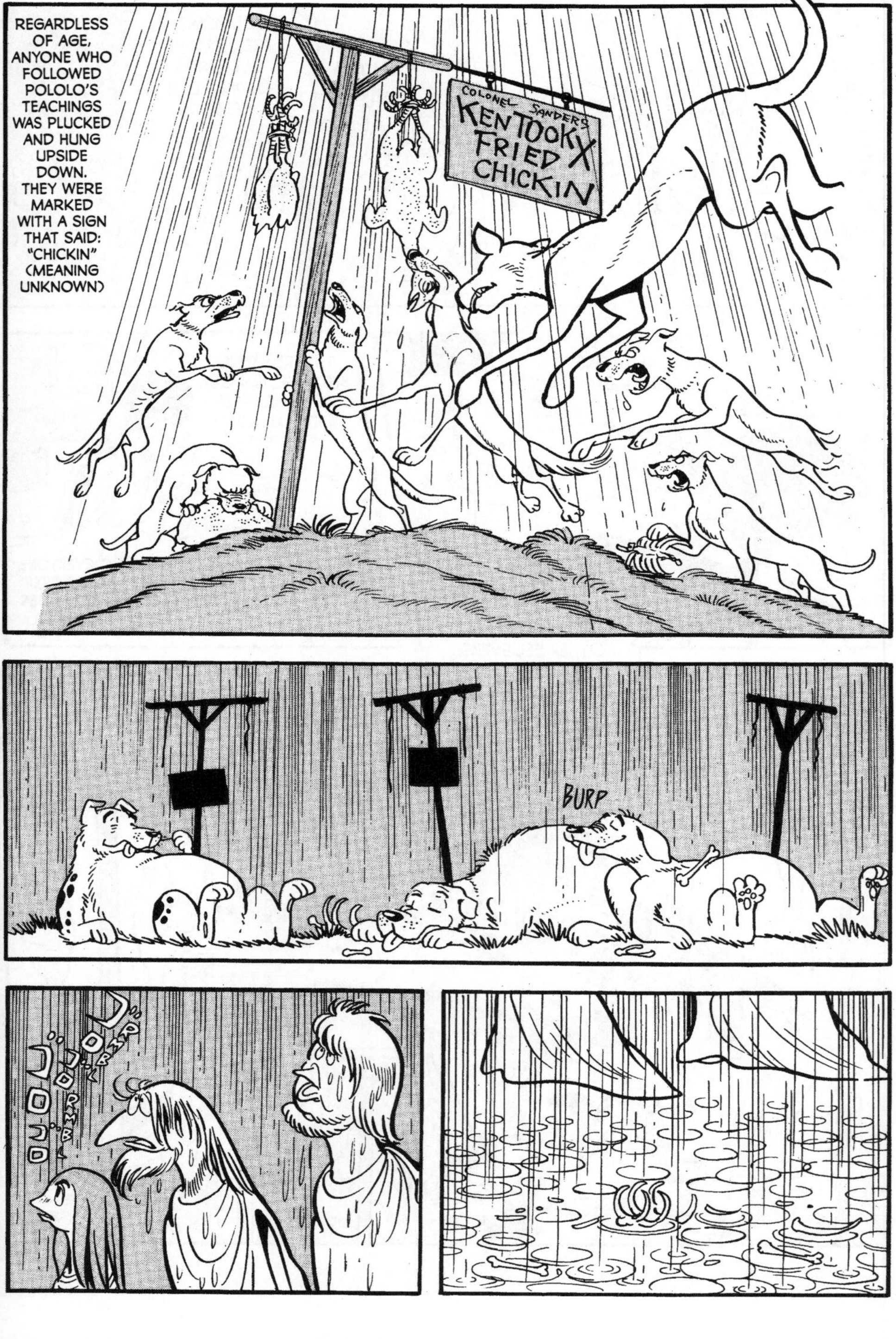
REGARDLESS OF AGE, ANYONE WHO FOLLOWED POLOLO'S TEACHINGS WAS PLUCKED AND HUNG UPSIDE DOWN. THEY WERE MARKED WITH A SIGN THAT SAID: "CHICKIN" (MEANING UNKNOWN)
COLONEL SANDERS
KENTOOKY FRIED CHICKIN
BURP

WE CAN'T EVEN FIND A DECENT PLACE TO STAY.
THE CHIEFTAIN'S INVESTIGATION HAS BEEN HARSHER THAN EXPECTED...
WE CAN'T GO ANY FURTHER IN THIS RAIN. PLEASE REST HERE FOR THE NIGHT.
SOMETHING'S WRONG WITH THAT FEMALE.
A HUMAN! THIS IS A HUMAN HUT.
NO MATTER WHAT HARDSHIPS AWAIT US, OUR LORD DOBLOOD WILL ALWAYS PROTECT US.
IT MUST BE FOR LIVESTOCK.
THIS HUT SMELLS LIKE PISS.

SHE'S DYING...
HUMANS SMELL AWFUL ...
SHE'S ABOUT TO STARVE TO DEATH!
LOOK. SHE ISN'T EVEN BEING FED.
IT APPEARS SHE'S BEING PUNISHED.
...BUT, IN THE PAST, HUMANS USED TO RECEIVE GOD'S BLESSING ON THIS EARTH.
THAT MAY BE TRUE...
HERE YOU GO.
B-BUT POLOLO, SHE'S JUST A STUPID BARN ANIMAL.
GIVE HER MY FOOD.
CHOMP
CHOMP
CHOMP
MUNCH
SNARF

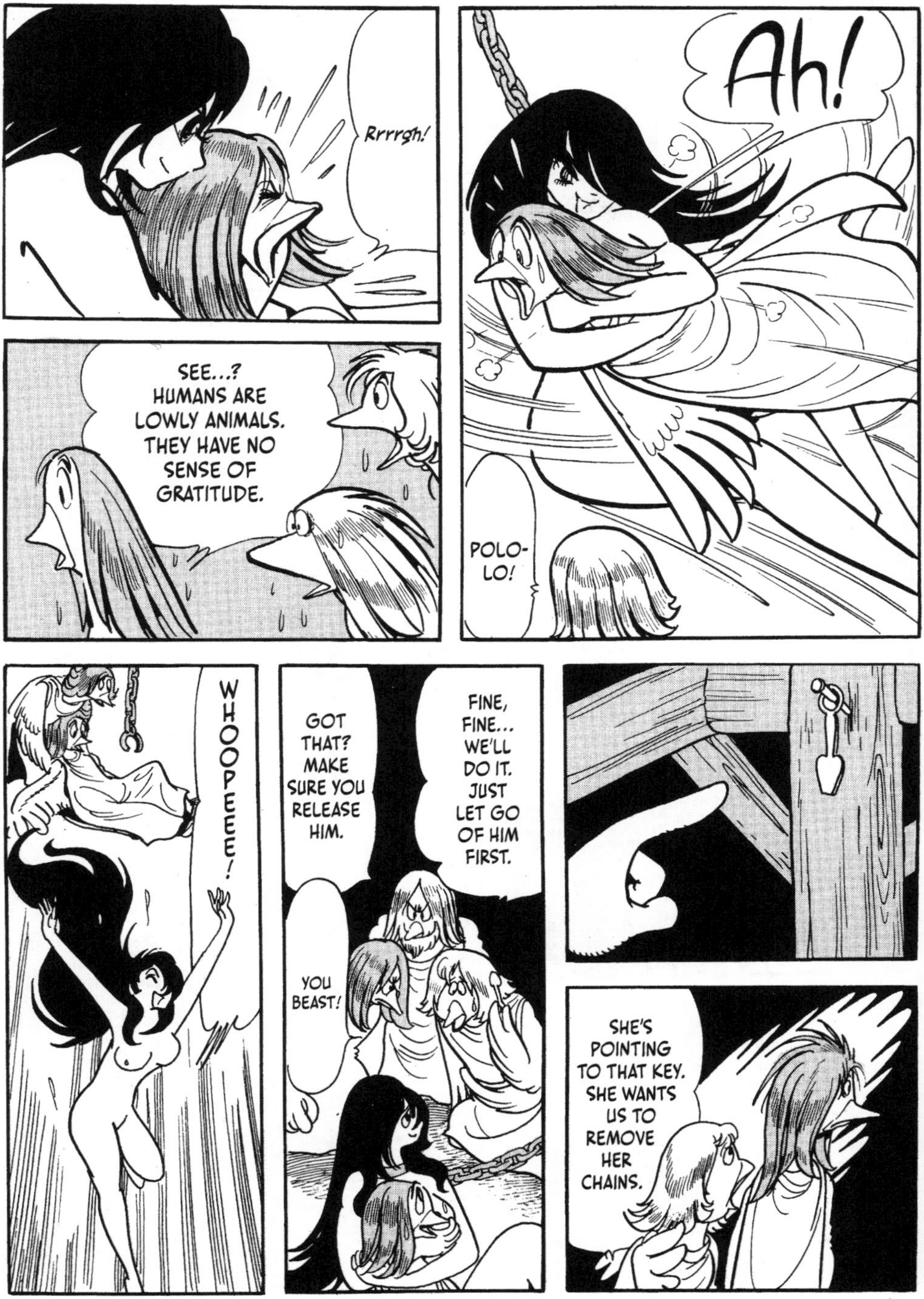
Rrrrgh!
Ah!
SEE...? HUMANS ARE LOWLY ANIMALS. THEY HAVE NO SENSE OF GRATITUDE.
POLOLO!
WHOOPEEE!
FINE, FINE... WE'LL DO IT. JUST LET GO OF HIM FIRST.
GOT THAT? MAKE SURE YOU RELEASE HIM.
YOU BEAST!
SHE'S POINTING TO THAT KEY. SHE WANTS US TO REMOVE HER CHAINS.

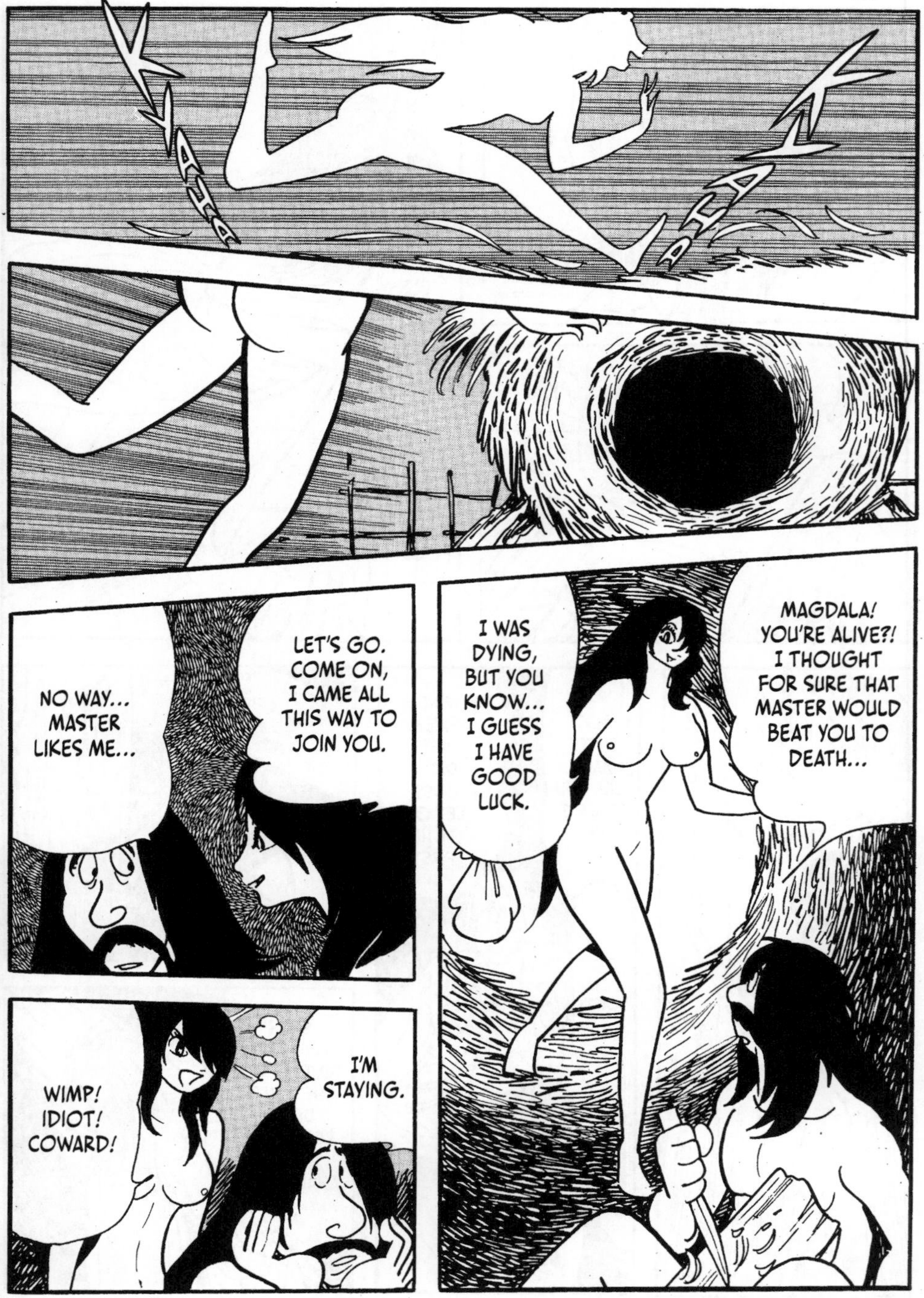
MAGDALA! YOU'RE ALIVE?! I THOUGHT FOR SURE THAT MASTER WOULD BEAT YOU TO DEATH...
I WAS DYING, BUT YOU KNOW... I GUESS I HAVE GOOD LUCK.
LET'S GO. COME ON, I CAME ALL THIS WAY TO JOIN YOU.
NO WAY... MASTER LIKES ME...
I'M STAYING.
WIMP! IDIOT! COWARD!

I COULD NEVER RUN AWAY WITH YOU...
NO WONDER MASTER IS FED UP WITH YOU.
MAGDALA, YOU KNOW WHY YOU WERE ALMOST KILLED, RIGHT? YOU DON'T DO YOUR JOB... YOU JUST GO FROM MAN TO MAN, DOING WHATEVER YOU PLEASE...
YOU KNOW WHAT PEOPLE CALL YOU? THE VIPER!
GYAAAH!
FINE... BYE.
SHOO! DON'T FOLLOW US! MASTER POLOLO, THIS FEMALE WON'T LEAVE...
LET HER BE. SHE LIKES ME.
Heheh... HEY...
LOW TIDE ↑

HOW DARE YOU STEAL FOOD! I'LL KILL YOU!

Eek! IT'S A FEMALE HUMAN!

BOING
AAH! MURDERER!
YOU'VE DONE IT AGAIN...
MAG-DALA!
SINCE YOU STARTED TRAVELING WITH ME...
...YOU'VE COMMITTED MURDER, BURGLARY, ASSAULT, FRAUD, AND TRAFFIC VIOLATIONS.
I LIKE YOU, BUT A CRIME IS A CRIME...
...COMMITTING RAPE... NO... BESTIALITY...
YOU'RE EVEN... *Hmm...*

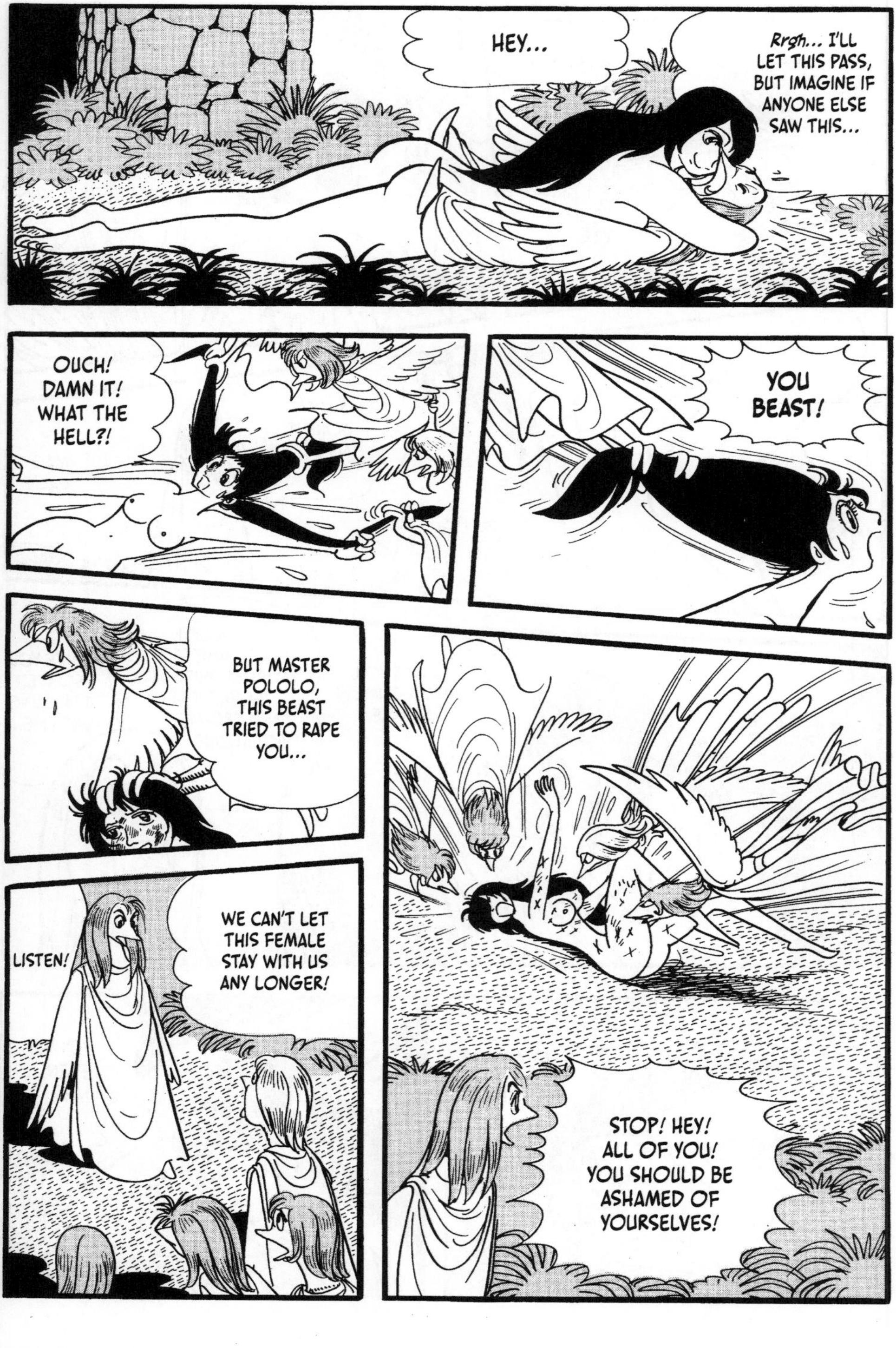
HEY...
Rrgh... I'LL LET THIS PASS, BUT IMAGINE IF ANYONE ELSE SAW THIS...
OUCH! DAMN IT! WHAT THE HELL?!
YOU BEAST!
BUT MASTER POLOLO, THIS BEAST TRIED TO RAPE YOU...
STOP! HEY! ALL OF YOU! YOU SHOULD BE ASHAMED OF YOURSELVES!
LISTEN!
WE CAN'T LET THIS FEMALE STAY WITH US ANY LONGER!

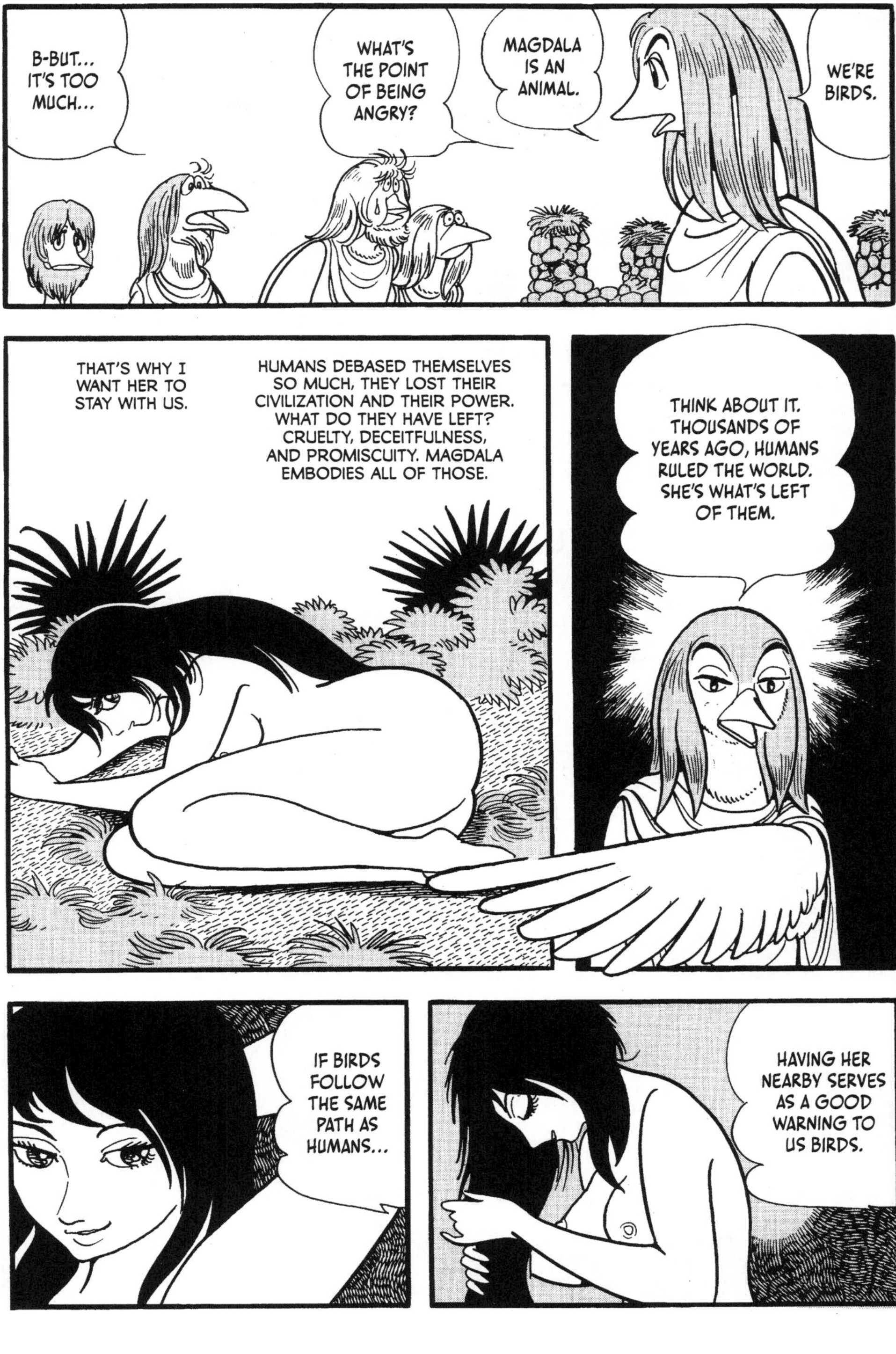
B-BUT... IT'S TOO MUCH...
WHAT'S THE POINT OF BEING ANGRY?
MAGDALA IS AN ANIMAL.
WE'RE BIRDS.
THAT'S WHY I WANT HER TO STAY WITH US.
HUMANS DEBASED THEMSELVES SO MUCH, THEY LOST THEIR CIVILIZATION AND THEIR POWER. WHAT DO THEY HAVE LEFT? CRUELTY, DECEITFULNESS, AND PROMISCUITY. MAGDALA EMBODIES ALL OF THOSE.
THINK ABOUT IT. THOUSANDS OF YEARS AGO, HUMANS RULED THE WORLD. SHE'S WHAT'S LEFT OF THEM.
IF BIRDS FOLLOW THE SAME PATH AS HUMANS...
HAVING HER NEARBY SERVES AS A GOOD WARNING TO US BIRDS.

DO THIS, AND YOU WILL BE SAVED!
REMOVE YOUR CLOTHES. ABANDON YOUR PROPERTY. SOAR THROUGH THE SKY, WHERE YOU'LL BE FREE FROM STATUS AND GREED.
BIRDS MUST LIVE LIKE BIRDS!
...OUR CIVILIZATION IS SURE TO END IN RUIN.
POLOLO'S MESSAGE THAT BIRDS SHOULD LIVE LIKE BIRDS INSPIRED THE MASSES – ESPECIALLY THE PROLETARIAN BIRDMEN. THEY ABANDONED EVERYTHING AND DEDICATED THEMSELVES TO FLYING IN THE SKY. SOME BIRDMEN IN THE RULING CLASS SAW THIS AS A BLATANT ACT OF REBELLION.
POLOLO BELIEVERS WERE BOILED WITH ONIONS...
IMPOSE THE HARSHEST PENALTY! MAKE THEM REGRET WHAT THEY'VE DONE!

THEY WERE FRIED FROM THE LEGS DOWN.
THEY WERE GROUND INTO MEATBALLS FOR SOUP.
LIGHTER PUNISHMENTS INCLUDED BEING FORCED INTO A STIFF POSITION WHILE DRINKING ONLY WATER FOR DAYS.
THE NUMBER OF POLOLO BELIEVERS IS NOT DECREASING.
DAMN IT! WE MUST CAPTURE POLOLO HIMSELF!
HE'S AN EVIL SORCERER WHO EATS AND SLEEPS WITH A FEMALE HUMAN.

WHAT? YOU'RE A DISCIPLE OF POLOLO'S?
YES, BUT I CAN'T TAKE IT ANYMORE.
HE SAYS WE SHOULD LIVE LIKE BIRDS... HE MAKES US EAT RICE BRAN AND DRINK MUDDY WATER.
IT'S GOOD YOU CAME TO ME. I'LL GIVE YOU SOME GOLD.
LORD...
YOU MUST LEAVE AT ONCE. SOLDIERS ARE APPROACHING!
SOMEBODY GAVE US UP!
MAGDALA, THIS IS GOODBYE. GO WHEREVER YOU LIKE.
WAIT.
YOU SAID YOU LIKED ME. I LIKE YOU, TOO. I'LL SAVE YOU.
I WON'T LET THOSE SOLDIERS LAY A HAND ON YOUR FEATHERS!
WAIT HERE.
SEE? I BROUGHT ALL THESE HUMAN BODYGUARDS. EVERY MAN ON EARTH WILL FIGHT FOR YOU IF I TELL THEM TO.

H-HE SAYS IF BIRDS FOLLOW THE SAME PATH AS HUMANS, OUR CIVILIZATION IS SURE TO MEET THE SAME FATE AS THEIRS.
HOW DARE HE?!
HE SAYS BIRDS DON'T NEED CLASSES OR STATUS.
WE DON'T NEED LAWS OR MONEY OR ARISTOCRACY.
BIRDS SHOULD SIMPLY FLY AS THEY PLEASE. FLYING IN THE SKY LEADS TO SALVATION. THAT'S WHAT HE SAYS.
AND YOU BELIEVE THAT? HUH?!
NO NEED FOR THE KING OR POLITICS OR THE STATE?!
NOT EVEN THE KING?
IS THAT ALL YOU HAVE TO SAY?!
KILL THEM!

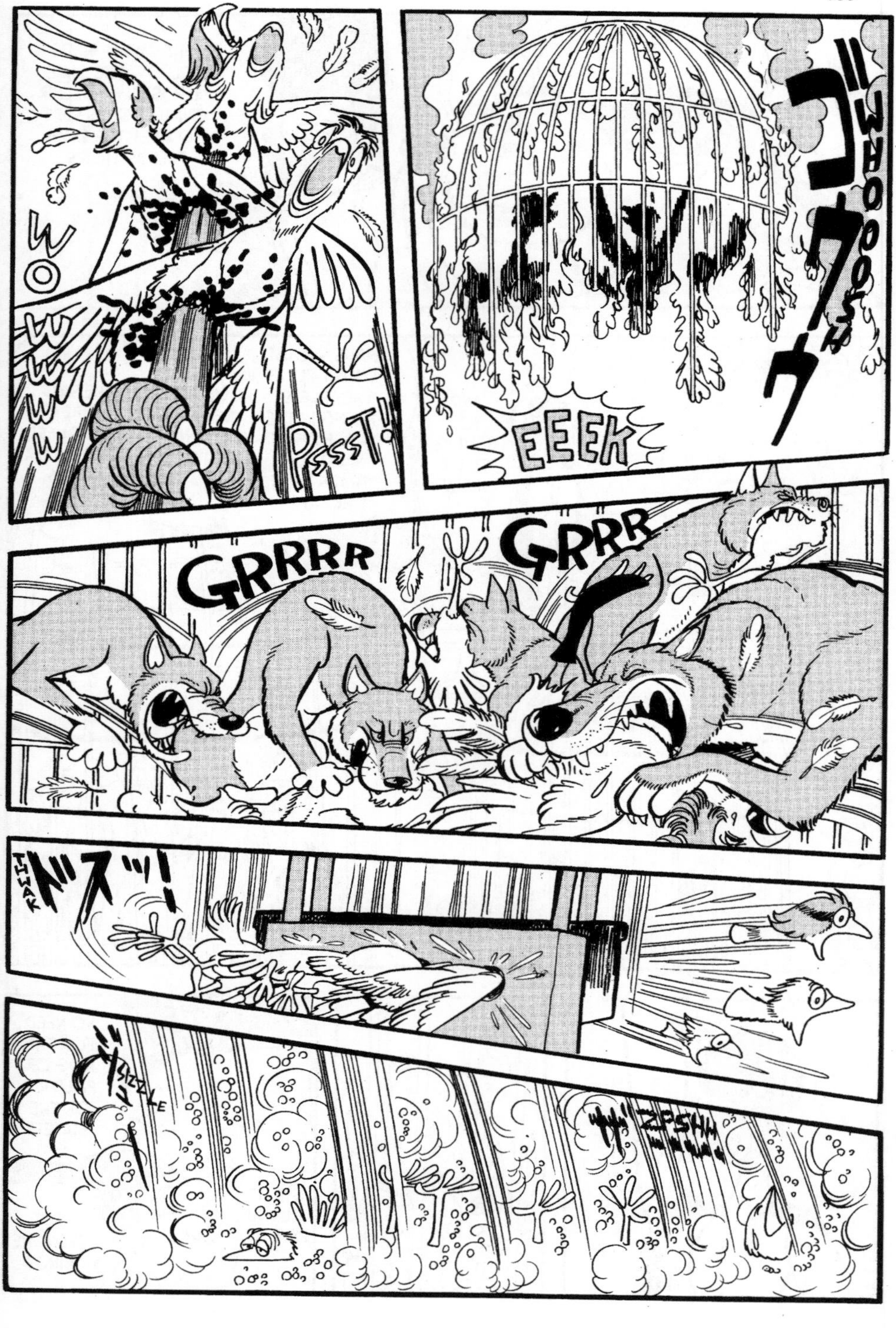
ゴウウ
WHOOOOOSH
EEEK
WOWWWW
PSSST!
GRRRR
GRRR
ズッ!
THWAK
SIZZLE
ZSHH

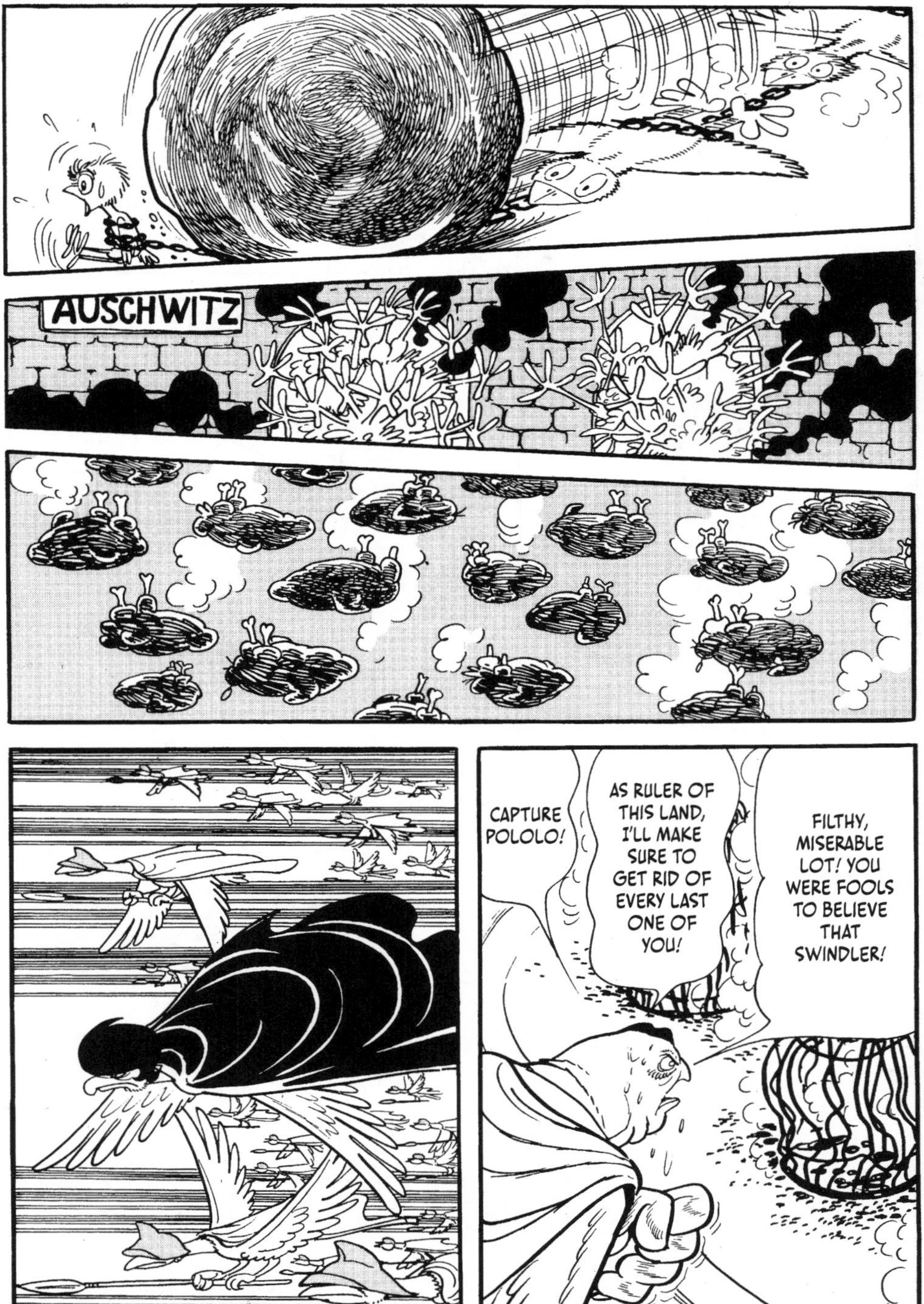
AUSCHWITZ
CAPTURE POLOLO!
AS RULER OF THIS LAND, I'LL MAKE SURE TO GET RID OF EVERY LAST ONE OF YOU!
FILTHY, MISERABLE LOT! YOU WERE FOOLS TO BELIEVE THAT SWINDLER!

THERE'S THE INSTI-GATOR!
THAT'S POLOLO!
YOU HAVE TWO LIMBS, BUT WE HAVE TWICE AS MANY!
DAMN... YOU... LOWLY HUMAN...
THAT MEANS WE HAVE THE UPPER HAND WHEN FIGHTING ON LAND.
RRGH
WHAK
SMASH

SIMMER DOWN, FOOLS!
WE'RE DONE, MAGDA-LA.
NOW LET US DO WHAT YOU PROMISED...
HEY! I'M FIRST!
BUT MAGDALA...
YOU ALL SAID YOU'D DO ANYTHING FOR ME. DIDN'T YOU?!
THE FIGHT IS NOT FINISHED. KEEP KILLING BIRDS UNTIL I SAY WE'RE DONE.
I DON'T WANT TO KILL NO BIRDS.
SHUT UP!
MAGDALA... I APPRECIATE THAT YOU WANT TO PROTECT ME, BUT...
HOLD IT. WE'RE HUMANS. YOU'RE A BIRD... DON'T WORRY ABOUT US.
WE'RE GOING TO WIPE OUT EVERY LAST BIRD THAT TRIES TO HARM POLOLO. GOT THAT?!

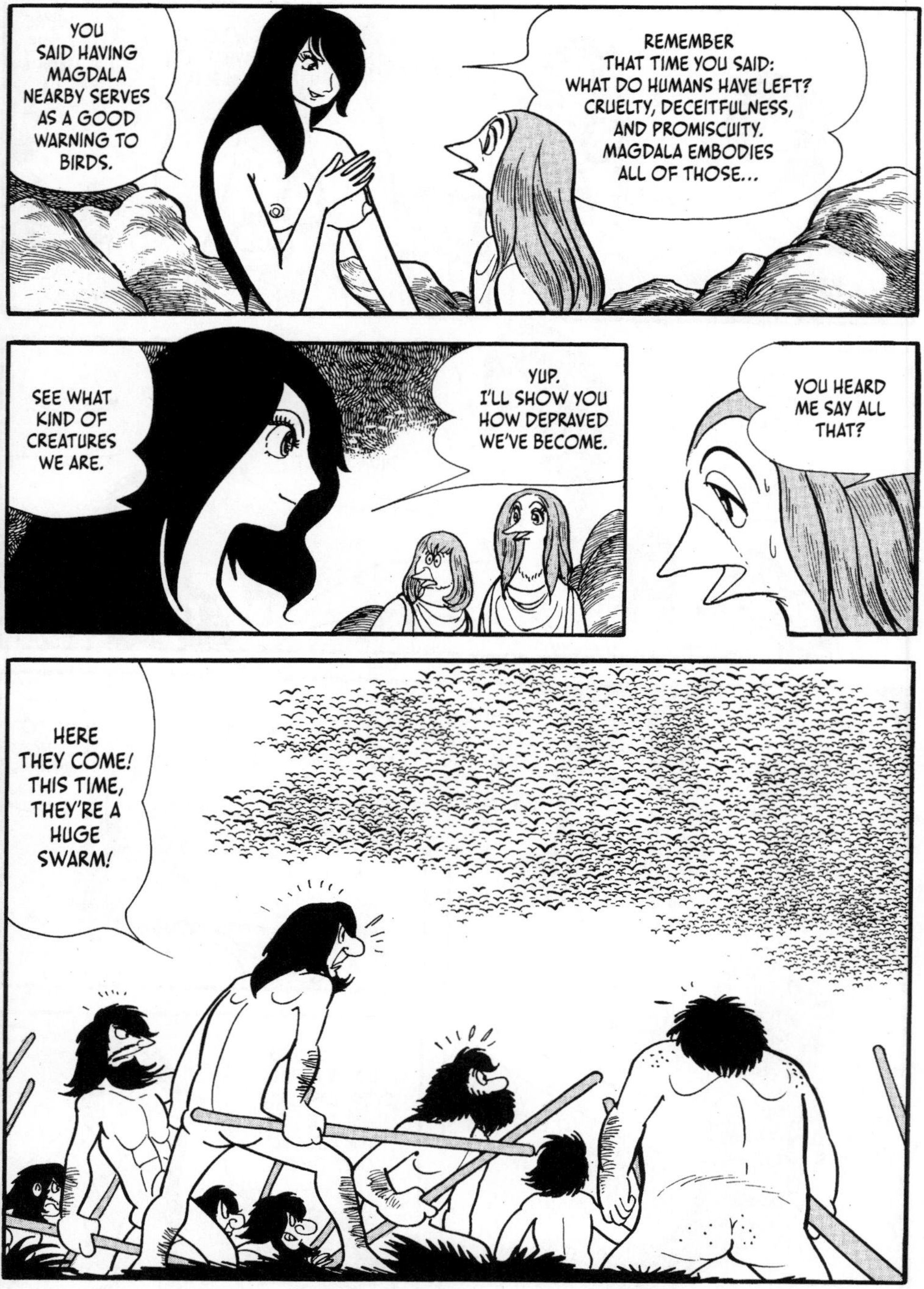
YOU SAID HAVING MAGDALA NEARBY SERVES AS A GOOD WARNING TO BIRDS.
REMEMBER THAT TIME YOU SAID: WHAT DO HUMANS HAVE LEFT? CRUELTY, DECEITFULNESS, AND PROMISCUITY. MAGDALA EMBODIES ALL OF THOSE...
YOU HEARD ME SAY ALL THAT?
YUP. I'LL SHOW YOU HOW DEPRAVED WE'VE BECOME.
SEE WHAT KIND OF CREATURES WE ARE.
HERE THEY COME! THIS TIME, THEY'RE A HUGE SWARM!

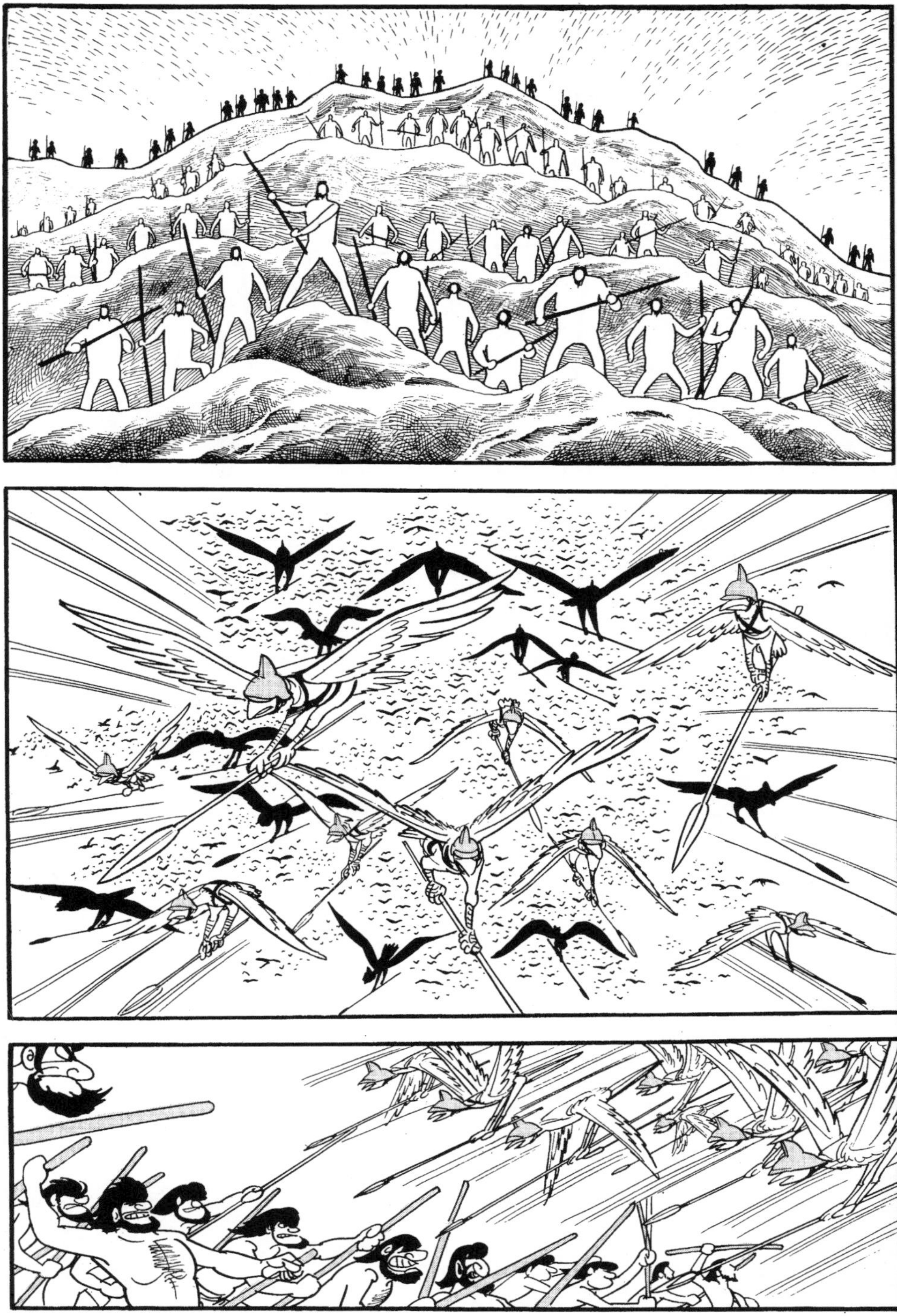

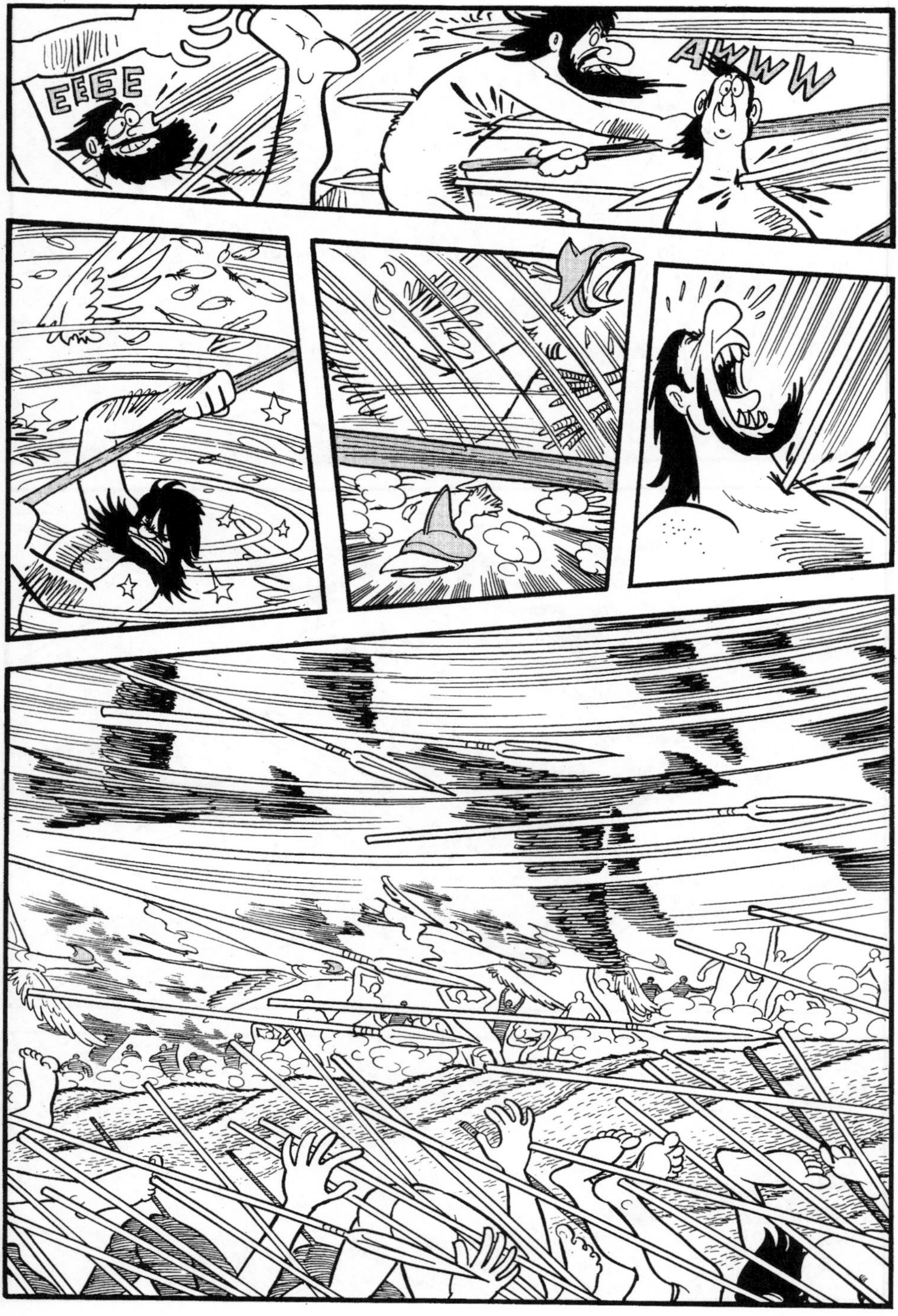
EEEE
AWWW

FWEE

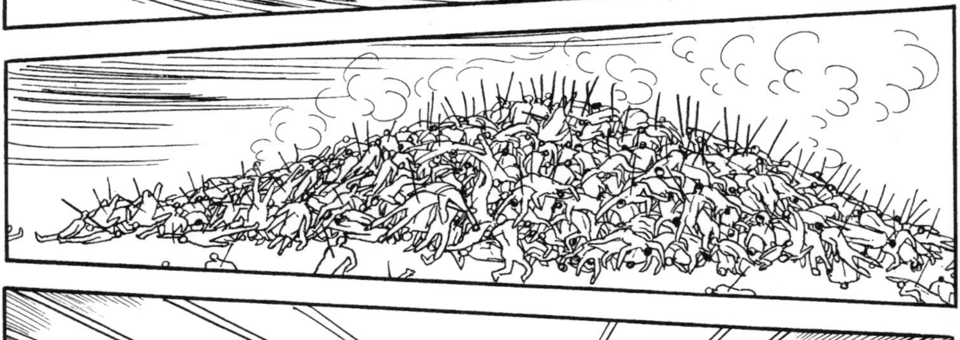

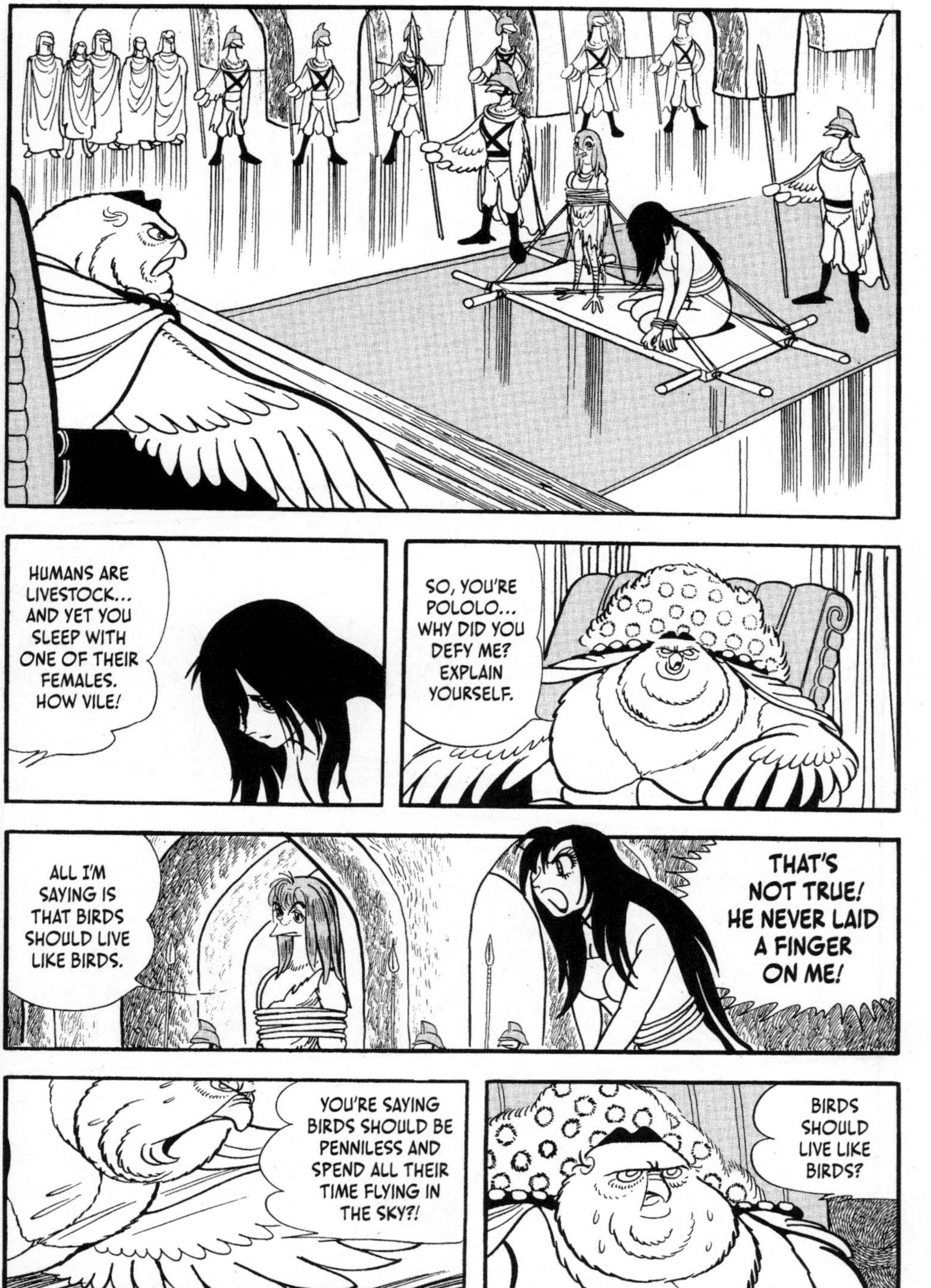
SO, YOU'RE POLOLO… WHY DID YOU DEFY ME? EXPLAIN YOURSELF.
HUMANS ARE LIVESTOCK… AND YET YOU SLEEP WITH ONE OF THEIR FEMALES. HOW VILE!
THAT'S NOT TRUE! HE NEVER LAID A FINGER ON ME!
ALL I'M SAYING IS THAT BIRDS SHOULD LIVE LIKE BIRDS.
BIRDS SHOULD LIVE LIKE BIRDS?
YOU'RE SAYING BIRDS SHOULD BE PENNILESS AND SPEND ALL THEIR TIME FLYING IN THE SKY?!

YOU WANT BIRDS TO EAT RICE BRAN AND GRAIN AND DRINK MUDDY WATER?!
BIRDS SHOULD HAVE PRIDE.
NO.
THEY SHOULD ABANDON THEIR STATUS AND PROPERTY AND PRIDE AND LIVE LIKE BUMS?!
YOUR SORCERY IS RESPONSIBLE FOR THAT!
...IS WHY THERE ARE SO MANY DEFORMED EGGS.
EATING ALL THAT RICH FOOD...
THAT'S THE BEST NUTRITION FOR BIRDS.
SILENCE!
SHUT UP!
YOU'RE NOW GUILTY OF LESE-MAJESTY AS WELL!
THAT'S ABSURD!
HOW DARE YOU ACCUSE THE KING OF IMITATING HUMANS!
O KING, OPEN YOUR EYES. YOU'RE TOO MUCH LIKE A HUMAN... IF BIRDS IMITATE THE WAYS HUMANS LIVED, IT WILL ONLY LEAD TO OUR DOWNFALL!

I SENTENCE THIS REBEL TO DEATH BY THE MOST PAINFUL METHOD!
AND THE SAME FOR THAT FEMALE HUMAN!
Hmph. THEY CALL ME THE VIPER. YOU CAN DO WHAT-EVER YOU WANT. I WON'T DIE! JUST WATCH!
SHUT UP, LIVESTOCK!
HELP!
Rrgh... FLESH-EATING ANTS... WHAT THE HELL...

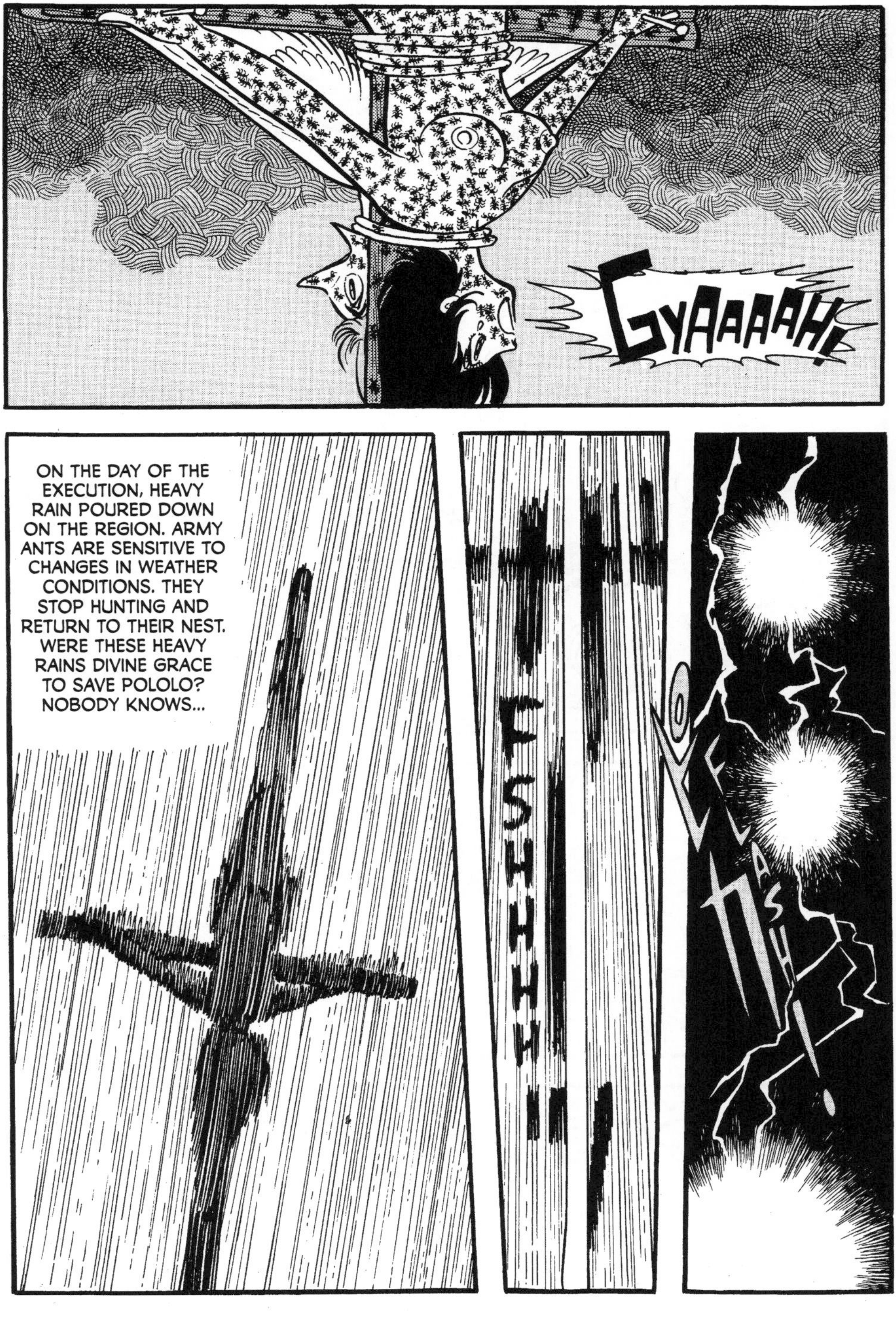
GYAAAAH!
ON THE DAY OF THE EXECUTION, HEAVY RAIN POURED DOWN ON THE REGION. ARMY ANTS ARE SENSITIVE TO CHANGES IN WEATHER CONDITIONS. THEY STOP HUNTING AND RETURN TO THEIR NEST. WERE THESE HEAVY RAINS DIVINE GRACE TO SAVE POLOLO? NOBODY KNOWS...
FSHHHH!!
FLASH!

THE RAIN FLOWED INTO RIVERS AND CAUSED FLOODS. THE KING'S MANSION, COMMONERS' HOMES, AND THE EXECUTION SITE ALL WASHED AWAY.

KING ODOLO THE 13TH WAS UNABLE TO FLY DUE TO HIS LAVISH DIET. THEY SAY HE DROWNED BEFORE ANYONE COULD RESCUE HIM...

A SEA OF MUD COVERED EVERYTHING IN SIGHT, AND BOTH ARISTOCRATS AND COMMON FOLK FLEW ABOVE IT, WITH NOWHERE TO GO.

THEY SAY THAT MAGDALA RIPPED POLOLO OFF THE CROSS AND SET HIM FREE.
MAGDALA'S CORPSE WAS FOUND WITH THE CROSS, BUT THERE WAS NO SIGN OF POLOLO.
SOME SAID THAT A FEW OF POLOLO'S FEATHERS REMAINED IN MAGDALA'S CLENCHED HAND.
SINCE THEN, BIRDMEN HAVE ALWAYS BELIEVED THAT THEIR SAINT POLOLO...
...WILL ONE DAY RETURN ON THE DAY OF FINAL JUDGMENT.

CHAPTER 13: MUTANT

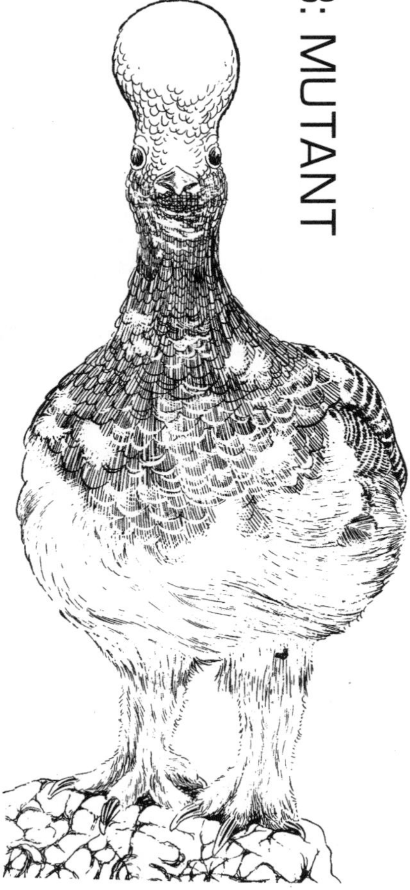

THE ESSENCE OF MUTATION IS GENETIC CHANGE. IN MANY CASES, GENE MUTATION INVOLVES CHANGES IN WHICH DOMINANT TRAITS BECOME RECESSIVE. HUMANS HAVE REGRESSED SIGNIFICANTLY, BUT ONE OUT OF EVERY MILLION IS BORN WITH THE INTELLIGENCE OF THEIR ANCIENT ANCESTORS. THIS APPEARS TO BE AN EXTREMELY RARE EXAMPLE OF GENETIC MUTATION.

Ha ha... Ha ha ha...
GREEDY FOOL...
BAK-HATZ!
ABMARAC YA!
SEKIY!

TAKE THIS ROTTEN TANGERINE AND SCRAM.
OUT OF THE WAY, APE!
WHY YOU LOUSY...
SPLAT
INOGUCHI!!
DOVAM
YAHOO
HURRAH
YAHOO

Ha ha! Ho ho!
ARE THE CARRIAGES TOO SHABBY TO DRIVE THROUGH THOSE APE-MEN?!
TEN FOOD CARRIAGES HAVE BEEN PLUNDERED IN THE UTSUZA DISTRICT.
HUMAN SANCTUARY
HE USES MAGIC...
NO, THEY HAVE A LEADER.
MAGIC? BY THE APE-MEN? DON'T BE RIDICULOUS.

IS THE OPPOSITION PARTY BEHIND THIS?
HOW DID HE GET SO SMART?
THE LEADER IS TERRIBLY CLEVER. YOU COULD EVEN SAY HE'S A GENIUS...
DUMB
DUMB
DUMB
DUMB
IF HE'S USEFUL, HE CAN WORK FOR US.
I WANT TO MEET HIM.
HUMAN SANCTUARY
ODDLY ENOUGH, BIRDMEN DID NOT RIDE HORSES. THEY USUALLY RODE DEER. HORSES WERE TOO LARGE FOR BIRDMEN TO HANDLE. WHEN RIDING STAGECOACHES, THEY USED BOTH HORSES AND DEER. THE FOOTSTEPS SOUNDED LIKE "DUMB, DUMB."*

*A joke referencing the Japanese word for "dumb," which is written with the kanji for "horse" and "deer."

LISTEN, APE-MEN! I HEAR YOU HAVE A CLEVER LEADER. I WANT TO MEET HIM.
THAT'S HIM! LOOK!
DAMN YOU!
KLUNK
ARGH!

MAYOR?
WHOA, YOU KNOW THAT WORD?
UTSUZA IS A HUMAN SANCTUARY. THERE SHOULD BE PLENTY OF FOOD THERE. THE LAND IS FERTILE.
HUMANS IN UTSUZA DISTRICT ALL HUNGRY. SOME DIE. BIRD NO LET HUMAN OUT.
LET HUMAN OUT UTSUZA. OR GIVE MORE FOOD. MAKE DECISION.
SO, YOU'RE THE LEADER OF THE VIOLENT APES...
HERE'S MY ANSWER.
YOU APE-MEN WILL NO LONGER GET AWAY WITH YOUR UNRULY BEHAVIOR.
GIVE MORE FOOD! OR OPEN SANCTUARY!
YOUR BODY IS PROOF OF THAT. YOU'RE CUT LIKE AN OX.
ANSWER NOW.

IF ANY OF YOU TRY TO LEAVE THE SANCTUARY, WE'LL STOP YOU WITH THIS THORN CANNON. WHO WANTS TO SEE WHAT IT CAN DO?
AIM FOR THE WILDCAT ON THAT MOUND.
CREAK

EEEK!
Z-BOOM
IT FIRES BARRENWORT THORNS. ONE SHOT CAN MAKE TWENTY OF YOU GO CRAZY AND DIE.
Mrow! Ah ah ah! Gwah!
GWAMP!
?
?
WHAT'S THAT?
...
Rrrr!

Rr...
HEY, STOP! NO WEAPONS!
Fwee!
DOKAN

HE THREW SOMETHING AND THEN THERE WAS LIGHTNING... IS MY LIVER TORN?
THAT'S THE MAGIC I WAS TELLING YOU ABOUT, SIR.
SIR... THERE'S NO TELLING WHAT DAMAGE HE CAN DO...
WE SHOULD SETTLE... LET'S GRANT SOME OF THEIR DEMANDS...
AND FIND OUT HOW TO MAKE THAT LIGHTNING...
WHAT'S YOUR NAME, APE-MAN?
PARENT DIE BEFORE GIVE NAME!
FINE, WE'LL CALL YOU WILDCAT.
I'LL TELL YOU WHAT, HUMANS!
WE'LL USE THIS YEAR'S SPECIAL BUDGET TO BUY FEED FOR UTSUZA DISTRICT.
DON'T YOU UNDERSTAND? I'M SAYING WE'LL GIVE YOU FOOD.
BUT...
...I HAVE ONE CONDITION.

IT OKAY. I GO. I WANT SEE TOWN LIFE.
NO! THIS MAN OUR HERO!
TO MAKE SURE YOU HONOR OUR DEAL.
YOU'RE COMING WITH US!
SHUT UP AND GET IN!
NO. I RIDE HORSE!
I BE BACK SOON!
BRAVO!!
BRAVO!
HOMO
REY!

YEAH, DON'T WORRY. YOUR PEOPLE SHOULD HAVE PLENTY TO EAT NOW.
YOU DELIVER FOOD UTSUZA?
THIS IS YOUR NEW PLACE, WILDCAT. MAKE YOURSELF AT HOME. WE JUST CAN'T LET YOU OUT. YOU'RE OUR HOSTAGE.
I READ AN ANCIENT TEXT THAT SAID APE-MEN USED TO LIVE SOPHISTICATED LIVES. THEY WERE HIGHLY INTELLIGENT.
HE'S NOT LIKE OTHER APE-MEN.
THAT DAMN WILDCAT... HE'S MAKING SOMETHING. SUCH FOCUS!

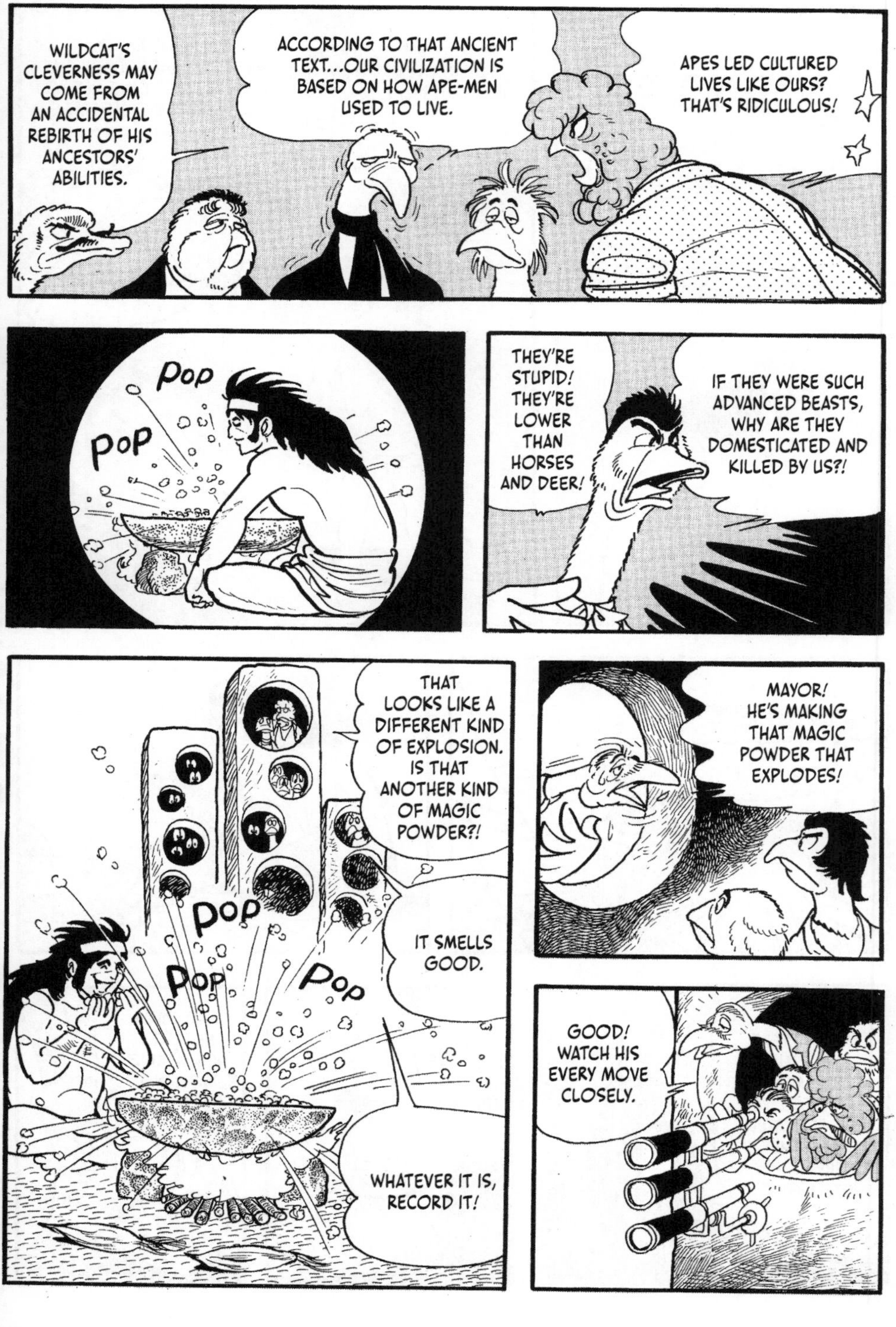

WILDCAT'S CLEVERNESS MAY COME FROM AN ACCIDENTAL REBIRTH OF HIS ANCESTORS' ABILITIES.
ACCORDING TO THAT ANCIENT TEXT...OUR CIVILIZATION IS BASED ON HOW APE-MEN USED TO LIVE.
APES LED CULTURED LIVES LIKE OURS? THAT'S RIDICULOUS!
POP
POP
THEY'RE STUPID! THEY'RE LOWER THAN HORSES AND DEER!
IF THEY WERE SUCH ADVANCED BEASTS, WHY ARE THEY DOMESTICATED AND KILLED BY US?!
THAT LOOKS LIKE A DIFFERENT KIND OF EXPLOSION. IS THAT ANOTHER KIND OF MAGIC POWDER?!
IT SMELLS GOOD.
POP
POP
POP
WHATEVER IT IS, RECORD IT!
MAYOR! HE'S MAKING THAT MAGIC POWDER THAT EXPLODES!
GOOD! WATCH HIS EVERY MOVE CLOSELY.

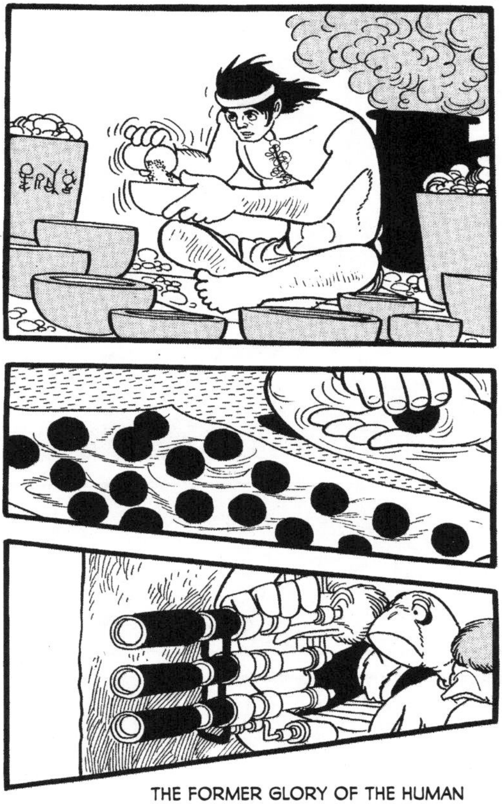

THE FORMER GLORY OF THE HUMAN
RACE – ITS SCIENTIFIC TECHNOLOGY AND
KNOWLEDGE – CANNOT BE PASSED ON
THROUGH HEREDITY. BUT THE TRAITS
OF BRAIN CELLS THAT DEVELOP SUCH
KNOWLEDGE ARE FOUND IN GENES,
AND THEY APPEAR IN ONE OUT OF EVERY
SEVERAL DOZENS OF MILLIONS OF PEOPLE!
HE IS ONE OF THOSE PEOPLE.

BOMP
MAKE HIM LOYAL TO US.
TREAT HIM LIKE ONE OF US. LET HIM BE A MEMBER OF SOCIETY.
GIVE HIM SOME CLOTHES AND SHOES.
HE'S A MONSTER!
TATANO-PRAST AND GERCO-NIUM AND A TRACE AMOUNT OF NO-BRONDATE POWDER. AND HEAT.
IF WE GIVE HIM MATERIALS, THERE'S NO TELLING WHAT HE'LL MAKE!
WILDCAT! THESE ARE GIFTS FROM THE MAYOR. BE GRATEFUL.
PUT THEM ON.

Heh heh heh! Ha ha ha!
WHOA!
I CAN EAT ANYTHING. AND BUY ANYTHING... Heh heh.
YOU'LL HAVE BIRD-MAN STATUS.
HERE'S YOUR CITIZEN CARD AND A PASS FOR THE SOCIAL CLUB.
HUH?
HEY! NO APE-MEN ALLOWED. GET LOST!
DAMN HIM...
I'LL PUT HIM IN HIS PLACE!

EEK! AN APE-MAN!
CITIZENS! ALLOW ME TO INTRODUCE MR. WILDCAT. HE'S A GENIUS APE-MAN SCIENTIST... HE INVENTED THAT MAGIC POWDER.
WE'VE MADE HIM AN HONORARY BIRDMAN!
IT'S GOOD TO SEE YOU, WILDCAT.
WE NEED TO TEACH HIM SOME MANNERS.
MUNCH MUNCH CHOMP CHOMP
I'VE SEEN YOUR WORK. IT'S QUITE IMPRESSIVE.
APE-MEN SMELL AWFUL.
HE'S BEEN PROMOTED, BUT HE'S STILL JUST A BEAST.
WELL, HE ACTS MUCH BETTER THAN MOST YOUTH TODAY.
HE LOOKS GOOD IN BIRDMEN CLOTHING.
WHY DON'T YOU WORK ON MY NEXT ELECTION CAMPAIGN?
NO BEAK. SUCH A STRANGE FACE.

Ah, MR. MAYOR.
MR. MAYOR, THE GOVERNOR OF THE SUNSET DISTRICT IS HERE.
I'VE HEARD ABOUT WILDCAT... IN MY DISTRICT, EXTREMIST RADICALS ARE THREATENING MY STATUS. I NEED SOMETHING POWERFUL TO DEAL WITH THEM.
THE BEST WAY TO CONTROL THE POPULATION IS THROUGH FORCE. THAT APE-MAN WOULD COME IN HANDY...
LEND HIM TO ME.
I'LL PAY YOU. AND I'LL SUPPORT YOU IN THE NEXT ELECTION.
SO HOW ABOUT IT? SELL HIM TO ME.
FIVE MILLION PIRONE!
NO, TEN MILLION!
I CAN'T, SIR.

...
GOOD DAY.
HE'S MY ASSET. AN IMPORTANT WEAPON.
I'M SORRY, IT DOESN'T MATTER HOW MUCH YOU OFFER.
HE DRANK TOO MUCH.
WHAT A DISGRACE!
Oof...
HOW DARE THAT WORM-EATING UPSTART REFUSE ME! I'LL SHOW HIM!
HE LONGS TO RETURN TO UTSUZA.
WHAT DOES HE WANT?
HE'S HOMESICK? THAT'S NOT GOOD.
WHAT WOULD MAKE HIM FORGET ALL THAT?
THAT DAMN GOVERNOR... HE WON'T TAKE NO FOR AN ANSWER. HE'LL KEEP TRYING TO STEAL WILDCAT.
MAKE SURE WILDCAT DOESN'T BETRAY US. LOCK HIM UP IN SOLITARY CONFINEMENT.
THAT WOULD MAKE HIM TURN AGAINST US.

A WOMAN. LET'S GIVE HIM A WOMAN.
A FEMALE APE FROM UTSUZA?
THAT WOULD ONLY FUEL HIS DESIRE TO RETURN HOME.
A BIRDWOMAN SHOULD BE FINE.
WHAT?! A BIRDWOMAN WITH AN APE-MAN?! THAT'S OUTRAGEOUS!
I'LL FIND A FEMALE WHO'S SUITABLE FOR AN APE-MAN.
I WON'T CONDONE BESTIALITY!
W-WATER...
Oof...
WHO ARE YOU?
I'M YOUR WOMAN, WILDCAT.
I NO NEED BIRDWOMAN! LEAVE!
THEY FORCED ME TO COME HERE.
NOW DO AS YOU WISH...

OW!
THAT'S ENOUGH...
GET OUT!
APE MAN NOT BIRDMAN. BIRDWOMAN NOT APE WOMAN...

TO CONTROL YOU. HE GAVE YOU BIRDMAN STATUS SO YOU'D KEEP MAKING THAT POWDER.
WHY MAYOR DO THIS?
I CAN'T GO HOME NOW. NOBODY WILL ASSOCIATE WITH A BIRDWOMAN WHO'S BEEN WITH AN APE-MAN...
SEE... THEY'RE WATCHING YOU.
NO!
I GO BACK UTSUZA!
MOVE! I GO HOME!
GET BACK IN YOUR NEST, BEAST!
OUCH!

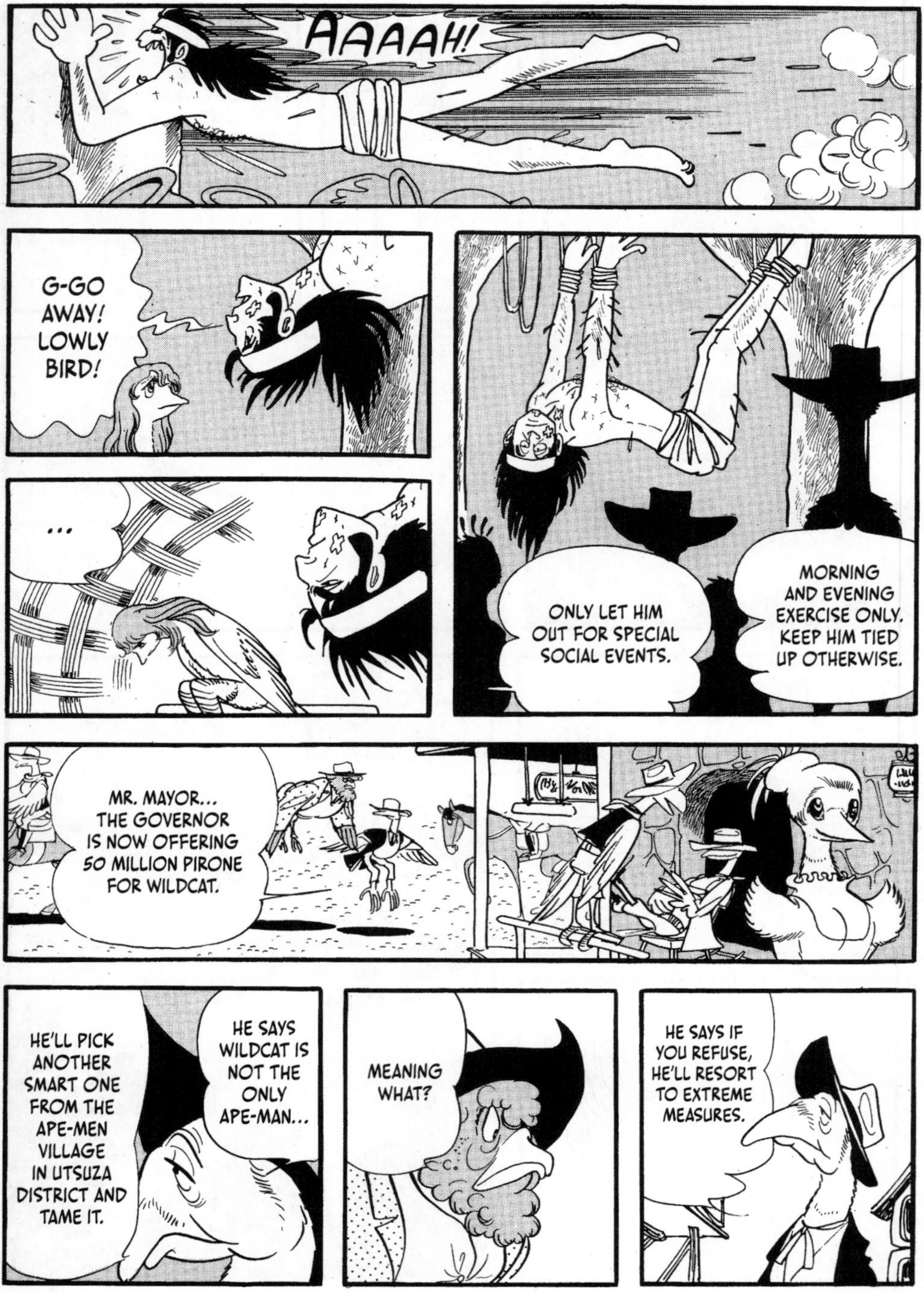
AAAAH!
G-GO AWAY! LOWLY BIRD!
...
ONLY LET HIM OUT FOR SPECIAL SOCIAL EVENTS.
MORNING AND EVENING EXERCISE ONLY. KEEP HIM TIED UP OTHERWISE.
MR. MAYOR... THE GOVERNOR IS NOW OFFERING 50 MILLION PIRONE FOR WILDCAT.
HE SAYS WILDCAT IS NOT THE ONLY APE-MAN...
HE'LL PICK ANOTHER SMART ONE FROM THE APE-MEN VILLAGE IN UTSUZA DISTRICT AND TAME IT.
MEANING WHAT?
HE SAYS IF YOU REFUSE, HE'LL RESORT TO EXTREME MEASURES.

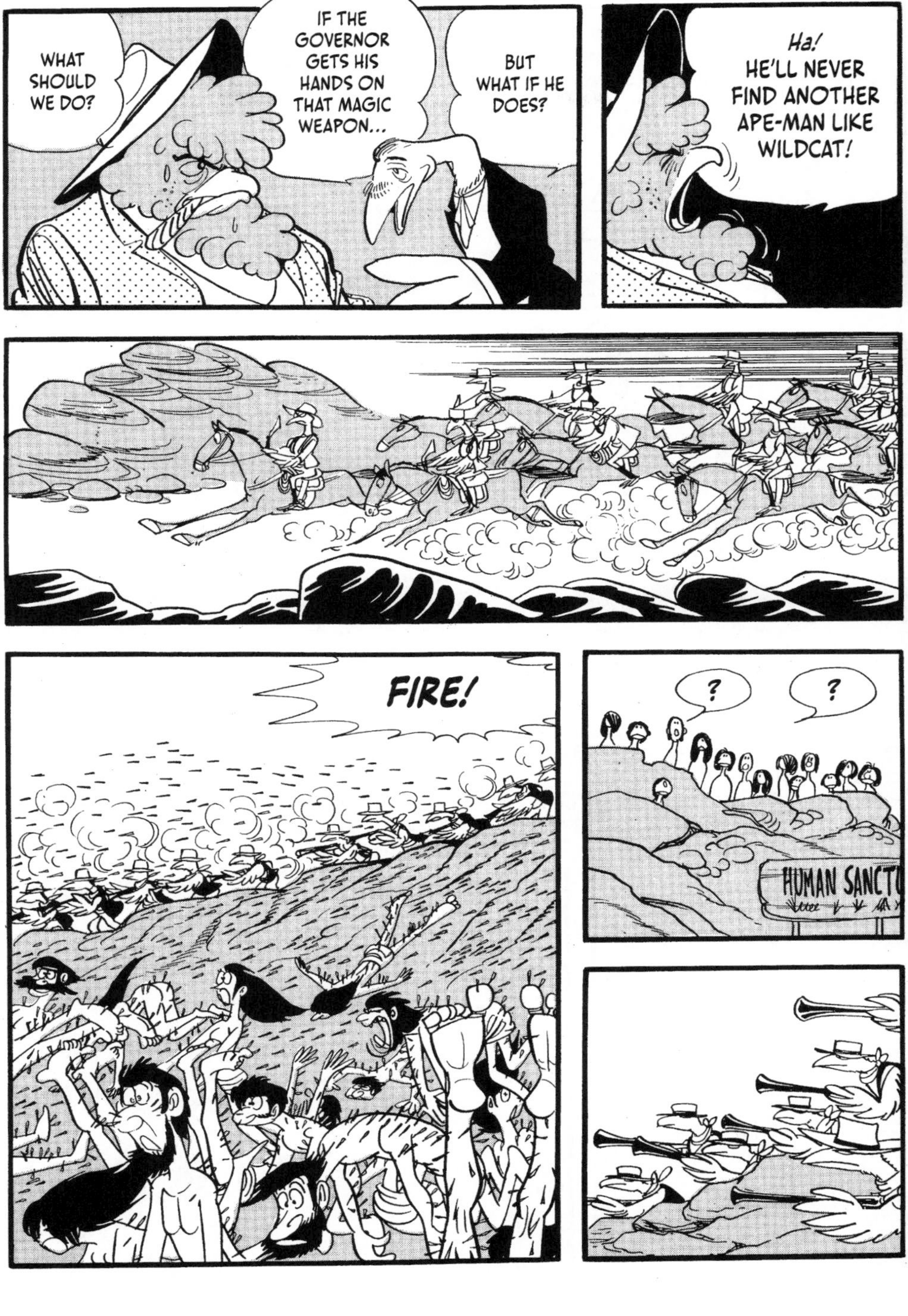
WHAT SHOULD WE DO?
IF THE GOVERNOR GETS HIS HANDS ON THAT MAGIC WEAPON...
BUT WHAT IF HE DOES?
Ha! HE'LL NEVER FIND ANOTHER APE-MAN LIKE WILDCAT!
FIRE!
?
?
HUMAN

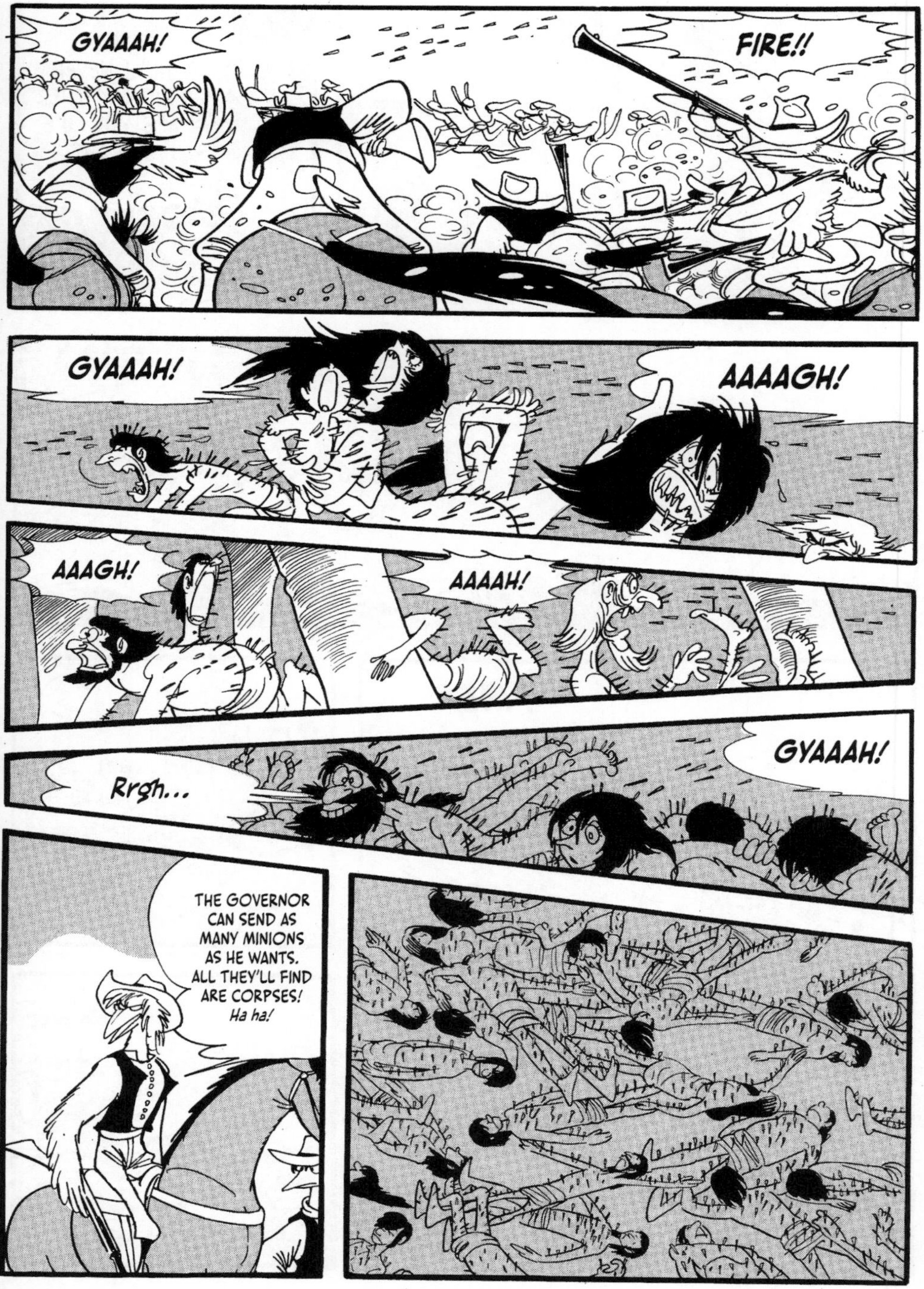
FIRE!!
GYAAAH!
AAAAGH!
GYAAAH!
AAAAH!
AAAGH!
GYAAAH!
Rrgh...
THE GOVERNOR CAN SEND AS MANY MINIONS AS HE WANTS. ALL THEY'LL FIND ARE CORPSES! *Ha ha!*

A WITNESS SAID THERE WERE PILES OF CORPSES...
MY FAMILY... PARENTS... BROTHERS... ALL KILLED?
WHAT?!
GAH!
GR-R-R
...
WHY? THEY DO NOTHING WRONG!!
WHY?! WHY KILL?!
YOU HELP ME?
YOU SAID NO GO HOME.
HELP MY WORK?
I...STUPID.

WHAT IS WILDCAT DOING?
ANOTHER EXPERIMENT.
ARE THEY GETTING ALONG?
SHE'S SERVING HIM WELL.
DOES HE KNOW WE KILLED THE APE-MEN IN UTSUZA DISTRICT?
I THINK HE'S HEARD...
MAYBE HE REALIZES WHAT WE'RE CAPABLE OF. HE'S AFRAID OF US NOW.
LOOK AT ALL THOSE EGGS! WHAT A DISGRACE!
SHE LAID ALL THOSE EGGS WITH A HUMAN!!
LOOK! THERE'S A STRANGE BLACK POWDER INSIDE!
THEY'RE SO HEAVY! ARE ALL HUMAN EGGS THIS HEAVY?
A MIXED BREED OF A HUMAN AND A BIRD? DISGUSTING!

TOMORROW IS THE MAYORAL ELECTION.
WHATEVER HAPPENS, THE TOWN WILL BE EMPTY.
HEY, Y'ALL! MY TREAT TONIGHT! HOP ON THE PERCH AND HAVE AT IT!
ALL I ASK IS THAT YOU VOTE FOR THE INCUMBENT.
HELL NO!

HOW ARE YOUR COCK-SPURS?
FINE. I'M NOT YOUNG ANYMORE, BUT I WON'T LOSE.
I NEED TO WIN ANOTHER TERM! OTHER-WISE, THE GOVERNOR WILL TAKE OVER THIS TOWN!
WHAT'S WRONG WITH KILLING APE-MEN?!
IT'S NOT ILLEGAL!
YOU'RE FAVORED TO WIN, BUT KILLING THE APE-MEN IN UTSUZA DISTRICT HAS UPSET THE FEMALES IN THE ANIMAL PROTECTION SOCIETY.
WHAT'S THE OUT-LOOK?
THEY THINK KILLING THEM BRINGS A CURSE.
STUPID SUPERSTI-TION!
SOME OF OUR YOUTH HAVE AN INSTINCTUAL INFERIORITY COMPLEX ABOUT THE APE-MEN.
SQUAAWK!!

SOMEONE WAS PEEPING AT MY NEST!
HONEY!
THAT'S HIM! PERVERT!
CATCH HIM!
CHECK OUTSIDE!
HEY! IT'S NOT A GUY. IT'S A FEMALE!
HOW DARE YOU PEEP AT THE MAYOR'S WIFE!
HEY, BABE! HOW ABOUT IT TONIGHT?
SHE'S A LOOKER.
Heh, SURE… BUT HEY…
THEN SHE'S NOT A PERVERT, UNLESS SHE'S A LESBIAN…
A FEMALE!

BESIDES! HE'S MUCH MORE PURE AND SINCERE THAN YOU LOT! HE HAS MORE CLASS THAN ANY BIRDMAN!
FILTHY MY ASS! WILDCAT HASN'T LAID A FINGER ON ME!
WHOA, THIS IS THAT APE-MAN'S BIRDWOMAN!
Y-YOU'RE RIGHT!
FILTHY WHORE!
IGNORE HER.
LEWD BITCH IS ON 'BOUT SOMETHIN'.
THIS ONLY CHANCE FOR REVENGE. ASK YOU HELP AGAIN TOMORROW. THEN FLY AWAY SOMEWHERE.
HOW IT GO?
THE TOWN WILL BE PRACTICALLY EMPTY TOMORROW MORNING. UNGUARDED NESTS EVERY-WHERE!

NO! I'LL STAY WITH YOU, WILDCAT! WHEREVER YOU GO!
I BE KILLED. IF FIGHT AND DIE, THEN GO PARADISE. CAN MEET TOP APE MAN.
I'LL FIGHT, TOO!
YOU, ME, NOT SAME. IF YOU DIE, NO PARADISE.
I DON'T CARE. I JUST WANT TO GO WITH YOU TO THE GATE.
KLANG
KLANG
KLANG
KLANG

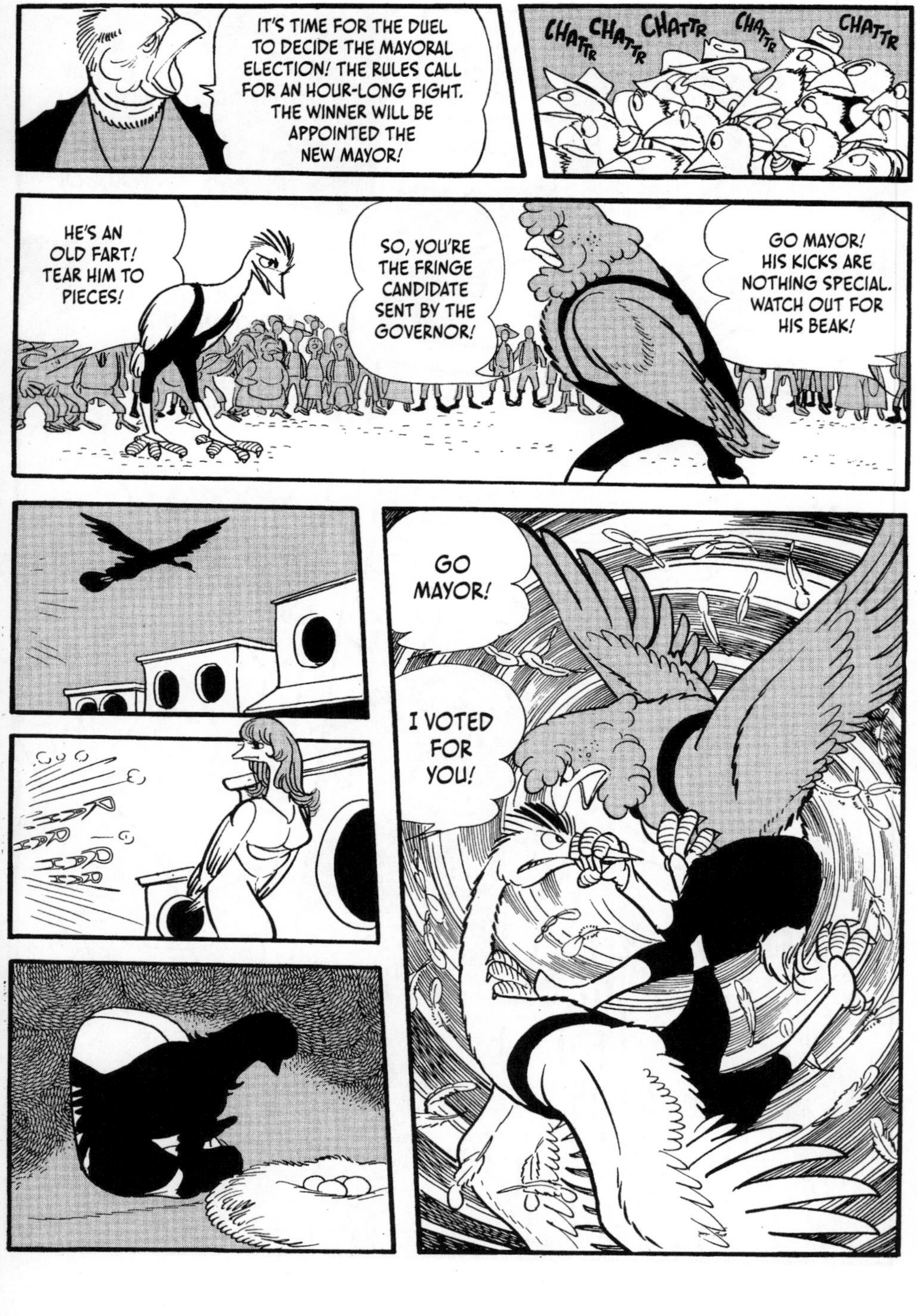
IT'S TIME FOR THE DUEL TO DECIDE THE MAYORAL ELECTION! THE RULES CALL FOR AN HOUR-LONG FIGHT. THE WINNER WILL BE APPOINTED THE NEW MAYOR!
CHATTR CHATTR CHATTR CHATTR CHATTR
HE'S AN OLD FART! TEAR HIM TO PIECES!
SO, YOU'RE THE FRINGE CANDIDATE SENT BY THE GOVERNOR!
GO MAYOR! HIS KICKS ARE NOTHING SPECIAL. WATCH OUT FOR HIS BEAK!
GO MAYOR!
I VOTED FOR YOU!

STAB HIS NECK!
HANG IN THERE, BOSS!
I'M MAYOR FOR ONE MORE TERM! Oof...
RAH
THOSE EGGS HOT. WILL BURN... BIRDWOMEN COME HOME AND HOLD EGGS... WATCH!
I SWITCHED THE EGGS IN MOST NESTS.

LET'S PARTY! DRINK UP!
ANY WORDS FOR YOUR CAMPAIGN STAFF?
CONGRATULATIONS, MAYOR!
FINE. I'LL BUY YOU ANYTHING YOU WANT!
YOU PROMISED ME A NEW ONE IF YOU WON...
WHY DON'T YOU GO REST IN YOUR NEST?

DOGAAANN
GYAAAH!
THE APE-MAN'S MAGIC POWDER! HE BETRAYED US!
GET OUT OF HERE!
MY WIFE!
AN EXPLOSION!
W-WHAT THE...?!

GWOOSH
B-B-BAM
BOOM
SQUAWK!
HOW DARE HE TURN MY DAUGHTER INTO YAKITORI!
WHERE'S THE APE-MAN?! FIND HIM AND TEAR HIM TO PIECES!
ALL FEMALES HAVE BEEN BLOWN TO PIECES!
MY WIFE EXPLODED!

AAAH!
GAAH!
HE'S GONE! HE RAN AWAY!
WHAT THAT?
TOO BAD YOU CAN'T FLY...
THEY'RE COMING FOR US. LET'S GO!
THIS RAGING FIRE WILL EVEN SCORCH HEAVEN. RESIDENTS ARE RUNNING AMOK. THIS IS THE END TIMES, THE DAY OF JUDGMENT THAT ST. POLOLO PROPHESIED. WE BIRDMEN HAVE SINNED... WE'RE CONSUMED BY POWER AND VANITY. SO GOD HAS TAKEN THE FORM OF AN APE-MAN AND PUNISHED US...

THEY COME. NO GET AWAY. BUT YOU FLY. ASK YOU FAVOR.
I WRITE HOW MAKE POWDER. YOU TAKE PAPER. SHOW APE MAN OTHER DISTRICT!
THIS HOW MAKE POWDER. OTHER APE MAN MAKE. NO MORE FEAR!
APE MAN NO DIE. NEXT HERO COME. CHASE BIRDMAN FROM APE MAN LAND.
I LOVE YOU, WILDCAT.
THANK. BUT YOU GO SAFE. I NO FORGET YOU.
WHAT'S YOUR REAL NAME? YOU HAVE A NAME, RIGHT?
I NO TELL BIRDMAN. BUT YOU OK. I GERONIMO.
DON'T DIE, GERONI-MO!
GERONIMO NO DIE! NO DIE 'TIL CHASE BIRDMAN AWAY!

THERE'S THE APE-MAN! FIRE!
FOOT!!

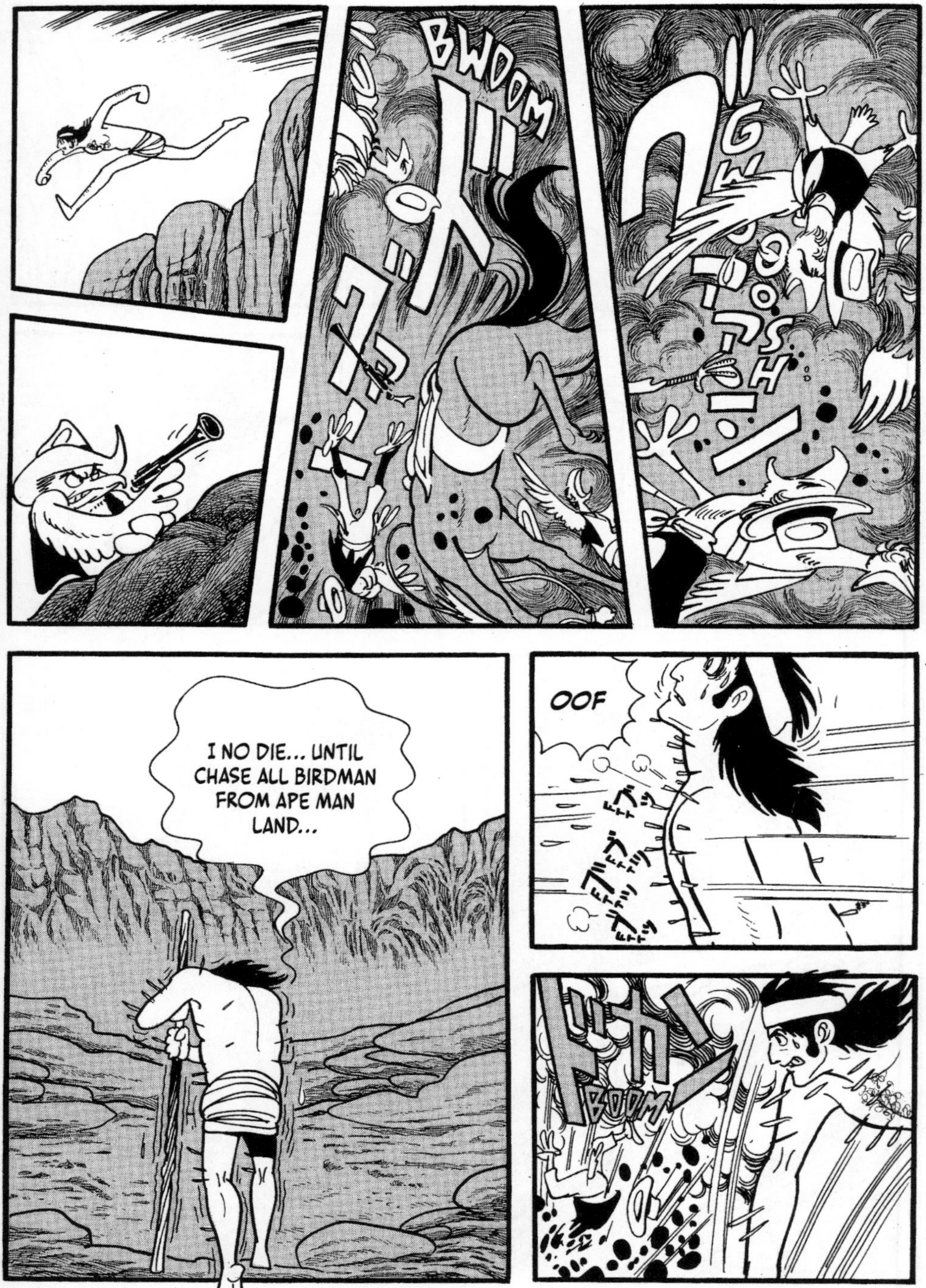
BWOOM
GWOOOSH
I NO DIE... UNTIL CHASE ALL BIRDMAN FROM APE MAN LAND...
OOF
BOOM

CHAPTER 14:

FALCO TINNUNCULUS MOLTHUS

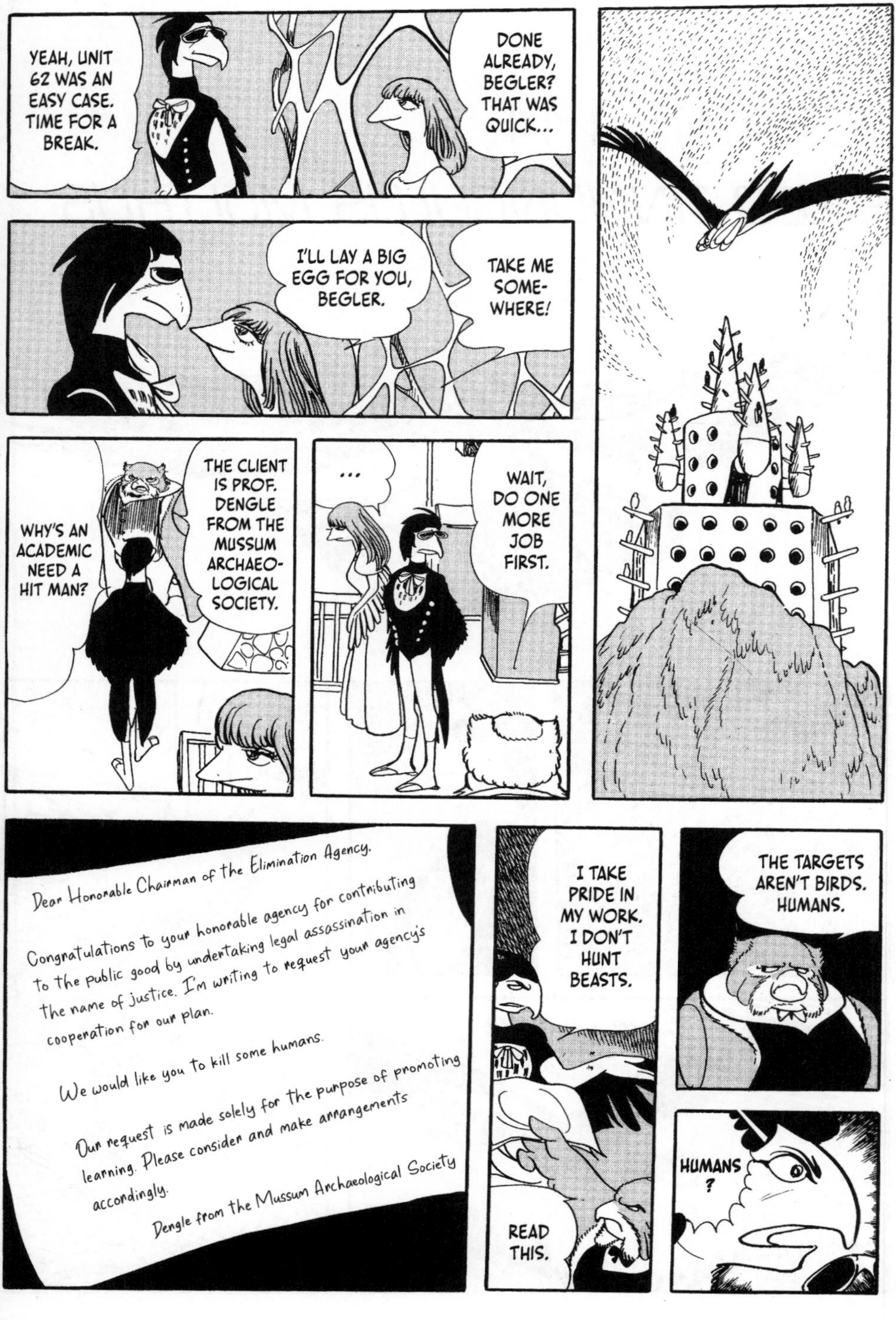
DONE ALREADY, BEGLER? THAT WAS QUICK...
YEAH, UNIT 62 WAS AN EASY CASE. TIME FOR A BREAK.
I'LL LAY A BIG EGG FOR YOU, BEGLER.
TAKE ME SOME-WHERE!
WAIT, DO ONE MORE JOB FIRST.
...
THE CLIENT IS PROF. DENGLE FROM THE MUSSUM ARCHAEO-LOGICAL SOCIETY.
WHY'S AN ACADEMIC NEED A HIT MAN?
I TAKE PRIDE IN MY WORK. I DON'T HUNT BEASTS.
THE TARGETS AREN'T BIRDS. HUMANS.
HUMANS?
READ THIS.
Dear Honorable Chairman of the Elimination Agency.
Congratulations to your honorable agency for contributing to the public good by undertaking legal assassination in the name of justice. I'm writing to request your agency's cooperation for our plan.
We would like you to kill some humans.
Our request is made solely for the purpose of promoting learning. Please consider and make arrangements accordingly.
Dengle from the Mussum Archaeological Society

THE CLIENT IS IMPRESSED WITH YOUR SKILLS.
THE COMPANY CONSIDERS THIS AN OFFICIAL JOB.
IT WILL BENEFIT ACADEMIA.
I WANT SOME TIME OFF.
FINE. SUIT YOURSELF.
TAKE A MONTH, AND THEN VISIT THE CLIENT.
MOST JOBS YOU'VE DONE ARE LOVE AFFAIRS.
KILL SOME HUMANS FOR A CHANGE.
TAKE ME TO A HEALTH RESORT.
FOLLOW ME.
OH, YES!
I LOVE YOU, BEGLER.

THERE'S A HUMAN.
AAAAH!
GYAAAH!
GOUGE THE EYES, AND THE REST IS EASY.
THEY'RE WEAKER THAN I THOUGHT.
I'LL LAY AN EGG FOR YOU.
HELL NO.
YOU'RE A REAL PRO.

TO HELL WITH CLINGY FEMALES.
MAKE ME A NEST.
YOU'RE MINE. I'LL NEVER LET YOU GO.
NO HARD FEELINGS. I'M JUST NOT A FAMILY MAN.
UNDERDANS ELIMINATION AGENCY? COME THIS WAY.
THIS IS PROFESSOR DENGLE.
I'M BEGLER, A CLASS 1 ELIMINA-TOR.
I AM POPOT. MANAGING DIRECTOR.

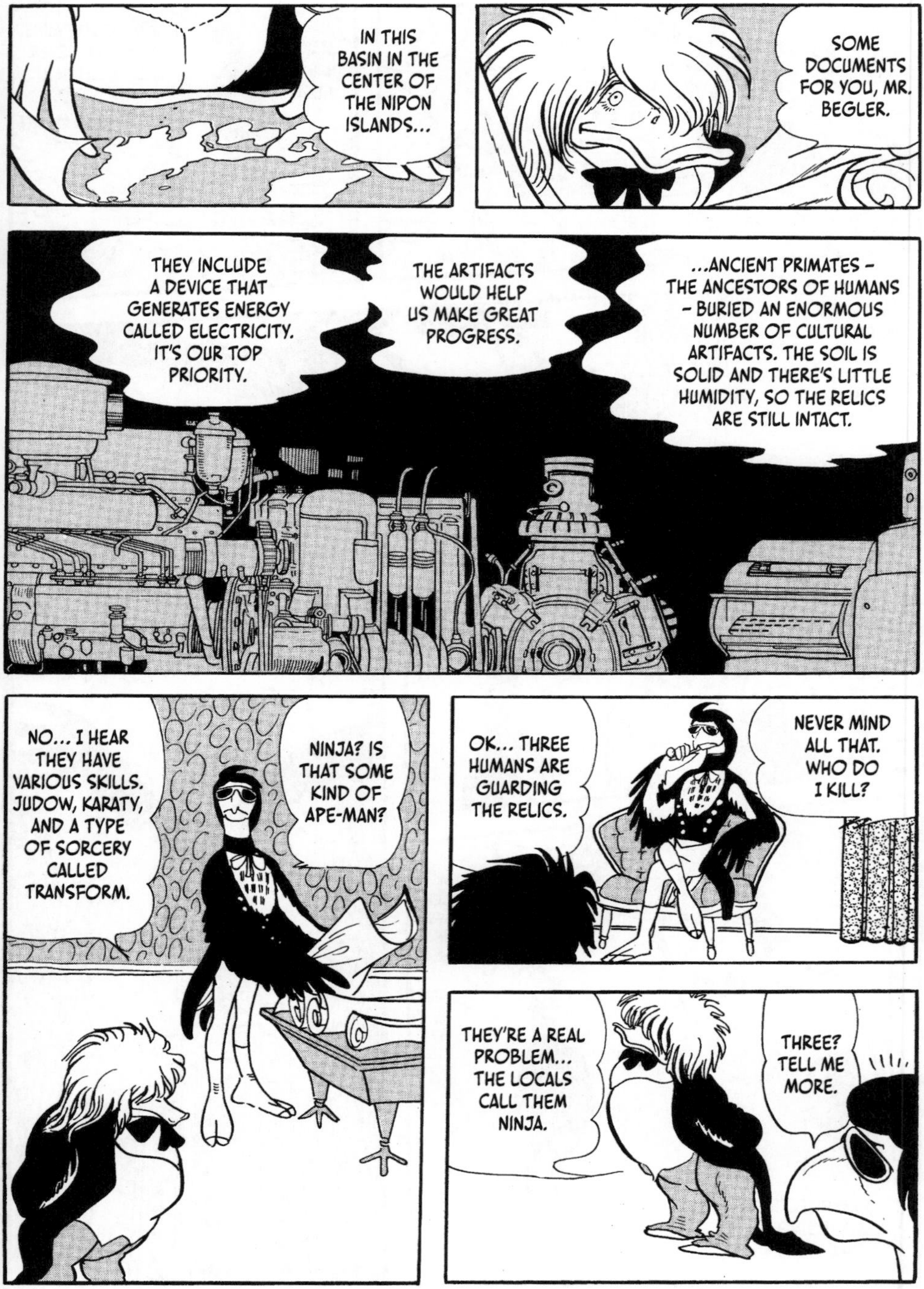
SOME DOCUMENTS FOR YOU, MR. BEGLER.
IN THIS BASIN IN THE CENTER OF THE NIPON ISLANDS...
...ANCIENT PRIMATES – THE ANCESTORS OF HUMANS – BURIED AN ENORMOUS NUMBER OF CULTURAL ARTIFACTS. THE SOIL IS SOLID AND THERE'S LITTLE HUMIDITY, SO THE RELICS ARE STILL INTACT.
THE ARTIFACTS WOULD HELP US MAKE GREAT PROGRESS.
THEY INCLUDE A DEVICE THAT GENERATES ENERGY CALLED ELECTRICITY. IT'S OUR TOP PRIORITY.
NEVER MIND ALL THAT. WHO DO I KILL?
OK... THREE HUMANS ARE GUARDING THE RELICS.
THREE? TELL ME MORE.
THEY'RE A REAL PROBLEM... THE LOCALS CALL THEM NINJA.
NINJA? IS THAT SOME KIND OF APE-MAN?
NO... I HEAR THEY HAVE VARIOUS SKILLS. JUDOW, KARATY, AND A TYPE OF SORCERY CALLED TRANSFORM.

WHAT DO YOU NEED?
DRAW-INGS OF THOSE THREE HUMANS.
THEY'RE UGLY BEASTS. THIS JOB SUCKS...
IF THEY SEND SCOUTS, THEY'LL BE HERE IN TWO OR THREE DAYS...
THINK THEY WILL?
YUP. YOU CAN TRUST WHAT BIRDS SAY TO EACH OTHER.
IS IT TRUE THEY'RE BRINGING AN ASSASSIN TO KILL US?
PROBABLY. BUT WE WON'T LET THEM TAKE THIS CASTLE.
WE'LL SLAUGHTER 'EM AND PLUCK THEIR FEATHERS ...
...RIGHT HERE IN FRONT OF OUR ANCESTORS' TREASURE!

WHAT DO YOU SEE?
NO SIGN OF 'EM YET.

OUR ANCESTORS DIDN'T GIVE A DAMN ABOUT BIRDS.
I WON'T LET 'EM LAY A FEATHER ON OUR ANCESTORS' RELICS.
I LEARNED THAT FROM THE RECORDS THEY LEFT.
BUT THESE THINGS CALLED CASSETTE TAPES...
...GAVE US KNOWL-EDGE.
...WE WERE LIKE THE OTHER APE-MEN. WE COULD BARELY SPEAK...
UNTIL WE FOUND THIS...

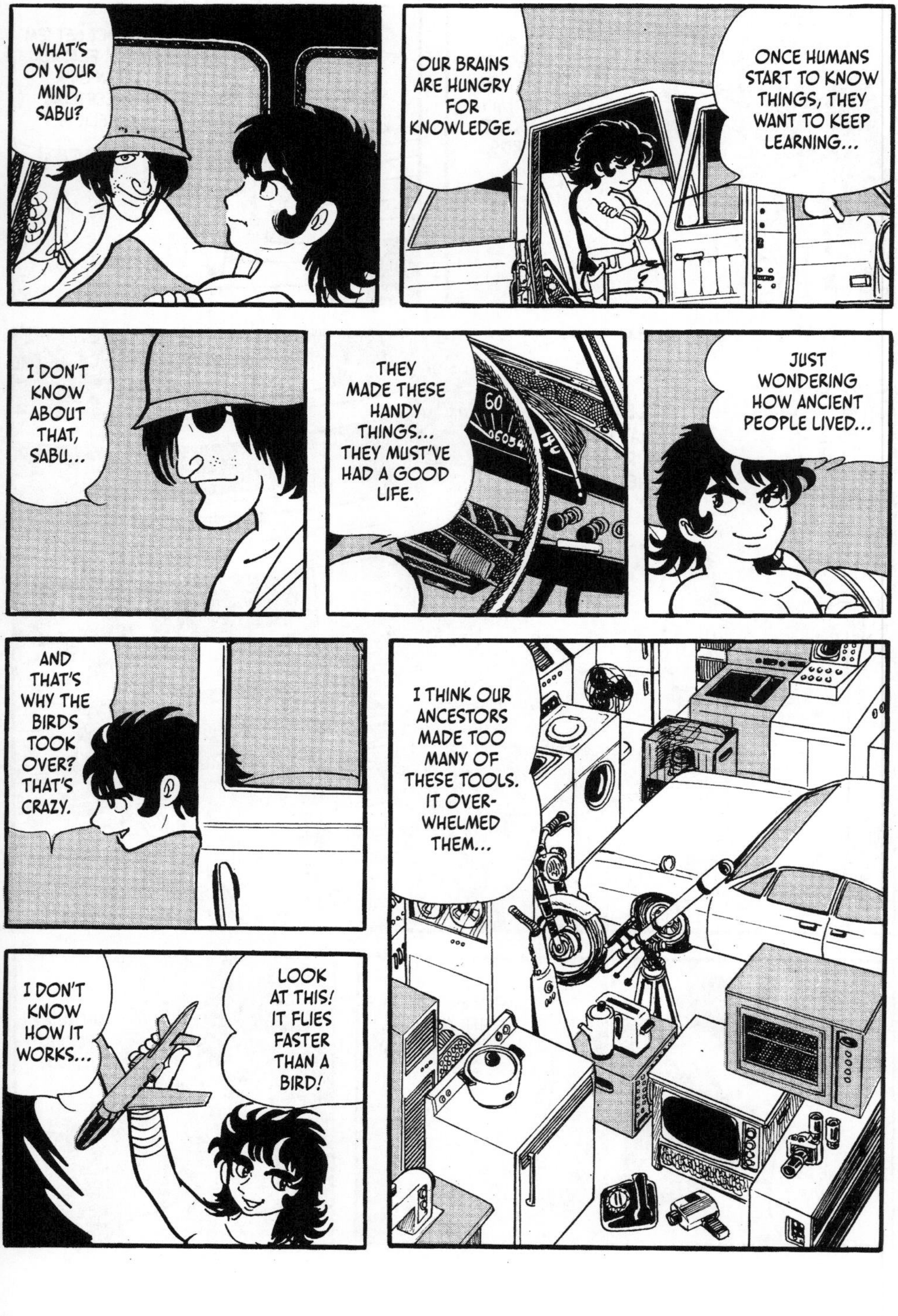
WHAT'S ON YOUR MIND, SABU?
OUR BRAINS ARE HUNGRY FOR KNOWLEDGE.
ONCE HUMANS START TO KNOW THINGS, THEY WANT TO KEEP LEARNING...
I DON'T KNOW ABOUT THAT, SABU...
THEY MADE THESE HANDY THINGS... THEY MUST'VE HAD A GOOD LIFE.
JUST WONDERING HOW ANCIENT PEOPLE LIVED...
AND THAT'S WHY THE BIRDS TOOK OVER? THAT'S CRAZY.
I THINK OUR ANCESTORS MADE TOO MANY OF THESE TOOLS. IT OVER-WHELMED THEM...
I DON'T KNOW HOW IT WORKS...
LOOK AT THIS! IT FLIES FASTER THAN A BIRD!

OUR ANCESTORS MADE THIS. HOW COULD THEY LOSE TO BIRDS?
THIS BIRD WAS SNOOPING ON US.
TELL ME ABOUT THE ASSASSIN. IS HE FAMOUS?
BEGLER? HE'S AN OFFICIAL ELIMINATOR WITH 200 KILLS.
GOOD. NOW LET'S KILL HIM.
WAIT.
WE'LL SEND HIM BACK WITH A GIFT.
YOU'RE LETTING HIM GO?
TAKE THIS. GIVE IT TO THAT BEGLER GUY.
DON'T OPEN IT BEFORE THEN.
NOW GO!
THAT'S A BOMB. IT'LL GO OFF WHEN OPENED. *Heh heh.*

WHERE ARE THE APE-MEN I'M TO KILL?
IT CONTAINS MANY RELICS FROM THE APE-MEN'S ANCIENT CIVILIZATION.
THIS IS TRULY EXCITING.
THAT'S THE ANCIENT SITE.
?
WHAT'S INSIDE?
A VILLAGER MUST HAVE FOUND IT AT THE SITE.
STOP!
WHO BROUGHT THIS?
THIS IS ONE OF THE RELICS!
HE LEFT IN A HURRY.
SOMEONE FROM THE VILLAGE BROUGHT THIS.
HMM.

PULL ON THIS.
I DON'T LIKE THIS.
DON'T OPEN IT.
GWABOOOOM
THAT WAS CLOSE. WE ALL WOULD'VE DIED...

IT'S COMING OUR WAY.
NOPE... I SEE A BLACK BIRD FLYING.
THEY'RE YAKITORI NOW.
THEY FELL FOR IT! SUCKERS!
I'LL SLAUGHTER YOU RIGHT NOW!
SHUT UP, YOU THIEF!
LOOK OUT, SABU!
Rrgh.
I'M BEGLER. I KNOW YOU'VE HEARD OF ME.
LISTEN, APE-MEN! IF YOU HAVE ANY PRIDE, FIGHT FAIR!
WHO WANTS TO DIE FIRST? TAKE ALL THE TIME YOU NEED.

SABU!

Heh heh heh. TOSS THAT FIRE STICK.
TOSS IT!
IF YOU DON'T, I'LL TEAR HIM IN TWO!
GOOD. NOW WALK.
AS PROMISED, I WON'T TEAR YOU APART.
BUT EITHER WAY, YOU'RE GOING TO DIE.
GET READY TO FLY OFF THIS CLIFF!
IF YOU WERE A BIRD, YOU COULD FLY TO SAFETY. BUT A WINGLESS APE-MAN WILL FALL 500 FUDELIN ONTO THE BEDROCK.
ICHI!

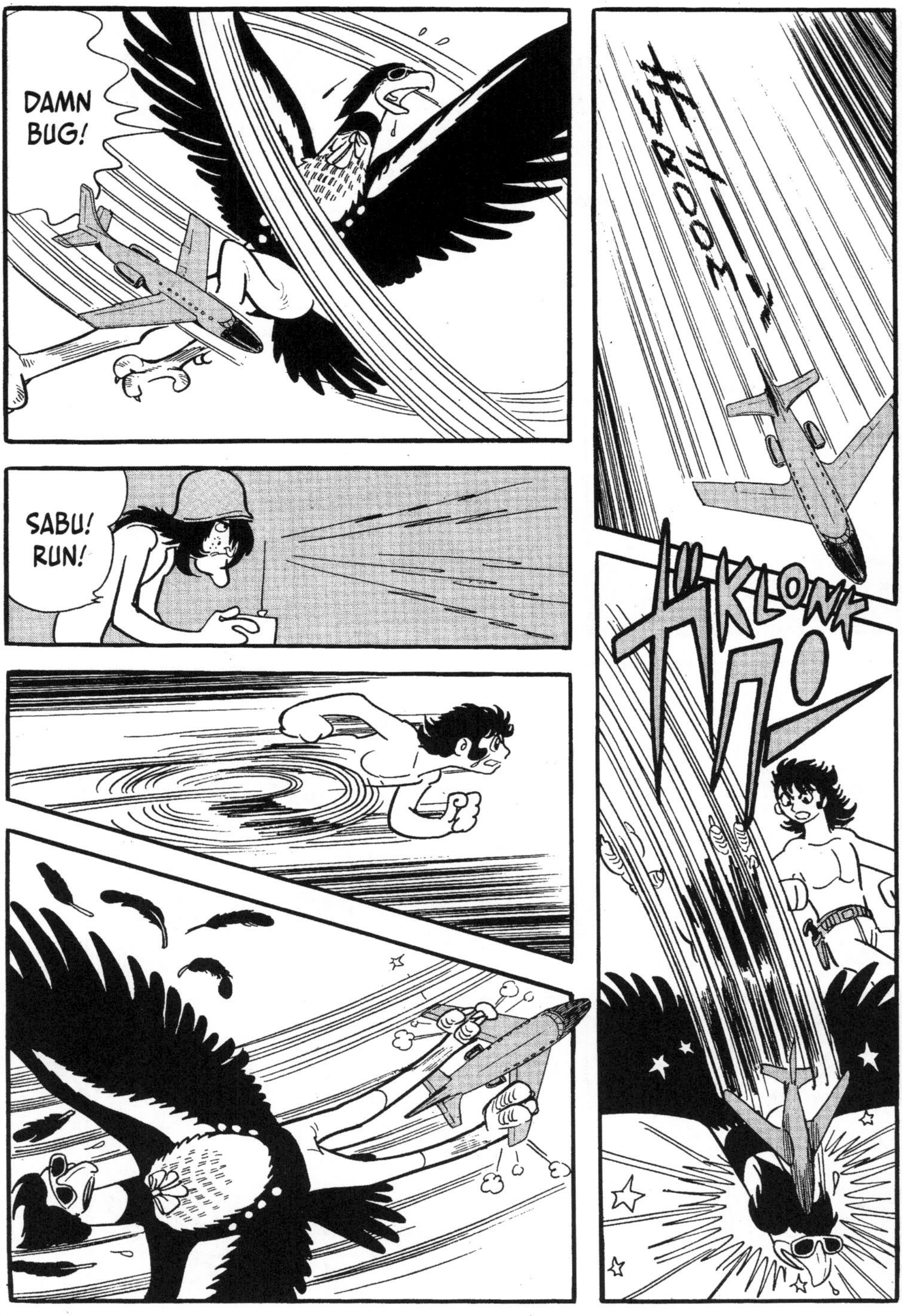
DAMN BUG!
SWOOSH
SABU! RUN!
KLONK

WHAT?! THAT THING ATTACKED ME!
YOU'VE COST US AN IMPORTANT STUDY PIECE, BEGLER.
A MAN-MADE TOOL. AN APE-MAN MUST'VE MADE IT.
WHAT'S YOUR PLAN?! SOME OLD-FASHIONED DUEL?
YOUR METHODS ARE HALF-ASSED!
WANT ME TO GET RID OF 'EM? MISS ME WITH THE ANNOYING REQUESTS.
MY ORDERS WERE TO KILL HUMANS. I'VE GOT NO TIME FOR THIS JUNK.
DON'T CHALLENGE THEM TO A DUAL. JUST JUMP INTO THAT NEST AND SLAUGHTER THEM!
KILLING IS AN ART. AND A RITUAL.
I'M A PROFESSIONAL. DON'T CONFUSE ME FOR SOME WANNABE HITMAN!
THEY MIGHT END IT ALL WITH AN EXPLOSION. THE RELICS WOULD BE LOST!
...THEM TO FEEL CORNERED.
I DON'T WANT...

WHATEVER YOU DO, KILL ALL THREE OF 'EM TOMORROW.
FINE.
AFTER ALL, YOU'RE MY CLIENT.
LISTEN CAREFULLY, DESCENDANTS. YOU'VE OPENED A TIME CAPSULE LEFT BY YOUR ANCESTORS.
IF YOU'RE STILL THE LORDS OF CREATION, WE CONGRATULATE YOU.
BUT YOU'RE PROBABLY IN A MESS, IN DECLINE. CIVILIZATION IS ENDING, RIGHT?

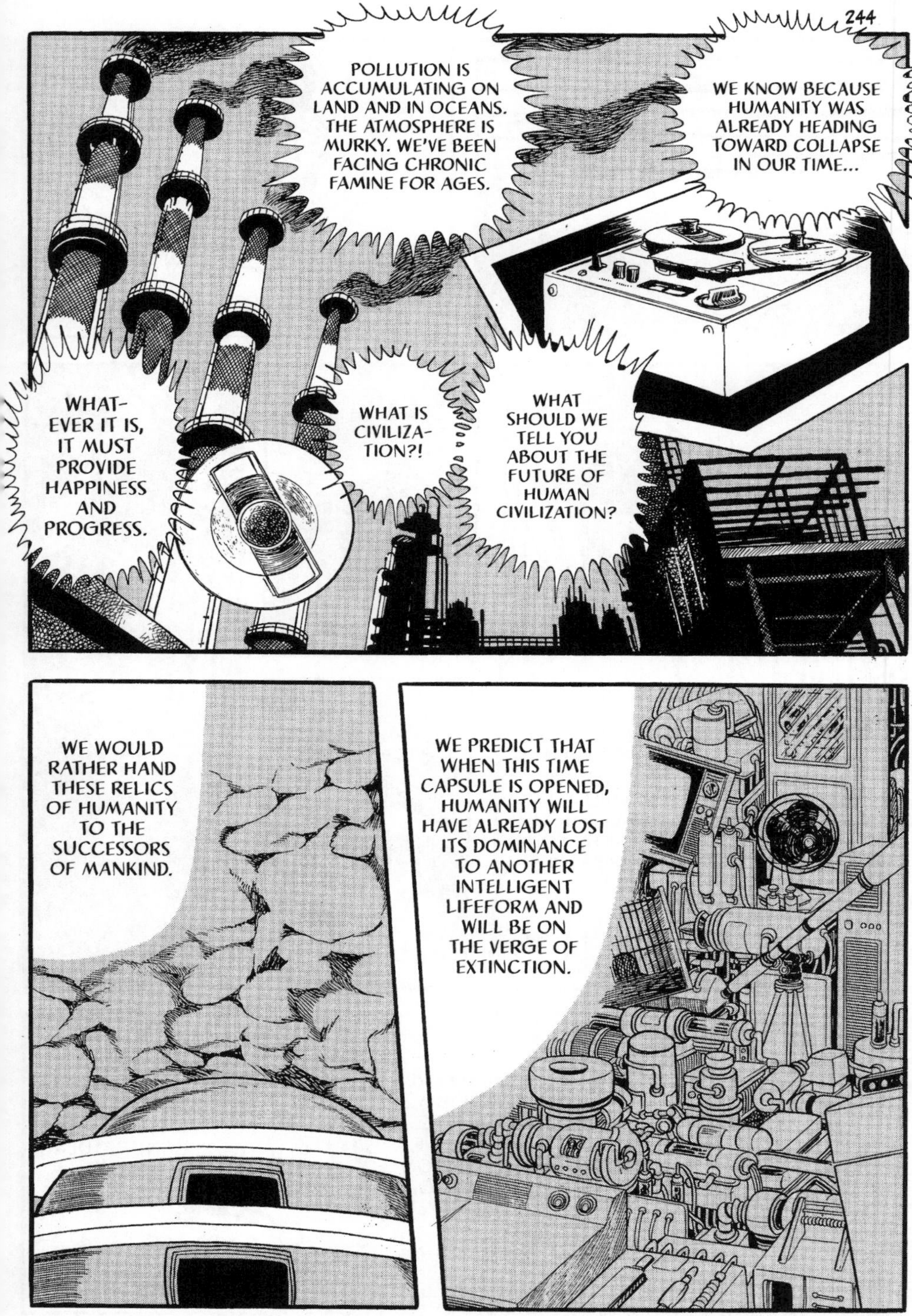
POLLUTION IS ACCUMULATING ON LAND AND IN OCEANS. THE ATMOSPHERE IS MURKY. WE'VE BEEN FACING CHRONIC FAMINE FOR AGES.
WE KNOW BECAUSE HUMANITY WAS ALREADY HEADING TOWARD COLLAPSE IN OUR TIME...
WHAT SHOULD WE TELL YOU ABOUT THE FUTURE OF HUMAN CIVILIZATION?
WHAT IS CIVILIZA-TION?!
WHAT-EVER IT IS, IT MUST PROVIDE HAPPINESS AND PROGRESS.
WE PREDICT THAT WHEN THIS TIME CAPSULE IS OPENED, HUMANITY WILL HAVE ALREADY LOST ITS DOMINANCE TO ANOTHER INTELLIGENT LIFEFORM AND WILL BE ON THE VERGE OF EXTINCTION.
WE WOULD RATHER HAND THESE RELICS OF HUMANITY TO THE SUCCESSORS OF MANKIND.

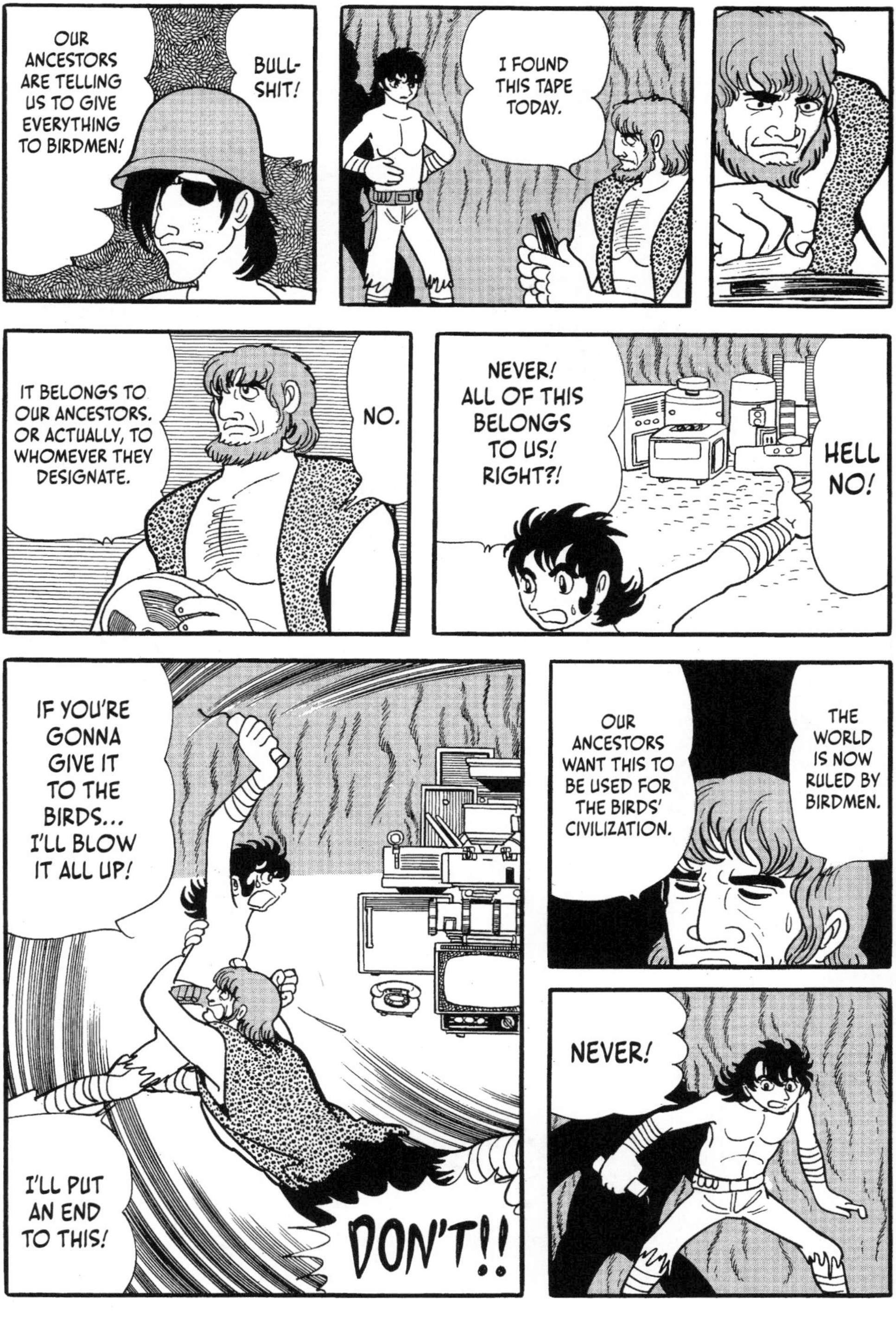
OUR ANCESTORS ARE TELLING US TO GIVE EVERYTHING TO BIRDMEN!
BULL-SHIT!
I FOUND THIS TAPE TODAY.
IT BELONGS TO OUR ANCESTORS. OR ACTUALLY, TO WHOMEVER THEY DESIGNATE.
NO.
NEVER! ALL OF THIS BELONGS TO US! RIGHT?!
HELL NO!
THE WORLD IS NOW RULED BY BIRDMEN.
OUR ANCESTORS WANT THIS TO BE USED FOR THE BIRDS' CIVILIZATION.
NEVER!
IF YOU'RE GONNA GIVE IT TO THE BIRDS... I'LL BLOW IT ALL UP!
I'LL PUT AN END TO THIS!
DON'T!!

HEAR ME OUT, SABU. WE'RE NOT GIVING THIS STUFF TO THE BIRDS AS PART OF A SURRENDER.
WE'RE GOING TO TEST THEM! SEE WHAT THEY DO WITH IT!
SETTLE DOWN!
GET A HOLD OF YOURSELF!
LISTEN TO ME.

YOU HEARD THAT TAPE. IT SAID OUR ANCESTORS STARTED MAKING ALL OF THESE THINGS, AND WHAT'S MORE, THEY WENT EXTINCT.
IF THAT'S TRUE, THEN ONCE THE BIRDS START USING THIS, THEY'LL ALSO FACE THEIR END.
WE'LL GET TO SEE HOW THEY COLLAPSE. NOT BAD, RIGHT?
WE WON'T LIVE TO SEE IT.
OF COURSE NOT. BUT IF BIRDMEN SUCCEED HUMAN CULTURE...
...THEY'RE GOING TO MAKE A LOT OF SILLY MISTAKES. I CAN'T WAIT!
WHAT DO YOU THINK?
SOUNDS GOOD...
THAT SETTLES IT. WE'LL HAND IT OVER TOMORROW.
SABU... GO TO SLEEP.
HEY...
WHAT?

I'M NOT OKAY WITH THIS.
WHY DID ICHI CHANGE HIS MIND SO FAST?
HE'S NOT LIKE US. HE THINKS DEEPLY.
HEARING THAT TAPE MADE HIM DISTRESSED. I SAW IT HAPPEN.
I'D NEVER SEEN HIM BAWL LIKE THAT.
BUT EVENTUALLY, HE REALIZED SOMETHING... HE FIGURED IT ALL OUT.
LET'S TAKE THAT TREASURE AND RUN.
FUCK NO! HOW WOULD WE CARRY ALL THAT STUFF?
I HAVE AN IDEA... WE'LL GIVE IT TO THE BIRDS...
...FOLLOW THEM, THEN TAKE IT BACK! WE COULD EVEN FORCE THEM TO TRANSPORT IT SOMEWHERE!
IF WE WORK TOGETHER, WE CAN FOOL THEM. WHAT DO YOU SAY?
Heh, I LIKE IT!
HAND IT OVER AND TAKE IT BACK... LET'S DO IT!

COME. I'LL GIVE YOU THE TREASURE. WE WON'T DO ANY-THING.
NOT SURREN-DERING, BUT I CHANGED MY MIND!
BE CAREFUL, BEGLER. WHAT ARE THEY TRYING TO PULL?
THAT HUMAN IS WAVING A STRANGE FLAG.
DOESN'T THAT MEAN THEY WANT A TRUCE?
ANCESTORS' LAST WORDS.
YOU'RE HANDING OVER ALL OF IT?
WHAT? WHY'D YOU CHANGE YOUR MIND?
Hmph! WHAT-EVER...
I DIDN'T THINK I'D GET MY HANDS ON THESE SO EASILY.
SIMPLY MIRACU-LOUS!
STUDYING ALL OF THIS COULD TAKE A LIFETIME...
FANTASTIC! THIS IS THE GREATEST DISCOVERY OF THE CENTURY!

I KNOW WHAT THEY'RE PLOTTING, PROFESSOR DENGLE.
DON'T TRUST THEM. LET'S KILL!
SILENCE, BEGLER!
THESE HUMANS ARE COOPERATING. NO NEED FOR SENSELESS VIOLENCE.
HEY, LISTEN!
THEY'RE GOING TO STEAL IT ALL BACK!
I WOULD NEVER!
CUT THE CRAP! I HEARD YOUR PLAN LAST NIGHT.
FROM THOSE TWO!
THEY'RE GOING TO FORCE YOU TO MOVE THE STUFF SOMEWHERE.
YOU BETRAYED ME, SABU?
DROP YOUR WEAP-ONS.
ICHI...

WHY ARE YOU DOING THIS? DAMN IT...
SCREW YOU, ICHI!
YOU'RE JUST GOING TO HAVE TO SIT STILL.
PRETTY IMPRESSIVE MORALS AND INTELLECT FOR A HUMAN.
ONCE I ESCORT YOU TO SAFETY, I'LL COME BACK AND UNTIE THEM.
WHY ARE YOU BEING SO COOPERATIVE NOW?
THERE'S NO POINT TRYING TO FIGHT HOW THINGS ARE.
OUR GLORY DAYS ARE IN THE PAST.
GLORY DAYS?
OF MON-KEYS...
NO WINGS OR TALONS... YOU APE-MEN CRAWLED ON THE GROUND, SCAVENGING... YOU HAVE NO IDEA WHAT GLORY IS.
HOW DARE YOU INSULT OUR ANCESTORS?! NEVER DO THAT AGAIN!

I'LL SAY IT AGAIN AND AGAIN! APE-MAN GLORY, MY ASS!
BEGLER... BOTH OF YOU! STOP!
BASTARD!
GWAAAA
WHAT'S THE MATTER WITH YOU?!
FINALLY! KILLING TIME!
D-DAMN... SCREW THIS!
CATCH 'EM, SABU!
I'LL CHECK ON ICHI.

YOU'RE FIRED, BEGLER!
FIRED?!
WHAT ABOUT YOUR CONTRACT WITH UNDERDANS?! YOU'RE GOING TO BREACH IT?!
IT SAYS HERE "IF ASSASSIN COMMITS ANY ACT THAT MARKEDLY HARMS CLIENT'S INTERESTS, ASSASSIN IS LIABLE FOR DAMAGE COMPENSATION."
WHAT?! OVER SOME LOWLY APE-MEN?!

THE JOB IS CANCELED. YOU HAVE NO MORE OBLIGATIONS. GOODBYE.
THIS MALE IS NOT AN ENEMY. HE WAS CO-OPERATING.
I WAS GOING TO TAKE HIM HOME AND PUT HIM IN CHARGE OF MY LIVE-STOCK.
SUIT YOURSELF. WE'RE NO LONGER RESPONSIBLE FOR YOUR ACTIONS.
THIS APE-MAN IS COMING WITH ME. HE CAN'T CARRY ANYTHING FOR YOU ANYWAY.
FAREWELL!!
THE JOB ISN'T DONE.
I'M STILL A CLASS 1 ELIMI-NATOR.
I WILL KILL!
NOW THEN...

YOU'RE ONE HELL OF A CLEVER BEAST.
I KNEW YOUR PLAN.
THEY REFUSE TO UNDER-STAND ANYTHING.
THOSE STUBBORN, THICK-HEADED GEEZERS...
THAT'S WHY YOU TIED UP YOUR BROTHERS AND LEFT THEM THERE.
YOU WERE GONNA DIE, HUH?
I COULD FIGURE OUT THAT MUCH...
YOU WERE GOING TO SET IT OFF ONCE WE REACHED OUR CITY. TENS OF THOUSANDS DEAD, RIGHT?
THE MACHINE ON YOUR BACK... THAT GENERATES SOME KIND OF TREMENDOUS ENERGY, RIGHT?
SO, YOU'RE A NINJA? YOU HAVE SPECIAL POWERS?

Shh! THAT'S HIM!
DAMN IT!
AND ICHI! HIS EYES ARE GOUGED...
KILLING IS ALL I LIVE FOR.

I'LL GO FIRST. IF I DIE...
...YOU KILL HIM, SABU.
THE OTHER TWO HAVE PROBABLY BROKEN FREE. THEY'LL CATCH UP ANY TIME NOW.
OR MAYBE THEY'VE ALREADY SPOTTED ME.
I WON'T HIDE. I'LL TAKE THEM ON, AND YOU CAN WATCH.
I'LL KILL 'EM BOTH!
AND THEN IT'LL BE YOUR TURN.

?
KCHK
Heh...
FEATHERS.
FUCKING BIRD
HAS NO CLUE
HOW TO
HIDE.

AAAH!
BANG
BANG
BANG
ONE DOWN !!
Rrgh.
?
I'LL FEED HIS HEAD TO THE DOGS!
FUCKER ...
SHIT...
JIRO!

COME OUT AND FACE ME! I'LL MAKE YOU PAY FOR WHAT YOU DID TO MY BROTHER!
FILTHY, BEAKED PIECE OF SHIT!
WHAT'S THE MATTER?! AFRAID TO DUEL?! PECKING AT THE GUTS OF A CORPSE IS ALL YOU'RE GOOD AT!
SCARED OF THIS FIRE STICK, AREN'T YOU?!

Heh heh... FINALLY. I'LL FINISH HIM WITH ONE SHOT.
DAMN IT! HE LIT THE DRY GRASS ON FIRE...
POOF
BANG BANG
BANG

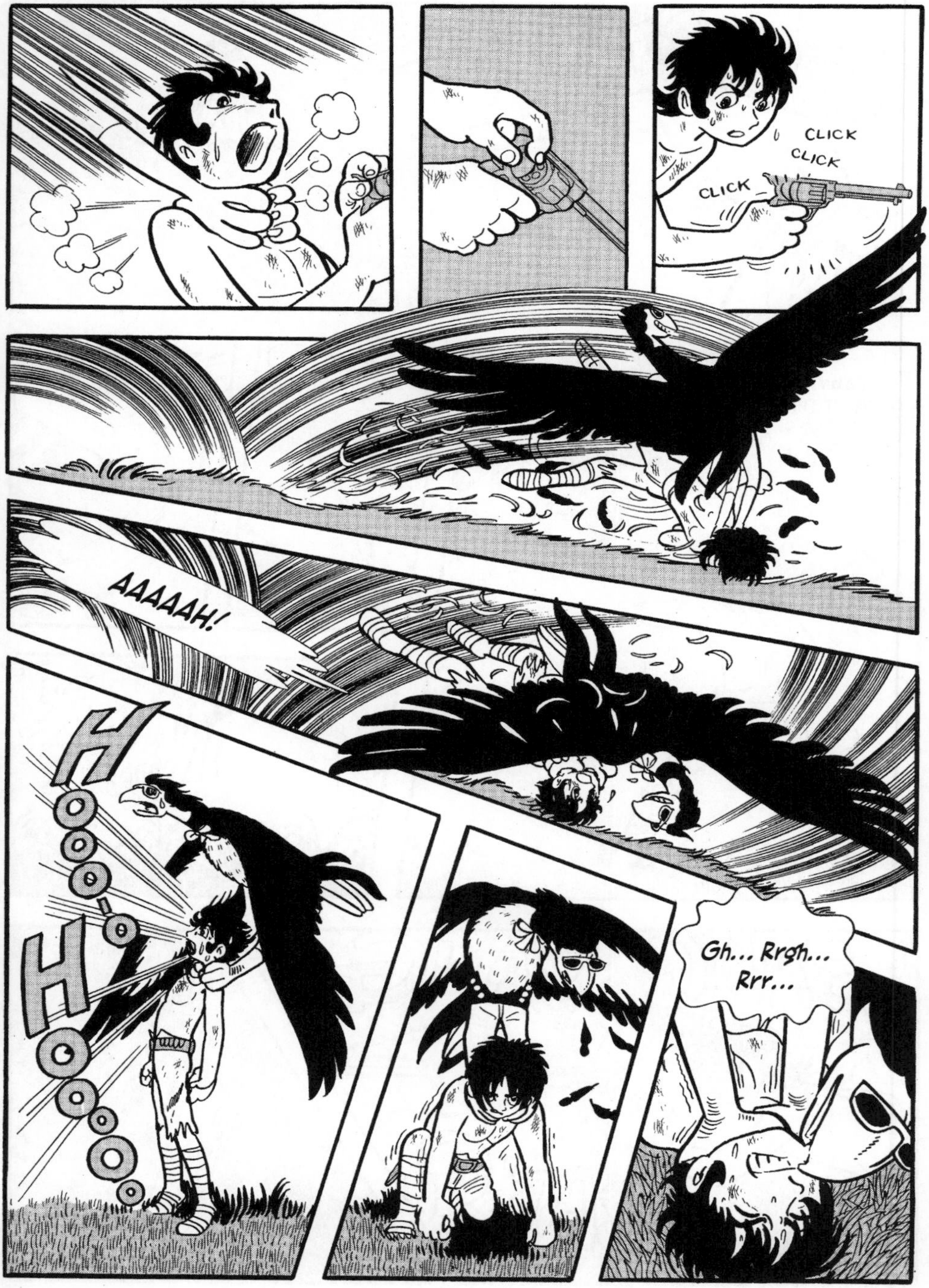
CLICK
CLICK
CLICK
AAAAAH!
HOOOO-O-HOOOOOO
Gh... Rrgh... Rrr...

HOOOO
HOOOO
HOOo-o
HOooo-o
AAAH!!
がっくり
SLUMP
YOU DID IT... ICHI...
S... SABU ...

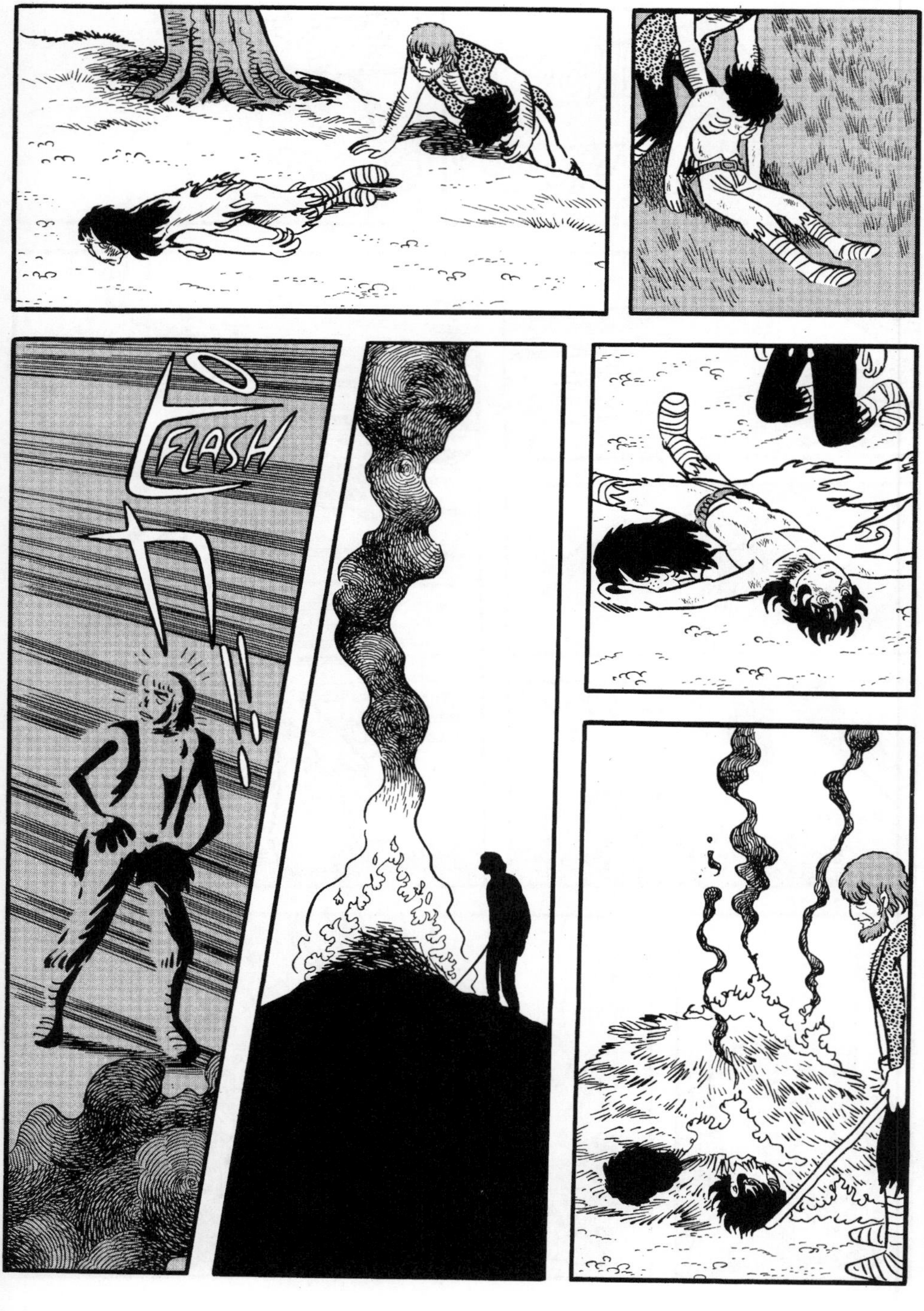
FLASH

B-B-B-B-BOOOOOM
JIRO... SABU... LOOK! ONE OF THOSE MACHINES WAS SOMETHING CALLED A NUCLEAR WEAPON. IT MUST HAVE BURST IN THE CENTER OF A BIRDMAN TOWN. THIS MEANS ALL OF OUR ANCESTORS' RELICS ARE GONE...
BIRDMEN MUST HAVE BEEN FIDDLING AROUND... THEY SET OFF THE DETONATION DEVICE. THEY FUCKED UP. JUST LIKE I KNEW THEY WOULD.
YOU'RE RIGHT... YOU SAW IT COMING...
B-BIRDMEN SCHOLARS AND POLITICIANS ARE FOOLS... THEY'RE JUST GOING TO REPEAT THE MISTAKES THAT HUMANS MADE...

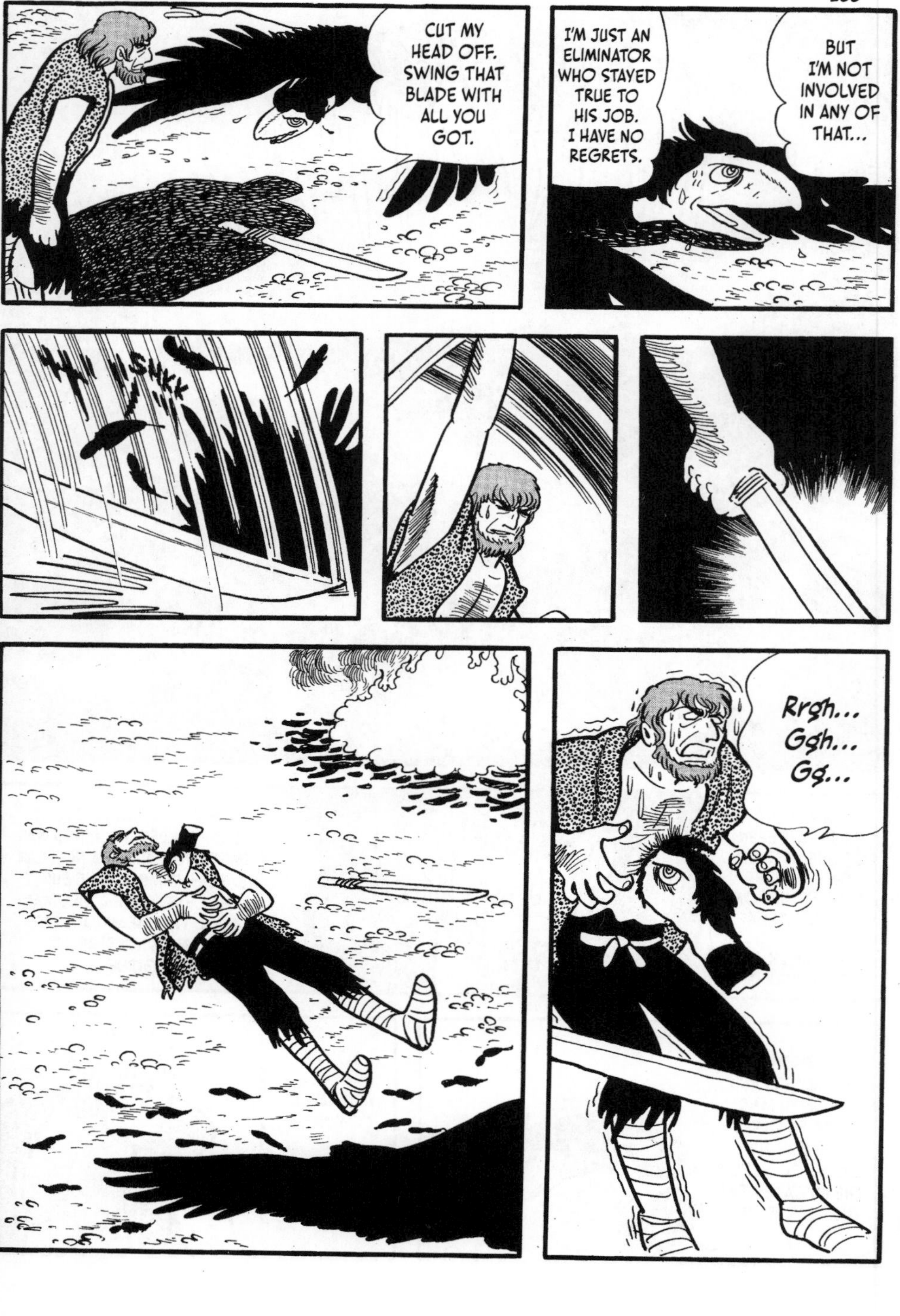
CUT MY HEAD OFF. SWING THAT BLADE WITH ALL YOU GOT.
BUT I'M NOT INVOLVED IN ANY OF THAT...
I'M JUST AN ELIMINATOR WHO STAYED TRUE TO HIS JOB. I HAVE NO REGRETS.
SHKK
Rrgh... Ggh... Gg...

CHAPTER 15: THE RED BEAK PARTY

I'LL TAKE ONE TEKA'S WORTH OF CLACARIA BERRIES AND FOUR PLUSS' WORTH OF POCHIRULUS BUDS.
MA'AM, WE'VE JUST ACQUIRED A NEW OVULATION SUPPRESSANT MADE OF SUDODORA MIXED WITH BRAN.
WON'T IT CAUSE DEFORMITY WHEN I EVENTUALLY LAY EGGS?
IT HAS NO SUCH SIDE EFFECTS. I ASSURE YOU.

PAY HIM.
HOW WOULD YOU LIKE TO PAY?
THEN GIVE ME ONE PLUSS' WORTH. IF I LIKE IT, I'LL ORDER MORE.
YES, MA'AM.
MA'AM... TAKE THE REAR EXIT.
!
A MARVELOUS EGG!
Heh heh heh heh
THERE'S NO NEED TO SNEAK OUT, MA'AM. YOU CAN USE THE MAIN ENTRANCE.
WE JUST NEED YOU TO COOPERATE WITH OUR POLICE INVESTIGATION FIRST.
GASP!

SHOW ME THE EGG THIS LADY GAVE YOU.
SHOW IT TO ME, DARK.
S-SHOW YOU WHAT, SIR?
KNOCK IT OFF.
MA'AM, WE KNOW THAT DARK SELLS OVULATION SUPPRESSANTS TO LADIES OF THE PROPERTIED CLASS.
THAT'S ILLEGAL, BUT LET'S FORGET ABOUT THAT FOR NOW.
B-BUT MY SHOP WOULD NEVER ACCEPT EGGS AS PAYMENT...
HOW CAN YOU ACCUSE ME OF THAT?!
THE REAL PROBLEM IS THAT HE COLLECTS EGGS AS PAYMENT. THE FERTILIZED ONES ARE DELIVERED TO A SECRET ORGANIZATION. EVENTUALLY, CHICKS ARE BORN.
WHAT DO YOU THINK HAPPENS TO THOSE ORPHAN CHICKS?
THEY'RE USED AS FOOD! THEY LINE THE DINNER TABLES OF CARNIVORES!
N-NO WAY!
I'M AN UPSTANDING CITIZEN. I WOULD NEVER DO SUCH A...

SOME CARNIVORES ATTACK AND DEVOUR THEIR COMPATRIOTS. IT'S A SERIOUS CRIME! PUNISHABLE BY DEATH UNDER THE LAW. BUT CARNIVORES GET NO SATISFACTION FROM EATING BEASTS AND INSECTS. THE URGE TO MAKE BLOOD SACRIFICES OF THEIR OWN KIND IS TOO STRONG TO RESIST.
SO THEY DEVISE CLEVER MEANS TO OBTAIN SACRIFICIAL VICTIMS AND SATISFY THEIR DESIRE TO INFLICT CRUELTY. FOR EXAMPLE, ONE SECRET ORGANIZATION CALLED THE RED BEAK PARTY ACQUIRES EGGS OF A CERTAIN SPECIES CONSIDERED TO BE PARTICULARLY DELICIOUS. THEY HATCH THE EGGS AND RAISE THE CHICKS AS FOOD. WE MUST PUT AN END TO SUCH BARBARIC PRACTICES!

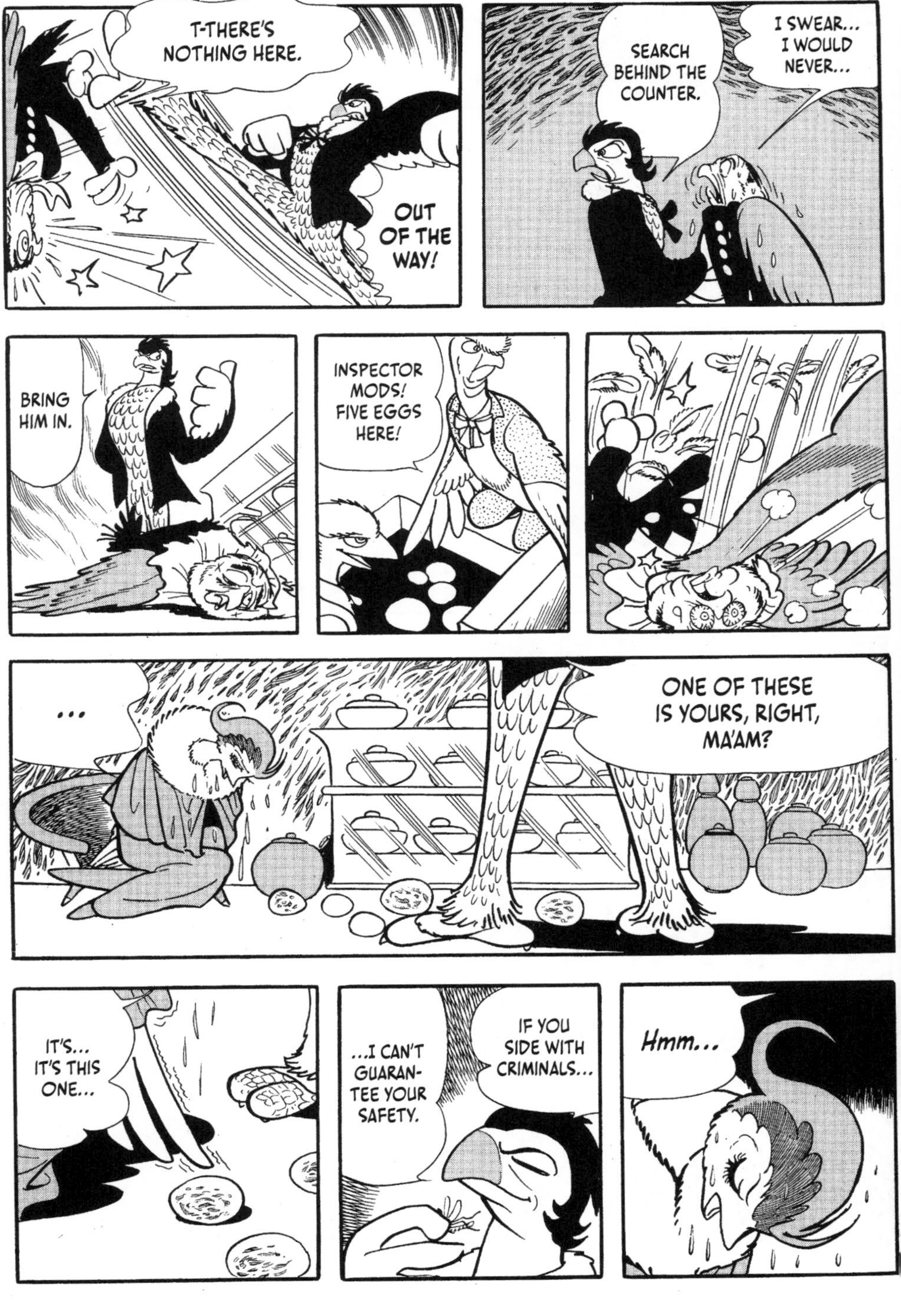
T-THERE'S NOTHING HERE.
OUT OF THE WAY!
SEARCH BEHIND THE COUNTER.
I SWEAR... I WOULD NEVER...
BRING HIM IN.
INSPECTOR MODS! FIVE EGGS HERE!
...
ONE OF THESE IS YOURS, RIGHT, MA'AM?
IT'S... IT'S THIS ONE...
IF YOU SIDE WITH CRIMINALS...
...I CAN'T GUARANTEE YOUR SAFETY.
Hmm...

GOOD GRIEF...
WILL THAT PHARMACIST CONFESS ABOUT THE RED BEAK PARTY?
PROBABLY NOT. IT'LL TAKE MORE THAN THAT TO CRACK THAT ORGANI-ZATION.
THEY'RE CANNIBALS! HOW CAN SUCH A BARBARIC CRIME GO UNPUNISHED?! OUR WORLD IS EVEN LOWER THAN THE APE-MEN'S!
BUT I'LL FIGURE OUT A WAY.
GOOD. AT SOME POINT, YOU'LL TESTIFY IN COURT. GIVE HIM YOUR NAME AND ADDRESS.
IF MY HUSBAND FINDS OUT ABOUT THIS EGG...
...I MADE WITH ANOTHER MALE... I'M FINISHED.
MA'AM, YOU ONLY HAVE YOURSELF TO BLAME.

HE'LL TALK BY TOMORROW.
BUT WE WON'T GET MUCH FROM HIM.
WHY DON'T YOU CONFESS? MAKE THINGS EASIER FOR YOURSELF.
I... I...
WHO'S THERE?!
CARNIVORES DO EXIST! EVEN IN THE POLICE...
DAMN!

I MISSED YOU, HONEY.
DO YOU WANT A DRINK BEFORE DINNER?
NO... I'LL EAT. NOT IN THE MOOD TO DRINK.
I HEAR I'M A MEAN DRUNK. DRINKING MAKES ME WANT TO STRANGLE THINGS WITH MY TALONS...
HOW ABOUT A TRIP OUT OF TOWN ON YOUR NEXT DAY OFF? GO HUNT SOME WILD MICE.

FRUSTRATION... YOU MIGHT BE RIGHT.
THEY SAID IT WAS GREAT FOR RELIEVING FRUSTRATION.
THE COUPLE ACROSS THE HALL WENT AND CAUGHT THIRTY SNAKES!
I HAD THE URGE TO POUNCE ON HER.
I SAW A LITTLE GIRL ON THE WAY HOME...
OUR FRUSTRATION IS NOT THE SEXUAL KIND. THAT'S THE PROBLEM...
!
OUR ANCESTORS WERE HAWKS AND KITES. THEIR FEROCITY RUNS IN OUR BLOOD. WE CAN'T ESCAPE IT.

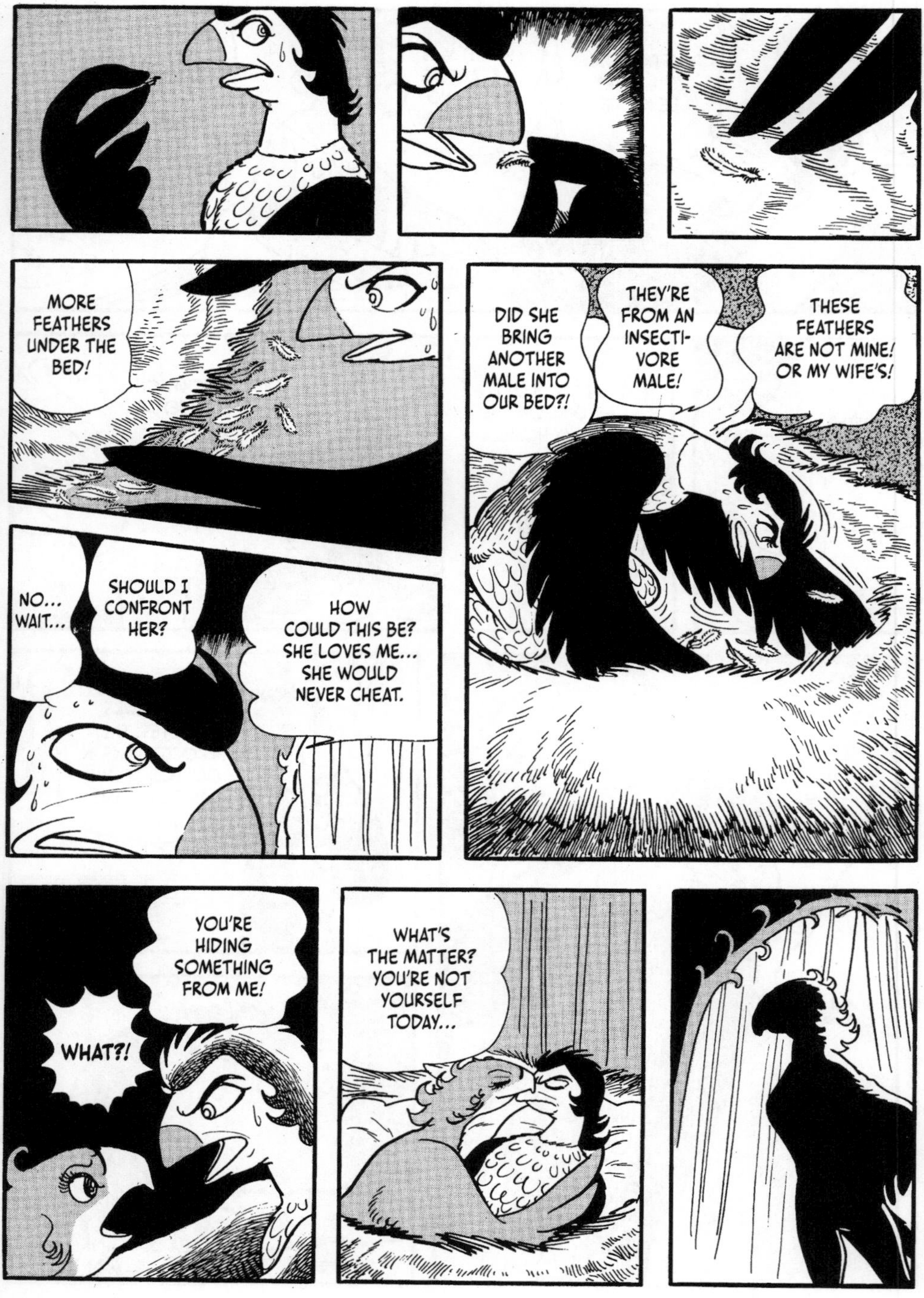
MORE FEATHERS UNDER THE BED!
THESE FEATHERS ARE NOT MINE! OR MY WIFE'S!
THEY'RE FROM AN INSECTIVORE MALE!
DID SHE BRING ANOTHER MALE INTO OUR BED?!
HOW COULD THIS BE? SHE LOVES ME... SHE WOULD NEVER CHEAT.
SHOULD I CONFRONT HER?
NO... WAIT...
WHAT'S THE MATTER? YOU'RE NOT YOURSELF TODAY...
YOU'RE HIDING SOMETHING FROM ME!
WHAT?!

YOU'RE GORGEOUS! IF YOU WANTED, YOU COULD CHARM ANY CARNIVORE MALE!
AND YET... YOU BROUGHT AN INSECT EATER IN HERE!
WHAT?! DON'T YOU SEE HOW MUCH I LONGED FOR YOU TO COME HOME?!
SOME OTHER MALE WAS IN THIS ROOM! WHILE I WAS OUT WORKING...AND YOU...!
TELL ME! WHOSE FEATHERS ARE THESE?! WHAT COLOR INSECTIVORE WAS HE?!
DON'T INTERROGATE ME!
IT'S TRUE... I HAD MR. PICONI OVER... FROM ACROSS THE HALL. BUT NOT FOR AN AFFAIR. IT WAS TO KILL HIM.
WHAT?!
I DIDN'T WANT YOU TO FIND OUT... EVERY TIME I'D SEE HIM, I HAD THIS URGE TO DEVOUR HIM.

YOU ATE HIM?! THOSE FEATHERS ARE WHAT'S LEFT OF HIS CORPSE?
W-WHY? HOW COULD YOU...
YOU'RE INSPECTOR MODS' WIFE!
I COULDN'T HELP IT...
EATING ANOTHER BIRD... YOU'LL GET THE DEATH PENALTY!
WELL, I'VE DONE WHAT I'VE DONE... IT'S TOO LATE NOW!
HELP ME, HONEY...
LISTEN, VENNE... THIS IS NOT THE DARK AGES. WE LIVE IN A CIVILIZED SOCIETY. INSECTIVORES AND CARNIVORES HAVE EQUAL RIGHTS.
LOOK AT MY BOSS... HE HAILS FROM A FAMILY OF THRUSHES.
WHAT THE HELL SHOULD I DO?! I HAVE TO HIDE THE EVIDENCE!
DID ANYONE SEE YOU BRING PICONI IN HERE?
OF COURSE NOT.
DISPOSE OF HIS FEATHERS! WHAT ABOUT BLOOD? ARE THERE ANY STAINS?

BURN IT, FOOL!
I WIPED THEM WITH THIS.
THINK ABOUT HOW TO DO THAT!
CAN YOU ACT LIKE YOU DON'T KNOW ANYTHING?
PICONI'S WIFE AND CHILDREN WILL MAKE A FUSS WHEN HE DOESN'T COME HOME.
NO! YOU EVIL HAG...
W-WHY DON'T WE JUST EAT THEM, TOO?
I... CAN'T...
YOU NEED AN ALIBI.
YOU'VE BEEN AWAY ON VACATION SINCE YESTERDAY.
SEND ME MAIL WHEN YOU GET THERE. DON'T COME BACK FOR A MONTH.
TAKE A VACATION! YEAH... DOESN'T MATTER WHERE. GO SOUTH. FLY AS FAR AWAY AS YOU CAN!
THAT'S CRAZY!

...
DAMN IT! HOW COULD SHE...?
KNOCK KNOCK
EXPRESS MAIL FROM AN UNKNOWN SENDER.
Inspector Mods, Release Dark immediately. Never involve yourself with the Red Beak Party again. Otherwise, we'll be forced to reveal that your wife is an official member of the Red Beak Party! Think about what would happen.

YOU'RE FREE TO GO.
INSPECTOR MODS! WHY DID YOU RELEASE HIM?! WE WERE SO CLOSE! HE MIGHT HAVE TOLD US EVERYTHING!
CHIEF, DARK IS A NOBODY.
NOW THAT HE'S FREE, HE COULD LEAD US TO SOMEONE IMPORTANT.
...

THESE'LL GROW BACK...
...IN THE AUTUMN.
YOU LOOK PITIFUL, DARK.
YIKES!
KNOW WHY MODS RELEASED YOU?
HUH?
WE MADE A DEAL. WITH THAT GUY RIGHT THERE.
FOOL.
NO... HE PROBABLY GAVE UP BECAUSE I WOULDN'T TALK.

I KNEW YOU'D COME, INSPECTOR.
INSPECTOR MODS!
WE HAVE A RARE GUEST. MAKE SURE TO TREAT HIM WELL.
DON'T WORRY. I'VE CLIPPED THEM.
ALLOW ME TO CHECK YOUR TALONS.
YES. THIS WAY, PLEASE.
I WANT TO MEET YOUR LEADER. MILLERS IS IN CHARGE OF THE RED BEAK PARTY IN THIS DISTRICT, RIGHT?
HOW DO YOU LIKE OUR STORAGE AREA? IMPRESSIVE, RIGHT?
SHUT UP! JUST TAKE ME TO HIM!

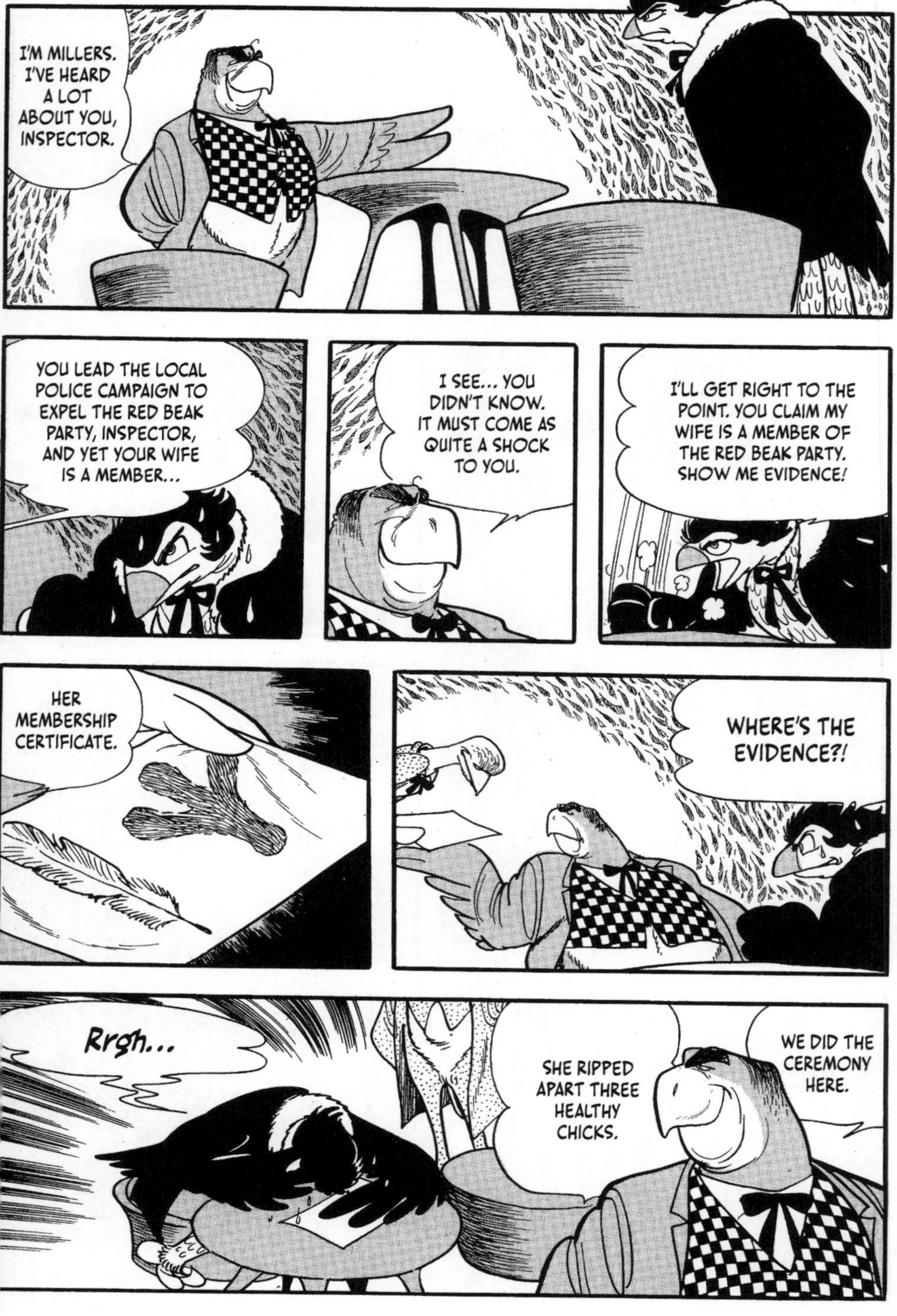
I'M MILLERS. I'VE HEARD A LOT ABOUT YOU, INSPECTOR.
YOU LEAD THE LOCAL POLICE CAMPAIGN TO EXPEL THE RED BEAK PARTY, INSPECTOR, AND YET YOUR WIFE IS A MEMBER...
I SEE... YOU DIDN'T KNOW. IT MUST COME AS QUITE A SHOCK TO YOU.
I'LL GET RIGHT TO THE POINT. YOU CLAIM MY WIFE IS A MEMBER OF THE RED BEAK PARTY. SHOW ME EVIDENCE!
HER MEMBERSHIP CERTIFICATE.
WHERE'S THE EVIDENCE?!
Rrgh...
WE DID THE CEREMONY HERE.
SHE RIPPED APART THREE HEALTHY CHICKS.

THAT UNGRATEFUL MURDERER!
HOW COULD SHE DO THIS TO ME?!
AS LONG AS YOU TURN A BLIND EYE, WE'LL GUARANTEE YOUR STATUS AND YOUR WIFE'S SAFETY.
THEN HOW CAN I DO MY JOB?!
DON'T WORRY. YOU'LL HAVE PLENTY OF CRIMINALS TO CATCH.
THE DOMDAY GROUP.
DOM- DAY?
THE LEADER OF THE NORTHERN DISTRICT YOU'RE IN A TURF WAR WITH?
YES. UNFORTUNATELY, THE RED BEAK PARTY IS DEALING WITH SOME INTERNAL CONFLICT.
THE DOMDAY GROUP IS RADICAL... THEY'RE SO PROGRESSIVE, THEY DON'T EVEN THINK. THEY DISRUPT PARTY UNITY.
I'LL GIVE YOU UPDATES ABOUT DOMDAY. YOU CAN ARREST THEM ALL.
IT'LL MAKE YOU LOOK GOOD AT WORK, INSPECTOR.
FOR NOW, I'LL TELL YOU WHERE DOMDAY'S HIDEOUT IS.
JUST MAKE SURE YOU DON'T BETRAY US. IF YOU DO...

GOOD. LET'S SEAL OUR PACT.
FINE... I GIVE YOU MY WORD.
...WE'LL GO PUBLIC ABOUT YOUR WIFE, AND WE'LL EXPOSE YOU FOR DEALING WITH US, TOO.
YOU WANT ME TO EAT THAT CHICK?
WHAT'S GOING ON?!
SLAP
SLAP
DO IT. YOU'LL NEVER WANT TO STOP.
EEEEK!
CRAZY BIRDIAC!
DON'T DO THIS!
EATING PREY YOU'VE TORN APART YOURSELF... THERE'S NOTHING LIKE IT. *Heh heh!*
I CAN'T!
WE'VE RAISED HIM SINCE BEFORE HE HATCHED. HE HAS NO CITIZENSHIP. HE'S MEANT TO BE EATEN.

WHAT ARE YOU WAIT-ING FOR?
FANTASTIC! NOW EAT. THE INTESTINES ARE ESPECIALLY DELICIOUS.
SEVERAL DAYS LATER...
WHAT WILL YOU HAVE FOR LUNCH, INSPECTOR?
THE USUAL. STEW MADE OF BEANS AND STEAMED BARLEY.
MODS... YOUR NEIGHBOR PICONI'S WIFE HAS REPORTED HIM MISSING. YOU'RE FRIENDS, RIGHT? WANT TO TAKE THE CASE?
HE'S PROBABLY HAVING AN AFFAIR. H-HE'LL SHOW UP EVENTUALLY.

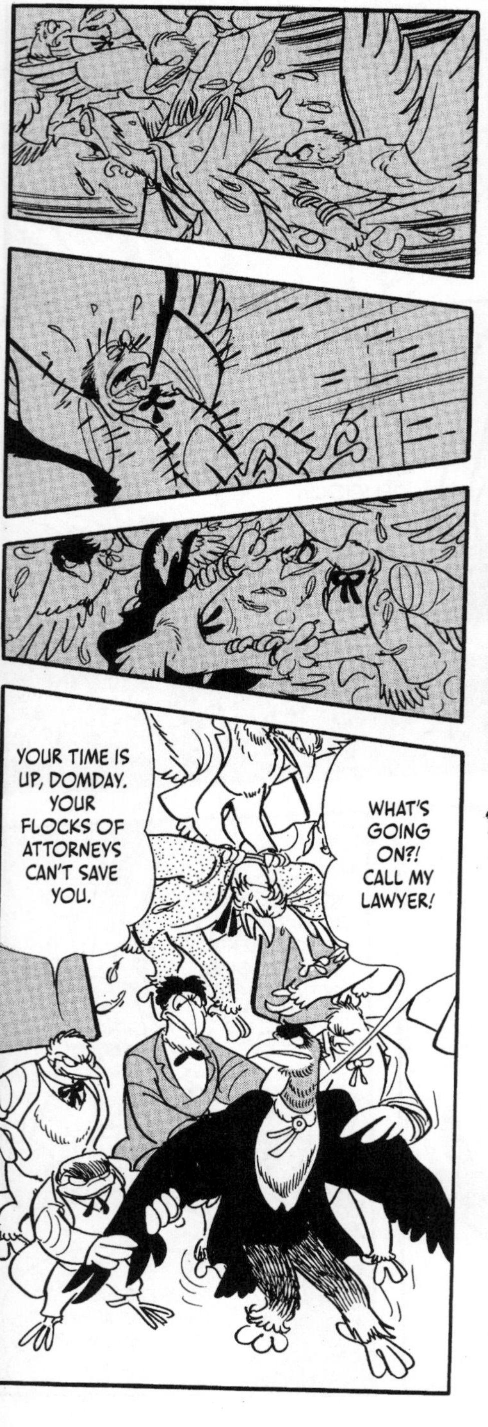
YOUR TIME IS UP, DOMDAY. YOUR FLOCKS OF ATTORNEYS CAN'T SAVE YOU.
WHAT'S GOING ON?! CALL MY LAWYER!

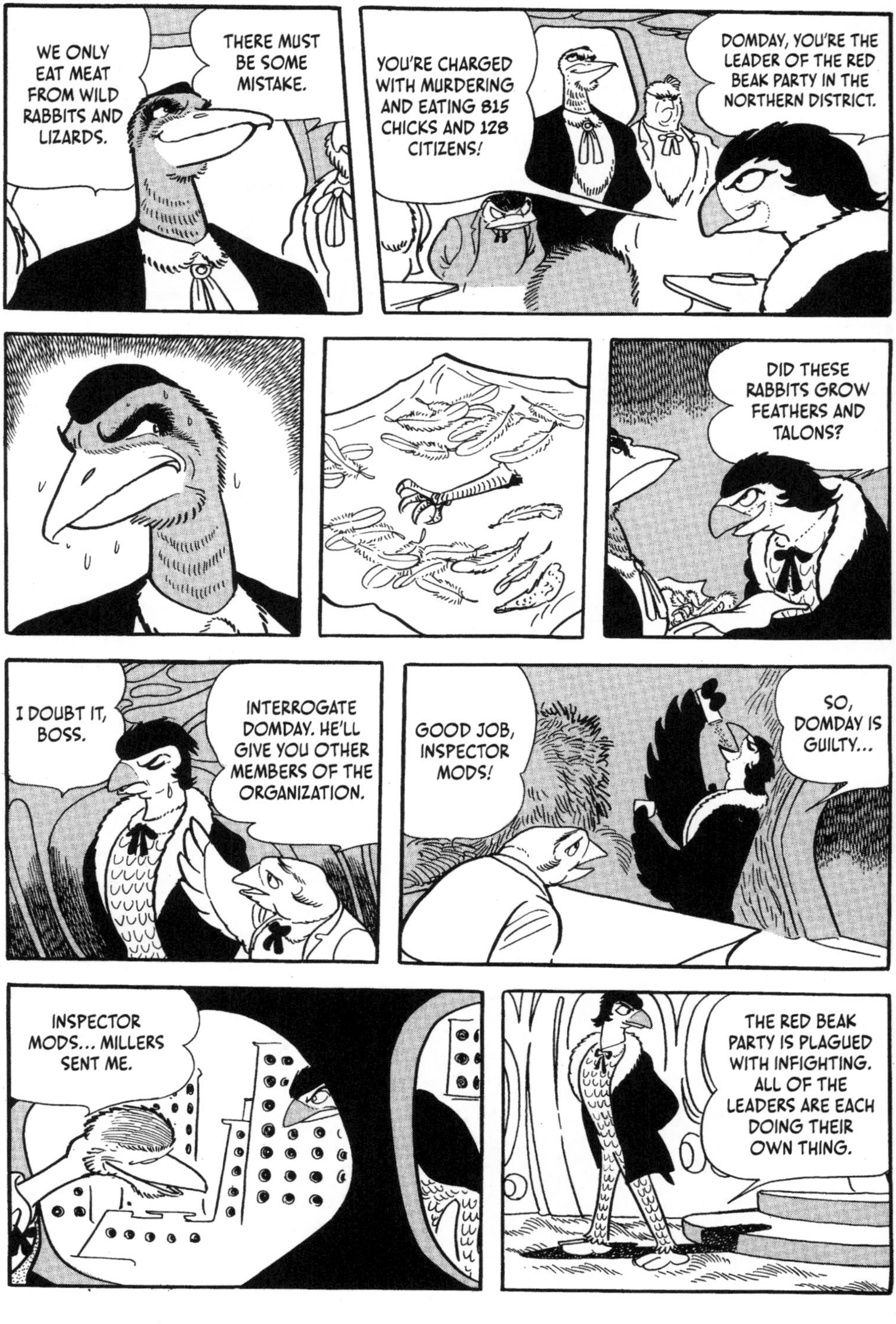
DOMDAY, YOU'RE THE LEADER OF THE RED BEAK PARTY IN THE NORTHERN DISTRICT.
YOU'RE CHARGED WITH MURDERING AND EATING 815 CHICKS AND 128 CITIZENS!
THERE MUST BE SOME MISTAKE.
WE ONLY EAT MEAT FROM WILD RABBITS AND LIZARDS.
DID THESE RABBITS GROW FEATHERS AND TALONS?
SO, DOMDAY IS GUILTY...
GOOD JOB, INSPECTOR MODS!
INTERROGATE DOMDAY. HE'LL GIVE YOU OTHER MEMBERS OF THE ORGANIZATION.
I DOUBT IT, BOSS.
THE RED BEAK PARTY IS PLAGUED WITH INFIGHTING. ALL OF THE LEADERS ARE EACH DOING THEIR OWN THING.
INSPECTOR MODS... MILLERS SENT ME.

IF SOMETHING HAPPENS AT THE CAMP SITE THREE DAYS FROM NOW... YOU'LL NEED TO LET IT SLIDE.
GIVE MILLERS MY REGARDS.
HE TOLD ME TO GIVE YOU THIS. IT'S ABOUT NORLON IN THE DISTRICT NORTH OF THE RIVER.
WHEN BIRDWOMEN WHO ARE ALREADY MOTHERS ARE ABOUT TO NEST, THEY PLACE THEIR CHILDREN IN VARIOUS CAMPS FOR EDUCATION AND MENTORSHIP.
THE CAMPS ARE SEVERAL HUNDREDS OF KILOMETERS AWAY. THE PRACTICE OF MAKING THE FLIGHT WITHOUT RESTING WAS A REMNANT OF AN ANCIENT CUSTOM CALLED "MIGRATION."
HATCHING EGGS AND EATING CHICKS WAS NO LONGER ENOUGH TO SATISFY THE CARNIVORES.
MILLERS AND HIS GROUP HAD DECIDED TO RAID THE CAMPS FOR MORE CHICKS.

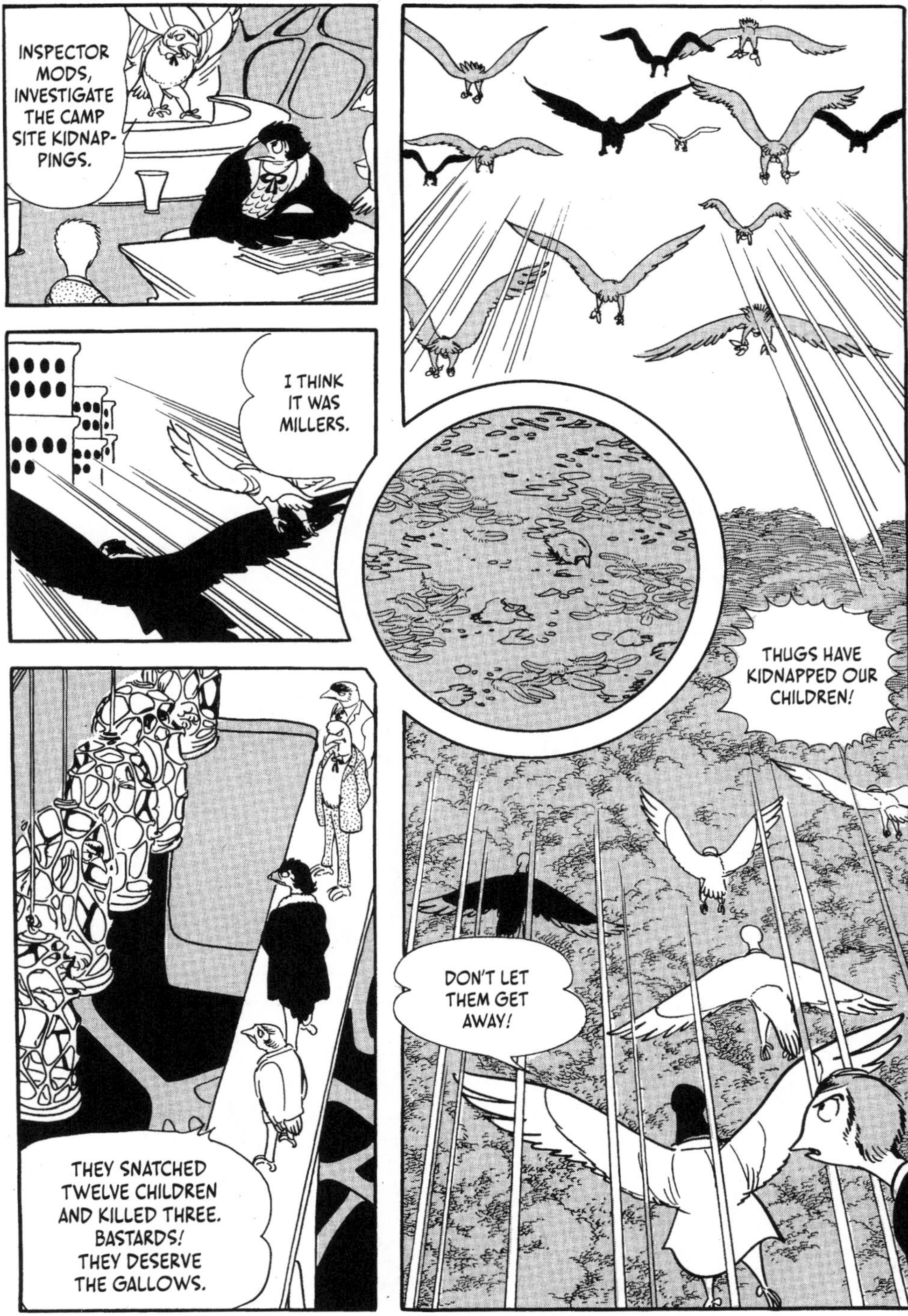
INSPECTOR MODS, INVESTIGATE THE CAMP SITE KIDNAPPINGS.
I THINK IT WAS MILLERS.
THEY SNATCHED TWELVE CHILDREN AND KILLED THREE. BASTARDS! THEY DESERVE THE GALLOWS.
THUGS HAVE KIDNAPPED OUR CHILDREN!
DON'T LET THEM GET AWAY!

WHO IS THAT BIRDWOMAN? YOU KNOW HER?
N-NO... NEVER SEEN HER BEFORE.
I SEE... WE'LL MAKE HER CONFESS EVENTUALLY.
VENNE!!
HONEY...
INSPECTOR...
OUR BOSS WANTS TO SEE YOU.
WHY IS VENNE ...?
DUMB BITCH!
I TOLD HER TO FLY FAR AWAY...
...BUT SHE JOINED THE RAID ON THE CAMP!

YOU KNOW WHAT THIS MEANS, INSPECTOR...
SHE'S A MEMBER OF THE PARTY. WHY WOULDN'T SHE BE THERE?
WHY'D YOU SEND OFFICERS TO THE CAMP SITE, INSPECTOR? I TOLD YOU NOT TO DO THAT.
IT WASN'T ME! THE LOCAL AGENCY SENT THEM!
WHY THE HELL'D YOU INVOLVE MY WIFE?!
YOU NEED TO RELEASE EVERYONE. NO MATTER WHAT IT TAKES.
IMPOSSIBLE! THEY WERE CAUGHT RED-HANDED! THEY'RE CLEARLY GUILTY!
SO YOU'RE FINE WITH YOUR WIFE GETTING THE DEATH PENALTY?
...

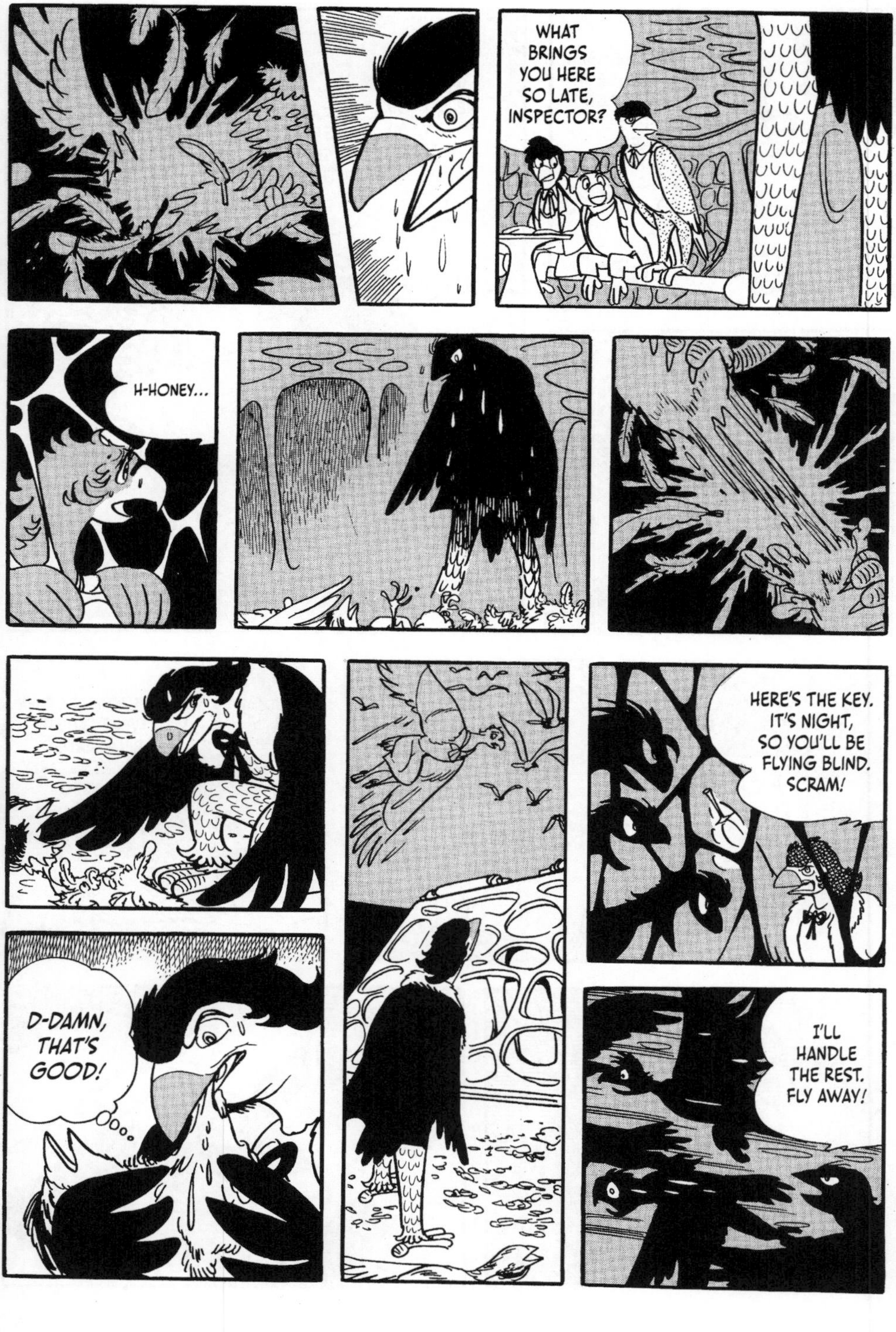
WHAT BRINGS YOU HERE SO LATE, INSPECTOR?
H-HONEY...
HERE'S THE KEY. IT'S NIGHT, SO YOU'LL BE FLYING BLIND. SCRAM!
D-DAMN, THAT'S GOOD!
I'LL HANDLE THE REST. FLY AWAY!

I NEED TO ASK YOU SOME QUESTIONS, INSPECTOR MODS.
LAST NIGHT, THE MILLERS GROUP ESCAPED AND ATE THREE GUARDS...
WE ANALYZED SOME FEATHERS FOUND AT THE SCENE.
THE ANALYSIS CONFIRMS THE FEATHERS ARE YOURS.
IT'S HARD TO BELIEVE, BUT WE HAVE EVIDENCE THAT YOU WERE THE ONE WHO KILLED THE GUARDS.
...THAT'S RIDICU-LOUS!

...
YOU DID IT TO FREE THAT FEMALE, DIDN'T YOU?
...
YOU FUCKED UP, MODS...
WE HAVE NO CHOICE. YOU'LL HAVE AN OPPORTUNITY TO ARGUE YOUR CASE. FOR NOW, YOU'RE UNDER ARREST!
FWSH
DON'T MAKE ME SAY IT!
WHO IS THAT FEMALE? WE'LL FIND OUT SOON, WHETHER YOU TALK OR NOT...

DID THE BLOOD OF YOUR ANCESTORS MAKE YOU DO IT? THIS IS OUTRAGEOUS!
MODS... YOU WERE MY LOYAL AND RELIABLE LIEUTENANT...
CAPTAIN, MEET SENATOR VERTICE.
C-COMMISSIONER!
I WASN'T AWARE YOU WERE COMING...
HE'S HERE ON BEHALF OF THE PRIME MINISTER...
THIS IS THE WORST SCANDAL IN THE HISTORY OF THE REGIONAL POLICE!
POLICE OFFICERS ARE PUBLIC SERVANTS! IF WORD GETS OUT THAT MEMBERS OF A CANNIBALISTIC GROUP HAVE INFILTRATED LAW ENFORCEMENT...
THE PRIME MINISTER IS EXTREMELY CONCERNED ABOUT THIS INCIDENT.

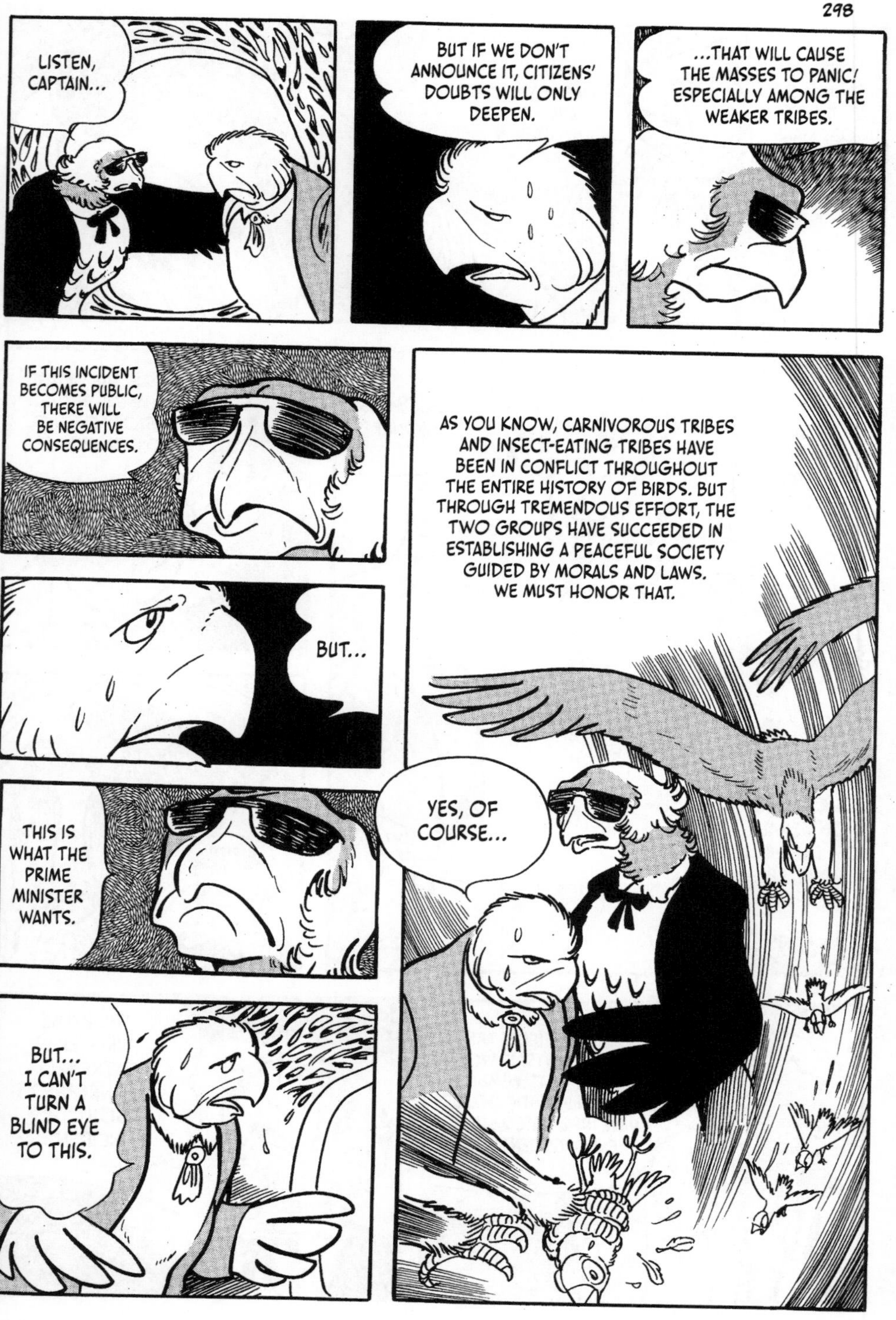
LISTEN, CAPTAIN...
BUT IF WE DON'T ANNOUNCE IT, CITIZENS' DOUBTS WILL ONLY DEEPEN.
...THAT WILL CAUSE THE MASSES TO PANIC! ESPECIALLY AMONG THE WEAKER TRIBES.
IF THIS INCIDENT BECOMES PUBLIC, THERE WILL BE NEGATIVE CONSEQUENCES.
BUT...
THIS IS WHAT THE PRIME MINISTER WANTS.
BUT... I CAN'T TURN A BLIND EYE TO THIS.
AS YOU KNOW, CARNIVOROUS TRIBES AND INSECT-EATING TRIBES HAVE BEEN IN CONFLICT THROUGHOUT THE ENTIRE HISTORY OF BIRDS. BUT THROUGH TREMENDOUS EFFORT, THE TWO GROUPS HAVE SUCCEEDED IN ESTABLISHING A PEACEFUL SOCIETY GUIDED BY MORALS AND LAWS. WE MUST HONOR THAT.
YES, OF COURSE...

THAT'S RIGHT. AND GO EASY ON THE RED BEAK PARTY.
THE PRIME MINISTER WOULD PREFER THAT. HE DOESN'T WANT THIS TO TURN INTO A BIG PROBLEM.
THEN WHAT ABOUT MODS?
EVEN IF PEACE IS SUPERFICIAL, THE MASSES FIND IT REASSURING.
I UNDERSTAND, SIR. SO WHAT WOULD YOU LIKE US TO DO? TURN A BLIND EYE?
YOU'RE A FINE CAPTAIN. VERY COOPERATIVE!
YES, SIR.
GIVE HIM A STERN WARNING AND RELEASE HIM.
YOU CAN FIRE HIM FOR DISCIPLINARY REASONS.

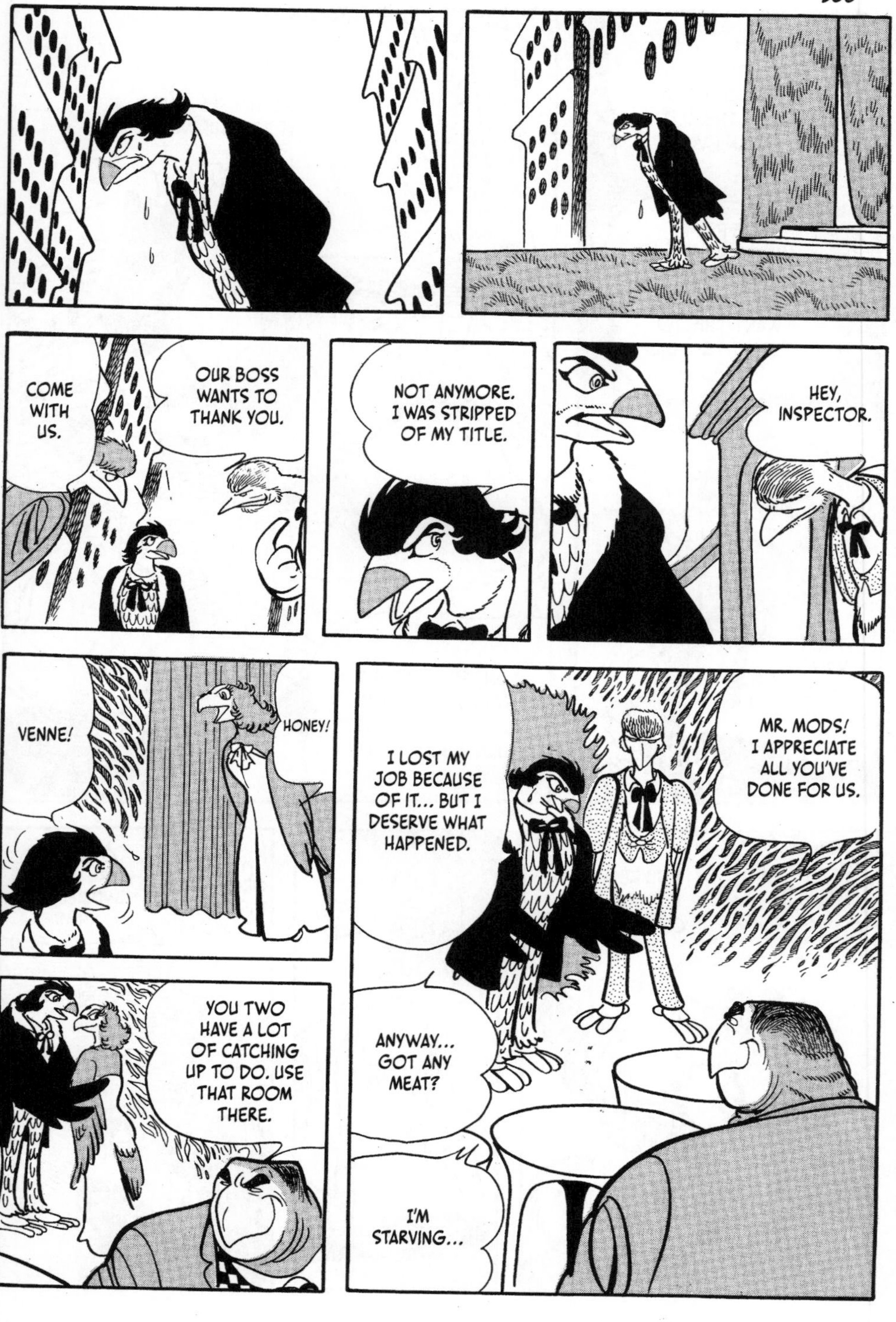
COME WITH US.
OUR BOSS WANTS TO THANK YOU.
NOT ANYMORE. I WAS STRIPPED OF MY TITLE.
HEY, INSPECTOR.
VENNE!
HONEY!
MR. MODS! I APPRECIATE ALL YOU'VE DONE FOR US.
I LOST MY JOB BECAUSE OF IT... BUT I DESERVE WHAT HAPPENED.
YOU TWO HAVE A LOT OF CATCHING UP TO DO. USE THAT ROOM THERE.
ANYWAY... GOT ANY MEAT?
I'M STARVING...

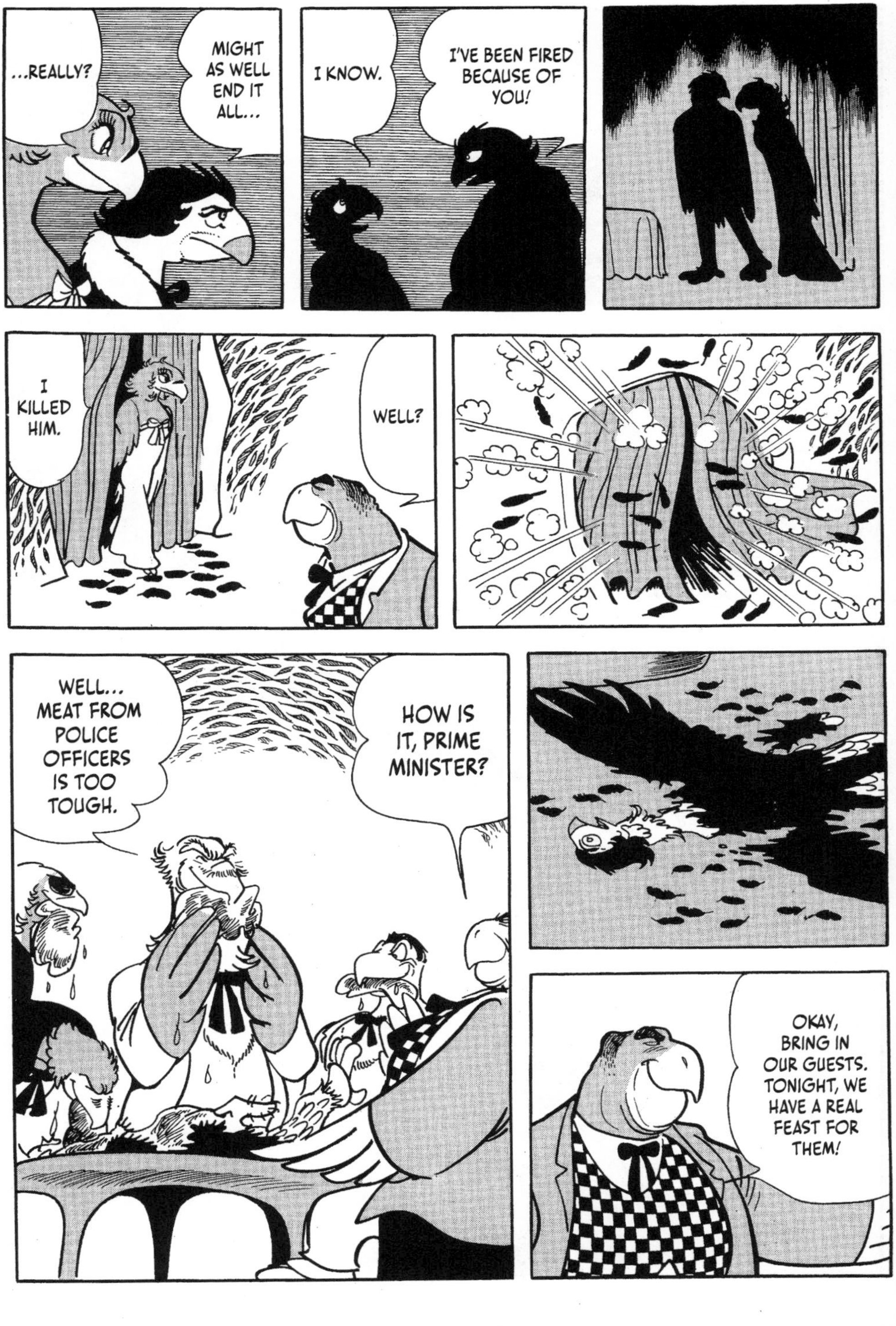
...REALLY?
MIGHT AS WELL END IT ALL...
I KNOW.
I'VE BEEN FIRED BECAUSE OF YOU!
I KILLED HIM.
WELL?
WELL... MEAT FROM POLICE OFFICERS IS TOO TOUGH.
HOW IS IT, PRIME MINISTER?
OKAY, BRING IN OUR GUESTS. TONIGHT, WE HAVE A REAL FEAST FOR THEM!

CHAPTER 16: JONGARA THE SEAGULL

WE HEAR THE COLD SEA OF TSUGARU SPLASHING AS USUAL.
BUT THE SEAGULLS ON THE SHORE COULDN'T CARE LESS ABOUT THE STORMY WEATHER.
THEY HAVE TRAPS SET UP TO CATCH ENTIRE SCHOOLS OF FISH.
THERE'S MORE FOOD THAN THEY COULD EVER NEED.

BUT A SEAGULL NAMED JONGARA WAS DIFFERENT.
THE SEAGULLS ACQUIRE RARE DELICACIES WITHOUT STEPPING FOOT INTO THE WATER. THEY'VE BECOME OBESE AND TOO LAZY TO FLY. ALL THEY TALK ABOUT IS WHO HAS THE SHINIEST FEATHERS.
EVERY DAY, HE DOVE INTO THE SEA AT TOP SPEED.
THE OTHER SEAGULLS WERE SUSPICIOUS OF HIM. THEY THOUGHT HE WAS WEIRD.
JONGARA CAUGHT AND ATE FISH. HE ONLY ATE WHAT HE CAUGHT HIMSELF.
BUT JONGARA IGNORED THEM.
THEY SAID HE SHOULD BUY FISH AT THE DISTRIBUTION CENTER.
JONGARA'S RELATIVES TOLD HIM NOT TO HUNT...

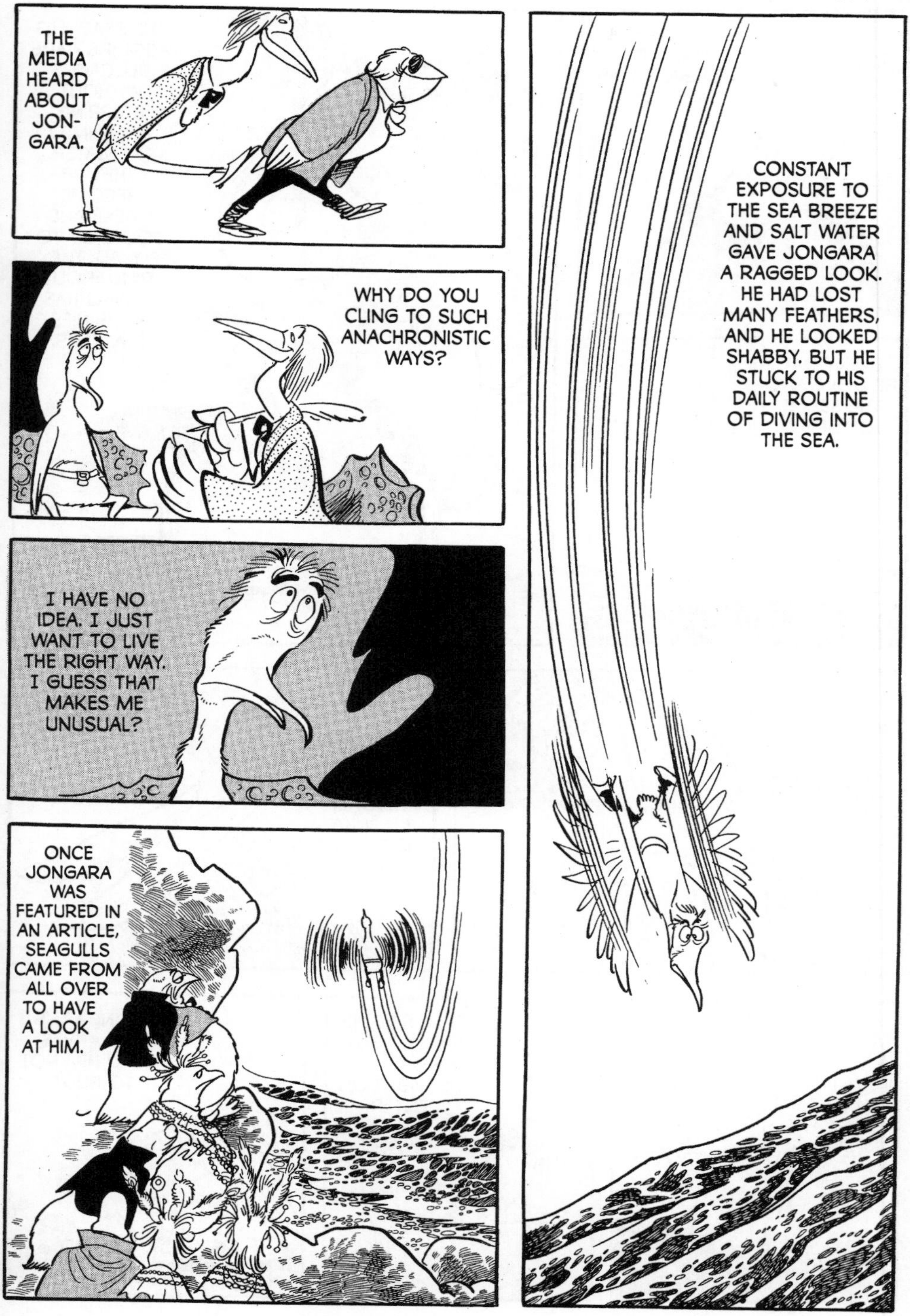
THE MEDIA HEARD ABOUT JON-GARA.
WHY DO YOU CLING TO SUCH ANACHRONISTIC WAYS?
I HAVE NO IDEA. I JUST WANT TO LIVE THE RIGHT WAY. I GUESS THAT MAKES ME UNUSUAL?
ONCE JONGARA WAS FEATURED IN AN ARTICLE, SEAGULLS CAME FROM ALL OVER TO HAVE A LOOK AT HIM.
CONSTANT EXPOSURE TO THE SEA BREEZE AND SALT WATER GAVE JONGARA A RAGGED LOOK. HE HAD LOST MANY FEATHERS, AND HE LOOKED SHABBY. BUT HE STUCK TO HIS DAILY ROUTINE OF DIVING INTO THE SEA.

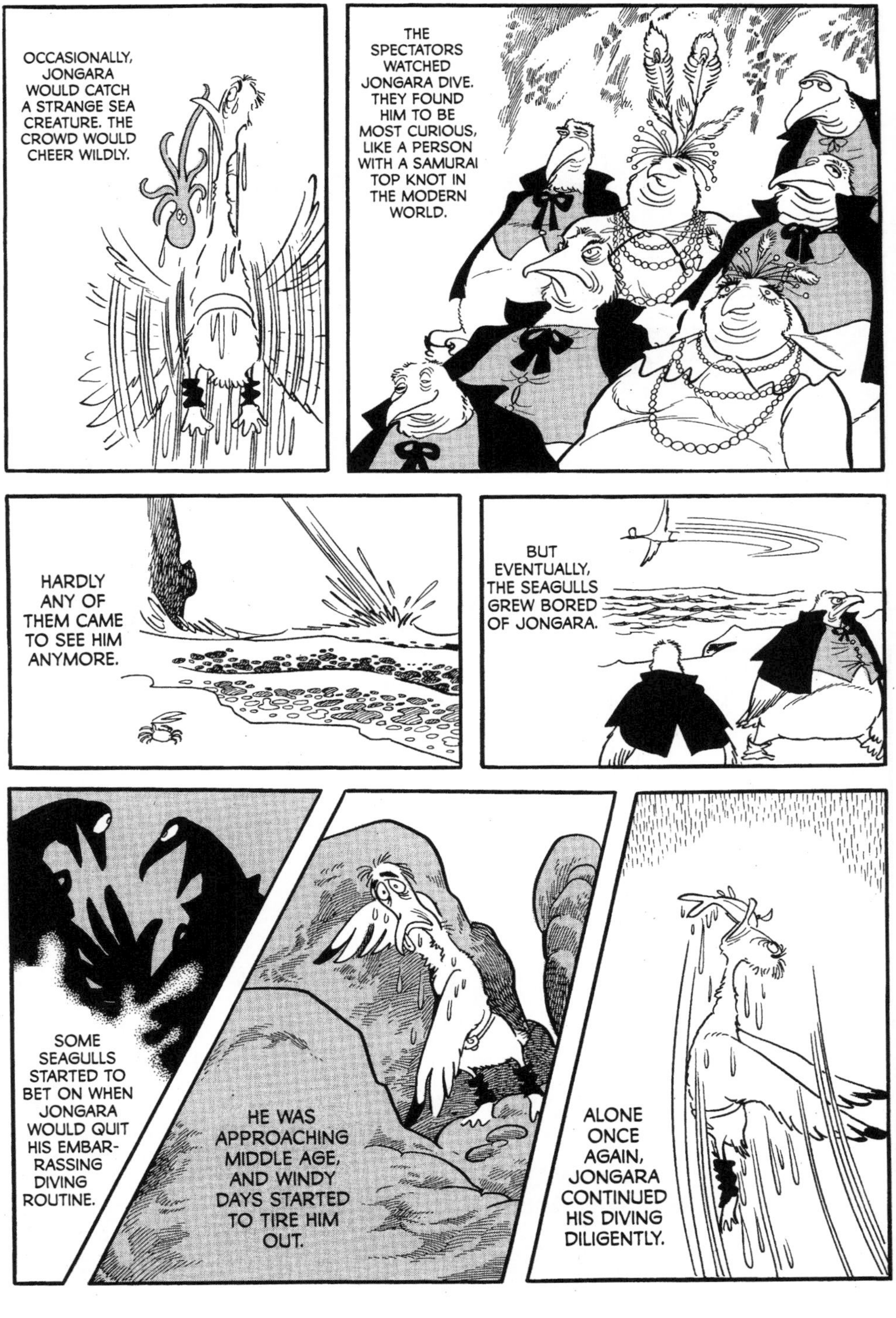
OCCASIONALLY, JONGARA WOULD CATCH A STRANGE SEA CREATURE. THE CROWD WOULD CHEER WILDLY.
THE SPECTATORS WATCHED JONGARA DIVE. THEY FOUND HIM TO BE MOST CURIOUS, LIKE A PERSON WITH A SAMURAI TOP KNOT IN THE MODERN WORLD.
HARDLY ANY OF THEM CAME TO SEE HIM ANYMORE.
BUT EVENTUALLY, THE SEAGULLS GREW BORED OF JONGARA.
SOME SEAGULLS STARTED TO BET ON WHEN JONGARA WOULD QUIT HIS EMBARRASSING DIVING ROUTINE.
HE WAS APPROACHING MIDDLE AGE, AND WINDY DAYS STARTED TO TIRE HIM OUT.
ALONE ONCE AGAIN, JONGARA CONTINUED HIS DIVING DILIGENTLY.

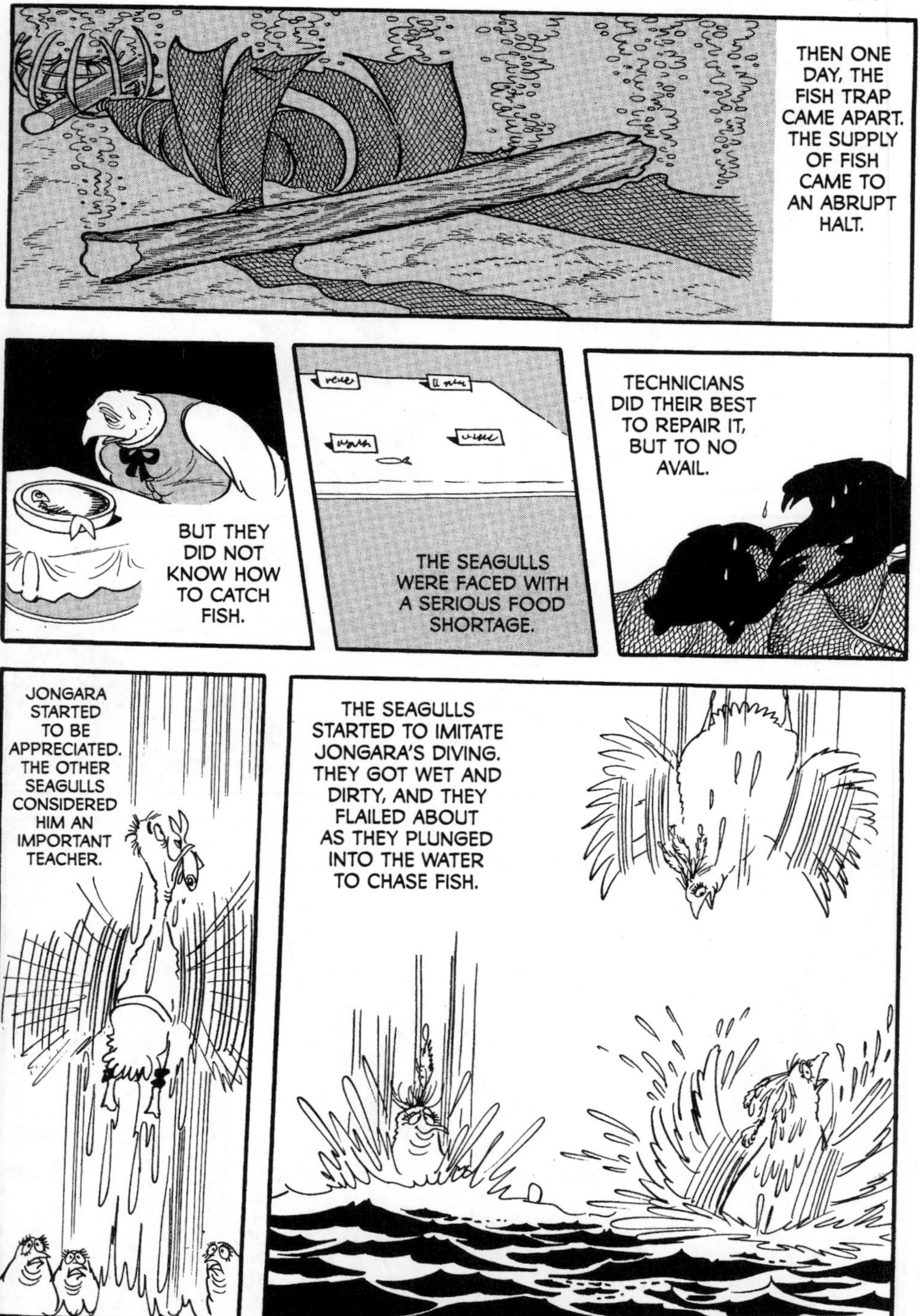
THEN ONE DAY, THE FISH TRAP CAME APART. THE SUPPLY OF FISH CAME TO AN ABRUPT HALT.
BUT THEY DID NOT KNOW HOW TO CATCH FISH.
THE SEAGULLS WERE FACED WITH A SERIOUS FOOD SHORTAGE.
TECHNICIANS DID THEIR BEST TO REPAIR IT, BUT TO NO AVAIL.
JONGARA STARTED TO BE APPRECIATED. THE OTHER SEAGULLS CONSIDERED HIM AN IMPORTANT TEACHER.
THE SEAGULLS STARTED TO IMITATE JONGARA'S DIVING. THEY GOT WET AND DIRTY, AND THEY FLAILED ABOUT AS THEY PLUNGED INTO THE WATER TO CHASE FISH.

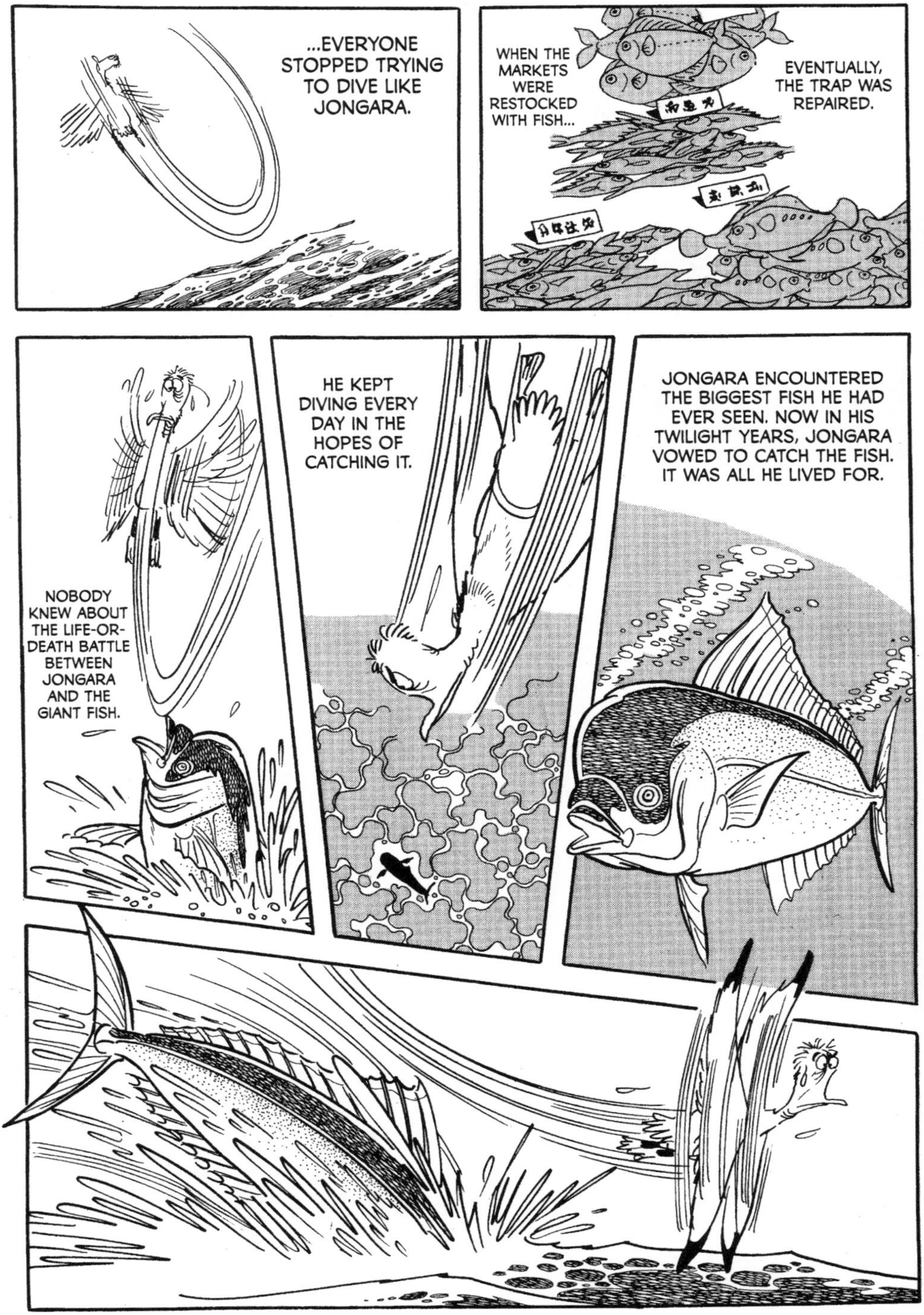
EVENTUALLY, THE TRAP WAS REPAIRED.
WHEN THE MARKETS WERE RESTOCKED WITH FISH...
...EVERYONE STOPPED TRYING TO DIVE LIKE JONGARA.
JONGARA ENCOUNTERED THE BIGGEST FISH HE HAD EVER SEEN. NOW IN HIS TWILIGHT YEARS, JONGARA VOWED TO CATCH THE FISH. IT WAS ALL HE LIVED FOR.
HE KEPT DIVING EVERY DAY IN THE HOPES OF CATCHING IT.
NOBODY KNEW ABOUT THE LIFE-OR-DEATH BATTLE BETWEEN JONGARA AND THE GIANT FISH.

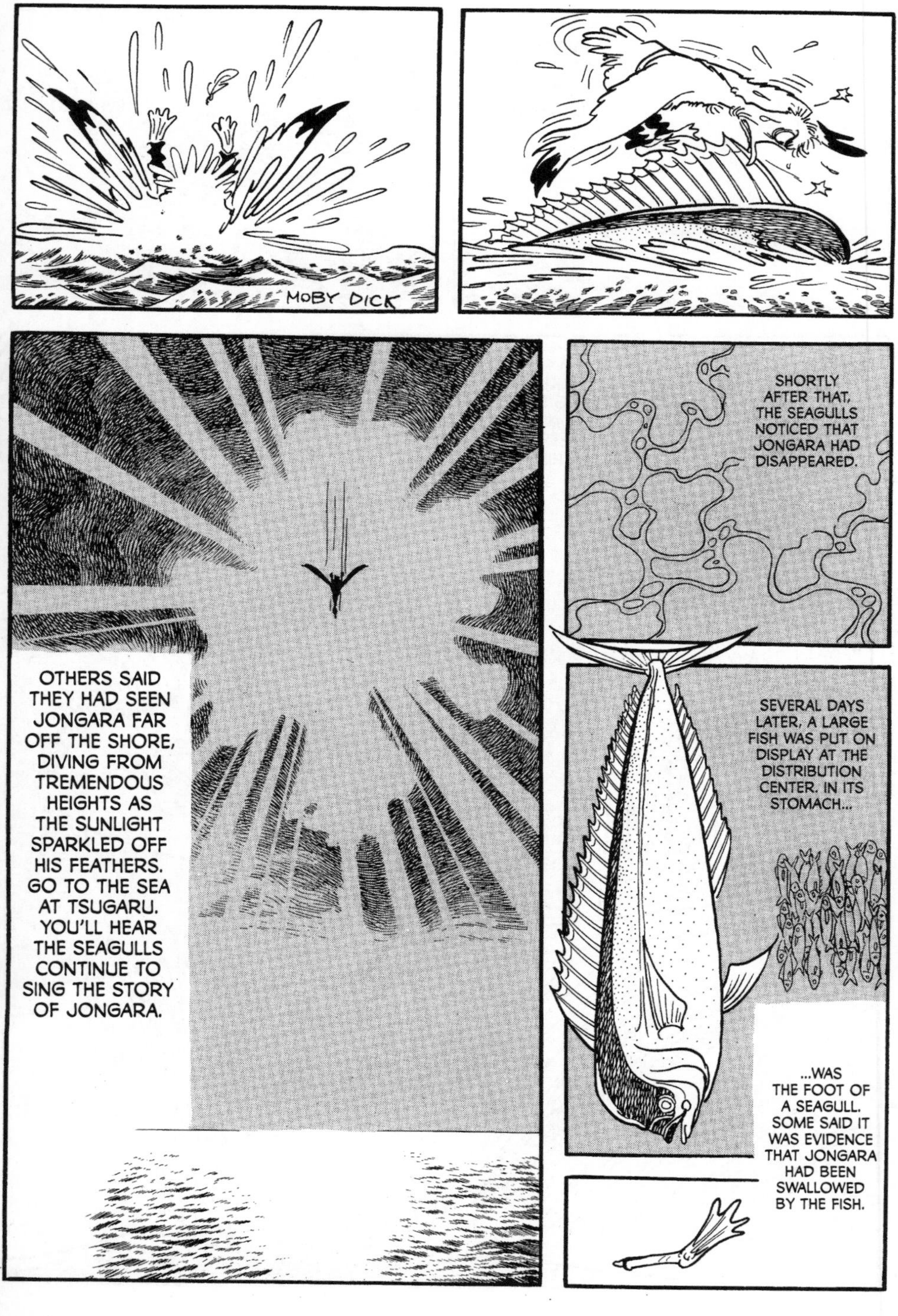
MOBY DICK
SHORTLY AFTER THAT, THE SEAGULLS NOTICED THAT JONGARA HAD DISAPPEARED.
OTHERS SAID THEY HAD SEEN JONGARA FAR OFF THE SHORE, DIVING FROM TREMENDOUS HEIGHTS AS THE SUNLIGHT SPARKLED OFF HIS FEATHERS. GO TO THE SEA AT TSUGARU. YOU'LL HEAR THE SEAGULLS CONTINUE TO SING THE STORY OF JONGARA.
SEVERAL DAYS LATER, A LARGE FISH WAS PUT ON DISPLAY AT THE DISTRIBUTION CENTER. IN ITS STOMACH...
...WAS THE FOOT OF A SEAGULL. SOME SAID IT WAS EVIDENCE THAT JONGARA HAD BEEN SWALLOWED BY THE FISH.

CHAPTER 17: THE BLUE HUMANS

I WOKE UP AT MIDNIGHT. THE COOL WIND CREPT THROUGH MY WINDOW, ALONG WITH A BLUISH WHITE SHADOW.

I GOT UP TO CLOSE THE WINDOW AND PEEKED OUT AT THE GARDEN.

WHAT I SAW ALMOST MADE ME SCREAM. HUMANS! TWO OF THEM!

I MUSTERED ENOUGH COURAGE TO FLY DOWN TO THE GARDEN AND SLOWLY APPROACH THE TWO HUMANS.
THEY WERE TRANSPARENT. I COULD LOOK RIGHT THROUGH THEM AT THE BLUE GROUND. GHOSTS! I TREMBLED IN FEAR. MOTHER HAD TOLD ME HUMANS USED TO LIVE IN THIS GARDEN, THOUSANDS OF YEARS AGO.
HELLO...
HELLO.
YOU CAN SPEAK! YOU EVEN KNOW MY LANGUAGE!
WHAT COUNTRY IS THIS?
WHAT DO YOU WANT, MISS GHOST?
THIS TOWN IS BORIDEAU, IN THE VELMEX SECTION OF ISCLARD CITY.
I'VE NEVER HEARD OF IT.

SEARCHING FOR WHAT?
WE'VE BEEN SEARCHING FOR A LONG TIME... A VERY, VERY LONG TIME...
MOTHER TOLD ME YOU HUMANS DIED OUT A THOUSAND YEARS AGO. WHY DID YOU COME BACK AS GHOSTS NOW?
GHOSTS? *Ha ha ha ha!*
YOU.
HUH? ME?
AND NOW WE FINALLY HAVE!
WE HUMANS HAVE ALWAYS DREAMED OF FINDING YOU!
COME WITH US!
NO!
I WON'T LET YOU TAKE ME AWAY! GO AWAY, HUMAN GHOSTS!

HELP!
CATCH HIM, MYTYL!
WE'RE NOT GHOSTS!
THEY PUT ME IN A GOLDEN CAGE.
FANTASTIC! WE'VE ACCOMPLISHED OUR MISSION!
WE DID IT, TYLTYL!
AS MY HOME DISAPPEARED INTO THE MISTY NIGHT, I CALLED OUT FOR HELP. BUT IT WAS NO USE.
THE TWO HUMANS STARTED TO RUN.

WE'RE HOME, GRANDMA! IT'S ME, MYTYL. WE FOUND THE BLUE BIRD! THE BIRD OF HAPPINESS!
TELL US, BIRD. ARE YOU HAPPY? ARE YOU THE BLUE BIRD OF HAPPINESS?
BUT WE'LL HAVE TO CHECK WHETHER IT'S ACTUALLY HAPPY.
THAT IS INDEED A BLUE BIRD.
WE HUMANS HAVE WISHED TO BE HAPPY FOR TENS OF THOUSANDS OF YEARS. THAT'S WHY WE'VE BEEN SEARCHING FOR YOU.
AM I HAPPY? NOT EVEN CLOSE!
HOW COULD WE BE HAPPY?!

I'M THE ONE WHO NEEDS TO FIND HAPPINESS!
MY LIFE IS JUST A SCHOOL ENTRANCE EXAM HELL. A CROWDED TRAFFIC HELL. A POLLUTED HELL.
OUR WORLD IS FILLED WITH GREED AND LIES AND VIOLENCE AND DISEASE. IT'S A HOPELESS HELL!
TYLTYL... MYTYL... THIS IS NOT THE BLUE BIRD.
THEN YOU'RE NO DIFFERENT FROM US HUMANS!
AAAH!
KILL IT!

*A Belgian writer whose play *The Blue Bird* is being referenced in this story

CHAPTER 18:
THE BALLAD OF LAP AND WILDA

LAP CARRIED THE STENCH OF GARBAGE IN THE MARSH. OF MUD AND ROTTEN THATCH. HE WAS ONE OF 28 SIBLINGS, BUT AN EPIDEMIC HAD KILLED 23 OF THEM. LAP'S REMAINING FAMILY WAS STARVING AND FREEZING.
THE TWO OF THEM FLEW IN THE MOONLIGHT, SEARCHING FOR A ROOST THAT WOULD PROVIDE LOVE AND COMFORT.

LAP WAS CHESTNUT COLORED. HIS HEAD WAS A DIRTY BROWN. WITH SPOTS AND GREY BALD SPOTS, HE LOOKED PITIFUL, SQUALID, AND DRAB. HE CARRIED THE STIGMA OF THE SKILLARD TRIBE ON HIS BODY. INSULTS, SYMPATHY, AND RIDICULE... HE ENDURED ALL OF THESE FROM A YOUNG AGE.

THE SKILLARD TRIBE! THEY INHABITED THE LOWEST CLASS, PASSED ON FROM PARENT TO CHILD, AND FROM CHILD TO DESCENDANT. A MISERABLE CASTE.
IN THE SAME WAY THAT HUMANS HAD DISCRIMINATED BASED ON SKIN COLOR, BIRDS STARTED DISCRIMINATING BASED ON FEATHER COMPLEXION, ACCESSORIES, AND SOFTNESS OF DOWN.

LAP REFUSED TO LEAVE THE MARSH. WHEN THE ARROGANT SONS OF THE PROPERTIED CLASS LOOKED FOR SOMEONE TO BULLY, LAP WAS THE OBVIOUS CHOICE.

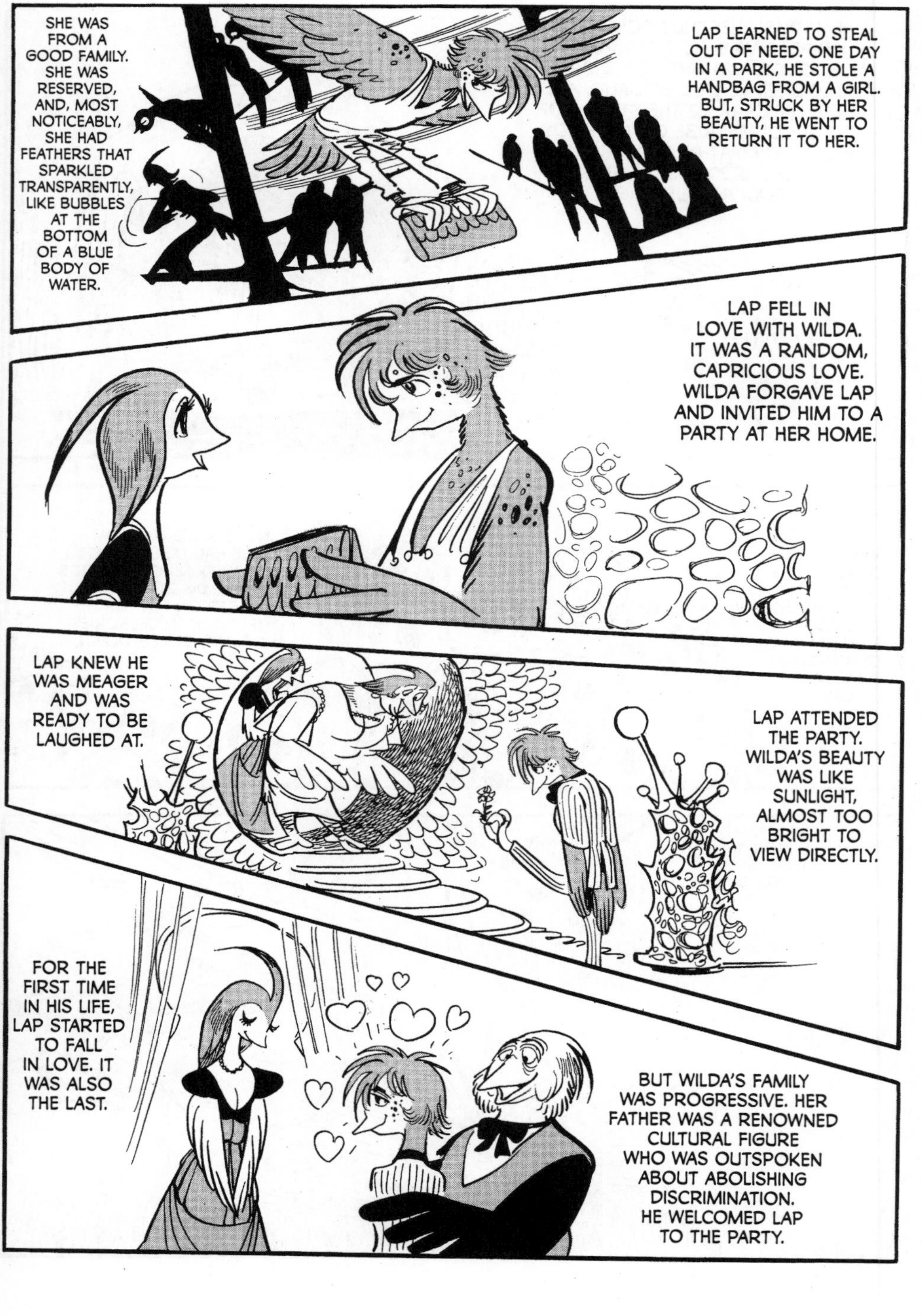
SHE WAS FROM A GOOD FAMILY. SHE WAS RESERVED, AND, MOST NOTICEABLY, SHE HAD FEATHERS THAT SPARKLED TRANSPARENTLY, LIKE BUBBLES AT THE BOTTOM OF A BLUE BODY OF WATER.
LAP LEARNED TO STEAL OUT OF NEED. ONE DAY IN A PARK, HE STOLE A HANDBAG FROM A GIRL. BUT, STRUCK BY HER BEAUTY, HE WENT TO RETURN IT TO HER.
LAP FELL IN LOVE WITH WILDA. IT WAS A RANDOM, CAPRICIOUS LOVE. WILDA FORGAVE LAP AND INVITED HIM TO A PARTY AT HER HOME.
LAP KNEW HE WAS MEAGER AND WAS READY TO BE LAUGHED AT.
LAP ATTENDED THE PARTY. WILDA'S BEAUTY WAS LIKE SUNLIGHT, ALMOST TOO BRIGHT TO VIEW DIRECTLY.
FOR THE FIRST TIME IN HIS LIFE, LAP STARTED TO FALL IN LOVE. IT WAS ALSO THE LAST.
BUT WILDA'S FAMILY WAS PROGRESSIVE. HER FATHER WAS A RENOWNED CULTURAL FIGURE WHO WAS OUTSPOKEN ABOUT ABOLISHING DISCRIMINATION. HE WELCOMED LAP TO THE PARTY.

LAP SEARCHED THE MARSH TO GATHER AS MANY FLOWERS AS HE COULD. HE GAVE THEM TO WILDA. ONE YEAR LATER, LAP FINALLY SAID:
"MARRY ME."
"ARE YOU SERIOUS, LAP?"
"YES, I PROMISE TO MAKE YOU HAPPY."
"I LOVE YOU, LAP."

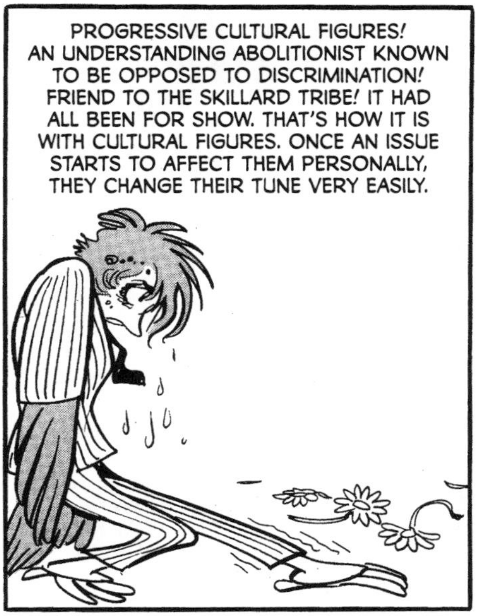
PROGRESSIVE CULTURAL FIGURES! AN UNDERSTANDING ABOLITIONIST KNOWN TO BE OPPOSED TO DISCRIMINATION! FRIEND TO THE SKILLARD TRIBE! IT HAD ALL BEEN FOR SHOW. THAT'S HOW IT IS WITH CULTURAL FIGURES. ONCE AN ISSUE STARTS TO AFFECT THEM PERSONALLY, THEY CHANGE THEIR TUNE VERY EASILY.

MARRIAGE WITH A SKILLARD? NEVER!
THAT WAS THE MOMENT WILDA'S FAMILY TURNED COLD ON LAP.

SOMEONE FROM THE PROUD RAINBOW BIRD TRIBE WOULD NEVER MARRY A LOWLY SKILLARD.
ACCORDING TO EUGENICS, YOUR REPRODUCTIVE FUNCTIONS ARE NOT A GOOD MATCH... THAT WAS THE EXCUSE WILDA'S FATHER GAVE.
IT HAD ALL BEEN A TRAP, DESIGNED TO MAKE LAP MORE MISERABLE THAN HE ALREADY WAS.
WILDA KEPT HER WORD. SHE CAME TO BE WITH LAP!
BUT NO!
"LET'S FLY AWAY," SAID LAP. "SOMEWHERE FAR," SAID WILDA. "FAR AWAY FROM MY PARENTS."

WILDA HAS BEEN KIDNAPPED! HER FAMILY CRIED OUT. THE POLICE SEARCHED FRANTICALLY.
THE BIRDS WERE IN UPROAR. THAT DAMN LAP! TEAR HIM TO PIECES!
LAP AND WILDA FLEW FAR AWAY IN THE MOON-LIGHT...
THE INVESTIGATION CLOSED IN ON THEM.
THE TWO OF THEM FLEW IN THE MOONLIGHT, SEARCHING FOR A ROOST THAT WOULD PROVIDE LOVE AND COMFORT.

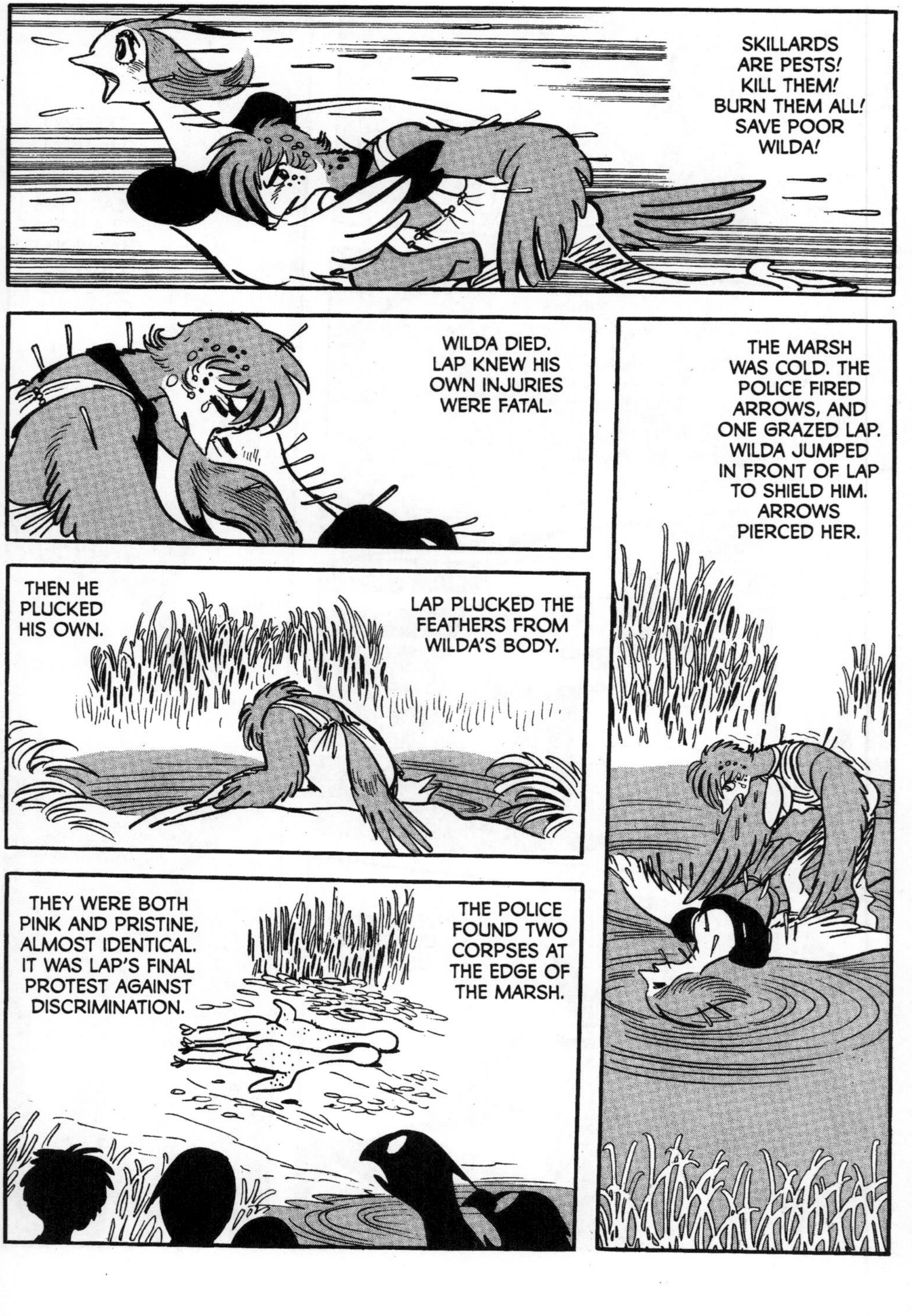
SKILLARDS ARE PESTS! KILL THEM! BURN THEM ALL! SAVE POOR WILDA!
THE MARSH WAS COLD. THE POLICE FIRED ARROWS, AND ONE GRAZED LAP. WILDA JUMPED IN FRONT OF LAP TO SHIELD HIM. ARROWS PIERCED HER.
WILDA DIED. LAP KNEW HIS OWN INJURIES WERE FATAL.
LAP PLUCKED THE FEATHERS FROM WILDA'S BODY.
THEN HE PLUCKED HIS OWN.
THE POLICE FOUND TWO CORPSES AT THE EDGE OF THE MARSH.
THEY WERE BOTH PINK AND PRISTINE, ALMOST IDENTICAL. IT WAS LAP'S FINAL PROTEST AGAINST DISCRIMINATION.

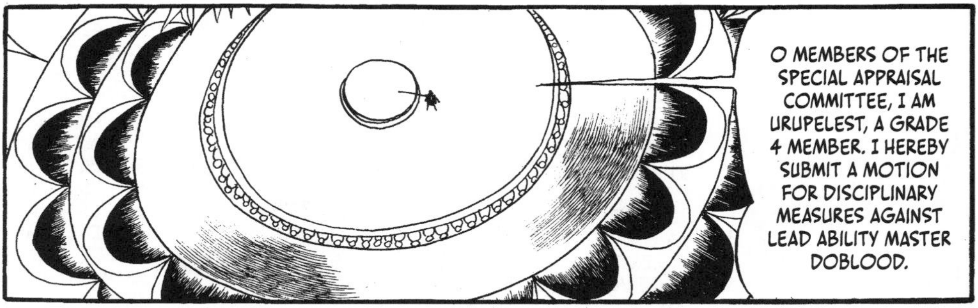
O MEMBERS OF THE SPECIAL APPRAISAL COMMITTEE, I AM URUPELEST, A GRADE 4 MEMBER. I HEREBY SUBMIT A MOTION FOR DISCIPLINARY MEASURES AGAINST LEAD ABILITY MASTER DOBLOOD.

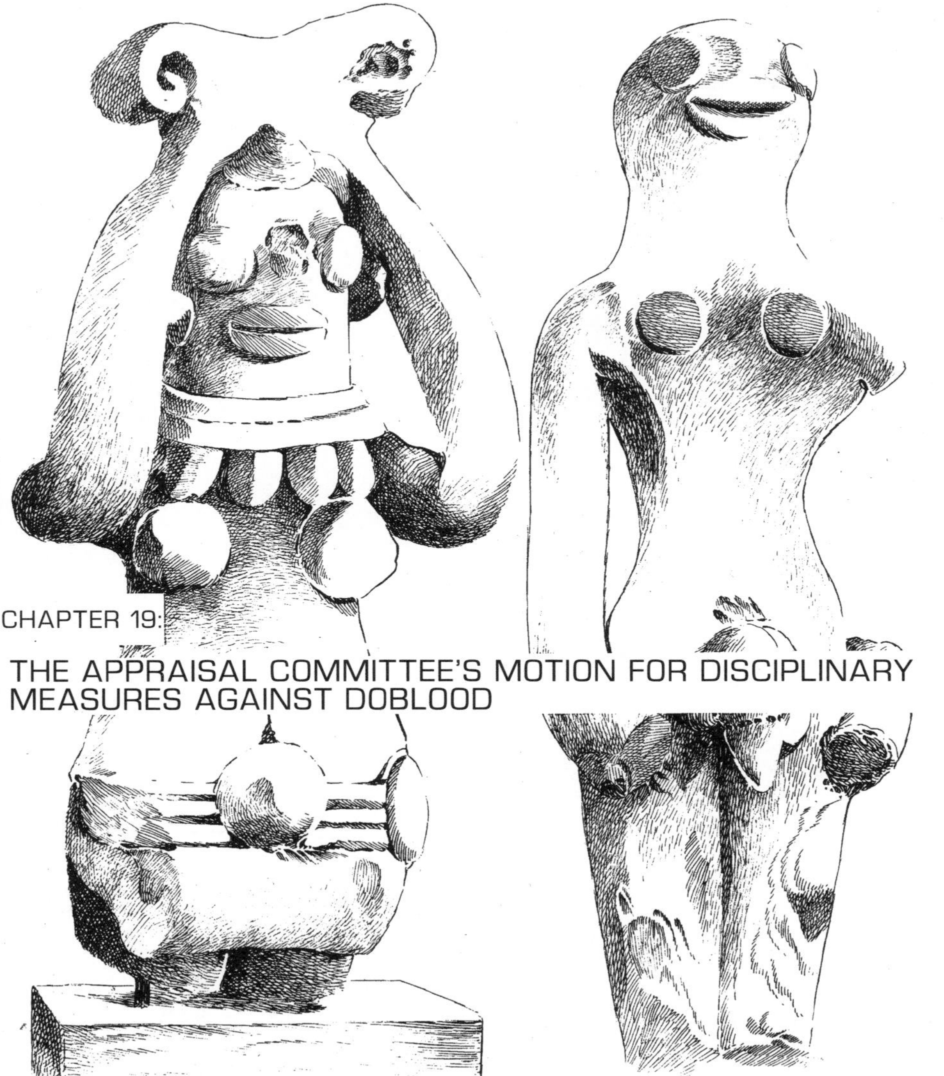

CHAPTER 19:

THE APPRAISAL COMMITTEE'S MOTION FOR DISCIPLINARY MEASURES AGAINST DOBLOOD

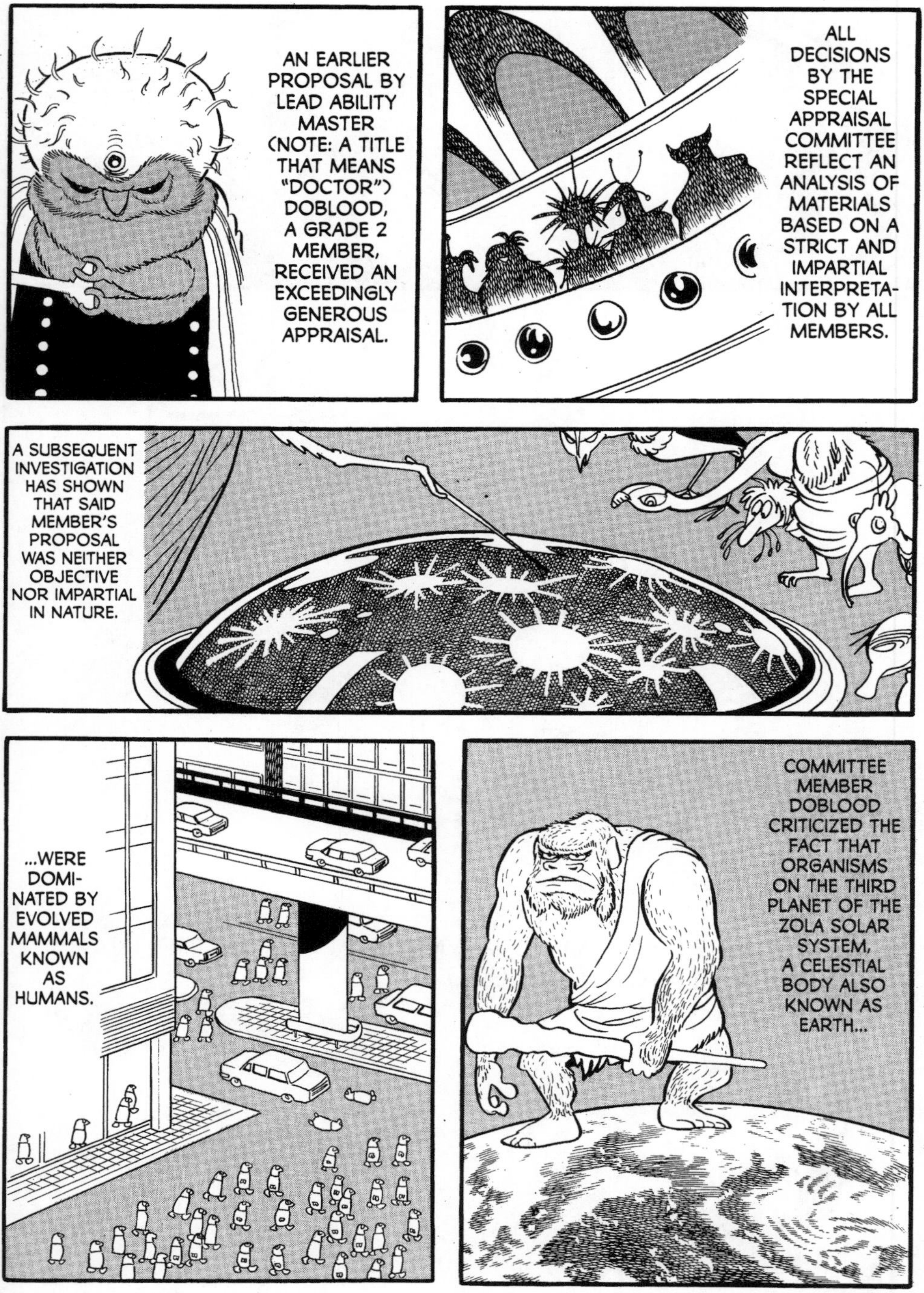
ALL DECISIONS BY THE SPECIAL APPRAISAL COMMITTEE REFLECT AN ANALYSIS OF MATERIALS BASED ON A STRICT AND IMPARTIAL INTERPRETA-TION BY ALL MEMBERS.
AN EARLIER PROPOSAL BY LEAD ABILITY MASTER (NOTE: A TITLE THAT MEANS "DOCTOR") DOBLOOD, A GRADE 2 MEMBER, RECEIVED AN EXCEEDINGLY GENEROUS APPRAISAL.
A SUBSEQUENT INVESTIGATION HAS SHOWN THAT SAID MEMBER'S PROPOSAL WAS NEITHER OBJECTIVE NOR IMPARTIAL IN NATURE.
COMMITTEE MEMBER DOBLOOD CRITICIZED THE FACT THAT ORGANISMS ON THE THIRD PLANET OF THE ZOLA SOLAR SYSTEM, A CELESTIAL BODY ALSO KNOWN AS EARTH...
...WERE DOMI-NATED BY EVOLVED MAMMALS KNOWN AS HUMANS.

CITING EVOLUTION THEORY, DOBLOOD USED THE 75TH PLANET OF IGNALGUM AS AN EXAMPLE TO PROPOSE THAT BIRDS, WITH THEIR ABILITY TO FLY, ARE THE MOST ADVANCED LIFEFORM AND SHOULD HAVE THE AUTHORITY TO RULE EARTH - NOT MAMMALS.

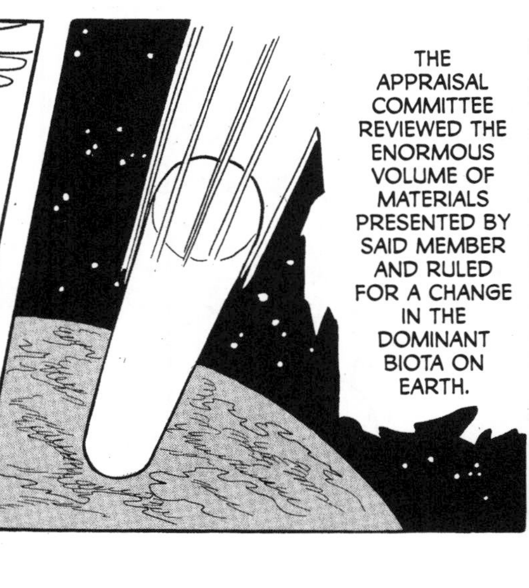
THE APPRAISAL COMMITTEE REVIEWED THE ENORMOUS VOLUME OF MATERIALS PRESENTED BY SAID MEMBER AND RULED FOR A CHANGE IN THE DOMINANT BIOTA ON EARTH.

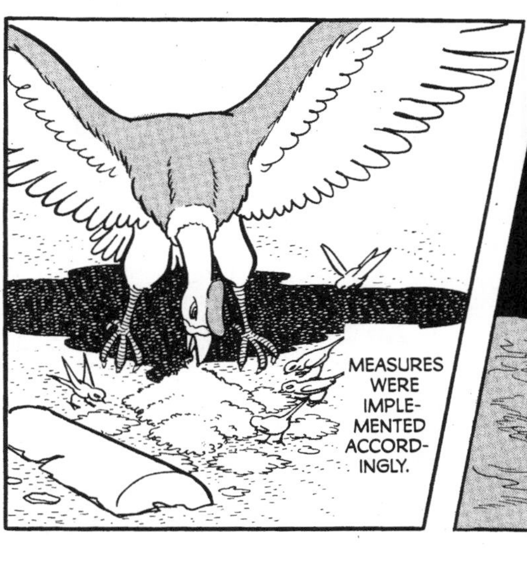
MEASURES WERE IMPLE-MENTED ACCORD-INGLY.

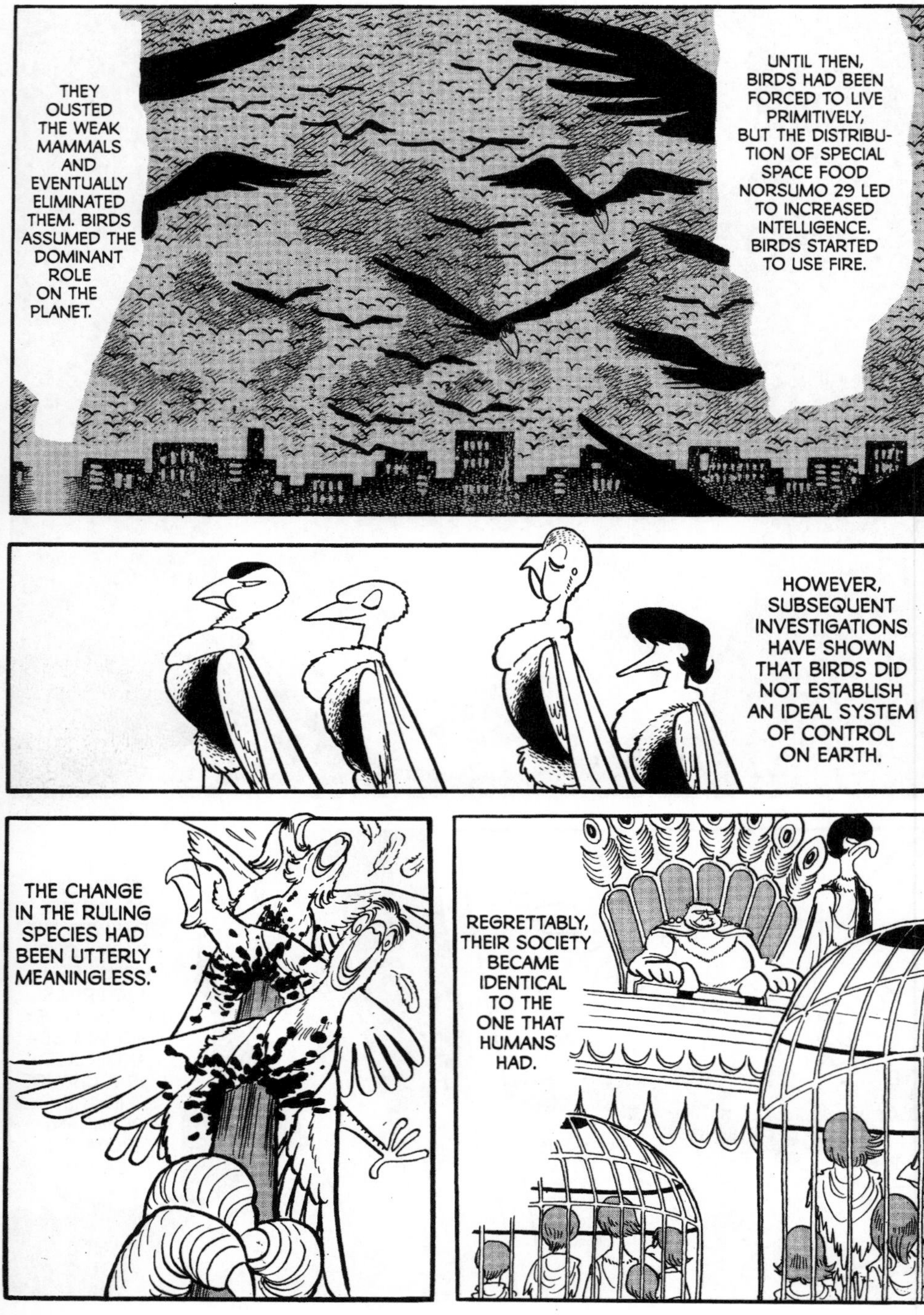
THEY OUSTED THE WEAK MAMMALS AND EVENTUALLY ELIMINATED THEM. BIRDS ASSUMED THE DOMINANT ROLE ON THE PLANET.
UNTIL THEN, BIRDS HAD BEEN FORCED TO LIVE PRIMITIVELY, BUT THE DISTRIBUTION OF SPECIAL SPACE FOOD NORSUMO 29 LED TO INCREASED INTELLIGENCE. BIRDS STARTED TO USE FIRE.
HOWEVER, SUBSEQUENT INVESTIGATIONS HAVE SHOWN THAT BIRDS DID NOT ESTABLISH AN IDEAL SYSTEM OF CONTROL ON EARTH.
THE CHANGE IN THE RULING SPECIES HAD BEEN UTTERLY MEANINGLESS.
REGRETTABLY, THEIR SOCIETY BECAME IDENTICAL TO THE ONE THAT HUMANS HAD.

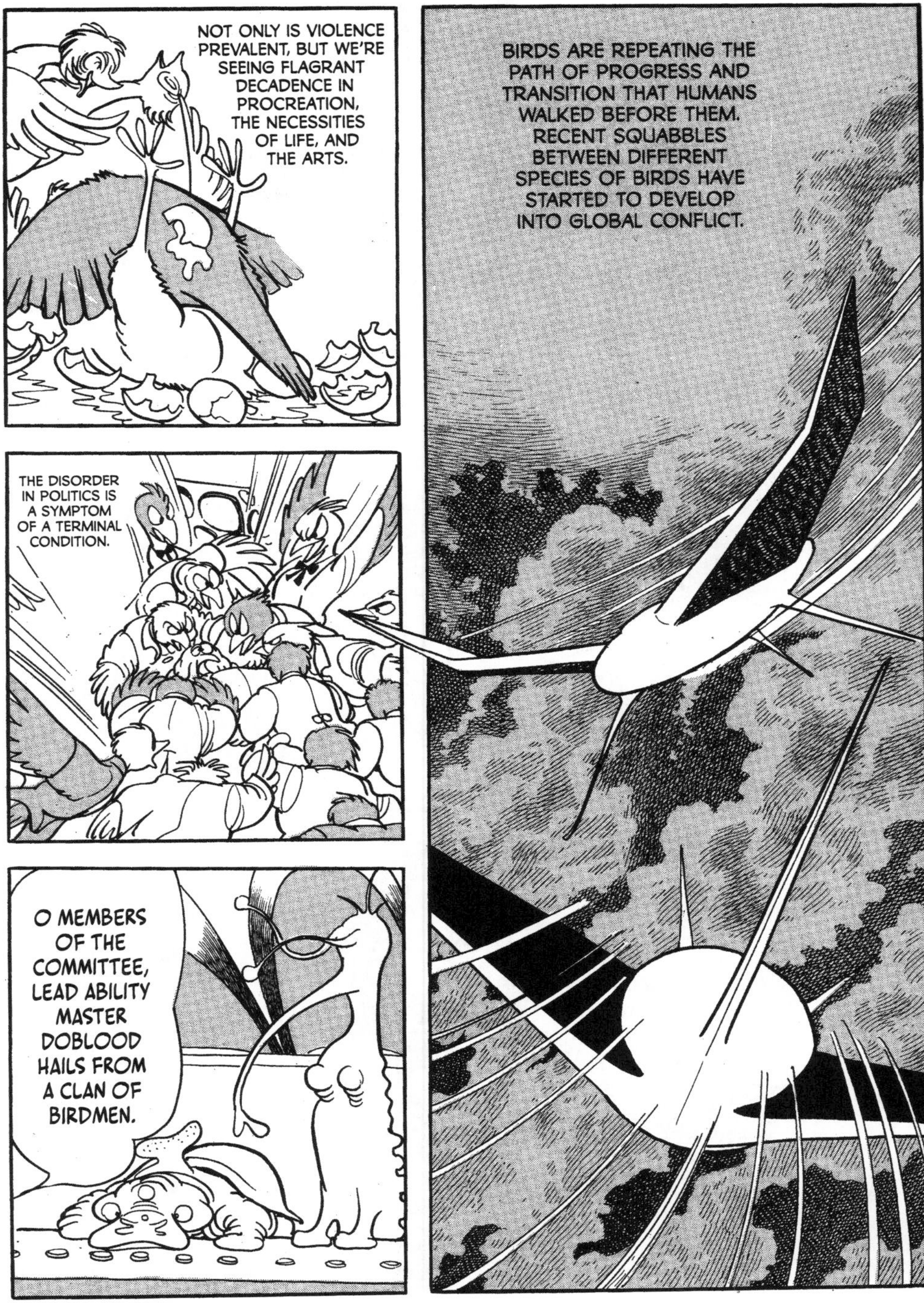
NOT ONLY IS VIOLENCE PREVALENT, BUT WE'RE SEEING FLAGRANT DECADENCE IN PROCREATION, THE NECESSITIES OF LIFE, AND THE ARTS.
THE DISORDER IN POLITICS IS A SYMPTOM OF A TERMINAL CONDITION.
O MEMBERS OF THE COMMITTEE, LEAD ABILITY MASTER DOBLOOD HAILS FROM A CLAN OF BIRDMEN.
BIRDS ARE REPEATING THE PATH OF PROGRESS AND TRANSITION THAT HUMANS WALKED BEFORE THEM. RECENT SQUABBLES BETWEEN DIFFERENT SPECIES OF BIRDS HAVE STARTED TO DEVELOP INTO GLOBAL CONFLICT.

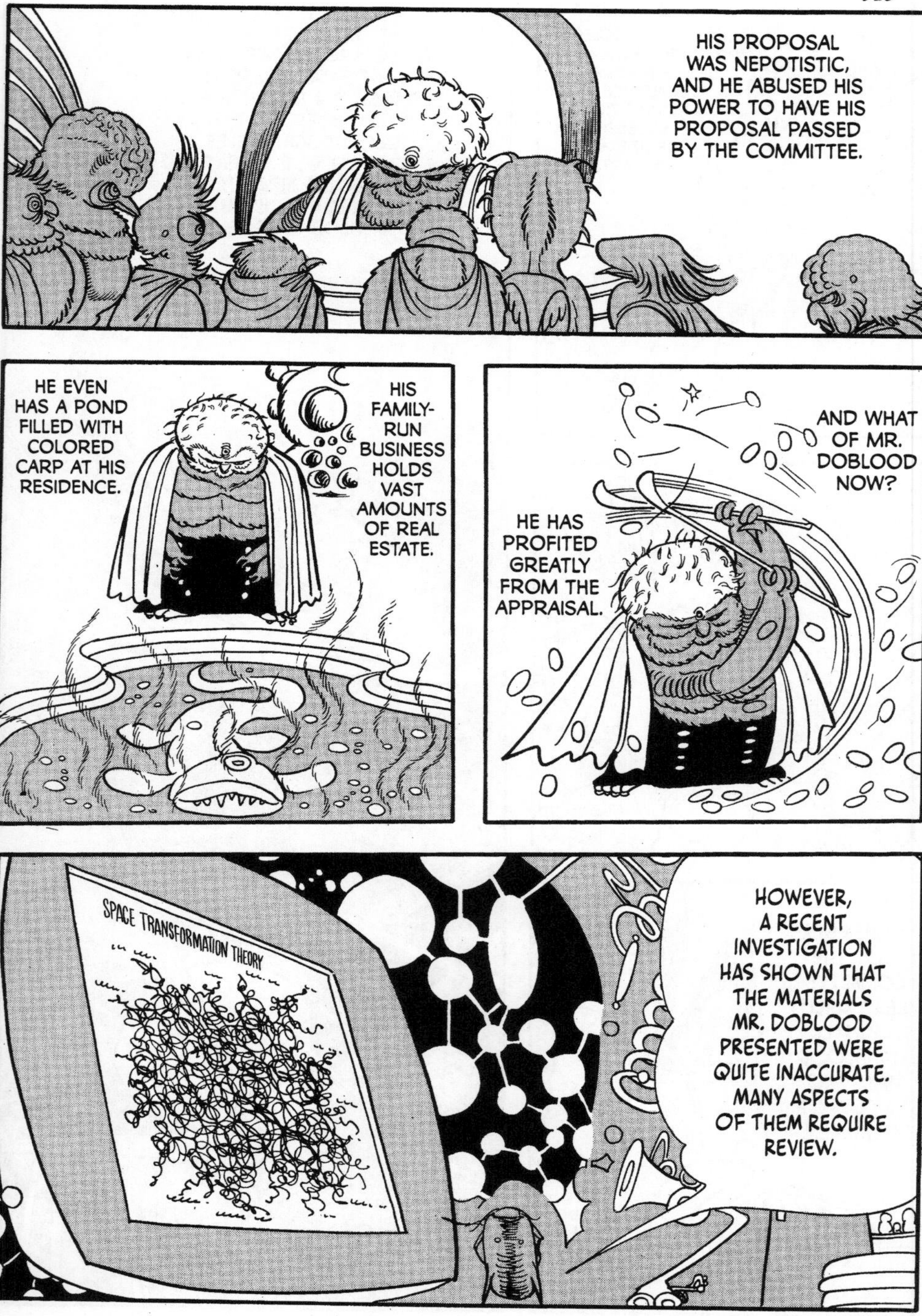
HIS PROPOSAL WAS NEPOTISTIC, AND HE ABUSED HIS POWER TO HAVE HIS PROPOSAL PASSED BY THE COMMITTEE.
HIS FAMILY-RUN BUSINESS HOLDS VAST AMOUNTS OF REAL ESTATE.
HE EVEN HAS A POND FILLED WITH COLORED CARP AT HIS RESIDENCE.
AND WHAT OF MR. DOBLOOD NOW?
HE HAS PROFITED GREATLY FROM THE APPRAISAL.
SPACE TRANSFORMATION THEORY
HOWEVER, A RECENT INVESTIGATION HAS SHOWN THAT THE MATERIALS MR. DOBLOOD PRESENTED WERE QUITE INACCURATE. MANY ASPECTS OF THEM REQUIRE REVIEW.

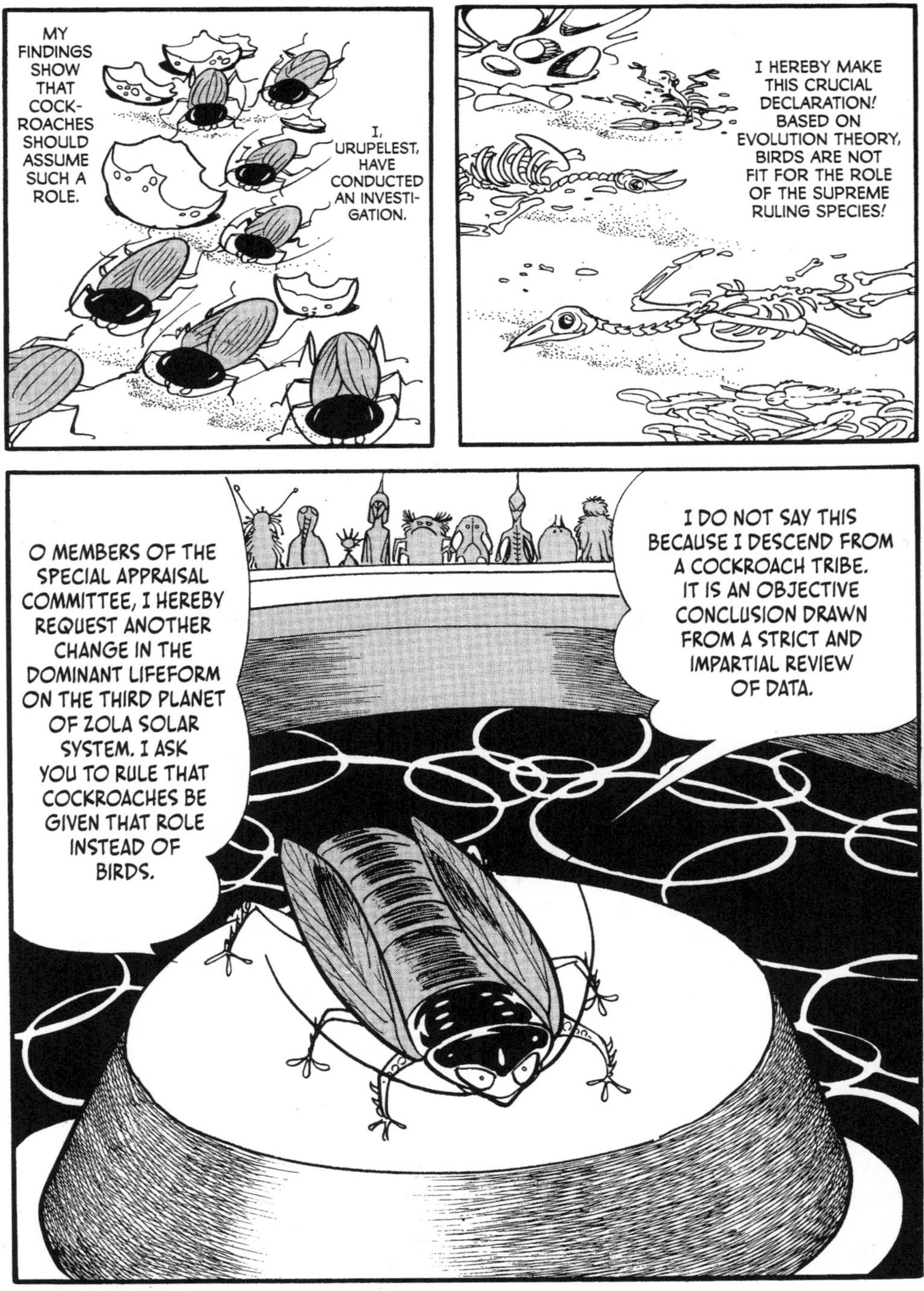
I, URUPELEST, HAVE CONDUCTED AN INVESTIGATION.
MY FINDINGS SHOW THAT COCKROACHES SHOULD ASSUME SUCH A ROLE.
I HEREBY MAKE THIS CRUCIAL DECLARATION! BASED ON EVOLUTION THEORY, BIRDS ARE NOT FIT FOR THE ROLE OF THE SUPREME RULING SPECIES!
O MEMBERS OF THE SPECIAL APPRAISAL COMMITTEE, I HEREBY REQUEST ANOTHER CHANGE IN THE DOMINANT LIFEFORM ON THE THIRD PLANET OF ZOLA SOLAR SYSTEM. I ASK YOU TO RULE THAT COCKROACHES BE GIVEN THAT ROLE INSTEAD OF BIRDS.
I DO NOT SAY THIS BECAUSE I DESCEND FROM A COCKROACH TRIBE. IT IS AN OBJECTIVE CONCLUSION DRAWN FROM A STRICT AND IMPARTIAL REVIEW OF DATA.

THE END

Afterword

(First appeared in Osamu Tezuka Complete Manga Works, Vol. 95, *Chōjin Taikei 2,* published by Kodansha on November 20, 1980)

Back when the SF Authors' Club held monthly meetings led by the late Mr. Masami Fukushima, Mr. Mori, who was deputy editor-in-chief of *S-F Magazine,* also attended each meeting.

On several occasions, he said: "Tezuka-san, please do another series for our magazine..." (It had been a long time since I wrote and drew *SF Fancy Free.*) I roused myself and decided to make a long-running science fiction spectacle adventure story.

Like a lot of people, I was a passionate fan of *The Martian Chronicles* by Bradbury and *City* by Simak. I had been wanting to depict a history of superhumans in episodic manga format, so I said: "Let's call it *Birdmen Chronicles.*"

But after the series was announced, I thought to myself: "Oh no*!*"

Many years earlier, in *The Adventures of Rock,* I had drawn birdmen characters called Epoom.

There would be no point in running something in *S-F Magazine* if I merely recycled something I'd done before.

Therefore, I decided to start with a low-key portrayal of the relationship between humans and birds.

Each month, there were only seven pages including the title page, so it took a long time to have enough material for a whole book.

During such time, Mr. Fukushima passed away and Mr. Mori left Hayakawa Shobō. Science fiction was on the verge of widespread popularity.

Even though I was only producing seven pages a month, it was no easy task writing and drawing for a magazine for die-hard fans. I ended up missing a lot of deadlines. At one point, I even inked some pages on a JAL flight during a trip to Kyushu. That was Chapter 13: Mutant. Mr. Noboru Baba was sitting next to me. I remember how exasperated he sounded: "How can you draw so quickly in these conditions?"

While drawing Chapter 10: Quail Hill, I received letters from manga fans in France and the US saying they liked the series. I wanted more overseas readers to take an interest, so I started drawing in a more Western style and used English for some of the sound effects.

Toward the end, there are many single-chapter stories. I did that because the series was running in a monthly magazine, and I thought that would be easier to understand.

After doing this series for a long time, I started to get bored of it, so I stopped.

Therefore, I never depicted the trajectory of the downfall of the birdmen.

Commentary on *Tomorrow the Birds*

Haruji Mori, Head of Archives, Tezuka Productions

This book [the Osamu Tezuka Complete Pocket-Sized Works edition of *Tomorrow the Birds,* Kodansha, 2011] contains all Osamu Tezuka manga that appeared in *S-F Magazine.*

The first issue of *S-F Magazine* was the February '60 issue. Osamu Tezuka debuted in the magazine in the July '61 issue in a roundtable discussion entitled *Will SF Die Out? – On the Launch of a Manned Satellite Ship* – with Kōbō Abe, Shin'ichi Hoshi, Mitsuo Harada, Jitsuo Kusaka, and Masami Fukushima. One of the participants in this roundtable discussion, Mitsuo Harada, is the author of *Kodomo no Tenmongaku* (Astronomy for Children), which Osamu Tezuka enjoyed reading as a child, and is also the father of Koremitsu Maetani, a manga creator famous for *Robotto Santōhei* (Robot Private Third Class). Up to the 18th issue, *S-F Magazine* had saddle stitch binding (also known as *maruze / maruse* [round back]), and since the 19th, it has had side stitch binding and the flat back you see today.

In the January '62 issue, Osamu Tezuka contributed the illustrated essay *Superman in Full Bloom – SF Comics Around the World –*, which was later rewritten and included in *Introduction to SF* published by Hayakawa Shobō in May '65.

On May 27, '65, the first Japan SF Convention (MEGCON) was held in Meguro-ku Kokaidō in Tokyo to commemorate the fifth anniversary of the founding of the fanzine *Uchūjin* [Space Dust] and the launch of S-F Magazine Club. Osamu Tezuka was among those who attended. The activities he participated in included drawing pictures using the letters in SF authors' names.

The September '62 issue includes an S-F Magazine Club Regular Meeting Report illustrated by Osamu Tezuka. According to this report, the 2nd Regular Meeting, which was held on July 8, featured Osamu Tezuka as the guest, with an SF quiz using manga.

In January '63, *Tetsuwan Atomu* (Mighty Atom [the show that became Astro Boy in the West]) started airing as the first 30-minute anime program on Japanese TV, so Osamu Tezuka would have been extraordinarily busy, but nonetheless, his *SF Fancy Free* ran from the February '63 issue to the March '64 issue (except in the March '63 issue and January '64 issue). The July '63 issue contains an interview conducted by Shōji Ōtomo entitled *People Who Make SF, Part 3: Osamu Tezuka.*

On March 5, '63, the Japan SF Authors' Club was founded, and Osamu Tezuka joined Sakyō Komatsu, Shin'ichi Hoshi, Ryū Mitsuse, Tōru Yano and others as a member.

On October 26 and 27, '63, the second Japan SF Convention (TOCON) was held at Mainichi Hall in Tokyo, and Osamu Tezuka wrote an essay entitled *SF Films and Me* that appeared in the program.

On August 20 and 21, '66, the 5th Japan SF Convention (MEICON) was held in Kankō Kaikan [Tourism Hall] in Nagoya, and the November '66 issue of *S-F Magazine* contains a report by Takumi Shibano detailing the convention. According to the report, Osamu Tezuka attended on the 21st and the anime *Songokū is Starting Soon, Mermaid, The Drop, Memory,* and *Tales from a Street Corner* were screened. Along with Sakyō Komatsu, Ryū Mitsuse, Norio Itō, and others, Osamu Tezuka received the 2nd Japan SF Fandom Award.

The August '64 Special Extra Issue of *S-F Magazine* contains the illustrated feature *Special Roundtable Meeting – The World Fair Creates the Future – Three SF Men Visit New York – Shin'ichi Hoshi, Hiroshi Manabe, MC: Masami Fukushima,* and the February '68 issue contains *New Year's Freewheeling Discussion on SF – Evaluations by SF People – Participants: Japan SF Authors' Club, MC: Masami Fukushima, Takashi Ishikawa.*

Doberman, which appeared in the February '70 issue, was drawn as a special New Year's feature in a bumper issue commemorating the 10th anniversary of the founding of *S-F Magazine. S-F Magazine* featured Japanese authors in its February issue each year, and this manga was included as part of that tradition. The February '71 issue contained *Ripe Planet,* and the March issue marked the start of *Tomorrow the Birds.* Kazuyoshi Fukumoto, who was Chief Assistant, remembers vividly how Osamu Tezuka's manager lamented: "It just doesn't make sense!" about Osamu Tezuka's decision to end the serialization of *Good Morning! Kusuko* in the Sunday edition of Mainichi Shimbun, which had been bringing in a high page rate estimated to be tens of thousands of yen per page, while continuing the serialization of *Tomorrow the Birds,* which had a low page rate estimated to be thousands of yen per page. To Osamu Tezuka, the page rate was not important. Presenting work in *S-F Magazine,* a magazine dedicated to science fiction, is what was meaningful to him.